A Book Of

COMPUTER NETWORKS-II

Semester IV : Paper - III

For Third Year B.Sc. Computer Science
As Per Revised Syllabus
Effective from June 2015

Rahul Patil
M.C.S.
Lecturer and Head of
Computer Science Department,
N.D.M.V.P. Samaj's K.T.H.M. College,
Nasik

Dr. Ms. Kavita A. Khobragade
M.Sc. (Computer Science), NET Ph.D.
Department of Computer Science,
Fergusson College,
Pune

NIRALI
PRAKASHAN
ADVANCEMENT OF KNOWLEDGE

N0896

COMPUTER NETWORKS-II   **ISBN 978-93-5164-911-3**

First Edition   :   **December 2015**
©   :   **Authors**

Published By :   **Polyplate**
NIRALI PRAKASHAN
Abhyudaya Pragati, 1312, Shivaji Nagar,
Off J.M. Road, Pune – 411005
Tel - (020) 25512336/37/39, Fax - (020) 25511379
Email : niralipune@pragationline.com

✦ DISTRIBUTION CENTRES

PUNE
Nirali Prakashan   :   119, Budhwar Peth, Jogeshwari Mandir Lane, Pune 411002, Maharashtra
            Tel : (020) 2445 2044, 66022708, Fax : (020) 2445 1538
            Email : bookorder@pragationline.com, niralilocal@pragationline.com
Nirali Prakashan   :   S. No. 28/27, Dhyari, Near Pari Company, Pune 411041
            Tel : (020) 24690204 Fax : (020) 24690316
            Email : dhyari@pragationline.com, bookorder@pragationline.com

MUMBAI
Nirali Prakashan   :   385, S.V.P. Road, Rasdhara Co-op. Hsg. Society Ltd.,
            Girgaum, Mumbai 400004, Maharashtra
            Tel : (022) 2385 6339 / 2386 9976, Fax : (022) 2386 9976
            Email : niralimumbai@pragationline.com

✦ DISTRIBUTION BRANCHES

JALGAON
Nirali Prakashan   :   34, V. V. Golani Market, Navi Peth, Jalgaon 425001,
            Maharashtra, Tel : (0257) 222 0395, Mob : 94234 91860

KOLHAPUR
Nirali Prakashan   :   New Mahadvar Road, Kedar Plaza, 1st Floor Opp. IDBI Bank
            Kolhapur 416 012, Maharashtra. Mob : 9850046155

NAGPUR
Pratibha Book Distributors   :   Above Maratha Mandir, Shop No. 3, First Floor,
            Rani Jhanshi Square, Sitabuldi, Nagpur 440012, Maharashtra
            Tel : (0712) 254 7129

DELHI
Nirali Prakashan   :   4593/21, Basement, Aggarwal Lane 15, Ansari Road, Daryaganj
            Near Times of India Building, New Delhi 110002
            Mob : 08505972553

BENGALURU
Pragati Book House   :   House No. 1, Sanjeevappa Lane, Avenue Road Cross,
            Opp. Rice Church, Bengaluru – 560002.
            Tel : (080) 64513344, 64513355,Mob : 9880582331, 9845021552
            Email:bharatsavla@yahoo.com

CHENNAI
Pragati Books   :   9/1, Montieth Road, Behind Taas Mahal, Egmore,
            Chennai 600008 Tamil Nadu, Tel : (044) 6518 3535,
            Mob : 94440 01782 / 98450 21552 / 98805 82331,
            Email : bharatsavla@yahoo.com

niralipune@pragationline.com | www.pragationline.com
Also find us on 🅵 www.facebook.com/niralibooks

Preface ...

We take an opportunity to present this book entitled as **"Computer Networks-II"** to the students of T.Y.B.Sc. Computer Science as per the revised syllabus, June 2015.

The book covers theory of Wired LANs, Wireless LAN, The Network Layer, Address Mapping, The Transport Layer, The Application Layer and Network Security.

A special word of thanks to Shri. Dineshbhai Furia, Mr. Jignesh Furia for showing full faith in us to write this book. We also thank to Mr. Amar Salunkhe and Mrs. Prachi Sawant of M/s Nirali Prakashan for their excellent co-operation.

Although every care has been taken to check mistakes and misprints, any errors, omission and suggestions from teachers and students for the improvement of this text book shall be most welcome.

Authors

Syllabus ...

1. Wired LANs [9 L]

1.1 IEEE Standards Data Link Layer, Physical Layer

1.2 Standard Ethernet MAC Sublayer – Frame Format, Frame Length, Addressing, Access Method

1.3 Physical Layer – Encoding and Decoding, 10Base5, 10Base2, 10Base-T, 10Base-F

1.4 Changes in the Standard – Bridged Ethernet, Switched Ethernet, Full Duplex Ethernet

1.5 Fast Ethernet – Goals, MAC Sublayer, Topology, Implementation

1.6 Gigabit Ethernet – Goals, MAC Sublayer, Topology, Implementation

1.7 Ten-Gigabit Ethernet – Goals, MAC Sublayer, Physical Layer

1.8 Backbone Networks Bus Backbone, Star Backbone, Connecting Remote LANs

1.9 Virtual LANs Membership, Configuration, Communication between Switches, IEEE standards, Advantages

2. Wireless LAN [2 L]

2.1 IEEE 802.11 Architecture – Basic Service Set, Extended Service Set, Station Types

2.2 Bluetooth Architecture – Piconet, Scatternet

3. The Network Layer [10 L]

3.1 Design Issues - Store-and-forward packet switching, Services Provided to the Transport Layer, Implementation of Connectionless Service, Implementation of Connection Oriented Service, Comparison of Virtual Circuit and Datagram subnets

3.2 Logical Addressing IPv4 Addresses – Address Space, Notations, Classful Addressing, Subnetting, Supernetting, Classless Addressing, Network Address Translation (NAT), (Enough problems should be covered on Addressing).

3.3 IPv4 Protocol - Datagram Format, Fragmentation, Checksum, Options

3.4 Routing Properties of routing algorithm, Comparison of Adaptive and Non-Adaptive Routing Algorithms

3.5 Congestion Control – Definition, Factors of Congestion, Difference between congestion control and flow control, General Principles of Congestion Control, Congestion Prevention Policies

3.6 Network Layer Devices – Routers

4. Address Mapping [4 L]

4.1 Protocol (ARP) - Cache Memory, Packet Format, Encapsulation, Operation, Four Different Cases, Proxy ARP, RARP, BOOTP, DHCP – Static Address Allocation, Dynamic Address Allocation, Manual and Automatic Configuration.

5. The Transport Layer [6 L]

5.1 Process-to-Process Delivery, Client Server Paradigm, Multiplexing and De-multiplexing, Connectionless Vs Connection-Oriented Service, Reliable Vs Unreliable

5.2 User Datagram Protocol (UDP) - Datagram Format, Checksum, UDP operations, Use of UDP

5.3 Transmission Control Protocol (TCP) TCP Services – Process-to-Process Communication, Stream Delivery Service, Sending and Receiving Buffers, Segments, Full –Duplex Communication, Connection oriented service, Reliable service

5.4 TCP Features – Numbering System, Byte Number, Sequence Number, Acknowledgement Number, Flow Control, Error Control, Congestion Control

5.5 TCP Segment – Format

6. The Application Layer [7 L]

6.1 Domain Name System (DNS) Name Space, Domain, Name Space, Distribution of Name Space, DNS in the Internet, Resolution

6.2 E-MAIL Architecture, User Agent, Message Transfer Agent-SMTP, Message Access Agent-POP3, IMAP4, Web Based Mail

6.3 File Transfer Protocol (FTP) Communication over control connection, Communication over Data Connection, Anonymous FTP

6.4 WWW Architecture, WEB Documents

6.5 HTTP - HTTP Transaction, Persistent and Non persistent Connection, Proxy Server

6.6 Devices- Gateways –Transport & Application Gateways

7. Network Security [10 L]

7.1 Introduction – Security Services – Message – Confidentiality, Integrity, Authentication, Non repudiation, Entity (User) – Authentication

7.2 Message confidentiality – Confidentiality with Asymmetric-Key Cryptography, Confidentiality with Symmetric-Key Cryptography

7.3 Cryptography Encryption Model, Substitution Cipher and Transposition Cipher (Problems should be covered)

7.4 Two Fundamental Cryptographic Principles

7.5 Communication Security Firewalls

7.6 Web Security Threats, Secure Naming, DNS Spoofing, Secure DNS, Self Certifying names

7.7 Mobile Code Security Java Applet Security, ActiveX, JavaScript, Viruses

7.8 Social Issues Privacy, Anonymous Remailers, Freedom of Speech, Stegnography, Copyright

Contents ...

❖❖❖

Wired LANs

Contents ...

Objectives...

- To Understand Wired LANs
- To Learn Ethernet and its Implementation
- To Sutdy Fast, Gigabit, Ten-Gigabit, Standard Ethernets
- To Learn Backbone Network Concepts
- To Understand VLANs

| 1.0 | INTRODUCTION

- In the first semester in Chapter 1, we learned that a Local Area Network (LAN) is a computer networks for the home and small business is designed for a limited geographic area such as a building or campus. Most LANs today are also linked to a Wide Area Network (WAN) or the Internet.

- LANs can be built using either wired or wireless technology. LAN supports several technologies such as Ethernet, Token Ring, Token Bus, FDDI, and ATM LAN. Today Ethernet is by far the dominant technology. Other technologies survived for a while.

- Wired networks are the most common type of Local Area Network (LAN) technology. A wired network (LAN) is simply a collection of two or more computers, printers, and other devices linked by Ethernet cables.

- In this chapter, we first discuss the IEEE standard project 802, interconnectivity between different LANs, and then focus on the Ethernet LANs.

- Fig. 1.1 shows an example of four computers connected in a traditional Ethernet LAN.

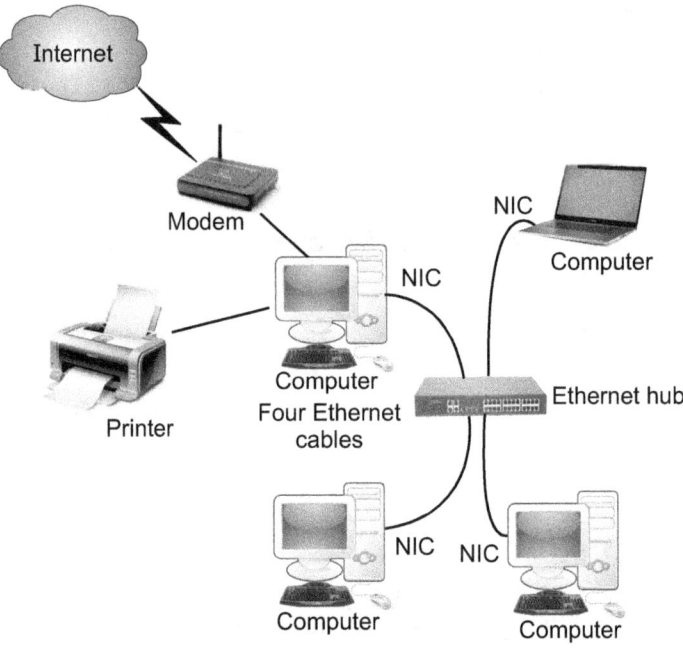

Fig. 1.1

- There are a number of advantages to using a wired LAN over a wireless one, including the following:

  1. **Speed:** Wired LANs almost invariably provide higher speed connections (basically due to the increased reliability).

  2. **Reliability:** Wired LANs tend to be much more reliable as they have a dedicated wire, suitably insulated, down which the router or server can converse with any clients.

  3. **Better Security:** It's more difficult to tap into a (suitably secured) wired LANs than a wireless one as there is no airborne signal that can be picked up.

  4. **Energy Saving:** Less electricity is consumed if your router can send a stream of electrons down a wire instead of having to broadcast on the airwaves.

- The disadvantages of Wired LAN are:

  1. **Difficult to Physical Setup:** Wired LANs require cables to be installed between your router, hub, switch, printer and computers location(s).

  2. **Security Problems:** Wired LANs may well require more stringent security setup in order to secure them properly.

3. **Mobility:** Wired LANs not provides wireless mobility.

4. **Compatibility:** Rather annoyingly, some manufacturers are assuming the use of Wi-Fi and are therefore not fitting a suitable RJ-45 port for a wired connection (e.g. virtually all touch-pads and a lot of printers).

5. **Cost:** High cost because of the cost of cables, hub, connectors etc.

6. **Time Consuming:** Ethernet cables must be run from each computer to another computer or to the central device like hub or switch. It can be time-consuming and difficult to run cables under the floor or through walls, especially when computers sit in different rooms.

1.1 | IEEE STANDARDS   (April 13)

- In 1985, the Computer Society of the IEEE started a project 'Project 802'. This project is used to set standards to enable inter-communication among equipment from a variety of manufacturers.

- Project 802 is aim to specify functions of the physical layer and the data link layer of major LAN protocols.

- The Institute of Electrical and Electronic Engineers (IEEE) developed a series of networking standards for LANs. These standards are collectively known as IEEE 802.

- These standards ensure that networking technologies developed by respective manufacturers are compatible to each other. This means that the cabling, networking devices, and protocols are all interchangeable when designed under the banner of a specific IEEE standard.

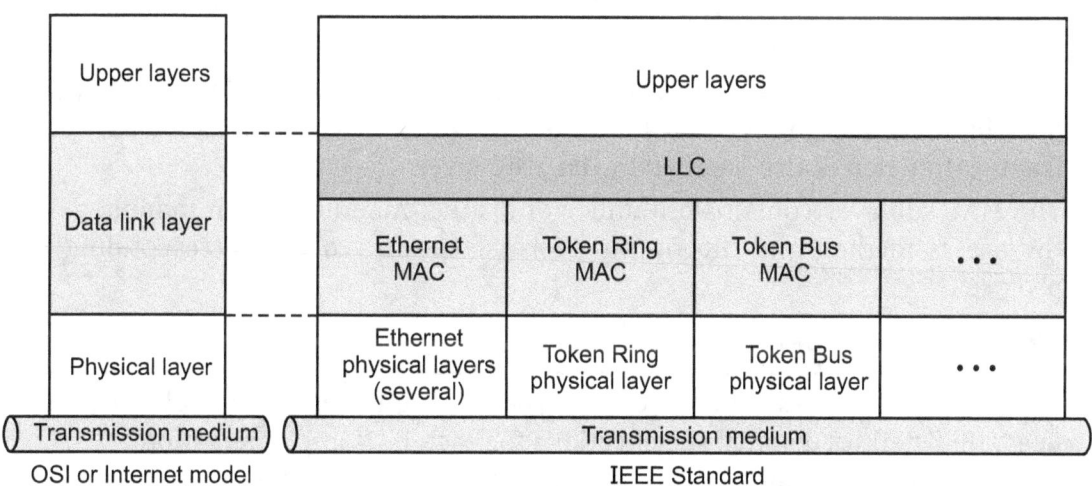

Fig. 1.2

- The relationship of the 802 Standard with the traditional OSI model is shown in the Fig. 1.2. The IEEE has subdivided the data link layer into two sub layers i.e. LLC (Logical Link Control) and MAC (Media Access Control).
- IEEE has also created different physical layer standards for several LAN protocols.
- Fig. 1.2 shows IEEE standards for WLANs.

1.1.1 Data Link Layer   (Oct. 12)

- The data link layer in the IEEE standard is divided into two sub layers i.e., LLC and MAC.

1. **Logical Link Control (LLC):**
- Data link layer offers several services. Out of which in IEEE Project 802, flow control, error control, and part of the framing srvices are collected into one sublayer called the logical link control. Framing is handled in both the LLC sublayer and the MAC sublayer.
- The LLC provides one single data link control protocol for all IEEE LANs whereas, MAC provides different protocols for different LANs.
- A single LLC protocol can provide interconnectivity between different LANs because it makes the MAC sublayer transparent.
- The purpose of the LLC is to provide flow and error control for the upper layer protocols.

2. **Media Access Control (MAC):**
- Access control is also one of the important function of Data link layer. In the first semester we studied that random access, controlled access, and channelization are the methods used for access control.
- For access control IEEE Project 802 has created a sublayer called media access control that defines the specific access method for each LAN.
- For example, it defines CSMA/CD as the media access method for Ethernet LANs and the token-passing method for Token Ring and Token Bus LANs. Part of the framing function is also handled by the MAC layer.
- The MAC sublayer contains a number of distinct modules. Each module defines the access method and the framing format specific to the corresponding LAN protocol.

1.1.2 Physical Layer

- The physical layer is dependent on the type and implementation of physical media used. IEEE defines detailed specifications for each LAN implementation.
- For example, although there is only one MAC sublayer for Standard Ethernet, there is a different physical layer specification for each Ethernet implementations.

1.2 | STANDARDS ETHERNET   (Oct. 14; April 15)

- The original Ethernet was developed in 1976 at Xerox's Palo Alto Research center (PARC).

- Ethernet is a standardized system for connecting computers to a Local Area Network (LAN).

- The Institute for Electrical and Electronic Engineers (IEEE) developed an Ethernet standard known as IEEE Standard 802.3.

- 802.3 standard defines rules for configuring an Ethernet network and also specifies how the elements in an Ethernet network interact with one another.

- Since then, it has gone through four generations i.e., Standard Ethernet (10 Mbps), Fast Ethernet (100 Mbps), Gigabit Ethernet (1 Gbps) and Ten-Gigabit Ethernet (10 Gbps) as shown in Fig. 1.3.

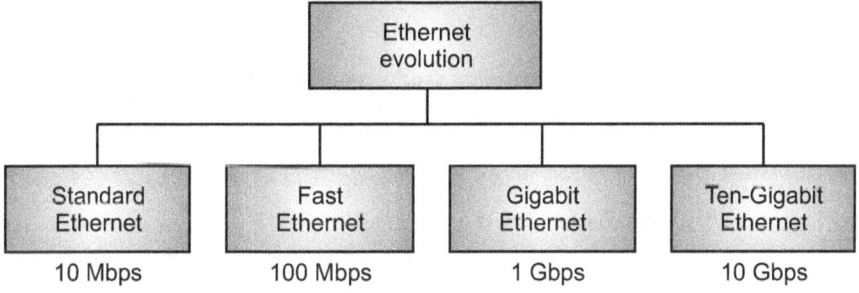

Fig. 1.3: Four generations of Ethernet evolution

1.2.1 MAC Layer

- In Standard Ethernet, the MAC (Media Access Control) sublayer governs the operation of the access method.

- MAC sub-layer also frames data received from the upper layer and passes them to the physical layer.

1.2.2 Frame Format

- The format of the Ethernet MAC frame is shown in the Fig. 1.4, and it contains several fields.

- Ethernet does not provide any mechanism for acknowledgment of received frames. Acknowledgments must be implemented at the higher layers.

Preamble : 56 bits of alternating 1s and 0s.
SFD : Start frame delimiter, flag (10101011)

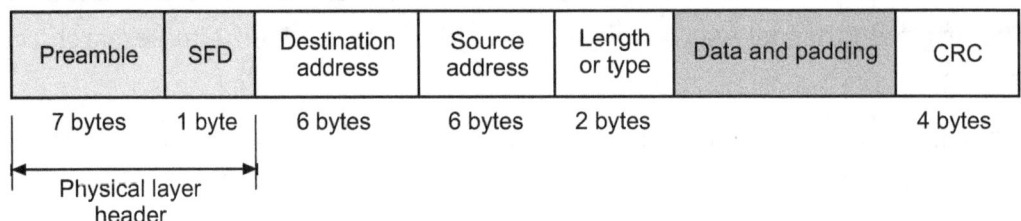

Fig. 1.4 : 802.3 Ethernet MAC frame

- The fields in the frame format are:

    1. **Preamble:** This is the first field of the 802.3 frame, which contains 7 bytes (56 bits) of alternating 0s and 1s. Which indicates the receiving system about the coming frame and enables it to synchronize its input timing. The preamble is actually added at the physical layer.

    2. **Start Frame Delimiter (SFD):** SFD is the second field in the frame. Size of this field is 1 byte (1 byte : 10101011). This field signals the beginning of the frame. The SFD warns the station or stations that this is the last chance for synchronization. The last 2 bits is 11 and alerts the receiver that the next field is the destination address.

    3. **Destination Address (DA):** The DA field is of 6 bytes and contains the physical address of the destination station or stations to receive the packet.

    4. **Source Address (SA):** The source address field is also 6 bytes and contains the physical address of the sender of the packet.

    5. **Length or type:** This field is defined as a type field or length field. Both uses are common. The original Ethernet used this field as the type field to define the upper-layer protocol using the MAC frame. The IEEE standard used it as the length field to define the number of bytes in the data field.

    6. **Data:** This field contains data encapsulated from the upper-layer protocols. Size of data is minimum of 46 and a maximum of 1500 bytes.

    7. **CRC:** This last field contains error detection information.

1.2.3 Frame Length

- Ethernet has forced restrictions about both the minimum and maximum lengths of a frame, as shown in Fig. 1.5.

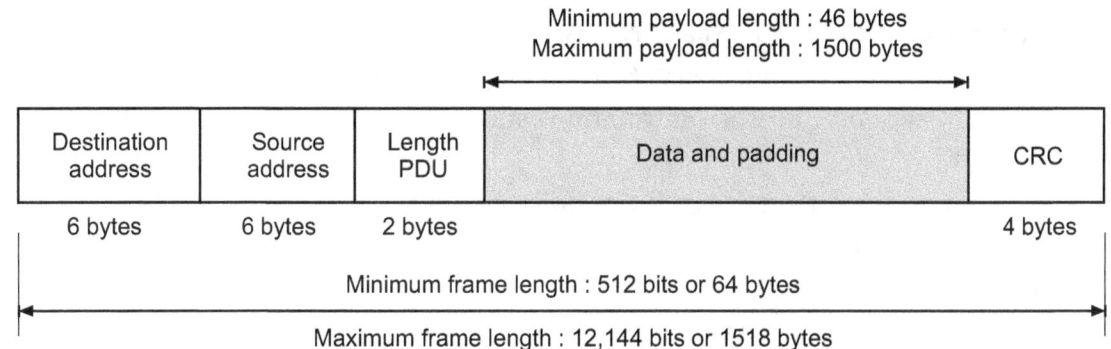

Fig. 1.5 : Minimum and maximum of Ethernet frame

- As we know CSMA/CD is used as access protocol in the Ethernet.
- The minimum length restriction is required for the correct operation of CSMA/CD. Minimum length of the Ethernet frame is 512 bits or 64 bytes.
- Frame contains 6 bytes of source address, 6 bytes of destination address, 2 bytes of length or type, and 4 bytes of CRC, total 18 bytes of header and trailer are required.
- The minimum length of data from upper layer is 64-18=46 bytes. If upper layer packet is less than this, padding (adding extra bits) is done.
- The maximum length of a Ethernet frame without preamble and SFD field defined by standard is 1518 bytes. If we subtract the 18 bytes of header and trailer, the maximum length of the payload is 1500 bytes.
- The maximum length restriction has following two reasons:
  1. Memory was very expensive when Ethernet was designed, this restriction helped to reduce the size of the buffer.
  2. The maximum length restriction prevents one station from taking the complete control of the shared medium, blocking other stations that have data to send.

1.2.4 Addressing

- Every station on an Ethernet network like a PC, workstation, printer etc., has its own Network Interface Card (NIC), installed inside the station.
- The NIC provides the station with 6-byte (48 bit) physical address.
- Fig. 1.6 shows physical address in hexadecimal notation.

06 : 01 : 02 : 01 : 2C : 4B

6 bytes = 12 hex digits = 48 bits

Fig. 1.6

Unicast, Multicast and Broadcast Addresses:

- As we know a source address is always a unicast address. The frame comes from only one station. But the destination address can be unicast, multicast or broadcast.
- Fig. 1.7 shows the difference between unicast address a multicast address.
- If the least significant bit of the first byte in a destination address is 0, the address is unicast; otherwise, it is multicast.

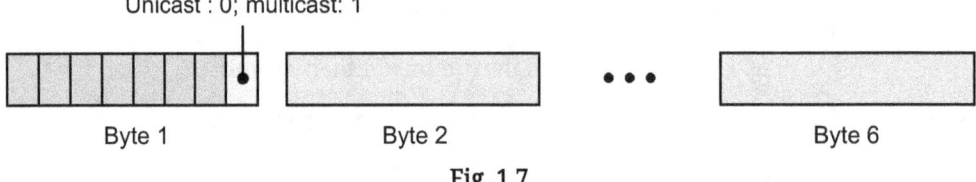

Fig. 1.7

- The broadcast address is a special case of the multicast address i.e., the recipients are all the stations on the LAN. A broadcast destination address contains all forty-eight (48) bits are 1s.

1.2.5 Access Method: CSMA/CD   (Oct. 11; April 12, 13)

- In the first semester, 6th chapter we already studied CSMA/CD protocol used in LANs.
- Standard Ethernet uses 1-persistent CSMA/CD (Carrier Sense Multiple Access/Collision Detection). 1-persistent mode waits for the medium to be idle, then transmits data.
- CSMA/CD is a type of contention protocol that defines how to respond when a collision is detected, or when two devices attempt to transmit packages simultaneously.
- In an Ethernet network, slot time is defined in bits. It is the time required for a station to send 512 bits. For example, for traditional 10mbps LAN it is 51.2µs and calculated as follows

  Slot time = round-trip time + time required to send the jam sequence

Slot Time and Collision :

- A 512 bit slot time allow proper functioning of CSMA/CD. To understand this let us consider two cases.

Case 1 :

- In the first case, the sender sends a minimum size packet of 512 bits. Before the sender can send the entire packet out, the signal travels through the network and reaches the end of the network.

- If there is another signal at the end of network collision occurs. The sender can send jam signal to abort the sending of a frame.
- The round trip time plus the time required to send the jam signal should be less than the time needed for the sender to send the minimum frame, 512 bits.

Case 2 :

- The sender must be aware of the collision before it has send the entire frame.
- In the second case, if the sender sends a frame larger than the minimum size, after sending first 512 bits, it is guaranteed that collision will not occur during the transmission of this frame.
- The entire medium belongs to the sender. The sender needs to listen for a collision only during the time the first 512 bits are sent.

Slot Time and Maximum Network Length:

- A relationship between the slot time and maximum length of the network is dependent on the propagation speed of the signal in the particular medium.

$$\text{Max Length} = \text{Propagation Speed} \times \text{Slot Time}/2$$

1.3 PHYSICAL LAYER

- Four common standard Ethernet physical layer implementations are shown in Fig. 1.8.

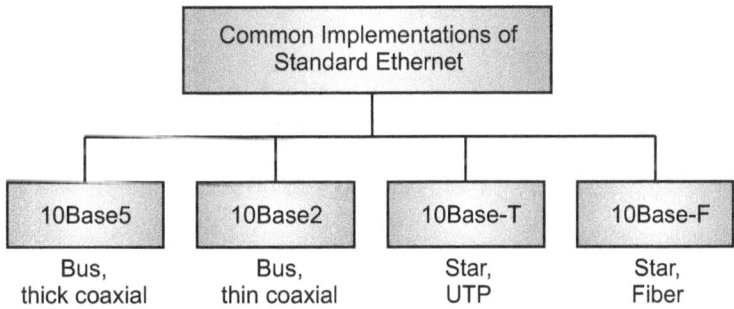

Fig. 1.8 : Categories of Standard Ethernet

1.3.1 Encoding and Decoding

- We know that Physical layer convert computer digital data into digital signals by using various methods and vice versa.
- In Standard Ethernet implementation (10 Mbps) sender converts data into a digital signal by using the Manchester scheme, at the receiver, received signals is interpreted as Manchester and decoded into data.
- Fig. 1.9 shows the encoding scheme for Standard Ethernet.

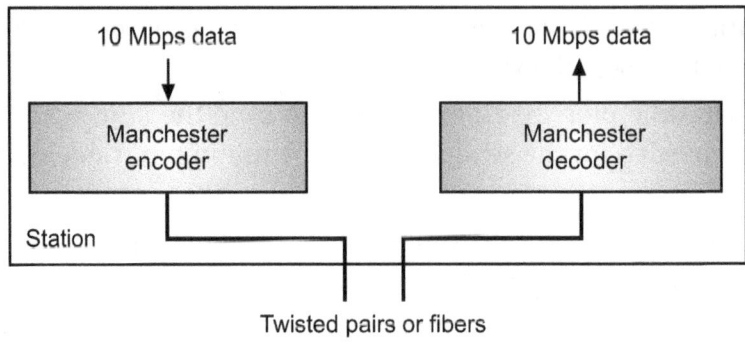

Fig. 1.9

1.3.2 10Base5   (Oct. 12)

- There are two types of 10Base5 Ethernet as explained below:

1. **10Base5: Thick Ethernet :**

- The first Ethernet implementation is called 10Base5, thick Ethernet, or Thicknet. 10Base5 was the first Ethernet specification used in bus topology.

- In 10Base5 specification external transceiver (transmitter and receiver) connected via a tap of a thick coaxial cable.

- Fig. 1.10 shows 10base5 implementation.

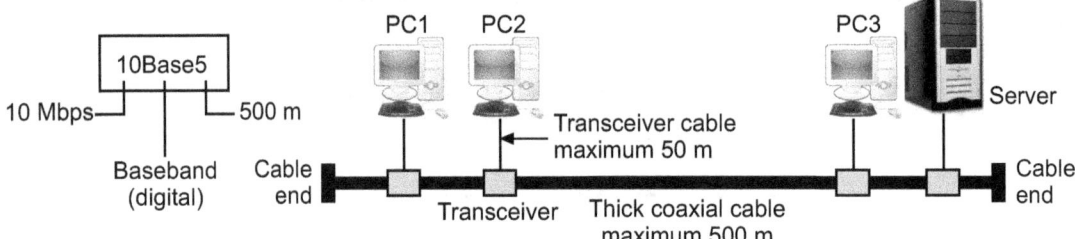

Fig. 1.10 : 10Base5 implementation

- The transceiver transmit, receive and detects collision. The transceiver is connected to a station via transceiver cable which provides separate path for sending and receiving. Collision can occur only in the coaxial cable.

- In 10Base5 implementation, the maximum length of coaxial cable should not exceed 500 m, otherwise, signal quality is degraded. If cable length is required more than 500 m, connecting device repeater is used.

2. **10Base5: Thin Ethernet :**

- The second implementation is called 10Base2, thin Ethernet, or Cheapernet.

- The cable used in this implementation is much thinner, more flexible and can be bent. Due to this cable can pass very close to the stations. The transceivers are built inside the Network Interface Card (NIC), which is installed inside the station.

1.3.3 10Base2

- 10Base2 also uses a bus topology, it is more cost effective than 10Base5.
- Thin coaxial is cheaper than thick and the tee (T) connectors are also cheaper than taps used in 10Base5.
- Installation of 10Base2 is simpler because the thin coaxial cable is very flexible.
- The length of each segment cannot exceed 185 m (close to 200 m) due to the high level of attenuation in thin coaxial cable.
- Fig. 1.11 shows the schematic diagram of a 10Base2 implementation.

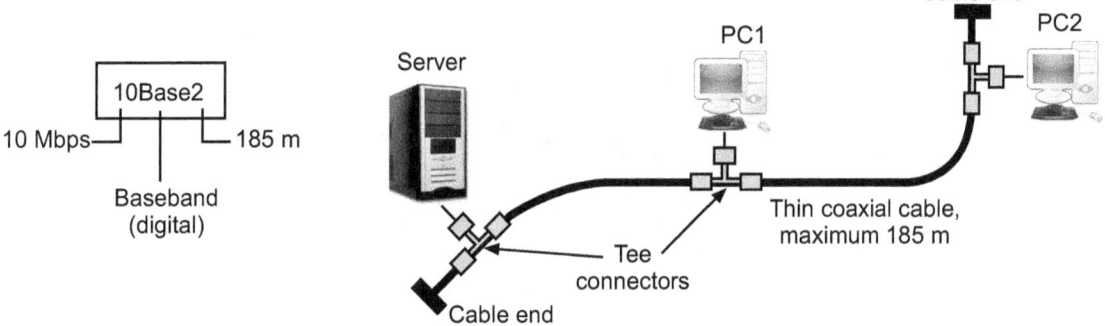

Fig 1.11 : 10Base2 implementation

1.3.4 10Base-T: Twisted-Pair Ethernet   (April 13)

- The third implementation is 10Base-T or twisted-pair Ethernet. 10Base-T uses physical star topology.
- All stations are connected to a hub or switch via two pairs of twisted pair. From these two pairs one pair is used for sending and other is used for receiving data in between the station and the hub.
- To minimize the effect of attenuation in the twisted pair, its length is defined as 100m only.
- Fig. 1.12 shows 10Base-T Ethernet implementation.

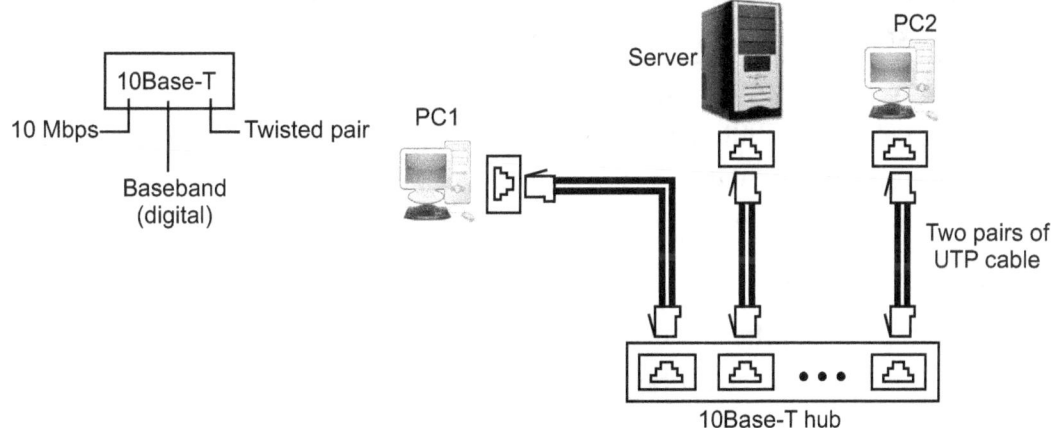

Fig. 1.12 : 10Base-T implementation

1.3.5 10Base-F: Fiber Ethernet

- 10Base-F uses a star topology to connect stations to a hub.
- The stations are connected to the hub using two fiber-optic cables as shown in the Fig. 1.13.

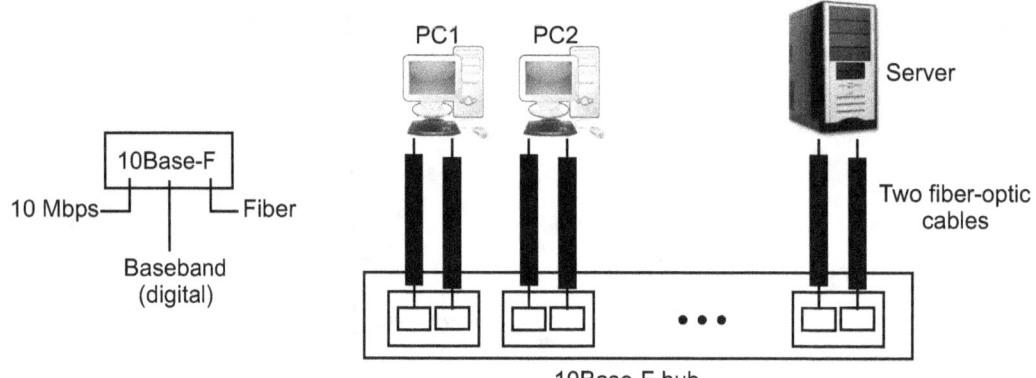

Fig. 1.13 : 10Base-T implementation

Summary of Standard Ethernet Implementation :

Sr. No.	Characteristics	10Base5	10Base2	10Base-T	10Base-F
1.	Media	Thick coaxial cable	Thin coaxial cable	2 UTP	2 Fiber
2.	Maximum length	500 m	185 m	100 m	2000 m
3.	Line encoding	Manchester	Manchester	Manchester	Manchester

1.4 │ CHANGES IN THE STANDARD

- In the previous topic we discussed standard Ethernet implementation which operates on 10 Mbps. But users are demanding higher data rates continuously.
- Before shifting to the higher data rates the 10-Mbps Standard Ethernet has gone through several changes. Some of these changes we discussed here.

1.4.1 Bridged Ethernet

- The first step in the Ethernet evolution was the division of a LAN by bridges.
- By using bridges two advantages are Bandwidth is raise and Separate collision domain.

1.   Raising the Bandwidth :

- The total capacity 10 Mbps of a unbridged Ethernet LAN is divided among all stations.

- The stations share the bandwidth of the network. If only one station from the network wants to send frame, it uses the total capacity (10 Mbps) of network. But if more than one station needs to use the network, the capacity is shared. For example, as shown in Fig. 1.14, if two stations have a lot of frames to send, they probably use the bandwidth alternately.

- When one station is sending, the other one is on hold from sending. In this case, each station on average, sends at a rate of 5 Mbps.

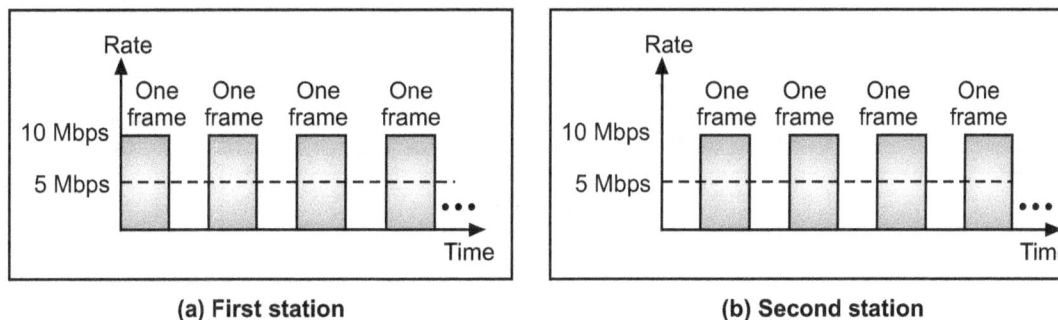

(a) First station   (b) Second station

Fig. 1.14 : Sharing bandwidth

- In computer networking a bridge as a internetworking device, divides the network into two or more networks. Bandwidth-wise, each network is independent.

- For example, in Fig. 1.15, a network with 12 stations is divided into two networks, each with 6 stations. Now each network has a capacity of 10 Mbps. The 10-Mbps capacity in each segment is now shared between 6 stations (actually 7 because the bridge acts as a station in each segment), not 12 stations.

(a) Without bridging

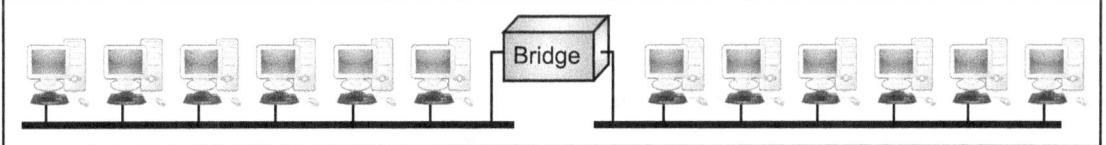

(b) With bridging

Fig. 1.15 : A network with and without a bridge

- In a network with a heavy load, each station theoretically is offered 10/6 Mbps instead of 10/12 Mbps. If we further divide the network, we can gain more bandwidth for each segment.

2. **Separating Collision Domains :**

- By using bridge we can separate the collision domain. Fig. 1.16 shows the collision domains for an unbridged and a bridged network.

- From the Fig. 1.16 we can say that the collision domain becomes very smaller and the probability of collision is reduced tremendously.

- Without bridging, 12 stations trying for access to the medium; with bridging only 3 stations trying for access to the medium.

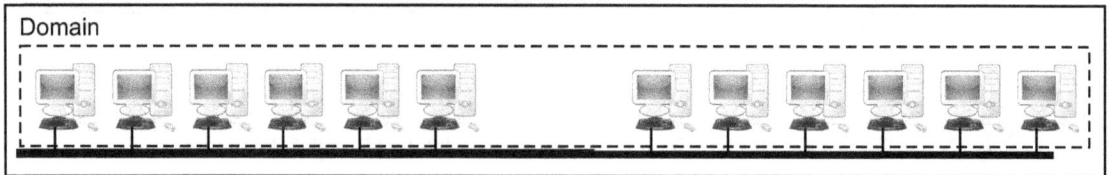

(a) Without Bridging

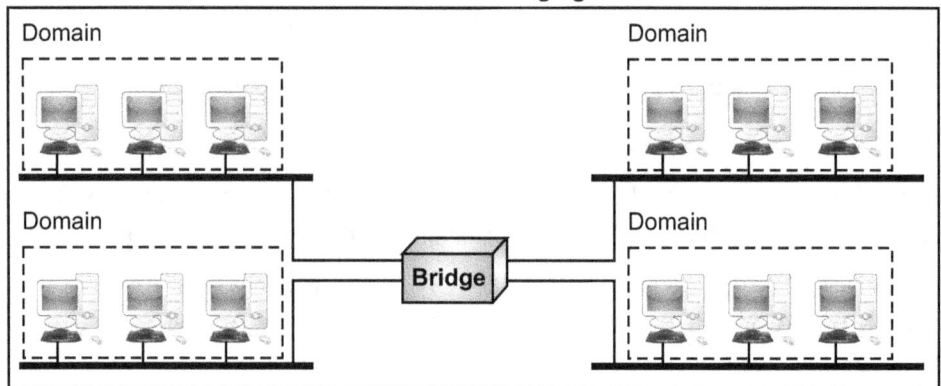

(b) With Bridging

Fig. 1.16 : Collision domains in an unbridged and a bridged network

1.4.2 Switched Ethernet   (April 11, 12)

- In the previous Section 1.4.1 we have seen that by using bridged LAN bandwidth is raised and we are having separate collision domain. Effect of this is performance of the network is increased. But by using bridges, we can not have N networks due to the limitations of number of ports.

- Instead of focusing on number of LANs, if we consider a single LAN with N stations, switched Ethernet is very good solution. The bandwidth is shared only between the station and the switch (5 Mbps each). The collision domain is also divided into N domains.

- A layer 2 switch is an N-port bridge that allows faster handling of the packets. Evolution from a bridged Ethernet to a switched Ethernet was a big step that opened the way to an even faster Ethernet.
- Fig. 1.17 shows a switched LAN.

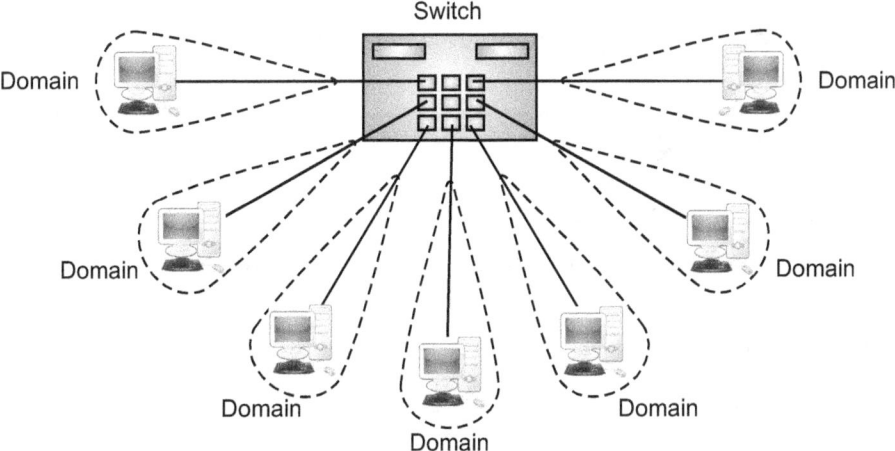

Fig. 1.17 : Switched Ethernet LAN

1.4.3 Full-Duplex Ethernet

- The 10Base2 and 10Base5 Ethernet implementations of LAN provides only half duplex communication.
- The sender can either transmit or receive, but not do both at same time. So to overcome this drawback, Full Duplex Ethernet implementation was introduced.
- The full duplex mode increases the capacity of each domain from 10 to 20 Mbps.
- Fig. 1.18 shows full duplex mode, separate links to transmit and receive data are used.

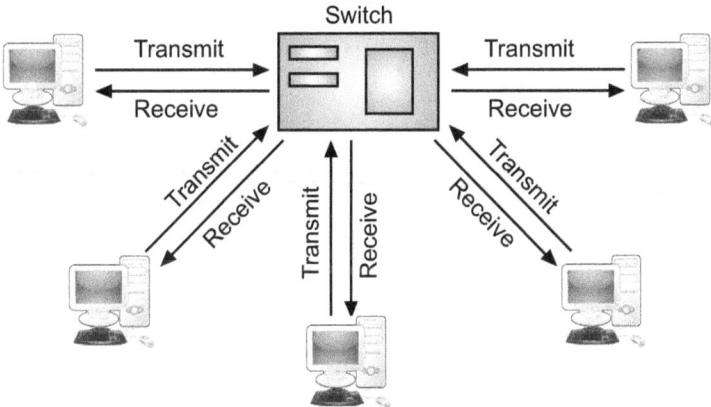

Fig. 1.18 : Full duplex switched Ethernet

- In full duplex switched Ethernet, each station is connected to the switch through two separate link. Each station or switch can send or receive independently.

- Every link is a point to point link. There is no need for carrier sensing and collision detection in full duplex switched Ethernet.

- The job of MAC sublayer is simple. There is no need of CSMA/CD in this implementation.

1.5 | FAST ETHERNET

- IEEE created fast Ethernet standard under the name 802.3μ.

- Fast Ethernet was designed to compete with LAN protocols such as FDDI or Fiber Channel.

- Fast Ethernet is 10 times faster than standard Ethernet and operates at 100 Mbps.

- Fast Ethernet is backward compatible to standard Ethernet.

Advantages of Fast Ethernet :

1. Fast Ethernet is a standards based technology used widely in the world. The performance is 10 times more than in traditional Ethernet. There also is a broad support from network, system and semiconductor industry.

2. Fast Ethernet is ten times faster (100Mbps) than regular 10BaseT networks (10Mbps).

3. Fast Ethernet is easy to set up.

4. Stronger error detection and correction.

5. Fast Ethernet hardware is available at prices that are only slightly higher than 10BaseT hardware.

6. Faster throughput for video, multimedia, graphics, Internet surfing, and other speed-intensive applications.

1.5.1 Goals

- Goals of Fast Ethernet are:

1. Upgrade the data rate to 100 Mbps.

2. Keep the same 48-bit address.

3. Make it compatible with Standard Ethernet.

4. Keep the same frame format.

5. Keep the same minimum and maximum frame length.

1.5.2 MAC Sublayer

- In the Fast Ethernet, the MAC sub layer is untouched. But bus topology is dropped and only star topology is kept. Star topology supports for half duplex and full duplex implementation.

- In half-duplex stations are connected via a hub, in full duplex stations are connected via switch.

- CSMA/CD is access method for half duplex and no need for CSMS/CD in full duplex.

Autonegotiation:

- Autonegotiation is a new feature added to Fast Ethernet.

- Autonegotiation allows a station or a hub a range of capabilities. It allows two devices to negotiate the mode or data rate of operation.

- Autonegotiation was designed particularly for the following purposes:

  1. To allow one device to have multiple capabilities.
  2. To allow incompatible devices to connect to one another. For example, a device with a maximum capacity of 10 Mbps can communicate with a device with a 100 Mbps capacity (but can work at a lower rate).
  3. To allow a station to check a hub's capabilities.

1.5.3 Physical Layer

- The physical layer in Fast Ethernet is more complicated than the Standard Ethernet. Some of the features of this layer are given below.

1.5.3.1 Topology   (Oct. 14)

- Fast Ethernet is designed to connect two or more stations together.

- If there are only two stations, they can be connected point-to-point as shown in Fig. 1.19.

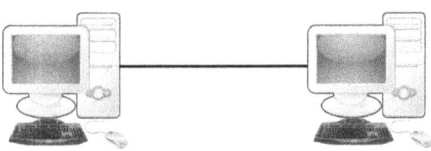

Fig. 1.19: Point to point

- Three or more stations need to be connected in a star topology with a hub or a switch at the centre as shown Fig. 1.20.

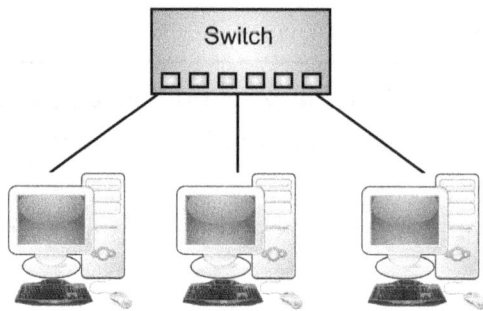

Fig. 1.20 : Star

1.5.3.2 Implementation

- Fig. 1.21 shows common Fast Ethernet implementation techniques.

- Fast Ethernet implementation at the physical layer can be categorized as either two-wire or four-wire.

  1. The two-wire implementation can be either category 5 UTP (100Base-TX) or fiber-optic cable (100Base-FX).

  2. The four-wire implementation is designed only for category 3 UTP (100Base-T4).

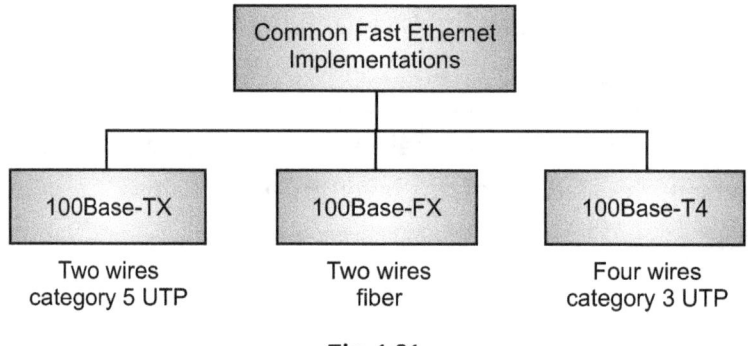

Fig. 1.21

- Fast Ethernet implementation at the physical layer can be categorized as either two-wire or four-wire.

Encoding :

- Manchester encoding scheme needs a 200-Mbaud bandwidth for a data rate of 100 Mbps.

- Three different encoding schemes are used for three different implementations, as shown in Fig. 1.22.

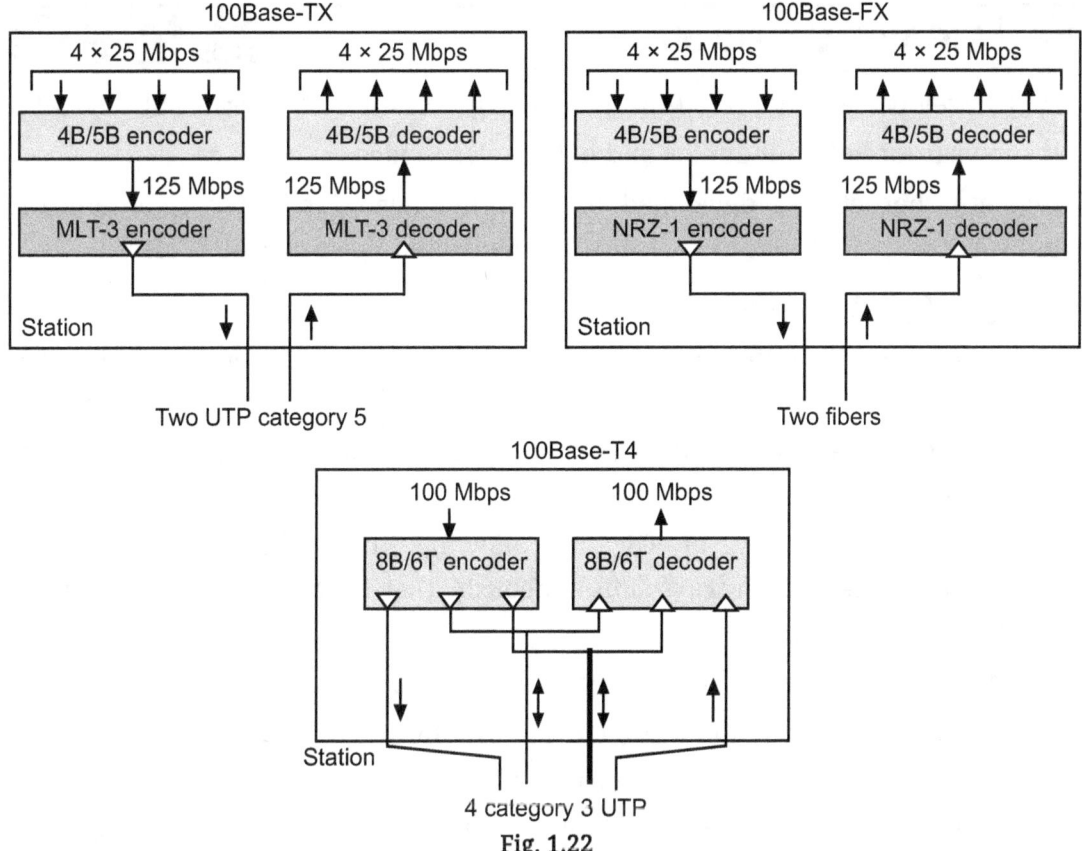

Fig. 1.22

1. **100Base-TX** : It uses two pairs of twisted-pair cable (either category 5 UTP or STP). For this implementation, the MLT-3 scheme was used. It supports a data rate of 125 Mbps.

2. **100Base-FX:** It uses two pairs of fiber-optic cables. 4B/5B encoding is used for this. It supports 100 to 125 Mbps, which can easily be handled by fiber-optic cable.

3. **100Base-T4:** It was designed to use category 3 or higher UTP. The implementation uses four pairs of UTP for transmitting 100 Mbps. 8B/6T encoding scheme was used. This means that 100 Mbps uses only (6/8) x 100 Mbps, or 75 Mbaud.

Summary of the Fast Ethernet Implementation :

Sr. No.	Characteristics	100Base-TX	100Base-FX	100Base-T4
1.	Media	Cat 5 UTP or STP	Fiber	Cat 4 UTP
2.	Number of wires	2	2	4
3.	Maximum length	100 m	185 m	100 m
4.	Block encoding	4B/5B	4B/5B	Two
5.	Line encoding	MLT-3	NRZ-I	8B/6T

| 1.6 | GIGABIT ETHERNET | (Oct. 11; April 13, 15) |

- IEEE developed a standard 802.3z, named Gigabit Ethernet, operates at 1000 Mbps.
- It supports for both full-duplex and half-duplex modes.
- Gigabit Ethernet was developed to meet the need for faster communication networks with applications such as multimedia and Voice over IP (VoIP).

Advantages of Gigabit Ethernet :

1. It is roughly 100 times faster than the regular Mbps Ethernet. This faster speed allows for faster research and content downloading while on the Internet.
2. Another advantage is the elimination of bottlenecks within the Internet service.
3. Full-duplex capacity of Gigabit, allowing the effective bandwidth to communicate in both ways simultaneously, therefore it increases the transfer rate.
4. Improving the traffic flow in overcrowded area.
5. Transferring large amounts of data across a network quickly.
6. Gigabit Ethernet offers performance enhancement for existing networks without having to change the cables, protocols and applications already in use.
7. Gigabit Ethernet cable may be a cheaper option than optical fiber.
8. Gigabit Ethernet cables are easier to install and setup.

Disadvantages of Gigabit Ethernet :

1. It is rather expensive.
2. The amount of bandwidth you have is not guaranteed.

1.6.1 Goals

- Goals of Gigabit Ethernet are :
1. Upgrade the data rate to 1 Gbps.
2. Make it compatible with Standard of Fast Ethernet.
3. Use the same 48-bit address.
4. Keep the same minimum and maximum frame length.
5. Keep the same frame format.
6. To support autonegotiation same as Fast Ethernet.

1.6.2 MAC Sublayer   (Oct. 14)

- To achieve 1 Gbps data rate, Gigabit Ethernet has two different approaches for medium access i.e., half-duplex and full-duplex.
- All Gigabit Ethernet implementation follow full-duplex approach, the half-duplex is used for compatible with the previous generations.

1. **Full-duplex Mode :**

- In full-duplex mode, there is a central switch connected to all computers or other switches. Every port of the switch has buffer to store data, data is stored until it is transmitted.
- Since, there is no collision in this mode, CSMA/CD is not used. The maximum length of cable is determined by the signal attenuation in the cable.

2. **Half-duplex Mode :**

- Gigabit Ethernet can also be used in half-duplex mode, but its very rare.
- In half-duplex mode, instead of a switch, hub is use in which collision might occur.
- The half-duplex approach uses CSMA/CD. The maximum length of the network is dependent on the minimum frame size.
  - (i) **Traditional:** In the traditional approach, the minimum length of the frame is same as traditional Ethernet (512 bits). The maximum length is 25 m. This length may be suitable if all the stations are in one room, but it may not even be long to connect the computers in one single office.
  - (ii) **Carrier Extension:** For longer network, the minimum frame length is increased. It is 512 bytes (4096 bits). The maximum length is 200 m.
  - (iii) **Frame Bursting:** Carrier extension is very inefficient if we have series of short frames to send. To improve efficiency, frame bursting is used. In this approach multiple frames with padding are send. These multiple frames look like one frame.   (Oct. 14)

1.6.3 Physical Layer

- The physical layer in Gigabit Ethernet is more complicated than that in Standard or Fast Ethernet.

1.6.3.1 Topology

- Gigabit Ethernet is designed to connect two or more stations.
- If there are only two stations, they can be connected point-to-point as shown in Fig. 1.23.

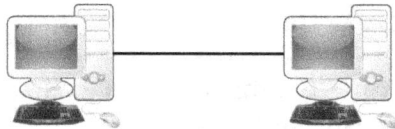

Fig. 1.23

- Three or more stations need to be connected in a star topology with a hub or a switch at the center as shown in Fig.   .

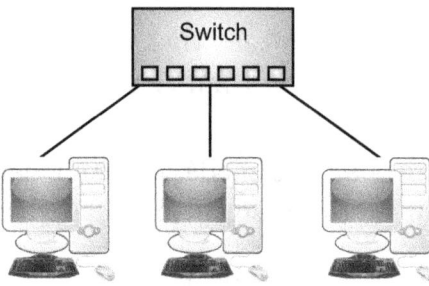

Fig. 1.24

- Another possible configuration is to connect several star topologies or let a star topology be part of another as shown in Fig. 1.25.

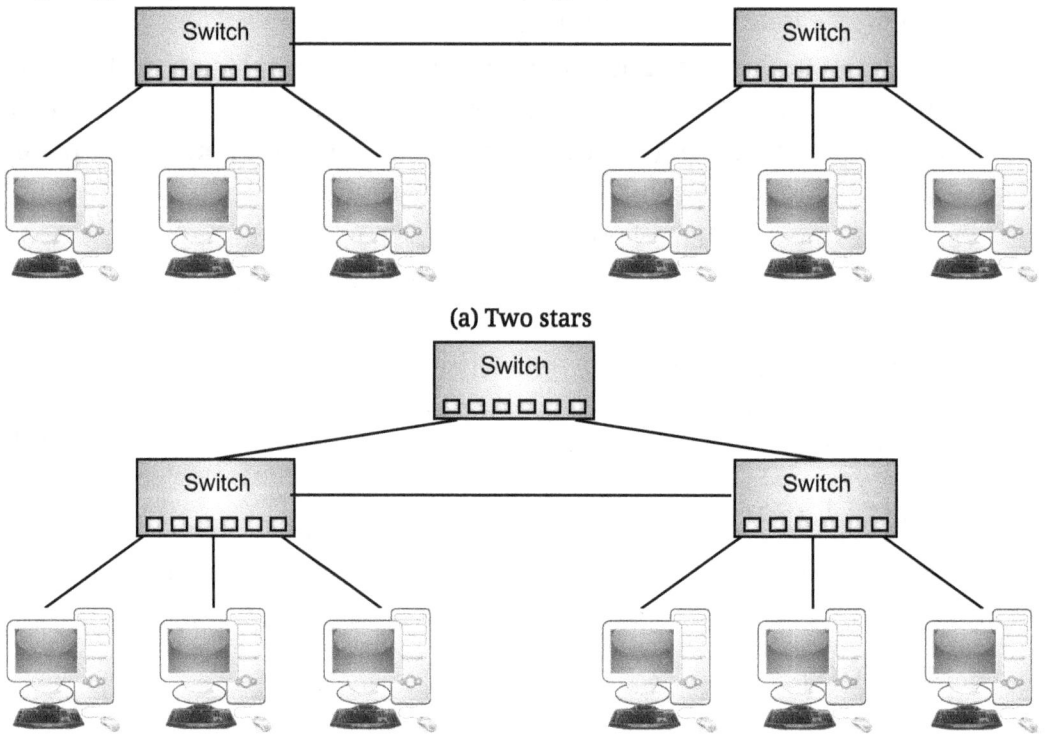

(a) Two stars

(b) Hierarchy of Stars

Fig. 1.25

1.6.3.2 Implementation

- Gigabit Ethernet implementations are shown in Fig. 1.26.
- Two different implementation of Gigabit Ethernet are two wires and a four Wire.
    1. The two-wire implementations use fiber-optic cable (1000Base-SX, short-wave, or 1000Base-LX, long-wave), or STP (1000Base-CX).
    2. The four-wire version uses category 5 twisted-pair cable (1000Base-T).

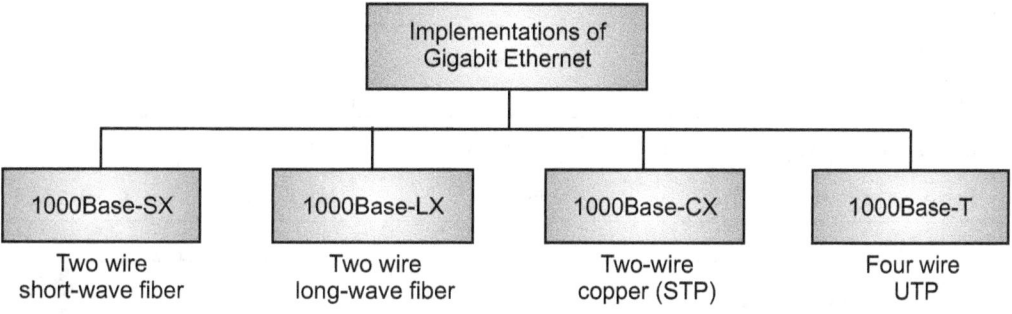

Fig. 1.26

Encoding :

- Fig. 1.27 shows the encoding/decoding schemes for the four implementations of Gigabit Ethernet.

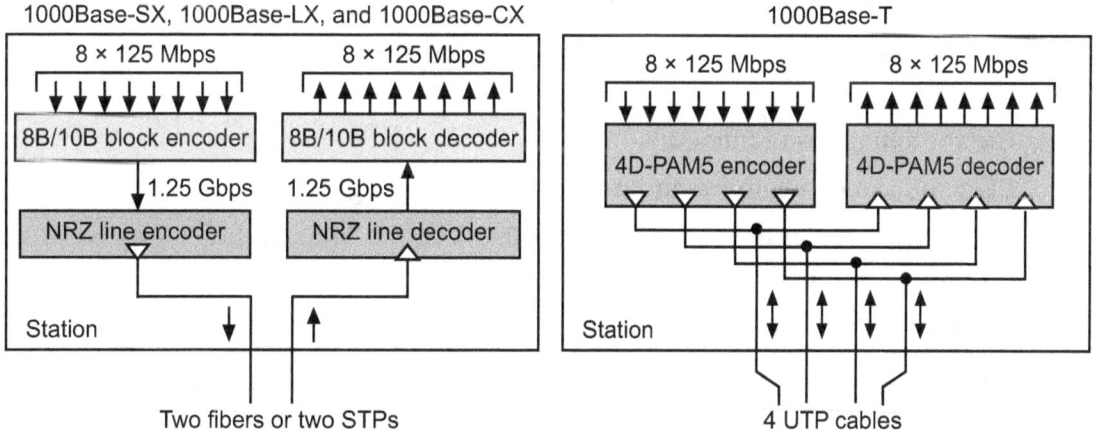

Fig. 1.27

- Gigabit Ethernet uses 8B/10B block encoding, resulting 1.25 Gbps.
- In the four-wire implementation, 4D-PAM5 encoding is used to reduce the bandwidth. Thus, all four wires are involved in both input and output; each wire carries 250 Mbps, which is in the range for category 5 UTP cable.

Summary of Gigabit Ethernet implementation :

Sr. No.	Characteristics	1000Base-SX	1000Base-LX	1000Base-CX	1000Base-T
1.	Media	Fiber short wave	Fiber long wave	STP	Cat 5 UTP
2.	Number of wires	2	2	2	4
3.	Maximum length	550 m	5000 m	25 m	100 m
4.	Block encoding	8B/10B	8B/10B	8B/10B	
5.	Line encoding	NRZ	NRZ	NRZ	4D-PAM5

1.7 | TEN-GIGABIT ETHERNET   (April 15)

- The IEEE developed a standard 802.3ae named as Ten-Gigabit Ethernet.

1.7.1 Goals

- The goals of the Ten-Gigabit Ethernet are:
  1. Upgrade the data rate to 10 Gbps.
  2. Make it compatible with Standard, Fast, and Gigabit Ethernet.
  3. Use the same 48-bit address.
  4. Use the same frame format.
  5. Keep the same minimum and maximum frame lengths.
  6. Allow the interconnection of existing LANs into a Metropolitan Area Network (MAN) or a Wide Area Network (WAN).
  7. Make Ethernet compatible with technologies such as Frame Relay and ATM

1.7.2 MAC Sublayer and Physical Layer

1. MAC Sublayer:
- Ten-Gigabit Ethernet operates only in full duplex mode.
- There is no need of CSMA/CD.
2. Physical Layer:
- The physical layer in Ten-Gigabit Ethernet is designed for using fiber-optic cable over long distances.

- Three implementations are the most common i.e. 10GBase-S, 10GBase-L and 10GBase-E.

Points of the Ten-Gigabit Ethernet implementations :

Sr. No.	Characteristics	10GBase-S	10GBase-L	10GBase-E
1.	Media	Short-wave 850-nm multimode	Long-wave 1310-nm single mode	Extended 1550-mm single mode
2.	Maximum length	300 m	10 km	40 km

1.8 BACKBONE NETWORKS   (April 11, 12)

- A backbone network or network backbone is a part of computer network.
- A backbone network allows several LANs to be connected. It provides a path for the exchange of information between different LANs or subnetworks.
- In a backbone network, no station is directly connected to the backbone; the stations are part of a LAN, and the backbone connects the LANs.
- The backbone is itself a LAN, each connection to the backbone is itself another LAN.
- Many different architectures are used as a backbone, most common are bus and the star.

1.8.1 Bus Backbone   (April 12)

- In a bus backbone, the topology of the backbone is a bus.
- The backbone uses the protocols that support a bus topology such as 10Base2 or 10Base5.
- Bus backbones are used as a distribution backbone to connect different buildings in an organization. Each building may comprise either a single LAN or another backbone (normally a star backbone).
- A example of a bus backbone is a LAN that connects single or multiple-floor buildings on a campus. Each single-floor building usually has a single LAN. Each multiple-floor building has a backbone (usually a star) that connects each LAN on a floor. A bus backbone can interconnect these LANs and backbones.
- Fig. 1.28 shows an example of a bridge-based backbone with four LANs. If a station in a LAN needs to send a frame to another station in the same LAN, the

corresponding bridge blocks the frame. However, if a station needs to send a frame to a station in another LAN, the bridge passes the frame to the backbone, which is received by the appropriate bridge and is delivered to the destination LAN. A bus network with a backbone offers greater reliability than a simple bus topology.

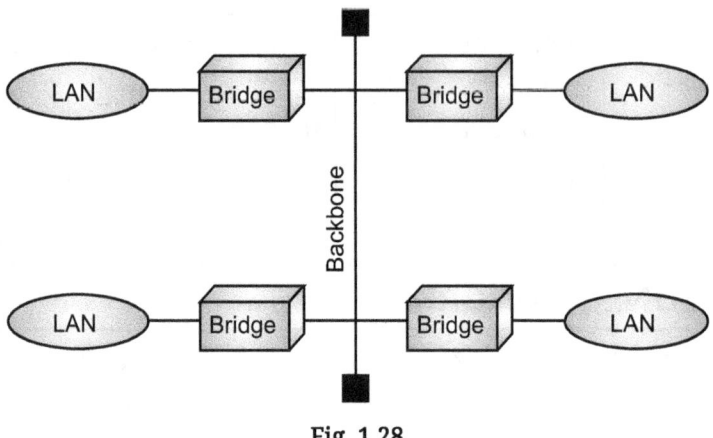

Fig. 1.28

1.8.2 Star Backbone   (April 12)

- A star backbone, also called a collapsed or switched backbone, the topology of the backbone is a star.

- In star backbone configuration, the backbone is just one switch that connects the LANs.

- Fig. 1.29 shows a star backbone. The switch does the job of the backbone and at the same time connects the LANs. Star backbones are mostly used as a distribution backbone inside a building.

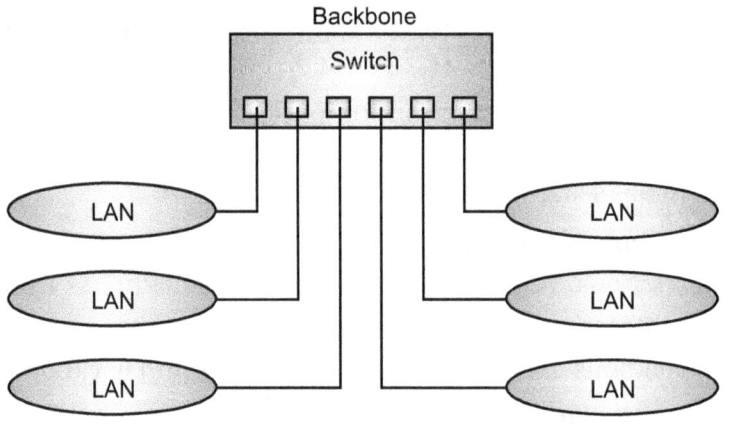

Fig. 1.29

- In a multi-floor building, we usually find one LAN that serves each particular floor.
- A star backbone connects these LANs. The backbone network, which is just a switch, can be installed in the basement or the first floor, and separate cables can run from the switch to each LAN.
- If the individual LANs have a physical star topology, either the hubs or switches can be installed on the corresponding floor, or all can be installed close to the switch.

1.8.3 Connecting Remote LANs

- For connecting remote LANs backbone networks are used. If a organization has several offices, each one having its own LAN and wish to connect them, this type of backbone networks are used.
- The connection can be done through bridges, so sometimes it is called as remote bridges.
- The bridges act as connecting devices connecting LANs and point-to-point networks, such as leased telephone lines or Asymmetric Digital Subscriber Line (ADSL) lines.
- The point-to-point network in this case is considered a LAN without stations.
- Fig. 1.30 shows a backbone connecting remote LANs.

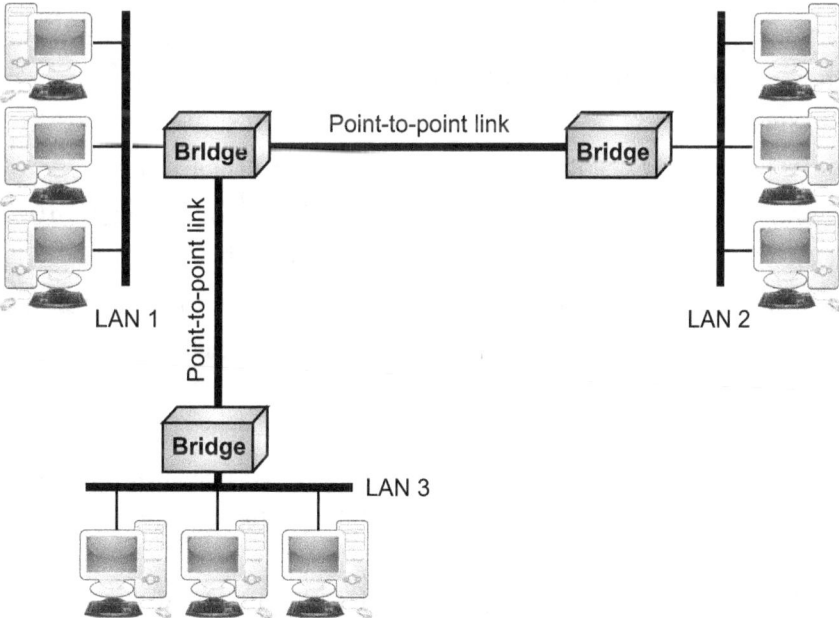

Fig. 1.30

1.9 | VIRTUAL LANs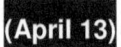

- A Virtual Local Area Network (VLAN) is a logical group of workstations, servers and network devices that appear to be on the same LAN despite their geographical location.

- We can define a virtual local area network (VLAN) as "a local area network configured by software, not by physical wiring".

Characteristics of VLAN :

1. Individual VLAN acts as a separate LAN, thus sharing the traffic among VLANs and reducing the congestion.

2. Workstations can be provided with full bandwidth at each port.

3. Relocation of terminals becomes easy.

4. Virtual LAN is software that is employed to provide multiple networks in single hub by grouping terminals connected to switching hubs. It is a LANs that is grouped together by logical addresses into a virtual LAN instead of a physical LAN through a switch. The switch can support many virtual LANs that operate with having different network addresses or as subnets. Users within a virtual LAN are grouped either by IP address or by port address, with each node attached to the switch via a dedicated circuit. Users also can be assigned to more than one virtual LAN.

5. The VLAN can be defined as a broadcast domain in which the broadcast address reaches all stations belonging to the VLAN. Communications within the VLAN can be secured, and between those two controlled separate VLANs.

6. A router is generally required to establish communication between VLANs.

- Fig. 1.31 shows a switched LAN in an engineering firm in which 10 stations are grouped into three LANs that are connected by a switch.

- The first four computer engineers work together as the first group, the next three computer engineers work together as the second group, and the last three computer engineers work together as the third group.

- The LAN is configured to allow this arrangement. But consider for a new project, if administrator needs two engineers from first, one from second and two from third group, the LAN configuration would need to be changed. The entire network need to be rewire.

- This problem may repeated for another project. In a switched LAN, changes in the work group mean physical changes in the network configuration.

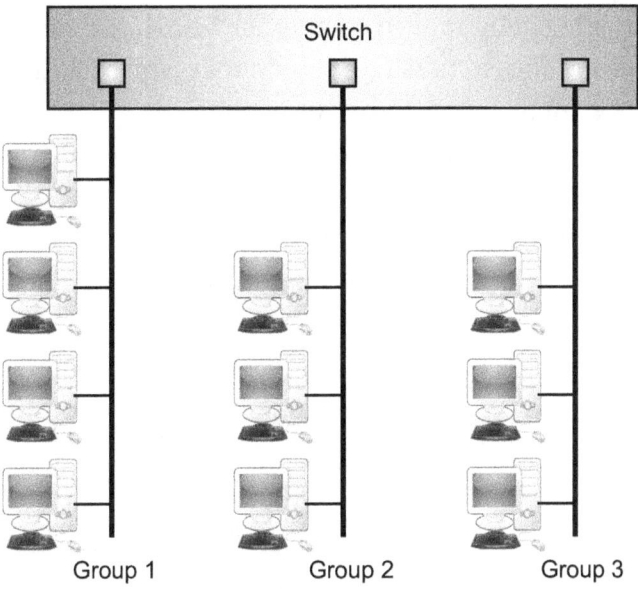

Fig. 1.31

- Fig. 1.32 shows the same switched LAN divided into VLANs. The whole idea of VLAN technology is to divide a LAN into logical, instead of physical, segments.

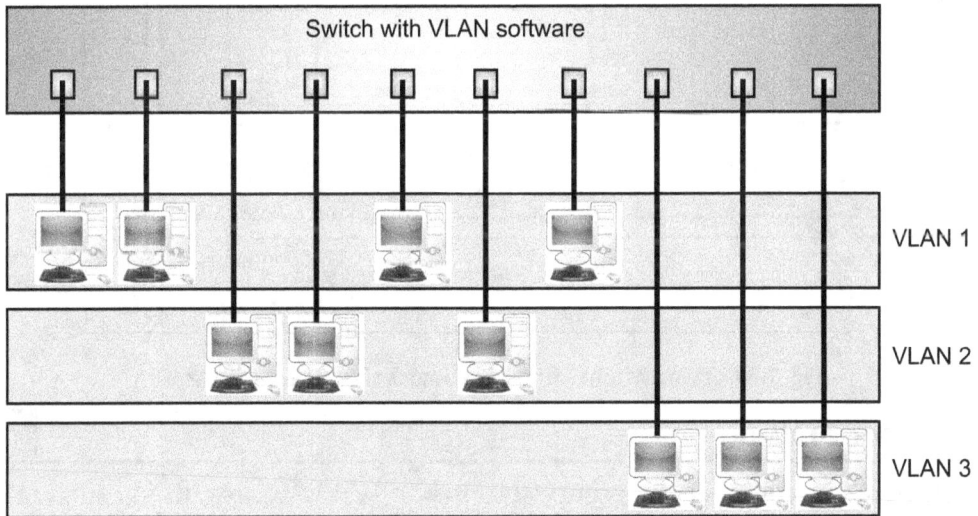

Fig. 1.32 : A Switch using VLAN software

- A LAN can be divided into several logical LANs called VLANs. Each VLAN is a work group in the organization.
- If a person moves from one group to another, there is no need to change the physical configuration. The group membership in VLANs is defined by software, not by hardware.

- Any station can be logically moved to another VLAN. All members belonging to a VLAN can receive broadcast messages sent to that particular VLAN.

- This means if a station moves from VLAN 1 to VLAN 2, it receives broadcast messages sent to VLAN 2, but no longer receives broadcast messages sent to VLAN 1. Moving engineers from one group to another through software is easier than changing the configuration of the physical network.

- VLAN technology even allows the grouping of stations connected to different switches in a VLAN.

- Fig. 1.33 shows a backbone local area network with two switches and three VLANs. Stations from switches X and Y belong to each VLAN.

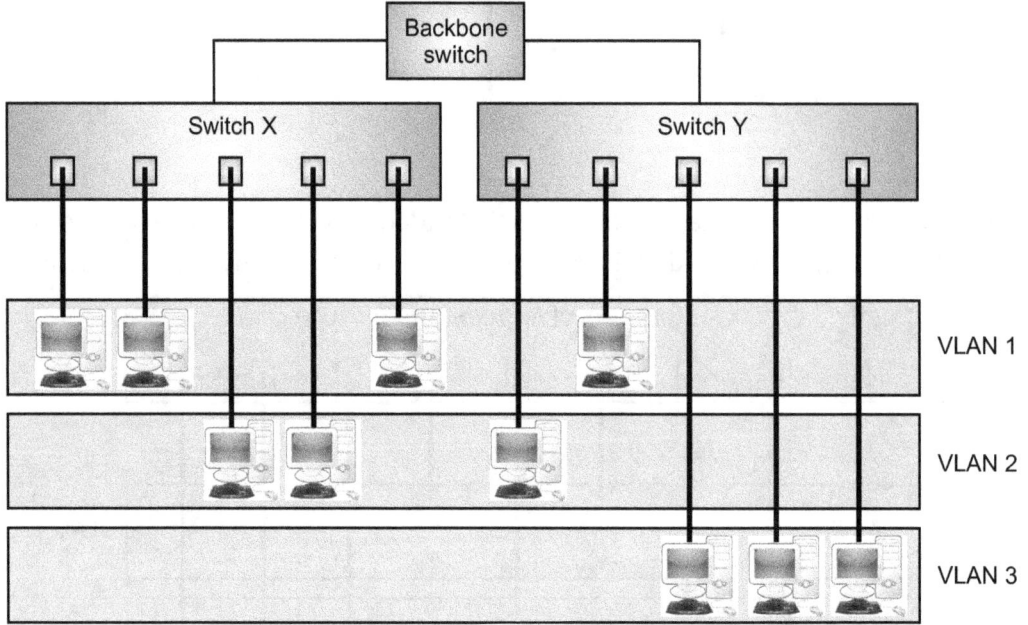

Fig. 1.33 : Two switches in a backbone using VLAN software

1.9.1 Membership   (Oct. 14)

- Different characteristics to group stations in a VLAN are used, such as port numbers, MAC addresses, IP addresses, IP multicast addresses, or a combination of two or more of these.

1. **Port Numbers:**

- Some VLAN vendors use switch port numbers as a membership characteristic.

- For example, in a bridge with four ports, ports 1, 2, and 4 belong to VLAN 1 and port 3 belongs to VLAN 2 (see Fig. 1.34).

Port	VLAN
1	1
2	1
3	2
4	1

Fig. 1.34: Assignment of ports to different VLAN's.

- The main disadvantage of this method is that it does not allow for user mobility. If a user moves to a different location away from the assigned bridge, the network manager must reconfigure the VLAN.

2. **MAC Addresses :**

- Some VLAN vendors use the 48-bit MAC address as a membership characteristic. The switch tracks the MAC addresses which belong to each VLAN (see Fig. 1.35).

- Since, MAC addresses form a part of the workstation's network interface card, when a workstation is moved, no reconfiguration is needed to allow the workstation to remain in the same VLAN. This is unlike Layer 1 VLAN's where membership tables must be reconfigured.

MAC Address	VLAN
1212354145121	1
2389234873743	2
3045834758445	2
5483573475843	1

Fig. 1.35: Assignment of MAC addresses to different VLAN's.

- The main problem with this method is that VLAN membership must be assigned initially. In networks with thousands of users, this is no easy task.

- Also, in environments where notebook PC's are used, the MAC address is associated with the docking station and not with the notebook PC.

- Consequently, when a notebook PC is moved to a different docking station, its VLAN membership must be reconfigured.

3. **IP Addresses :**

- Some VLAN vendors use the 32-bit IP address as a membership characteristic.

- For example, the administrator can stipulate that stations having IP addresses 181.34.23.67, 181.34.23.72, 181.34.23.98, and 181.34.23.112 belong to VLAN 1.

4. **Multicast IP Addresses :**

- Some VLAN vendors use the multicast IP address as a membership characteristic.
- Multicasting at the IP layer is now translated to multicasting at the data link layer.

5. **Combination :**

- Recently, the software available from some vendors allows all these characteristics to be combined.
- The network administrator can choose one or more characteristics when installing the software. In addition, the software can be reconfigured to change the settings.

1.9.2 Configuration

- How are the stations grouped into different VLANs? Stations are configured in one of three ways i.e. manual, automatic, and semiautomatic.

  1. **In a Manual Configuration** the administrator uses the VLAN software to manually assign the stations into different VLANs at setup. Later migration from one VLAN to another is also done manually. Note that this is not a physical configuration; it is a logical configuration. The term manually here means that the network administrator types the port numbers, the IP addresses, or other characteristics, using the VLAN software.

  2. **In an Automatic Configuration**, the stations are automatically connected or disconnected from a VLAN using criteria defined by the administrator. For example, the administrator can define the project number as the criterion for being a member of a group. When a user changes the project, he or she automatically migrates to a new VLAN.

  3. **A Semiautomatic Configuration** is somewhere between a manual configuration and an automatic configuration. Usually, the initializing is done manually, with migrations done automatically.

1.9.3 Communication Between Switches

- In a multi-switched backbone, each switch must know not only which station belongs to which VLAN, but also the membership of stations connected to other switches.

- For example, in Fig. 1.33, switch X must know the membership status of stations connected to switch Y, and switch Y must know the same about switch X.

- Three methods have been devised for this purpose named as table maintenance, frame tagging, and time-division multiplexing.

    1. **Table Maintenance:** In this method, when a station sends a broadcast frame to its group members, the switch creates an entry in a table and records station membership. The switches send their tables to one another periodically for updating.

    2. **Frame Tagging:** In frame tagging method, when a frame is traveling between switches, an extra header is added to the MAC frame to define the destination VLAN. The frame tag is used by the receiving switches to determine the VLANs to be receiving the broadcast message.

    3. **TDM (Time-Division Multiplexing):** In TDM method, the connection (trunk) between switches is divided into timeshared channels. For example, if the total number of VLANs in a backbone is five, each trunk is divided into five channels. The traffic destined for VLAN 1 travels in channel 1, the traffic destined for VLAN 2 travels in channel 2, and so on. The receiving switch determines the destination VLAN by checking the channel from which the frame arrived.

1.9.4 IEEE Standard

- In 1996, IEEE passed a standard called 802.1Q, which defines format for frame tagging.

- This 802-1Q standard also defines format to be used in multi switched backbones and allow to use multivendor equipments in VLAN.

1.9.5 Advantages of VLANs

- There are several advantages to using VLANs. Some of them are listed below:

    1. **Security :** VLANs provide an extra measure of security. People belonging to the same group can send broadcast messages with the guaranteed assurance that users in other groups will not receive these messages.

    2. **Cost and Time Reduction :** VLANs can reduce the migration cost of stations going from one group to another. Physical reconfiguration takes time and is costly. Instead of physically moving one station to another segment or even to another switch, it is much easier and quicker to move it by using software.

    3. **Creating Virtual Work Groups :** VLANs can be used to create virtual work groups. For example, in a campus environment, professors working on the same project can send broadcast messages to one another without the necessity of belonging to the same department. This can reduce traffic if the multicasting capability of IP was previously used.

4. **Performance** : In networks where traffic consists of a high percentage of broadcasts and multicasts, VLAN's can reduce the need to send such traffic to unnecessary destinations.

5. **Simplified Administration** : Seventy percent of network costs are a result of adds, moves, and changes of users in the network. Every time a user is moved in a LAN, re-cabling, new station addressing, and reconfiguration of hubs and routers becomes necessary. Some of these tasks can be simplified with the use of VLAN's. If a user is moved within a VLAN, reconfiguration of routers is unnecessary. In addition, depending on the type of VLAN, other administrative work can be reduced or eliminated.

SUMMARY

➤ As technology advances in society the need for wired and wireless networking has become essential. Wired networking has different hardware requirements and the range and benefits are different. Wireless networking takes into consideration the range, mobility, and the several types of hardware components needed to establish a wireless network.

➤ Wired networks, also called Ethernet networks, are the most common type of Local Area Network (LAN) technology.

➤ A wired network is simply a collection of two or more computers, printers, and other devices linked by Ethernet cables.

➤ The Institute of Electrical and Electronic Engineers (IEEE) developed a series of networking standards to ensure that networking technologies like 802.3 for Ethernet, 802.11 for wireless networks etc.

➤ The data link layer in the IEEE standard is divided into two sub layers i.e., LLC and MAC. The LLC provides one single data link control protocol for all IEEE LANs. IEEE Project 802 has created a sublayer called media access control that defines the specific access method for each LAN.

➤ The physical layer is dependent on the implementation and type of physical media (electrical, mechanical etc.) used. IEEE defines detailed specifications for each LAN implementation.

➤ The original Ethernet was created in 1976 at Xerox's Palo Alto Research Center (PARC). Ethernet is a standardized system for connecting computers to a LAN.

➤ A standard Ethernet network can transmit data at a rate up to 10 Megabits per second (10 Mbps).

➤ A standard Ethernet network can transmit data at a rate up to 10 Megabits per second (10 Mbps). 10Base5 is also called as thick Ethernet or Thicknet.

➤ 10Base2 is also called as thin Ethernet or Cheapernet.

➤ There are several types of optical fiber 10-Mbps Ethernet, the most common is called as 10Base-F.

➤ The first step in the Ethernet evolution was the division of a LAN by bridges. Bridges have two effects on an Ethernet LAN i.e., they raise the bandwidth and they separate collision domains.

➤ In the case of individual hosts, the switch replaces the repeater and effectively gives the device full 10 Mbps bandwidth (or 100 Mbps for Fast Ethernet) to the rest of the network. This type of network is sometimes called a desktop switched Ethernet.

➤ Full-duplex Ethernet switching has the ability to send and receive data at the same time. The full-duplex mode increases the capacity of each domain from 10 to 20 Mbps.

➤ Fast Ethernet is a version of Ethernet with a 100 Mbps data rate.

➤ The need for an even higher data rate resulted in the design of the Gigabit Ethernet protocol (1000 Mbps). IEEE created Gigabit Ethernet under the name 802.3z.

➤ 10 Gigabit Ethernet (10GE, 10GbE, or 10 GigE) is a group of computer networking technologies for transmitting Ethernet frames at a rate of 10 gigabits per second (10×109 or 10 billion bits per second).

➤ A backbone network or network backbone is a part of computer network infrastructure that interconnects various pieces of network, providing a path for the exchange of information between different LANs or sub-networks.

➤ In a bus backbone, the topology of the backbone is a bus. The backbone itself can use one of the protocols that support a bus topology such as 10Base2 or 10Base5.

➤ In a star backbone, sometimes called a collapsed or switched backbone, the topology of the backbone is a star.

➤ In star backbone configuration, the backbone is just one switch (that is why it is called, erroneously, a collapsed backbone) that connects the LANs.

➤ Connecting Remote LANs is a type of backbone network is useful when a company has several offices with LANs and needs to connect them. The connection can be done through bridges, so sometimes it is called as remote bridges.

➤ A Virtual Local Area Network (VLAN) is a logical group of workstations, servers and network devices that appear to be on the same LAN despite their geographical distribution.

➤ Three methods have been devised for this purpose named as table maintenance, frame tagging, and time-division.

➤ There are several advantages to using VLANs like Cost and Time Reduction and security.

PRACTICE QUESTIONS

1. What is Wired LAN?
2. What is IEEE standard?
3. Explain Standard Ethernet in detail.
4. Describe CSMA/CD in short.
5. What is bridged Ethernet?
6. Explain Data Link and Physical layer of IEEE standards.
7. With the help of diagram describe encoding and decoding of physical layer.
8. Write short notes on:
   (i) 10Base5   (ii) 10Base2   (iii) 100Base-TX   (iv) 100base-T4
9. What is Virtual LAN?
10. List goals of Fast Ethernet.
11. Explain MAC sublayer of Fast Ethernet.
12. What is Ten-gigabit Ethernet? Explain in detail.
13. What is meant by backbone networks?
14. Enlist advantages of VLANs.
15. What is Gigabit Ethernet? List its goals.
16. How to connect remote LAN? Explain with diagram.
17. List out advantages of VLANs.
18. What are the advantages and disadvantages of wired LANs?

UNIVERSITY QUESTIONS AND ANSWERS

April 2011

1. Explain all common fast Ethernet implementation.   [5 M]
Ans. Please refer to Section 1.5.3.1.
2. Write short note on switched Ethernet.   [5 M]
Ans. Please refer to Section 1.4.2.
3. Name the topologies used in backbone networks.   [1 M]
Ans. Please refer to Section 1.8.

October 2011

1. Write short note on Gigabit Ethernet.   [5 M]
Ans. Please refer to Section 1.6.
2. Explain CSMA/CD.   [5 M]
Ans. Please refer to Section 1.2.5.

April 2012

1. Write a short note on switched ethernet.   [5 M]
Ans. Please refer to Section 1.4.2.

2.   Explain CSMA/CD.   [5 M]
Ans. Please refer to Section 1.2.5.
3.   What are backbone networks ? Explain any two backbone networks.   [5 M]
Ans. Please refer to Section 1.8.

October 2012

1.   Give the function of LLC Sublayer.   [1 M]
Ans. Please refer to Section 1.1.1 Point (1).
2.   Write a note on 10Base5.   [5 M]
Ans. Please refer to Section 1.3.2.

April 2013

1.   Define 10 Base -T cabling.   [1 M]
Ans. Please refer to Section 1.3.4.
2.   Specify the purpose of using 802.2 and 802.11 IEEE standards.   [1 M]
Ans. Please refer to Section 1.1.
3.   Write note on CSMA/ CD.   [5 M]
Ans. Please refer to Section 1.2.5.
4.   What is gigabit ethernet ?   [5 M]
Ans. Please refer to Section 1.6.
5.   Explain advantages of VLAN.   [5 M]
Ans. Please refer to Section 1.9.

October 2014

1.   State the formula to calculate maximum length for traditional Ethernet. [1 m]
Ans. Please refer to Section 1.2.
2.   State the concept of frame bursting used in MAC sublayer of Gigabit
      Ethernet.   [1 m]
Ans. Please refer to Section 1.6.2 Point (2) (iii).
3.   State the topology used by fast Ethernet. Also write a note on implementation
      of fast Ethernet.   [5 M]
Ans. Please refer to Sections 1.5.3.1 and 1.5.3.2.
4.   Explain different attributes used to assign membership in VLAN.   [5 M]
Ans. Please refer to Section 1.9.1.

April 2015

1.   Why is the system called ethernet ?   [1 M]
Ans. Please refer to Section 1.0.
2.   What is Ethernet ? What are its types ?   [5 M]
Ans. Please refer to Sections 1.1, 1,2, 1,5, 1,6, 1,7.

❖❖❖

Wireless LAN

Contents ...

Objectives...

- To Understand Basic Concept of Wireless LAN
- To Study Arcitecture of 802.11
- To Learn Bluetooth Concepts

2.0 | INTRODUCTION   (April 12, 13)

- We know that LANs can be of two types i.e., Wired LAN and Wireless LAN.

- In the previous chapter we discussed about Wired LAN, in this chapter we concentrate on Wireless LAN IEEE 802.11, and Bluetooth, a technology for small wireless LANs.

- Now-a-days, wireless LANs can be found everywhere like college campuses, in office buildings, and in many public areas.

- A Wireless Local Area Network (WLAN) is a wireless computer network that links two or more devices using a wireless distribution method.

Advantages Wireless LAN :

1. **Convenience :** All notebook computers and many mobile phones are equipped with the Wi-Fi technology to connect directly to a wireless LAN.

2. **Increased mobility and Collaboration :** Users who use wireless LAN in a roam around the office or to different floors without losing their connection. Similarly, Voice over Wireless LAN technology gives them roaming capabilities with their voice communications.

3. **Improved responsiveness :** A wireless LAN can improve customer service by connecting employees to the information they need.

4. **Productivity :** A wireless LAN offers staff and others convenient access to information and your company's important applications. Visitors (such as customers, contractors, or vendors) can use a wireless LAN for secure guest access to the Internet and to their business data.

5. **Ease of Setup :** Since, a wireless LAN does not require running physical cables through a location, installation can be quick and cost-effective. A wireless LAN also makes it easier to bring network connectivity to hard-to-reach locations, such as a warehouse or factory floor.

6. **Scalability :** A wireless LAN can typically expand with existing equipment, while a wired network might require additional cables and other materials.

7. **Security :** Controlling and managing access to your wireless LAN is important to its success. Advances in WiFi technology provide robust security protection, so your data is easily available through the wireless LAN only to the people you allow access.

8. **Cost :** It can cost less to operate a wireless LAN, which eliminates or reduces wiring costs during office moves, reconfigurations, or expansions.

9. **Easier network expansion :** Companies that need to add employees or reconfigure offices frequently can benefit from the flexibility that a wireless LAN provides.

Disadvantages of Wireless LAN :

1. **Reliability :** Like any radio frequency transmission, wireless networking signals are subject to a wide variety of interference, as well as complex propagation effects that are beyond the control of the network administrator.

2. **Range :** The typical range of a common 802.11g network with standard equipment is on the order of tens of metres. While sufficient for a typical home, it will be insufficient in a larger structure. To obtain additional range, repeaters or additional access points will have to be purchased. Costs for these items can add up quickly. Other technologies are in the development phase, however, which feature increased range, hoping to render this disadvantage irrelevant.

3. **Speed :** The speed on most wireless networks (typically 1-108 Mbit/s) is reasonably slow compared to the slowest common wired.

4. **Security :** Wireless LAN transceivers are designed to serve computers throughout a structure with uninterrupted service using radio frequencies. Because of space and cost, the antennas typically present on wireless networking cards in the end computers are generally relatively poor.

5. **QoS :** WLAN offer typically lower QoS. Lower bandwidth due to limitations in radio transmission and higher error rates due to interference.

6. **Proprietary solutions :** Slow standardization procedures lead to many proprietary solutions only working in an homogeneous environment.

Applications of Wireless LANs:

- Wireless LANs have many applications in the real world. Applications of wireless LANs are as follows :

  1. Network managers in dynamic environments minimize the overhead of moves, adds, and changes with wireless LANs, thereby reducing the cost of LAN ownership.

  2. Doctors and nurses in hospitals are more productive because handheld or notebook computers with wireless LAN capability deliver patient information instantly.

  3. Warehouse workers use wireless LANs to exchange information with central databases and increase their productivity.

  4. Consulting or accounting audit teams or small workgroups increase productivity with quick network setup.

  5. Network managers installing networked computers in older buildings find that wireless LANs are a cost-effective network infrastructure solution.

  6. Training sites at corporations and students at universities use wireless connectivity to facilitate access to information, information exchanges, and learning.

2.1 | IEEE 802.11 ARCHITECTURE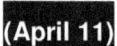

- IEEE defines a standard for wireless LAN, named IEEE 802.11, which covers the physical and data link layers.

- The IEEE 802.11 standard defines two different services BSS and ESS as explained below :

1. Basic Service Set (BSS): (Oct. 11, 12)

- BSS is a building block for a Wireless LAN.

- A BSS is made up of stationary or mobile wireless station and an optional central base station, known as Access Point (AP).

- The BSS without an AP is a stand- alone network and called as ad hoc architecture. Such type of networks cannot send data to other BSSs.

- Stations can form a network without the need of AP. Stations can locate one another and agree to be part of a BSS.

- A BSS with an AP is called as infrastructure network. All stations in such architecture are communicating through an AP.

- Fig. 2.1 shows two sets of IEEE 802.11 standard.

BSS : Basic Service Set
AP : Access Point

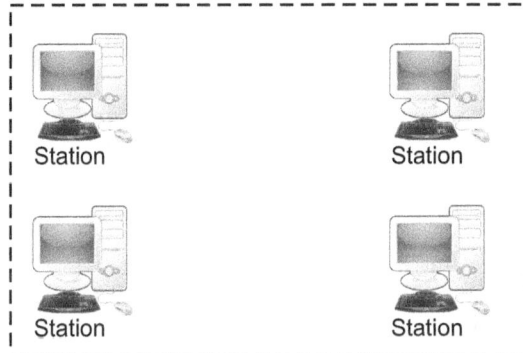
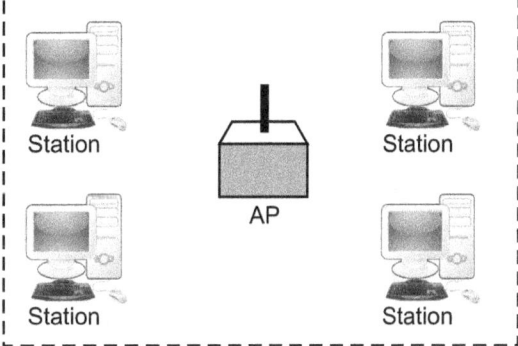

Ad hoc network (BSS without an AP)   Infrastructure (BSS with an AP)

Fig. 2.1

2. Extended Service Set (ESS):

- An extended service set is made up of two or more BSSs with APs.

- The BSSs are connected through a distribution system, which is a wired LAN. The distribution system connects the APs in the BSSs.

- ESS uses two types of stations, i.e., mobile and stationary stations.

- The mobile stations are the normal stations in the BSS. The stationary stations are AP stations that are part of a wired LAN.

- Communication between two stations from two different BSSs are taken place via., two APs. But when stations are within reach of one another, they can communicate directly, without the use of AP.

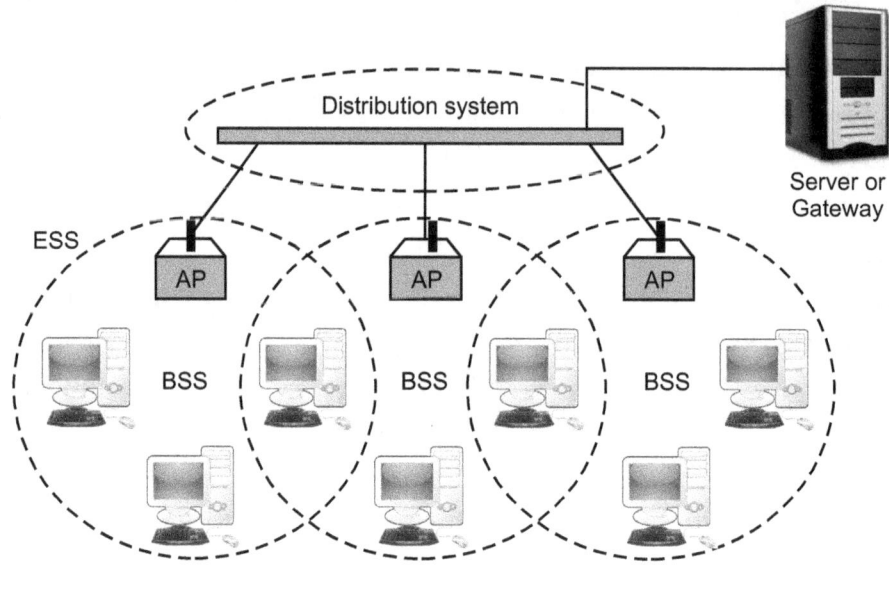

Fig. 2.2

Station Types: (Oct. 12)

- Based on mobility, IEEE 802.11 defines three types of stations in a wireless LAN, as given below:

  1. **No-transition:** A station with no-transition mobility is either stationary (not moving) or moving only inside a BSS.

  2. **BSS-transition:** A station with BSS-transition mobility can move from one BSS to another, but the movement is in one ESS only.

  3. **ESS-transition:** A station with ESS-transition mobility can move from one ESS to another.

MAC Sublayer:

- IEEE 802.11 defines two MAC sublayers, Distribution Co-ordination Function (DCF) and Point Co-ordination Function (PCF).

- Fig. 2.3 shows the relationship between the two MAC sublayers, the LLC sublayer and the physical layer.

- CSMA/CA (Carrier Sense Multiple Access with Collision Avoidance) is the protocol used to access method defined by IEEE at the MAC sublayer is called the Distribution Co-ordination Function (DCF).

- The Point Co-ordination Function (PCF) is an optional access method which is implemented in an infrastructure network and not in ad hoc network. It is implemented on top of the DCF and is used for time sensitive transmission.

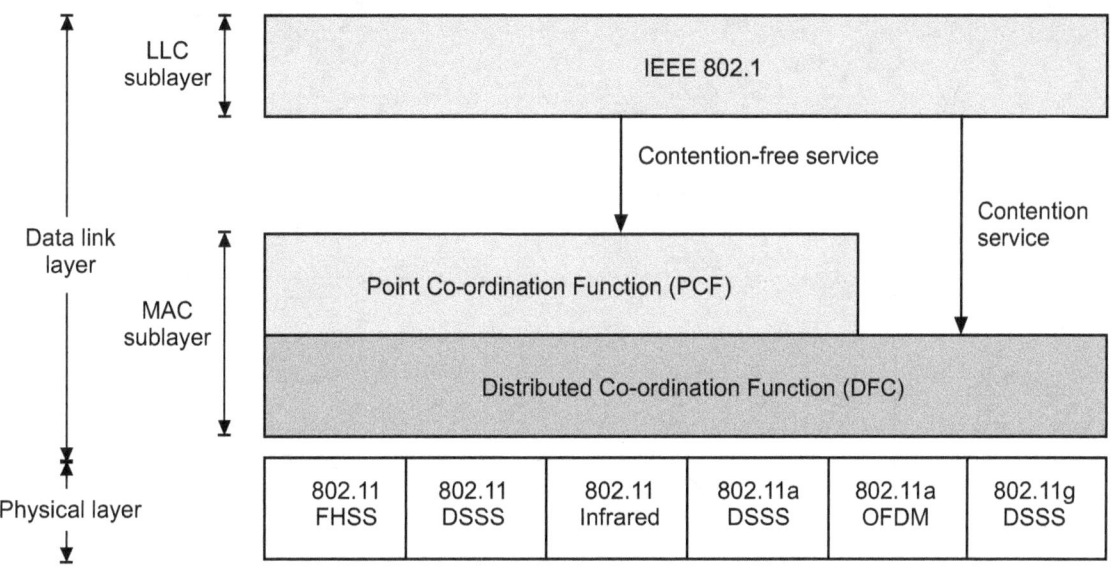

Fig. 2.3

- In wireless LAN, CSMA/CD cannot be implemented because of following reasons:

  1. For collision detection, a station must be able to send data and receive collision signals at the same time, which increases bandwidth requirements.

  2. Collision may not be detected because of the hidden station problem.

  3. The distance between stations can be great. Signal fading could prevent a station at one end from hearing a collision at the other end.

- Fig. 2.4 shows data exchange and control frames used in CSMA/CA. Before sending a frame, the source station senses the medium. There are two options:

  1. The channel uses a persistence strategy with back-off until the channel is idle.

  2. After the station found to be idle, the station waits for a period of time called the Distributed InterFrame Space (DIFS), then the station sends a control frame Request To Send (RTS).

- After receiving the RTS and waiting for a period Short Inter Frame Space (SIFS), the destination sends a control frame called Clear To Send (CTS). This control frame indicates to source that the destination station is ready to receive data.

- The source then waits for time equal to SIFS and then sends data. After receiving data, destination waits for time equal to SIFS and sends acknowledgement to the source.

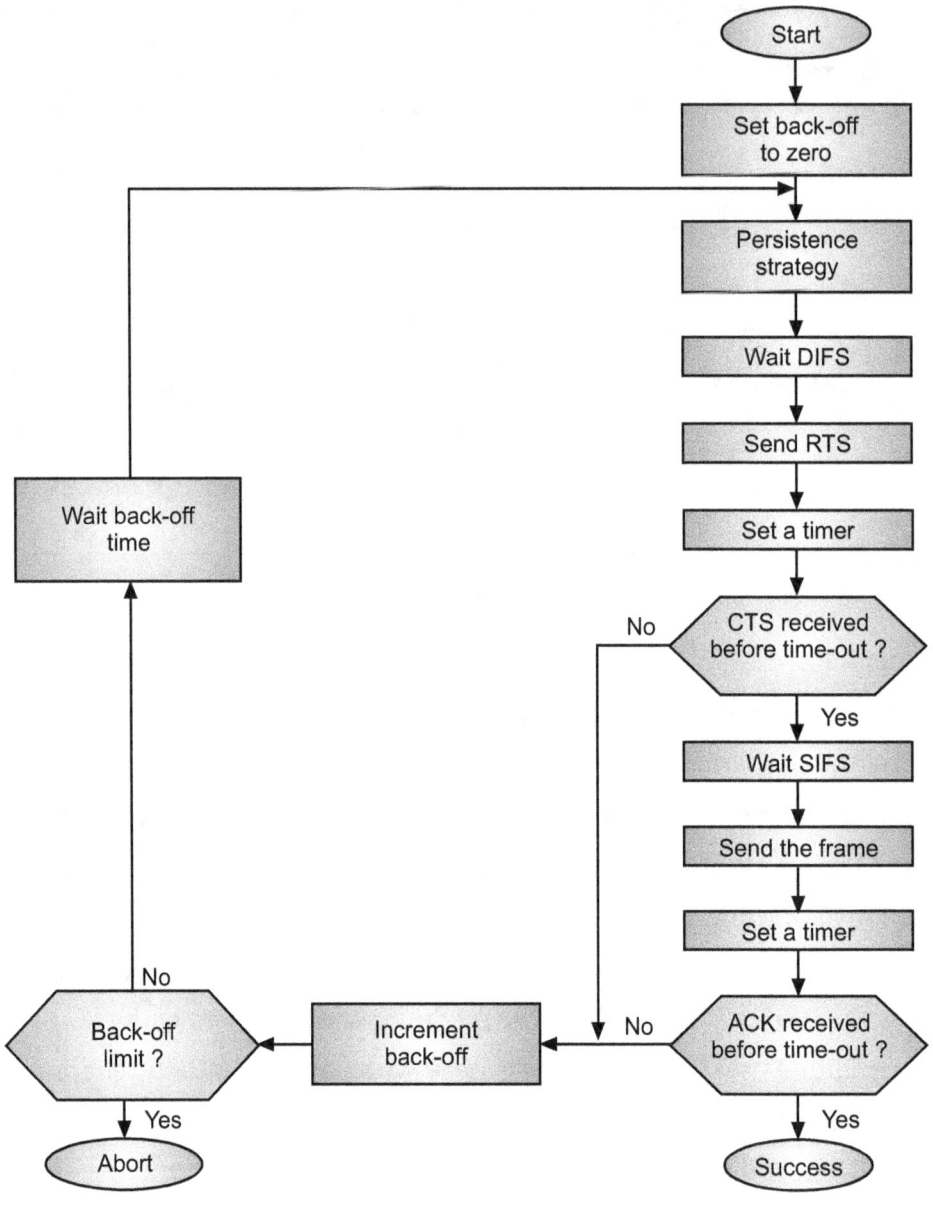

Fig. 2.4

Network Allocation Vector (NAV) :

- It's interesting to see how is the collision avoidance handled by the protocol. CSMA/CA protocol uses a feature called NAV. When a station sends RTS frame, it also includes the total time that is needed to occupy the channel.

- The stations that are affected by this transmission create a timer called NAV, that shows how much time these stations should not sense the channel. Each time a station accesses the system and sends RTS frame, other station starts NAV.

- Two or more stations may try to send RTS frames at the same time. These control frames may collide and destroy. The sender assumes there has been a collision if it has not received a CTS from the receiver. In such situation, sender tries again. This concept is known as collision during handshaking.

Frame Format :

- The MAC layer consists of nine fields as shown in Fig. 2.5.

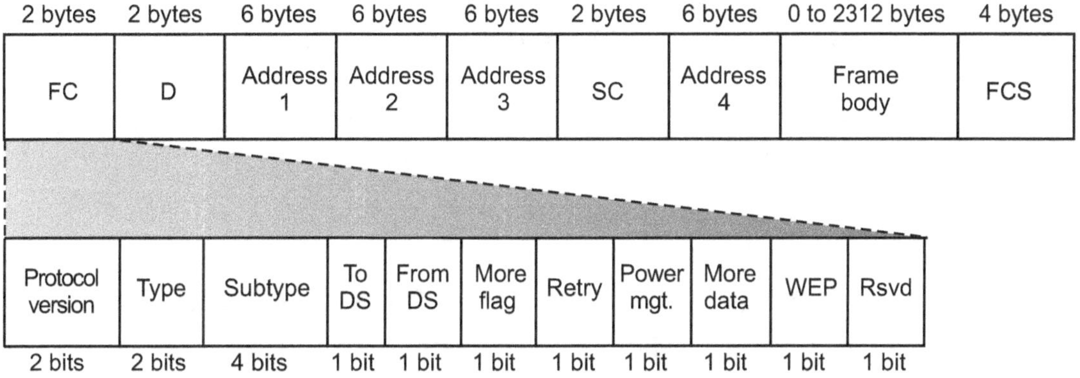

2 bytes	2 bytes	6 bytes	6 bytes	6 bytes	2 bytes	6 bytes	0 to 2312 bytes	4 bytes
FC	D	Address 1	Address 2	Address 3	SC	Address 4	Frame body	FCS

Protocol version	Type	Subtype	To DS	From DS	More flag	Retry	Power mgt.	More data	WEP	Rsvd
2 bits	2 bits	4 bits	1 bit	1 bit	1 bit	1 bit	1 bit	1 bit	1 bit	1 bit

Fig. 2.5: MAC layer frame format

1. **Frame Control (FC):** The FC field is 2 bytes long and defines the type of frame and some control information.

- The subfields of FC field are listed below:

    (i) **Version** : Current version is 0.

    (ii) **Type** : Type of information: management (00), control (01), or data (10).

    (iii) **Subtype** : Subtype of each type.

    (iv) **To DS** : Defined later.

    (v) **From DS** : Defined later.

    (vi) **More flag** : When set to 1, means more fragments.

    (vii) **Retry** : When set to 1, means retransmitted frame.

    (viii) **Pwr mgt** : When set to 1, means station is in power management mode.

    (ix) **More data** : When set to 1, means station has more data to send.

    (x) **WEP** : Wired equivalent privacy (encryption implemented).

    (xi) **Rsvd** : Reserved.

2. **D:** In all frames, this field defines the duration of the transmission that is used to set the value of NAV.

3. **Addresses:** There are four address fields, each 6 bytes long. The meaning of each address field depends on the value of the To DS and From DS subfields.

To DS	From DS	Address 1	Address 2	Address 3	Address 4
0	0	Destination	Source	BSS ID	N/A
0	1	Destination	Sending AP	Source	N/A
1	0	Receiving AP	Source	Destination	N/A
1	1	Receiving AP	Sending AP	Destination	Source

4. **Sequence control:** This field defines the sequence number of the frame to be used in flow control.

5. **Frame body:** This field between 0 to 2312 bytes contains information based on the type and the subtype defined in the FC field.

6. **FCS:** This field is used for error detection.

Frame Types :

- IEEE 802.11, wireless LAN defines three types of frames, as explained below:

   1. **Management Frames:** Management frames are used for the initial communication between stations and access points.

   2. **Control Frames:** Control frames are used for accessing the channel and acknowledging frames.

   3. **Data Frames:** Data frames are used for carrying data and control information.

2.2 | BLUETOOTH   (April 11)

- Bluetooth is a wireless LAN technology used to connect devices of different functions such as telephones, computers like laptop or desktop, notebooks, cameras, printers and so on.

- The Bluetooth specifications are developed and licensed by the Bluetooth Special Interest Group. Bluetooth technology is a short-range wireless radio technology that allows electronic devices to connect to one another.

- Generally, Bluetooth has a range of up to 30 ft. or greater, depending on the Bluetooth Core Specification Version. Newer devices, using newer versions of Bluetooth, have ranges over 100 ft.

- A Bluetooth LAN is an ad hoc network, which means that the network is formed spontaneously. The devices find each other and make a network.

- Bluetooth is an open specification for short-range wireless transmission of voice and data. It provides a simple, low-cost seamless wireless connectivity between portable handheld devices.

- Bluetooth technology is the implementation of a protocol defined by the IEEE 802.15 standard.

- The standard defines a wireless Personal Area Network (PAN) operable in an area the size of a room or a hall.

2.2.1 Bluetooth Architecture   (Oct. 11; April 12, 13)

- Bluetooth architecture defines two types of networks i.e., Piconet and Scatternet.

1. Piconet :   (Oct. 11; April 12, 15)

- Piconet is a Bluetooth network that consists of one primary (master) node and seven active secondary (slave) nodes.

- Thus, piconet can have upto eight active nodes (1 master and 7 slaves) or stations within the distance of 10 meters.

- There can be only one primary or master station in each piconet.

- The communication between the primary and the secondary can be one-to-one or one-to-many.

- Fig. 2.6 shows typical piconet.

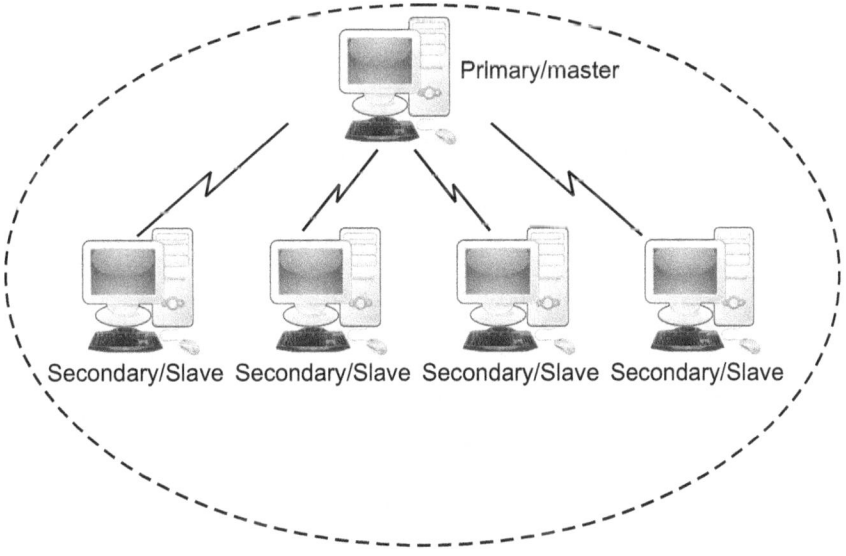

Fig. 2.6 : Piconet

- All communication is between master and a slave. Salve-slave communication is not possible.

- In addition to seven active slave station, a piconet can have upto 255 parked nodes. These parked nodes are secondary or slave stations and cannot take part in communication until it is moved from parked state to active state.

2. **Scatternet :**   (Oct. 11; April 15)

- Scattemet is formed by combining various piconets.

- A slave in one piconet can act as a master or primary in other piconet.

- Such a station or node can receive messages from the master in the first piconet and deliver the message to its slaves in other piconet where it is acting as master. This node is also called bridge slave.

- Thus, a station can be a member of two piconets.

- A station cannot be a master in two piconets.

- Fig. 2.7 shows scatternet.

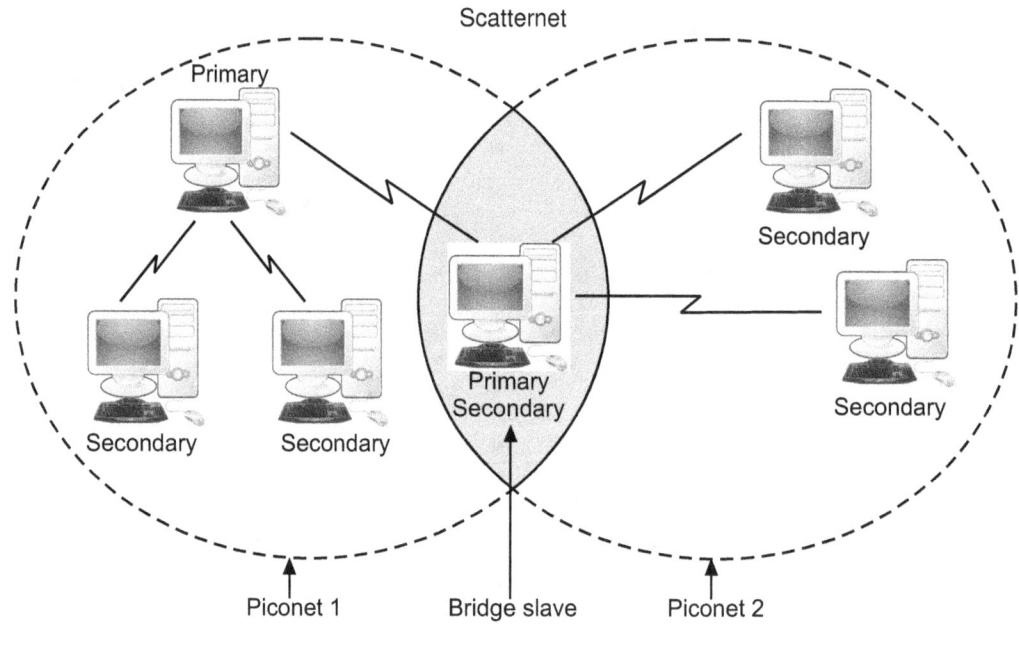

Fig. 2.7

2.2.2 Advantages and Disadvantages of Bluetooth

- Bluetooth technology is leading the future of wireless connections between different technological devices.

- Bluetooth is built into a variety of different devices including: phones, iPods, headsets, and even medical equipment.

Advantages of Bluetooth Technology:

1. It is cheaper in cost.
2. Easy to install and setup.
3. It makes connecting to different devices convenient.
4. Setting up a Bluetooth connection between two devices is quick and easy.
5. It is wireless technology.
6. It is free to use if the device is installed with it
7. Bluetooth doesn't need any configuration to start a connection and perform file transfers.
8. Bluetooth is actually inexpensive.
9. Bluetooth is automatic i.e., when two or more devices enter a range of up to 30 feet of each other, they will automatically begin to communicate without you having to do anything.
10. Bluetooth is standardized wireless, meaning that a high level of compatibility among devices is guaranteed.
11. Bluetooth devices almost always avoid interference from other wireless devices.
12. As a result of Bluetooth using low power signals, the technology requires very little energy and will use less battery or electrical power as a result. This is an excellent benefit for mobile devices.
13. The standard for Bluetooth will allow compatible devices to share data and voice communications. This is great for mobile phones and headsets.

Disadvantages of Bluetooth :

1. Bluetooth make it much more open to interception and attack. For this reason, security is a very key aspect to the Bluetooth specification.
2. It only allows short range communication between devices
3. It can only connect two devices at once
4. It can lose connection in certain conditions
5. Bluetooth only offers 1 MBps data transfer rate.

2.2.3 Bluetooth Applications   (April 15)

- Now-a-days, Bluetooth technology is used for several computer and non computer application:
  1. It is used for providing communication between peripheral devices like wireless mouse or keyboard with the computer.

2. It is used by modern healthcare devices to send signals to monitors.

3. It is used by modern communicating devices like mobile phone, PDAs, palmtops etc to transfer data rapidly.

4. It is used for dial up networking. Thus allowing a notebook computer to call via a mobile phone.

5. It is used for cordless telephoning to connect a handset and its local base station.

6. It also allows hands-free voice communication with headset.

7. It also enables a mobile computer to connect to a fixed LAN.

8. It can also be used for file transfer operations from one mobile phone to another.

SUMMARY

➢ A WLAN (Wireless Local Area Network) is a wireless computer network that links two or more devices using a wireless distribution method within a limited area such as a home, school, computer laboratory, or office building.

➢ IEEE 802.11 refers to the set of standards that define communication for wireless LANs. IEEE 802.11 has defined the Basic Service Set (BSS) as the basic building block of wireless LAN.

➢ A BSS is made of stationary or moving wireless stations and a central base station called as the Access Point (AP). AP is a device that provides access to the DS by providing DS services.

➢ DS (Distribution System) is used to interconnect a set of BSS and integrated local area networks to create an extended service set.

➢ An Extended Service Set (ESS) is a set of two or more wireless APs connected to the same wired network that defines a single logical network segment bounded by a router (also known as a subnet).

➢ IEEE 802.11 defines three types of stations on the basis of their mobility in wireless LAN. These are No-transition Mobility, BSS-transition Mobility and ESS-transition Mobility.

➢ Reliable data delivery, access control and security are the three main functions provided by the IEEE 802.11 MAC layer.

➢ IEEE 802.11 defines two MAC sub-layers i.e. the Distributed Co-ordination Function (DCF) and Point Co-ordination Function (PCF).

➢ The DCF is used in BSS having no access point. DCF uses CSMA/CA protocol for transmission.

➢ PCF method is used in infrastructure network. In this Access point is used to control the network activity. PCF uses centralized, contention free polling access method.

➢ A wireless LAN defined by IEEE 802.11 has three categories of frames i.e., Management frame, Control frame and Data frame.

➢ Bluetooth is a wireless LAN technology used to connect devices of different functions such as telephones, computers like laptop or desktop, notebooks, cameras, printers and so on a range of up to 30 ft. to 100 ft.

➢ Bluetooth architecture defines two types of networks: i.e., Piconet (consists of one primary (master) node and seven active secondary (slave) nodes) and Scattemet (formed by combining various piconets).

PRACTICE QUESTIONS

1. What is Wireless LAN?
2. State advantages and disadvantages of wireless LAN.
3. Enlist applications of WLAN.
4. What is Bluetooth?
5. With neat diagram explain architecture of bluetooth.
6. Define piconet and scatternet.
7. What are the applications of bluetooth.
8. List advantages and disadvantages of bluetooth.

UNIVERSITY QUESTIONS AND ANSWERS

April 2011

1. Based on mobility IEEE 802.11 supports which types of stations ?   [1 M]
Ans. Please refer to Section 2.1.

2. What is bluetooth ?   [1 M]
Ans. Please refer to Section 2.2.

October 2011

1. BSS without AP is called as adhoc architecture. Justify.   [1 M]
Ans. Please refer to Section 2.1 Point (1).

2. Give any two differences between piconet and scatternet.   [1 M[
Ans. Please refer to Section 2.2.1.

April 2012

1. What is piconet ?   [1 M]

Ans. Please refer to Section 2.2.1 (Point (1).

2. Which services are defined by IEEE 802.11 ?   [1 M]

Ans. Please refer to Section 2.0.

3. Differentiate between wireless LAN and Bluetooth.   [5 M]

Ans. Difference between Wireless LAN and Bluetooth given below :

Sr. No.	Bluetooth	Wireless LAN
1.	It is a short range technology standard which allows devices to communicate in a wireless manner.	It refers to a network that connects two or more devices by using wireless data connections over short distances.
2.	The distance range is 30 feet to 100 feet.	The distance range is Up to 400 feet.
3.	It requires low bandwidth (not for transferring large files).	It requires high bandwidth.
4.	Bluetooth has generally lower speed.	Wireless LAN is much faster compared to Bluetooth.
5.	Lower cost.	Cost is much more expensive than Bluetooth.
6.	Bluetooth chips have lower power consumption - less drain on battery.	It requires more power consumption.
7.	It is less secure.	More secure.
8.	Fairly simple to use. Can be used to connect upto seven devices at a time. It is easy to switch between devices or find and connect to any device.	It is more complex and requires configuration of hardware and software.

4. Explain Bluetooth Architecture.   [5 M]

Ans. Please refer to Section 2.2.1.

October 2012

1.   What do you mean by infrastructure network in the perspective of BSS ?

[1 M]

Ans. Please refer to Section 2.1 Point (1).

2.   Explain the IEEE 802.11 station types.   [5 M]

Ans. Please refer to Page 2.5.

April 2013

1.   Which standard is used for wireless LAN ?   [1 M]

Ans. Please refer to Section 2.0.

2.   Explain Bluetooth Architecture.   [5 M]

Ans. Please refer to Section 2.2.1.

April 2015

1.   State the applications of Wireless LAN.   [1 M]

Ans. Please refer to Section 2.2.3.

2.   What is piconets and scatternet ?   [2 M]

Ans. Please refer to Section 2.2.1 Points (1) and (2).

❖❖❖

The Network Layer

Contents ...

Objectives...

- To Understand Network Layer
- To Study Logical Addressing
- To Learn IPv4 Protocol and Routing
- To Understand Congestion Control and Routers

| **3.0** | **INTRODUCTION** | (Oct. 14) |

- In the seven layer OSI model of computer networking, the network layer is layer 3. Network layer receives services from data link layer and gives services to transport layer.
- Fig. 3.1 (a) shows function of network layer.

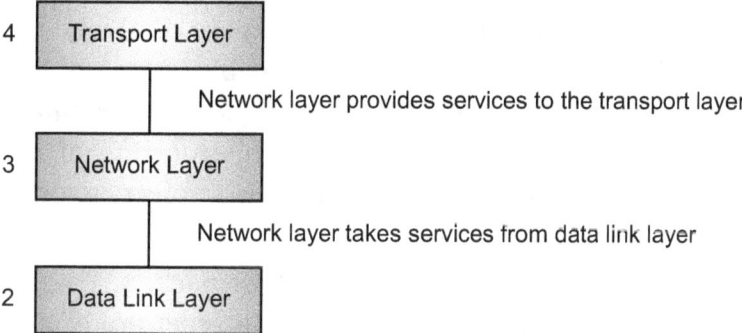

Fig. 3.1 : (a)

- Fig. 3.1 (b) shows position of network layer in OSI Model.

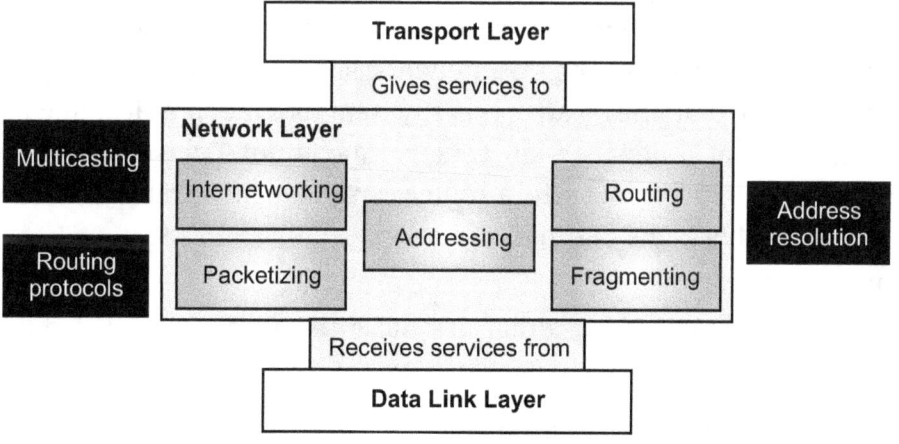

Fig. 3.1 (b) : Position of Network Layer

3.2

- The network layer is responsible for the delivery of individual packets from the source to the destination host.

- Network layer is also responsible for routing mechanism, addressing, internetworking, packetizing and fragmentation etc.

Tasks/Functions Performed by Network Layer :

1. **Internetworking:** One of the main responsibilities of network layer is to provide internetworking between different networks. It provides logical connection between different types of network. It is because of this layer, we can combine various different networks to form a bigger network.

2. **Logical addressing:** Large number of different networks can be combined together to from bigger networks or internetwork. In order to identify each device on internetwork uniquely, network layer defines an addressing scheme. Such an address distinguishes each device uniquely and universally.

3. **Routing:** When independent networks or links are combined together to create internet works, multiple routes are possible from source machine to destination machine. The network layer protocols determine which route or path is best from source to destination. This function of network layer is known as routing. Network layer routes frames among networks.

4. **Packetizing:** The network layer receives the data from the upper layers and creates its own packets by encapsulating these packets. The process is known as packetizing. This packetizing in done by Internet Protocol (IP) that defines its own packet format. The network layer encapsulates packets received from upper layer protocols and makes new packets out of them.

5. **Fragmentation:** Fragmentation means dividing the larger packets into small fragments. The maximum size for a transportable packet in defined by physical layer protocol. For this, network layer divides the large packets into fragments so that they can be easily sent on the physical medium. If it determines that a downstream router's Maximum Transmission Unit (MTU) size is less than the frame size, a router can fragment a frame for transmission and re-assembly at the destination station.

Other Issues :

- There are other Internet issues that are not directly related to the duties of the network layer :

1. **Address resolution :** When a packet is to be delivered from host to destination, it passes from one node to the next. Network layer provides only host-to-host

addressing, the data link layer requires physical (MAC) addresses for node to node delivery. There must be a method to map these two addresses. Address Resolution Protocol (ARP) is used for this mapping.

2. **Multicasting :** Today, another issue in the Internet is multicasting. There is one source and many destinations. Multicasting is becoming a very important issue in the Internet because of multimedia. Multimedia in the form of audio and video, need multicasting routes to reach many destinations.

3. **Routing protocols :** A routing protocol is a combination of rules and procedures that lets routers in an internet inform each other of changes. It allows routers to share Information about the Internet on their neighborhood. It helps to a router to know about failure of another network. The routing protocols also include procedures for combining information received from other routers.

3.1 | NETWORK LAYER DESIGN ISSUES

- The design issues of network layer include :
  1. Store and Forward Packet Switching
  2. The services provided to the transport layer.
  3. Internal design of the subnet.
  4. Routing.
  5. Congestion control.
  6. Internetworking etc.
- The following sections discuss above issues in detail.

3.1.1 Store and Forward Packet Switching

- Store and forward is a communication technique in which information is sent to an intermediate station where it is kept and sent at a later time to the final destination or to another intermediate station.

- The major components of the system are the carrier's equipment (routers connected by transmission lines), shown inside the shaded oval, and the customers' equipment, shown outside the oval.

- Host H1 is directly connected to one of the carrier's routers, A, by a leased line. In contrast, H2 is on a LAN with a router, F, owned and operated by the customer. This router also has a leased line to the carrier's equipment.

- We have shown F as being outside the oval because it does not belong to the carrier, but in terms of construction, software, and protocols, it is probably no different from the carrier's routers.

- Fig. 3.2 shows the environment of the network layer protocols.

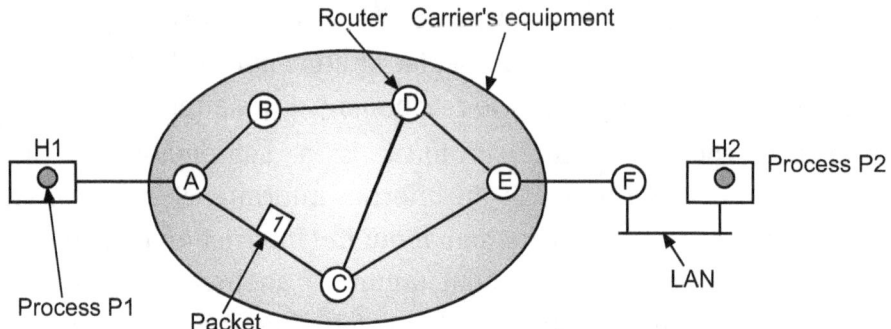

Fig. 3.2

- This equipment is used as a host with a packet to send transmits it to the nearest router, either on its own LAN or over a point-to-point link to the carrier. The packet is stored there until it has fully arrived so the checksum can be verified.

- Then it is forwarded to the next router along the path until it reaches the destination host, where it is delivered. This mechanism is store-and-forward packet switching.

3.1.2 Services Provided to the Transport Layer

- Network layer provides services to transport layer. Network layer services are designed with the following goals in mind :

  1. The services should be independent of the router technology.

  2. The transport layer should be shielded from the number, type and topology of the routers present.

  3. The network addresses made available to the transport layer should use a uniform numbering plan, even across LANs and WANs.

- With above goals, the network layer should provide connection oriented service or connectionless service. The Internet offers connectionless network layer service, ATM networks offer connection oriented service.

3.1.3 Implementation of Connectionless Service

- We know that network layer provides connection oriented and connectionless services to its users. Depending upon the type of service, two different organizations are possible.

- If connectionless service is offered, packets are injected into the subnet individually and routed independently of each other. No advance setup is needed.

- In this context, the packets are frequently called datagrams (in analogy with telegrams) and the subnet is called a datagram subnet.

- If connection-oriented service is used, a path from the source router to the destination router must be established before any data packets can be sent.

- This connection is called a VC (Virtual Circuit), in analogy with the physical circuits set up by the telephone system, and the subnet is called a virtual-circuit subnet.

- In this section we will examine datagram subnets; in the next one we will examine virtual-circuit subnets.

- Let us now see how a datagram subnet works. Suppose that the process P1 in Fig. 3.3 has a long message for P2. It hands the message to the transport layer with instructions to deliver it to process P2 on host H2.

- The transport layer code runs on H1, typically within the operating system. It prepends a transport header to the front of the message and hands the result to the network layer, probably just another procedure within the operating system.

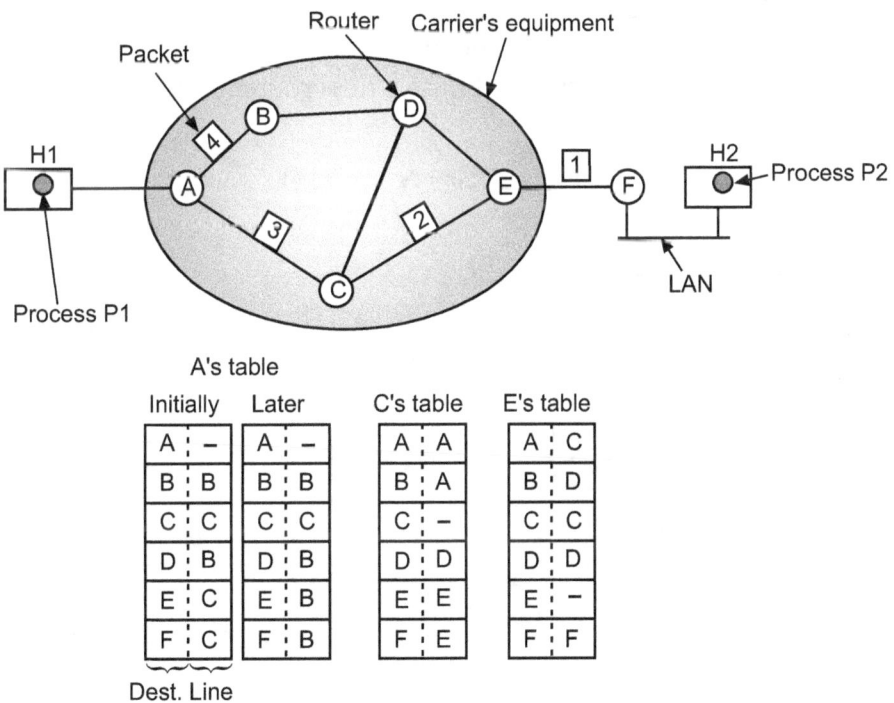

Fig. 3.3 : Routing with a datagram subnet

- Let us assume that the message is four times longer than the maximum packet size, so the network layer has to break it into four packets, 1, 2, 3, and 4 and sends each of them in turn to router A using some point-to-point protocol, for example, PPP.

- At this point the carrier takes over. Every router has an internal table telling it where to send packets for each possible destination. Each table entry is a pair consisting of a destination and the outgoing line to use for that destination.

- Only directly-connected lines can be used. For example, in Fig. 3.3, A has only two outgoing lines—to B and C—so every incoming packet must be sent to one of these routers, even if the ultimate destination is some other router. A's initial routing table is shown in the Fig. 3.3 under the label "initially."

- However, something different happened to packet 4. When it got to A it was sent to router B, even though it is also destined for F. For some reason, A decided to send packet 4 via. a different route than that of the first three.

- Perhaps it learned of a traffic jam somewhere along the ACE path and updated its routing table, as shown under the label "later." The algorithm that manages the tables and makes the routing decisions is called the routing algorithm.

3.1.4 Implementation of Connection Oriented Service

- For connection oriented service, we need a virtual-circuit subnet. The idea behind virtual circuits is to avoid having to choose a new route for every packet sent, as in Fig. 3.4.

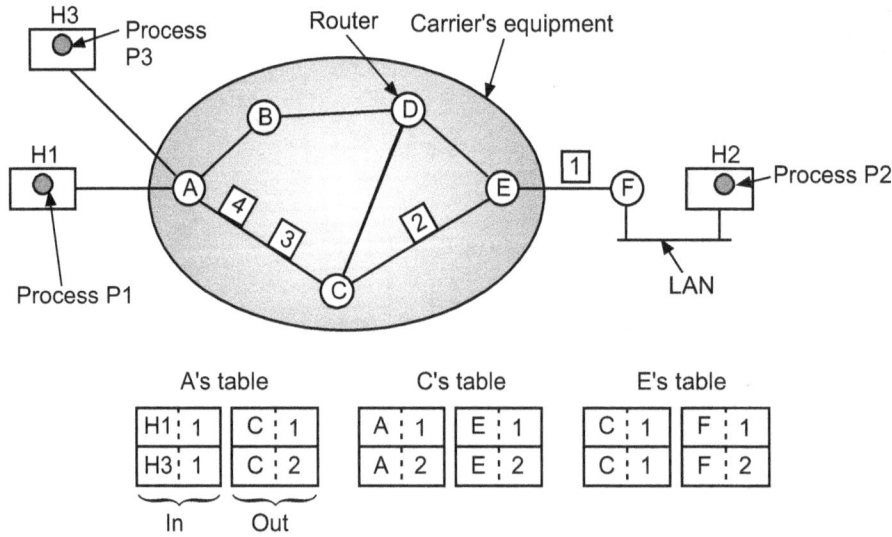

Fig. 3.4 : Routing within a virtual-circuit subnet

- Instead, when a connection is established, a route from the source machine to the destination machine is chosen as part of the connection setup and stored in tables inside the routers. That route is used for all traffic flowing over the connection, exactly the same way that the telephone system works.

- When the connection is released, the virtual circuit is also terminated. With connection-oriented service, each packet carries an identifier telling which virtual circuit it belongs to.

- As an example, consider the situation of Fig. 3.4. Here, host H1 has established connection 1 with host H2.

- It is remembered as the first entry in each of the routing tables. The first line of A's table says that if a packet bearing connection identifier 1 comes in from H1, it is to be sent to router C and given connection identifier 1. Similarly, the first entry at C routes the packet to E, also with connection identifier 1.

- Now let us consider what happens if H3 also wants to establish a connection to H2. It chooses connection identifier 1 and tells the subnet to establish the virtual circuit. This leads to the second row in the tables.

- Note that we have a conflict here because although A can easily distinguish connection 1 packets from H1 from connection 1 packets from H3, C cannot do this. For this reason, A assigns a different connection identifier to the outgoing traffic for the second connection.

- Avoiding conflicts of this kind is why routers need the ability to replace connection identifiers in outgoing packets. In some contexts, this is called label switching.

3.1.5 Comparison of Virtual Circuit and Datagram Subnets (April 15)

- Both virtual circuits and datagrams have advantages and disadvantages. The major issues are :

  1. **Bandwidth :** In virtual circuit subnet, only circuit number (route number) is given as a destination address on a datapacket which is very short. Whereas in datagram subnet, packets requires full destination address. So we can say that in datagram subnet, bandwidth required is more than virtual circuit subnet.

  2. **Setup time :** Virtual circuit requires a setup phase, which takes time and consume resources. But routing becomes easy in virtual circuit because router just uses the circuit number to index into a table to find out where the packet goes. In datagram subnet, no advance setup is needed. But a more complicated lookup procedure is required to locate the entry for the destination.

3. **Space in router memory :** If datagram subnet is used, router needs to know and have entry for every possible destination. So memory requirements are more in datagram subnet. Whereas virtual circuit subnet just needs an entry for each virtual circuit. So space required in router memory is less.

4. **Congestion control :** In virtual circuit subnet, congestion can be avoided by allocating the resources in advance. For example, buffers, bandwidth, CPU cycles etc., when the connection is established with datagram subnet, congestion avoidance is more difficult.

5. **Reliability :** Virtual circuits have a vulnerability problem. If a router crashes and looses its memory, all the virtual circuits passing through it will have to be aborted. In contrast, if a datagram router goes down, only those users whose packets were queued in the router at that time will lost. Other packets may be routed by another route.

- All these differences are summarized in the Table 3.1.

Table 3.1 : Difference between Datagram Subnet and Virtual Circuit Subnet (April 15)

Sr. No.	Issue	Datagram Subnet	Virtual-Circuit Subnet
1.	Circuit setup	Not needed.	Required.
2.	Addressing	Each packet contains the full source and destination address.	Each packet contains a short VC number.
3.	State information	Routers do not hold state information about connections.	Each VC requires router table space per connection.
4.	Routing	Each packet is routed independently.	Route chosen when VC is set up, all packets follow it.
5.	Effect of router failures	None, except for packets lost during the crash.	All VCs that passed through the failed router are terminated.
6.	Quality of service	Difficult.	Easy if enough resourced can be allocated in advance for each VC.
7.	Congestion control	Difficult.	Easy if enough resources can be allocated in advance for VC.

| 3.2 | **LOGICAL ADDRESSING** |

- We know that communication at the network layer is host-to-host i.e. source to destination, computer-to-computer.

- A computer somewhere in the world needs to communicate with another computer somewhere else in the world, (using Internet).

- The packets transmitted by source computer may pass through several LANs or WANs before reaching at destination computer.

- For such communication, to identify every device uniquely on Internet, we need a global addressing scheme, called as logical addressing.

- A logical address is given to all hosts connected to Internet and this logical address is called Internet Protocol Address or IP address.

- Today, we use the term IP address (Internet Protocol address) to mean a logical address in the network layer of the TCP/IP protocol suite. By using an IP address we can identify a computer or device on a TCP/IP network.

- There are two types of IP addresses IPv4 and IPv6.

- IPv4 addresses are 32 bits in length; this gives us a maximum of 2^{32} addresses.

- The need for more addresses motivated a new design of the IP layer called the new generation of IP or IPv6 (IP version 6).

- The IPv6 addresses uses 128-bit addresses, which give much greater flexibility in address allocation.

- In this chapter we discussed only IPv4 addressing mechanism.

3.2.1 IPv4 Addresses

- Internet Protocol version 4 (IPv4) is the fourth version in the development of the Internet Protocol (IP).

- IPv4 is one of the core protocols of standards-based internetworking methods in the Internet.

- An IPv4 address is a 32-bit address that uniquely and universally defines the connection of a device such as a computer or a router to the Internet.

- IP addresses are unique. Each address defines one, and only one, connection to the Internet.

- Two devices on the Internet can never have the same address at the same time. An address is assigned to a device for a time period, generally by ISP (Internet service provider) and then taken away and assigned to another device.

- The IPv4 addresses are universal in the sense that the addressing system must be accepted by any host that wants to be connected to the Internet.

Address Space :

- IPv4 protocol defines addresses that has an address space. An address space is the total number of addresses used by the protocol.

- IPv4 uses 32-bit addresses, which means the address space is 2^{32} or 4,294,967, 296 (more than 4 billion), this means if there were no restrictions, more than 4 billion devices could be connected to the Internet.

Notations :

- IPv4 addresses are defined by two different types of notations i.e., Binary notation and Dotted decimal notation.

1. **Binary Notation :**

- In binary notation method, to represent binary address, '0' and '1' are used.

- Length of address is 32 bits, which is grouped into 4 octet. Each octet is referred to as a byte. But such addresses are difficult to remember.

- For example, 01010111 10010101 00011101 00000011

2. **Dotted Decimal Notation :**   (Oct. 11)

- Representing a IPv4 address by using binary notation is very long and not easier to read.

- To make the IPv4 address more compact and easier to read, Internet addresses are usually written in dotted decimal form. Dots are used to separate the bytes.

- For example, 117.146.15.10.

- Fig. 3.5 shows IPv4 address in both binary and dotted decimal notation. Each byte (octet) is 8 bits, each number in dotted-decimal notation is a value ranging from 0 to 255.

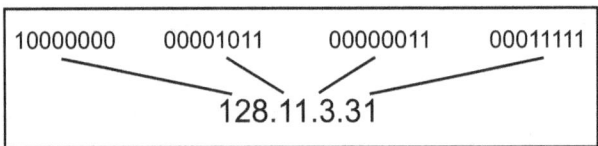

Fig. 3.5 : Dotted decimal notation and binary notation for IPv4

3.2.2 Classful Addressing   (Oct. 11)

- IPv4 addressing uses the concept of classes. This architecture is called classful addressing.

- Although classful addressing scheme is becoming obsolete, it is worth to understand it.

- In classful addressing, the address space is divided into five classes : A, B, C, D and E. Each class occupies some part of the address space.

- We can find the class of address just by checking the first few bits, if address is binary notation and checking the first byte if address is dotted decimal. Fig. 3.6 shows both methods.

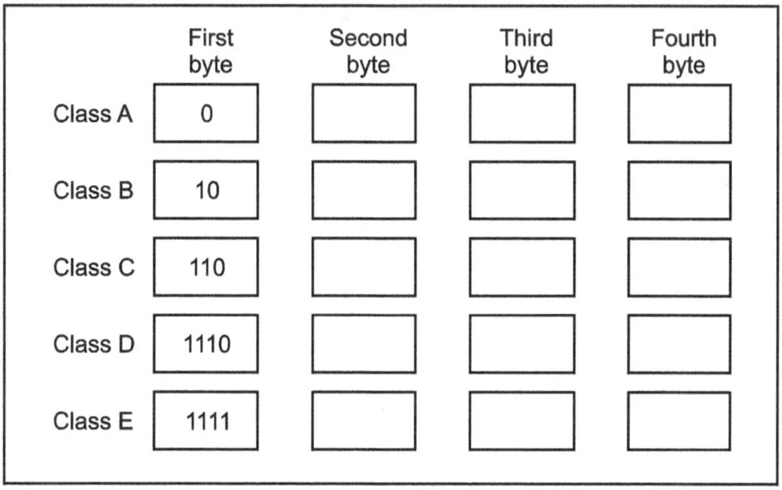

	First byte	Second byte	Third byte	Fourth byte
Class A	0			
Class B	10			
Class C	110			
Class D	1110			
Class E	1111			

(a) Binary notation

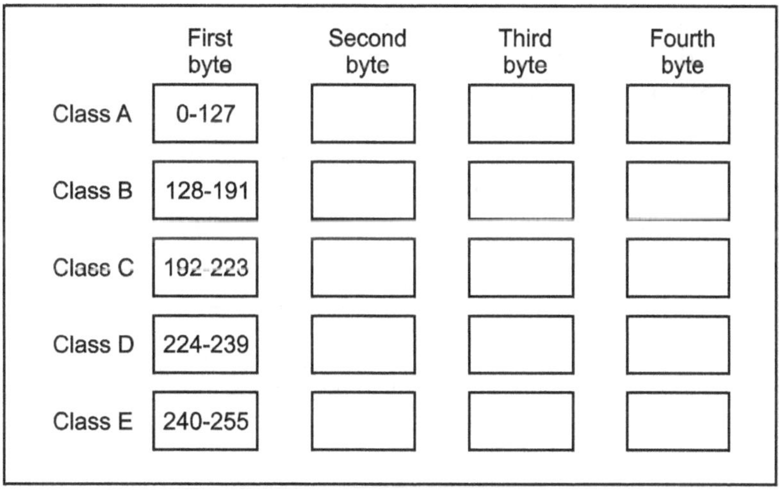

	First byte	Second byte	Third byte	Fourth byte
Class A	0-127			
Class B	128-191			
Class C	192-223			
Class D	224-239			
Class E	240-255			

(b) Dotted decimal notation

Fig. 3.6 : Finding the classes in binary and dotted decimal notation

Classes and Blocks :

- One problem with classful addressing is that each class is divided into a fixed number of blocks with each block having a fixed size as shown in Table 3.2.

Table 3.2: Number of blocks size in classful IPv4 addressing

Class	Number of blocks	Block size	Application
A	128	16, 777, 216	Unicast
B	16, 387	65, 536	Unicast
C	2, 097, 152	256	Unicast
D	1	268, 435, 456	Multicast
E	1	268, 435, 456	Reserved

- Class A addresses were designed for large organizations with a large number of attached hosts or routers.
- Class B addresses were designed for mid-size organizations with tens of thousands of attached hosts or routers.
- Class C addresses were designed for small organizations with a small number of attached host or routers.
- Class D addresses were designed for multicasting and class E addresses were reserved for future use.

Netid and Hostid :   (Oct. 11; April 15)

- In classful addressing, an IP address in class A, B or C is divided into Netid and Hostid. Netid and Hostid are varying in lengths depending on class of the address. Fig. 3.7 shows Netid and Hostid.
- In class A, one byte defines Netid and three bytes defines the Hostid. In class B, two bytes defines the Netid and two bytes defines the Hostid. In class C, three bytes defines the Netid and one byte defines the Hostid.

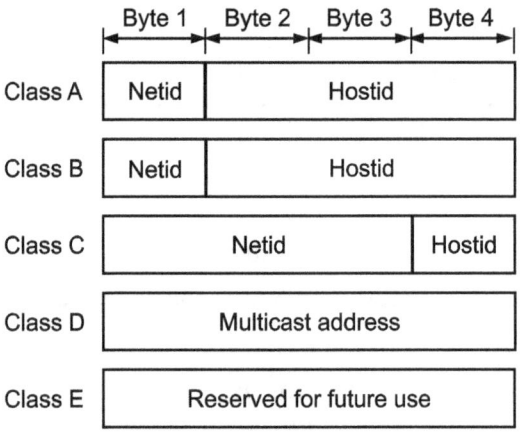

Fig. 3.7 : Netid and Hostid

For example :

(1) 00000001 00001011 00001011 11101111

    The first bit of this address, is 0. This is a class A address.

    Since it is class A address Netid is 00000001 and

    Hostid is 00001011 00001011 11101111

(2) 130. 45. 23. 120

    The first byte of this address is in between 128 to 191, so this address is class B.

    Its Netid is   130. 45. 0. 0 and

    Hostid is   23. 120

Mask :

- Netid and Hostid is predetermined in classful addressing. We can also use a mask (default mask), a 32 bit number made up of contiguous 1s is followed by contiguous 0s to find Netid and Hostid.

- The masks for classes A, B and C are shown in Table 3.3.

Table 3.3 : Default mask for classful addressing

Class	Binary	Dotted decimal	CIDR
A	11111111 00000000 00000000 00000000	255. 0. 0. 0	/8
B	11111111 11111111 00000000 00000000	255. 255. 0. 0	/16
C	11111111 11111111 11111111 00000000	255. 255. 255. 0	/24

- The mask can help to find netid and the hostid. For example, the mask for class A address has eight 1s, which means the first 8 bits of any address in class A define the netid, the next 24 bits define the hostid.

- The last column of shows Table 3.3 the mask in the form /n where n can be 8, 16 or 24 in classful addressing. This notation is also called slash notation or Classless Interdomain Routing (CIDR).

3.2.3 Subnetting   (April 12, 15)

- If an organization was granted a large block in class A or B, it could divide the addresses into several continuous groups and assign each group to smaller networks (called subnets).

- Subnetting increases the number of 1s in the mask.

3.2.4 Supernetting

- When most of the class A and class B addresses were depleted, there was a huge demand for midsize blocks. The size (only 256) of class C was not sufficient. Even a midsize organization needs more than 256 addresses. Supernetting is solution for this.

- In supernetting, an organization can combine several class C blocks to create a larger range of addresses.
- Several networks are combined to create a supernetworks or a supernet.

Address Depletion:

- Since the drawbacks in classful addressing and the Internet is growing very fastly, shortage of available addresses comes into picture.
- The continuous and fast growth of Internet led to the shortage of the available addresses. Yet the number of devices on the Internet is much less than the 2^{32} address space. We have run out of class A and class B addresses, and class C block is too small for most mid-size organizations.
- One solution for this problem is idea of classless addressing. Classful addressing, which is almost obsolete, is replaced with classless addressing.

3.2.5 Classless Addressing

- To solve the address depletion problem and give more organizations access to Internet, classless addressing was designed and implemented. No classes are used but the addresses are still granted in blocks.

Address Blocks :   (Oct. 14; April 15)

- In classless addressing, when a computer or number of computers or any device needs to be connected to the Internet, an ISP (Internet Service Provider) grants a block (range) of addresses.
- The size of block i.e., number of addresses varies based on the nature and number of computers (entity). For example : A single home user may require one address whereas an organization may requires more.
- An ISP may be given thousands or hundreds of thousands addresses based on number of customers it may serve.
- To make it simple, the Internet authorities impose three restrictions on classless address blocks :
  1. The addresses in a block must be contiguous, one after another.
  2. The number of addresses in a block must be a power of 2 (1, 2, 4, 8, 16, ...).
  3. The first address must be evenly divisible by the number of addresses.
- Fig. 3.8 shows block of 16 addresses granted to a small business.

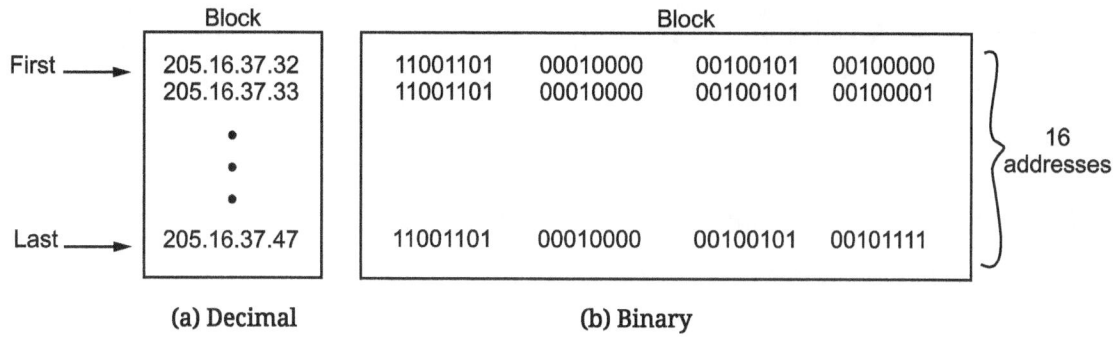

Fig. 3.8 : A block of 16 addresses granted to a small organization

- From the Fig. 3.8, we can say all the addresses are contiguous. The number of addresses are 16 which is power of 2. The first address, when converted to a decimal number is 3, 440, 387, 360 which is evenly divisible by 16.

Mask :

- A better way to define block of addresses is to select any address in the block and the mask.
- The mask is 32 bit number in which the n left most bits are 1s and the 32-n right most bits are 0s.
- In IPv4 addressing, a block of addresses can be defined as x.y.z.t/n, where x.y.z.t defines one of the addresses and the /n defines the mask.
- The addresses and the /n notation completely define the whole block, (the first address, the last address and the number of addresses).

First Address :

- The first address in the block can be found by setting the right most 32-n bits to 0s.
- For example : A block of addresses is granted to a small organization. We know that one of the addresses is 205.16.37.39/28. What is the fist address in the block?

  The binary representation of the given address is :

      11001101 00010000 00100101 00100111.

  If we set 32 – 28 right most   bits to 0, we get,

      11001101 0001000 00100101 00100000,

  Which is represented as 205. 16. 37. 32, is the first address.

Last Address :

- The last address in the block can be found by setting the right most 32 – n bits to 1s.

  For example : Find the last address for the block 205. 16. 37. 39/28.

  The binary representation of a given address is :

      11001101 00010000 00100101 00100111.

If we set 32 – 28 = 4 right most bits to 1, we get,

    11001101 00010000 00100101 00101111, which is represented in binary as 205. 16. 37. 47 is a last address.

Number of Addresses :

- The number of addresses in the block can be found by using the formula 2^{32-n}.

- For example : Find the number of addresses in 205.16.37.39/28 used in the address block.

    Here ,   n = 28

    ∴ 2^{32-n} = 2^{32-28}

                                = 2^4

                                = 16

    The number of addresses are 16.

Network Addresses :

- In IP addressing, network address concept is used. When a block of addresses are allocated to a organization, it is free to allocate the addresses to the devices that need to be connected to the Internet.

- The first address in the block is normally not assigned to any device, it is used as the network address that represents the organization to the rest of the world. Rest of the world identify that network by first address.

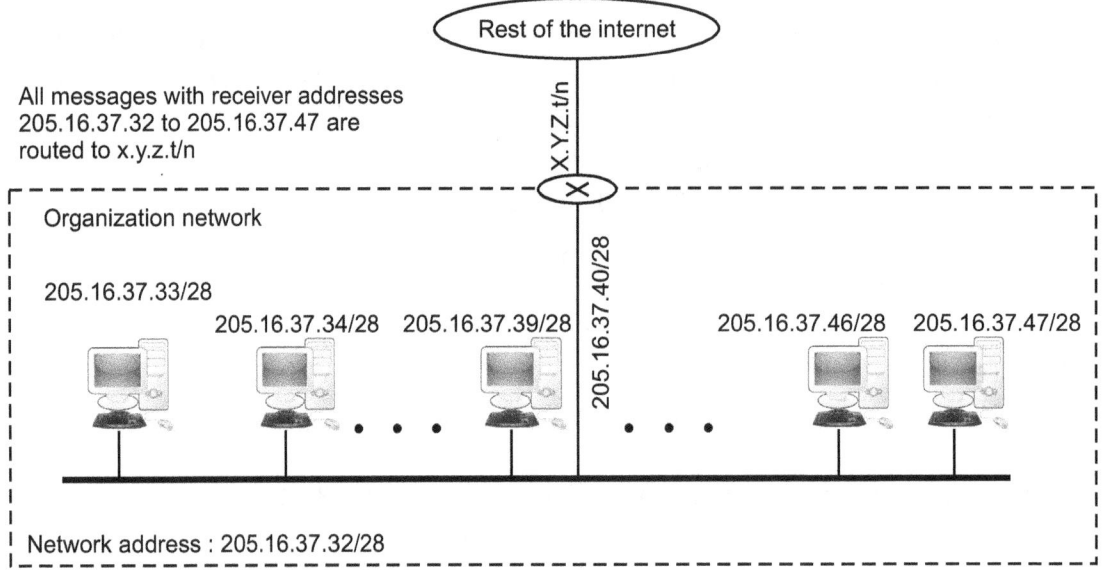

Fig. 3.9 : A network configuration for the block 205.16.37.32/28

- From Fig. 3.9, we can say organization network is connected to the Internet via a router. The router has two addresses one for organization network and one for rest of the word, i.e. the addresses 205.16.37.40/28 and x.y.z.t/n. All messages are destined for addresses in the organization block (205.16.37.32 to 205.16.37.47) are sent to x.y.z.t/n.

- The first address in a block is normally not assigned to any device, it is used as the network address that represents the organization to the rest of the world.

Hierarchy:

- IP addresses like any other identifiers, have levels of hierarchy.

- For example: A phone number 02025512336 is having STD code first, then area code and phone number.

Two-Level Hierarchy: No Subnetting :

- When not subnetted, IP address defines two levels of hierarchy. Each address in the block can be considered as a two-level hierarchical structure, the leftmost n bits (prefix) define the network; the rightmost 32-n bits define the host.

- Fig. 3.10 shows two levels of hierarchy in an IPv4 address.

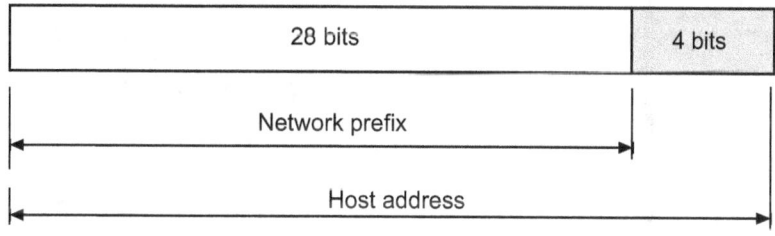

Fig. 3.10

Three-Levels of Hierarchy: Subnetting :

- An organization which is granted a large block of address creates small networks subnets. All available addresses are distributed among these subnets.

- For rest of the world, the organization is still identified by one IP address, however internally there are several subnets. All messages are sent to the router address that connects the organization to the rest of the Internet.

- The router routes the messages to the appropriate subnet. Small subblocks of addresses are assigned to specific subnets. The organization and it's subnets have its own mask.

- Consider, as an example an organization is given the block 17.12.40.0/26, which contains 64 addresses. The organization has three offices and needs to divide the addresses into three subblocks of 32,16, and 16 addresses.

- We can find the new masks by using:

  1. Suppose the mask for the first subnet is n 1, then 2^{32-n1} must be 32, which means that n1=27.

  2. Suppose the mask for the for the second subnet is n2, then 2^{32-n2} must be 16, which means that n2=28.

  3. Suppose the mask for the third subnet is n3, then 2^{32-n3} must be 16, which means that n3=28.

- We have the mask 27, 28, 28 with the organization mask being 26. Fig. 3.11 shows this configuration.

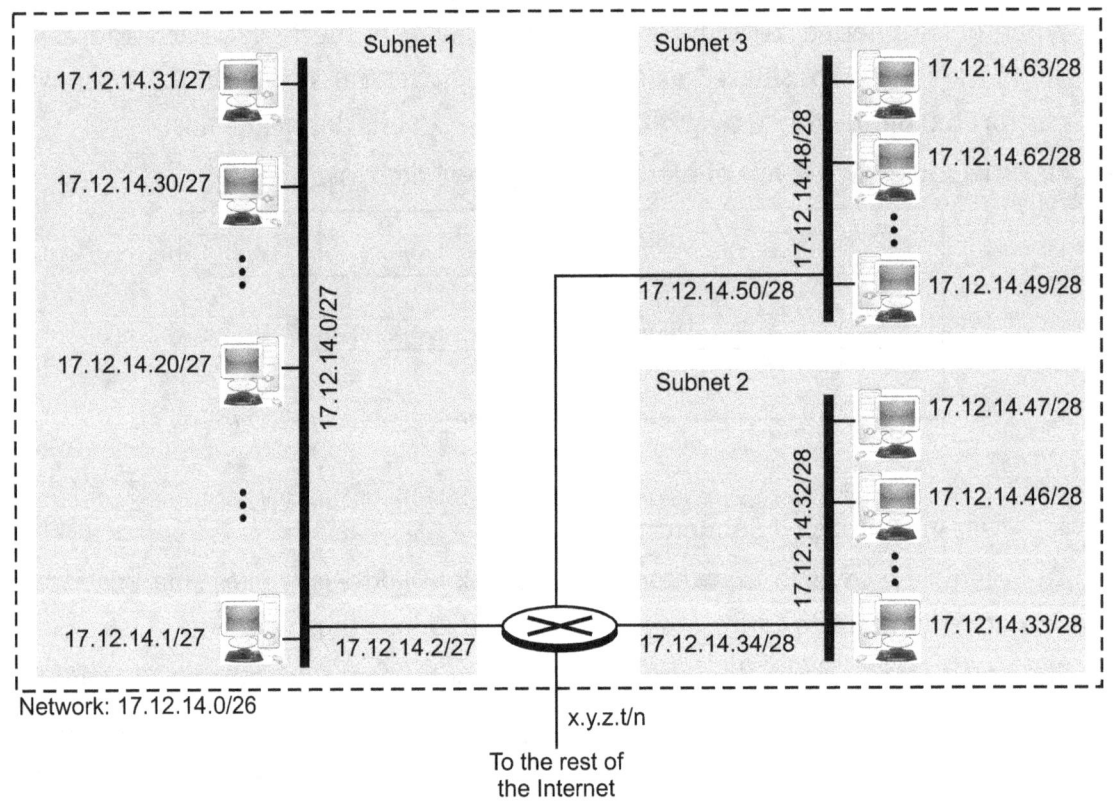

Fig. 3.11

- Through subnetting, we have three levels of hierarchy. It is shown in the Fig. 3.12.

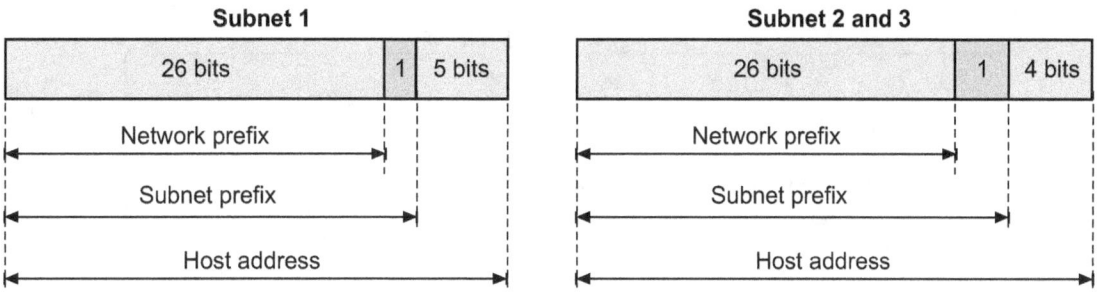

Fig. 3.12

More Levels of Hierarchy:

- In classless addressing the number of hierarchical levels are not restricted.
- An organization can divide the granted block of addresses into subblocks. Each subblock is further subdivided into smaller subblocks, and so on.

Address Allocation:

- The responsibility of address allocation is given to a global authority called the Internet Corporation for Assigned Names and Addressed (ICANN).
- ICANN assigns a large block of addresses to an ISP. This large block is distributed to it ISP's customers. This is called address aggregation: many blocks of addresses are aggregated in one block and granted to one ISP.

3.2.6 Network Address Translation (NAT)   (April 11; Oct. 11)

- The number of home users and small businesses who want to use Internet is day-by-day increasing. In earlier days, users are connected to the Internet for specific time by dial-up lines.
- ISP assigns a block of addresses to its user. An address is assigned to a user when it is needed.
- Today dial-up connections are not that much used. Home users and small businesses can be connected by an ADSL lines (Broadband) or cable modem with high speeds.
- Additionally users requires more addresses for their small networks. With the shortage of addresses, this is serious problem. A solution to this problem is Network Address Translation (NAT).
- With NAT, a user using large set of addresses internally and only one or small set of addresses for outside world.
- To separate the addresses used inside and outside the Internet authorities reserved three sets of addresses as private addresses. These are given in Table 3.4.

Table 3.4 : Addresses for private networks

Range	Total
10.0.0.0 to 10.255.255.255	2^{24}
176.16.0.0 to 172.31.255.255	2^{20}
192.168.0.0 to 192.168.255.255	2^{16}

- All the addresses shown in the above Table 3.4 are unique inside the organization, but they are not unique globally. Any organization can use these addresses without permission from the Internet authorities.

- Out of these addresses, if any address is used as a destination address, router will not forwards such packet.

- Fig. 3.13 shows a simple implementation of NAT.

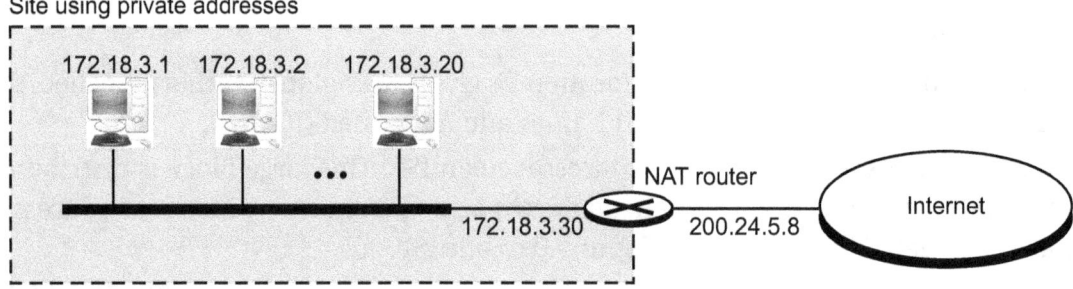

Fig. 3.13 : A NAT implementation

- Fig. 3.13 shows the private network using private addresses. The router that connects the network to the global address uses one private address and one global address.

- The private network is transparent to the rest of the Internet. The rest of the Internet sees only NAT router with the address 200.24.5.8.

Address Translation :

- Fig. 3.14 shows an example of address translation.

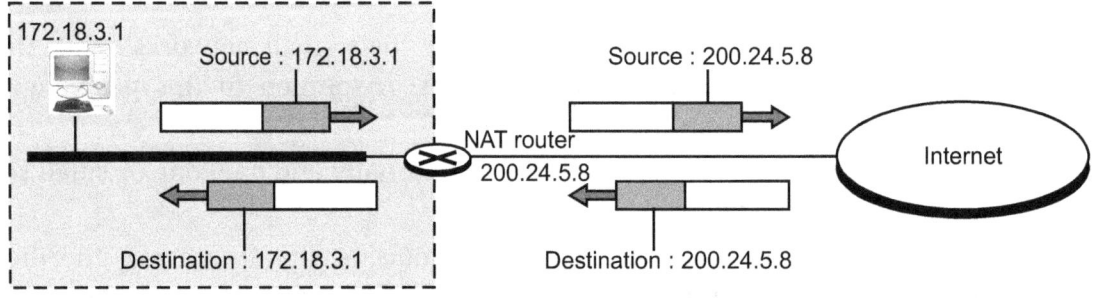

Fig. 3.14 : Addresses in NAT

- Each outgoing packet goes through NAT router, which replaces the source address in the packet with global NAT address.
- Each incoming packet also pass through the NAT router, which replaces the destination address in the packet with the appropriate private address.

Translation Table :

- When packets are going from the network, address translation is very simple.
- Only source address of packet is changed and NAT router's address is asigned. But when packets are coming from the Internet with destination address of a NAT router, how does the NAT router know the destination address to deliver it.
- Because there may be tens or hundreds of private IP addresses, each belonging to one specific host. To solve this problem NAT router using a translation table.

1. Using One IP Address:

- A translation table has only two columns i.e., the private address and the external address (destination address for a packet).
- Router makes a note of the source address of the outgoing packet. It also makes note of the destination address where the packet is going.
- When the response comes back from the destination, the router uses the source address of the packet (as the external address) to find the private address of the packet. Fig. 3.15 shows this concept.

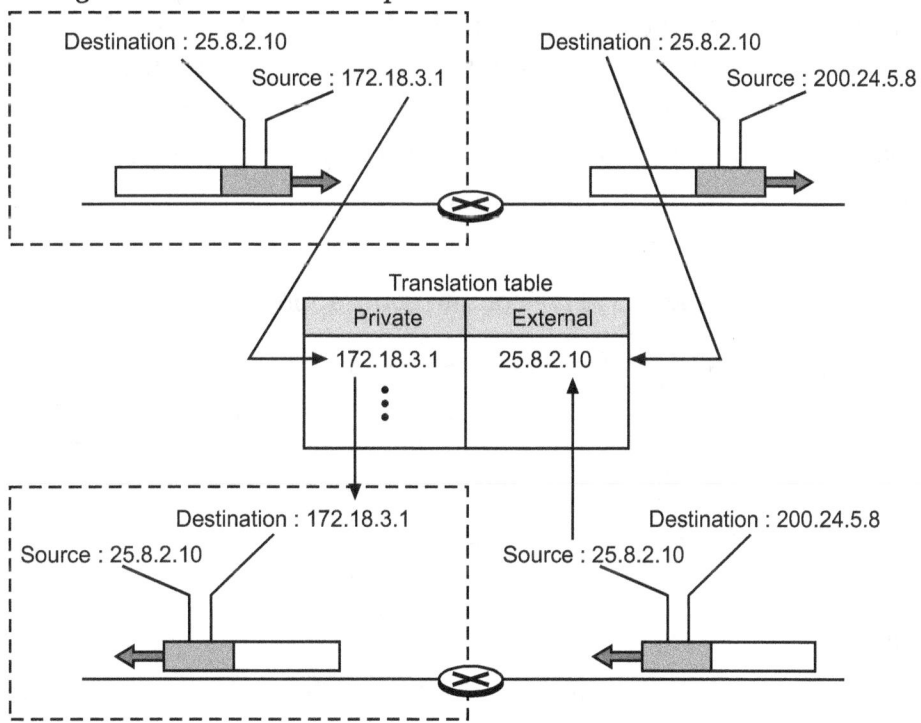

Fig. 3.15: NAT address translation

- Note that in this strategy, communication must be initiated by a private network. NAT is mostly used by ISPs. ISPs assign single address to its customer, which may using number of private addresses. Generally communication with the Internet is always initiated by customers.

2. **Using a Pool of IP Addresses :**
- NAT router has only one global address, only one private network host can access the same external host. To remove this drawback, the
- NAT router uses a pool of global addresses.
- For example, instead of using only one global address (200.24.5.8), the NAT router can use four addresses (200.24.5.8, 200.24.5.9, 200.24.5.10, and 200.24.5.11). In this case, four private network hosts can communicate with the same external host at the same time because each pair of addresses defines a connection.

3. **Using Both IP Addresses and Port Numbers :**
- To allow a many-to-many relationship
- between private-network hosts and external server programs, more information
- in the translation table is required.
- For example, suppose two hosts with addresses 172.18.3.1 and 172.18.3.2 inside a private network need to access the HTTP server on external host 25.8.3.2. If the translation table has five columns, instead of two, that include the source and destination port numbers of the transport layer protocol, the ambiguity is eliminated.
- Table 3.5 shows an example of such a table.

Table 3.5 : Five-column translation table

Private Address	Private Port	External Address	External Port	Transport Protocol
172.18.3.1	1400	25.8.3.2	80	TCP
172.18.3.2	1401	25.8.3.2	80	TCP
...	...	...	...	...

NAT and ISP :
- Suppose an ISP is granted 1000 addresses, but has 10,000 customers. Every customer is assigned a private network address.

- The ISP translates every 10,000 source addresses in outgoing packets to one of the 1000 global addresses. It translates the global destination address in incoming packets to the corresponding private address, (See Fig. 3.16).

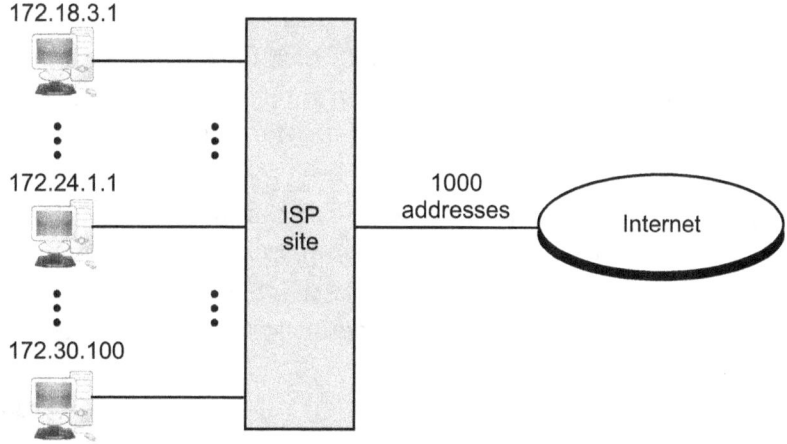

Fig. 3.16 : An ISP and NAT

3.3 | IPv4 PROTOCOL

- Internet Protocol version 4 (IPv4) is the fourth revision of the IP and a widely used protocol in data communication over different kinds of networks as a delivery mechanism.

- Fig. 3.17 shows the position of IPv4 in the Internet model.

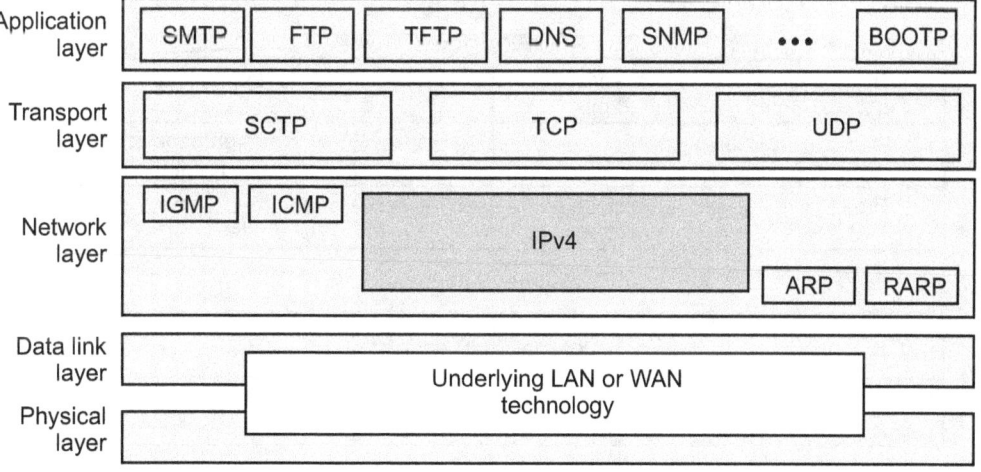

Fig. 3.17

- IPv4 protocol has the responsibility of identifying hosts based upon their logical addresses and to route data among them over the underlying network.
- IPv4 is an unreliable and connectionless datagram protocol, which does not provide error control or flow control mechanisms (except for error detection on the header). IP is also called best effort delivery protocol.
- For example, post office. Post office does its best to deliver the mail but does not always succeed and does not take any guarantee of delivery. If an unregistered letter is lost, post office does not inform to the original sender about loss or damage.
- IP is also do the same, if a datagram is lost or damage, IP will not inform to the original sender and damaged datagram is simply discarded.
- IPv4 is connectionless protocol for a packet switched network. Datagrams sent by the same source to the same destination could arrive out of order. IPv4 relies on the higher layer for reliability.

3.3.1 Datagram   (April 11; Oct. 12)

- In IPv4, packets are called as datagram, which is a basic transfer unit associated with a packet-switched network.
- The delivery, arrival time, and order of arrival need not be guaranteed by the network.
- Fig. 3.18 shows IPv4 datagram format.

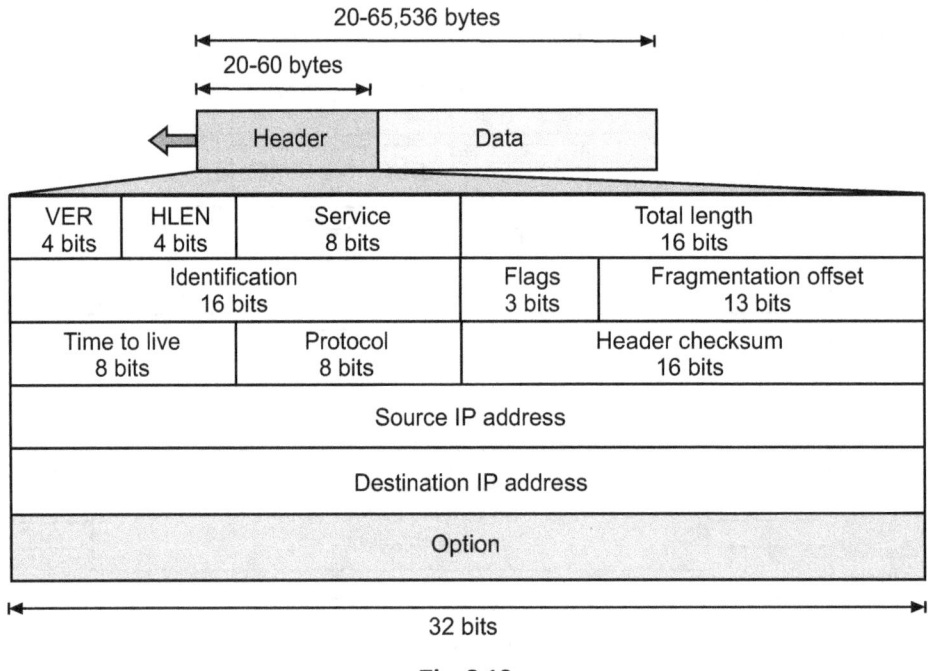

Fig. 3.18

- A datagram is a variable length packet which contains two parts i.e., header and data. The header is in between 20 to 60 bytes in length and contains information required to routing and delivery.

1. **Version (VER):** This 4 bit fields defines the current version of IPv4. Currently the version is 4. This field tells the IPv4 software running in the processing machine that the datagram has format of version 4 and all fields must be treated as version 4.

2. **Header Length (HLEN):** This 4 bit field defines the total length of the header. The length of the header is variable (between 20 to 60 bytes). When there are no options, the header length is 20 bytes, and value is 5(5 × 4 =20). When option field is at its maximum size, the value of this field is 15(15 × 4 = 60).

3. **Services :** This 8 bit field previously known as service type, is now called differentiated services. Both implementations are shown in Fig. 3.19.

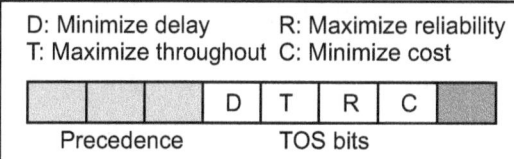

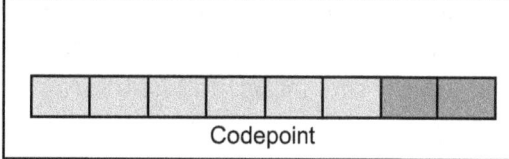

(a) **Service type**   (b) **Differentiated services**

Fig. 3.19

(i) **Service type:** First 3 bits are called precedence bits, the next 4 bits are Type Of Services (TOS) bits and the last bit is not used.

   (a) **Precedence :** This three bit subfield ranging from 0(000 in binary) to 7(111 in binary). This field defines priority of the datagram in issues such as congestion. If a router is congested, it discards some datagrams. Datagrams with the lowest priority is discarded first.

   (b) **TOS Bits:** This 4 bit subfield defines types of services. We can have 5 different types of services as listed in following table.

Table 3.6 : Types of Services

TOS Bits	Description
0000	Normal (default)
0001	Minimize cost
0010	Maximize reliability
0100	Maximize throughput
1000	Minimize delay

(ii) **Differentiated services:** The first 6 bits made the codepoint subfield, and the last 2 bits are not used.

4. **Total length :** This 16 bits field defines the total length of the datagram including the header. IPv4 datagram maximum size is 65,535, of which 20 to 60 bytes are the header and the rest is data from upper layer.

Length of data = Total length – Header length

5. **Identification :** This field is used in fragmentation.

6. **Flags:** This field is used in fragmentation.

7. **Fragmentation Offset:** This field is used in fragmentation.

8. **Time to live:** Every datagram has a limited lifetime on Internet. This field is used to control the maximum number of hops (routers) visited by the datagram. When a source sends a datagram, it stores a number in this field. This value is approximately double the maximum number of routes between any two hosts. Every time datagram visits a router, router decrements this number by 1. If this value, after being decremented, is zero, the router discards the datagram assuming the datagram lost the route.

   On Internet, routing tables of routers may be corrupted. A datagram may travel between two or more routers for long time without delivered to the destination. This field limits the lifetime of a datagram.

   This field also limits the journey of the packet. For example, if source wants that packet should not leave the home network, then it can store 1 in this field. When the packet arrives at the first router, this value is decremented to 0 and the datagram is discarded.

9. **Protocol:** This 8 bit field defines the higher level protocol that uses the services of IPv4. IPv4 protocol carries data from different other protocol(TCP, UDP, ICMP, etc.), the value of this field helps the receiving network layer know to which protocol the data belong.

10. **Checksum:** This field is used for error detection.

11. **Source address:** This 32 bit field defines the source address of a datagram.

12. **Destination address:** This 32 bit field defines the destination address of a datagram.

3.3.2 Fragmentation   (Oct. 14)

- Now, we will discuss fragmentation of IPv4 datagram in details.
- To reach upto destination, datagram may travel through different networks. Every router decapsulates the IPv4 datagram from the frame it receives, processes it, and then encapsulates it in another frame.

- The format and size of a frame depends upon the type of a network. Two networks may have different frame format and different sizes.

- For example : If a router connects a LAN to a WAN, it receives a frame in the LAN format and sends a frame in the WAN format.

- Each data link layer protocol has its own frame format in most protocols. Maximum Transfer Unit (MTU) defines the maximum size of the data field. The value of the MTU depends on the physical network protocol.

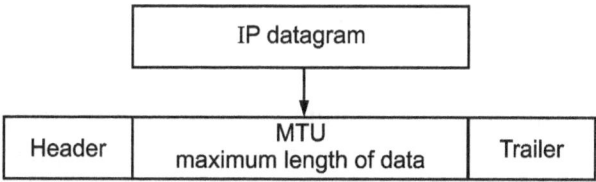

Fig. 3.20 : Maximum Transfer Unit (MTU)

Table 3.7 : MTU for some networks

Protocol	MTU
Hyperchannel	65,535
Token ring (16 mbps)	17,914
Token ring (4 mbps)	4,464
FDDI	4,352
Ethernet	1,500
X.25	576
PPP	296

- To make the IPv4 protocol independent of the physical network, length of IPv4 datagram equal to 65,535 bytes. This makes a transmission more efficient if we use a protocol with an MTU of this size. However, for other physical networks, we must divide the datagram, so that it can pass through these networks. This is called fragmentation.

- When a datagram is a fragmented, every fragment has its own header. Most of the fields are repeated and some are changed in fragments. A fragmented datagram can be fragmented if required. A datagram can be fragmented several times before it reaches to the final destination.

- In IPv4, datagram can be fragmented by the source or routers in the path. But reassembly of datagram is done only by the destination host. Because every fragmented datagram may be routed independently by different routes and we can never control or guarantee which route a fragmented datagram may take. All these fragments arrive at destination host. So the reassembly is done at final destination.

- The host or router that fragments a datagram must change the values of three fields i.e., Flags, fragmentation offset and total length. Other fields are copied as it is.

Fields Related to Fragmentation :

- The fields related to fragmentation are identification, flags and fragmentation offset. These fields are described below.

1. Identification :

- This 16 bit field identifies a datagram originating from the source host. Identification and source address uniquely defines a datagram as it leaves the source host. For uniqueness, IPv4 protocol uses a counter.

- When datagram is send, IPv4 copies the current value of the counter to the identification field and increments the counter by 1.

- When a datagram is fragmented, this value is copied to all fragments so that all fragments have the same identification number. This identification number helps the destination host at the time of reassembly.

2. Flags :

- From the 3 bits, first bit is reserved.

- The second bit is called the do not fragment bit. If its value is 1, the machine must not fragment the datagram. If it cannot pass the datagram, it must discard it. If the value is 0, the datagram can be fragmented if necessary.

- The third bit is called the more fragment bit. If its value is 1, means the datagram is not the last fragment, more fragments are coming after this. If its value is 0, it means this is the only or last fragment.

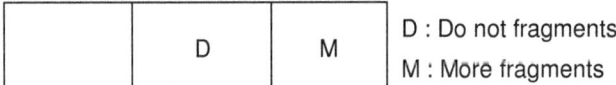

D : Do not fragments
M : More fragments

Fig. 3.21 : Flags used in fragmentation

3. Fragmentation Offset :

- This 13 bit field shows the position of the fragment with respect to the whole datagram.

- Fig. 3.22 shows a datagram with a data size of 4000 bytes fragmented into three fragments.

- The bytes in the original datagram are 0 to 3999. The first fragment carries 0 to 1399 bytes. The offset for this datagram is $\frac{0}{8}$ = 0. The second fragments carries 1400 to 2799, the offset is $\frac{1400}{8}$ = 8 = 175. The third one carries 2800 to 3999 bytes. The offset value is $\frac{2800}{8}$ = 350.

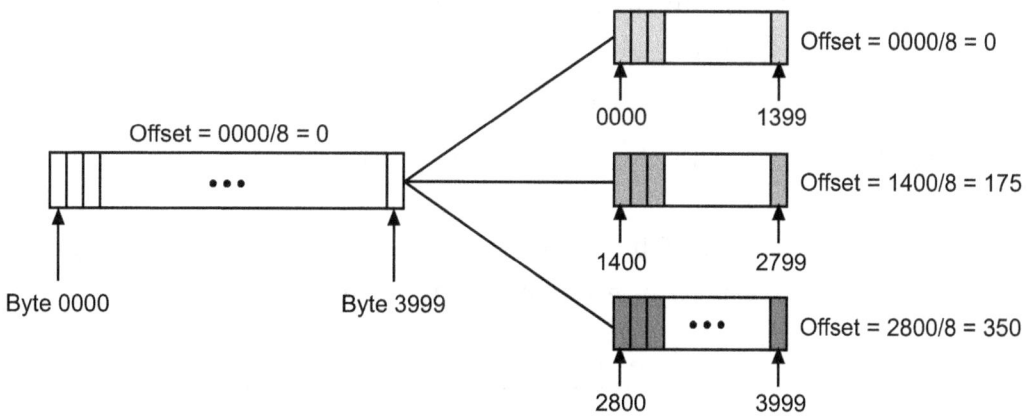

Fig. 3.22 : Fragmentation example

- Fig. 3.23 shows an expanded view of the fragments in Fig. 3.22.

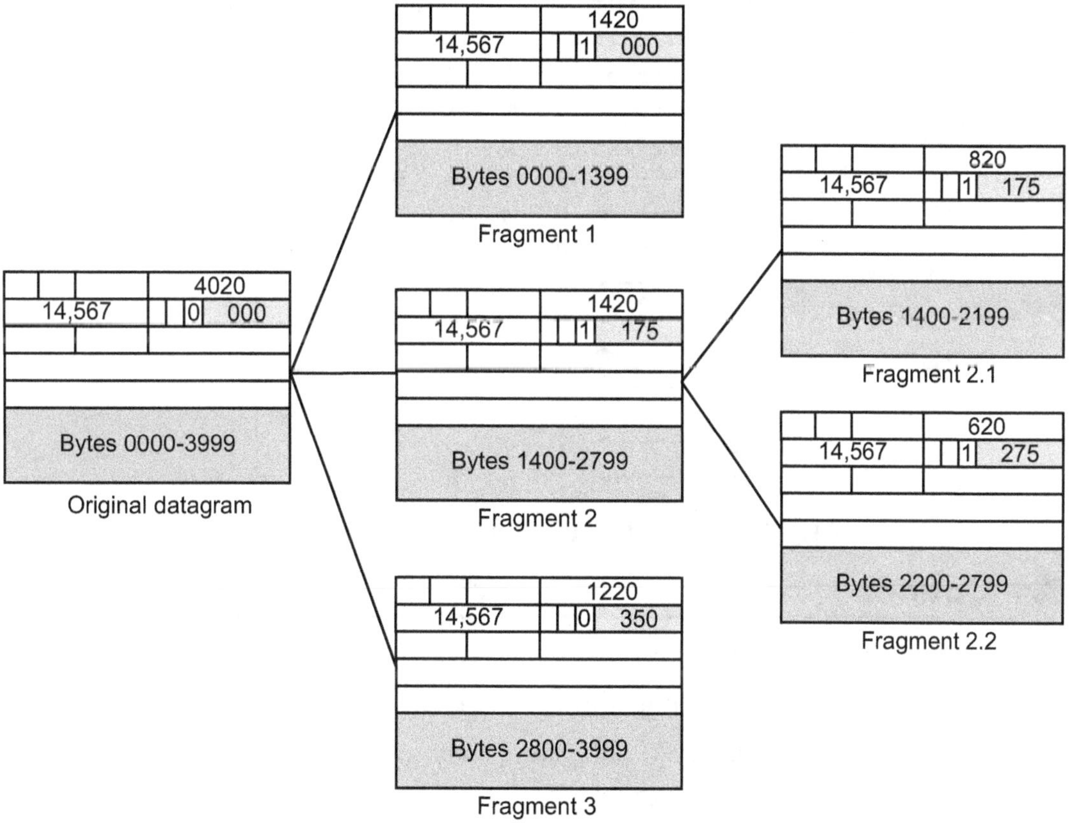

Fig. 3.23 : Detailed example

3.3.3 Checksum

- To compute checksum in IPv4, the value of the checksum field is set to 0. Then the entire header is divided into 16 bit sections and added together. The result (sum) is complemented and inserted into the checksum field.

- The checksum covers only the header, not the data.

- Fig. 3.24 shows an example of a checksum calculation for IPv4 header without options.

- The header is divided into 16 bit sections. All the sections are added and the sum is complemented. The result is inserted in the checksum field.

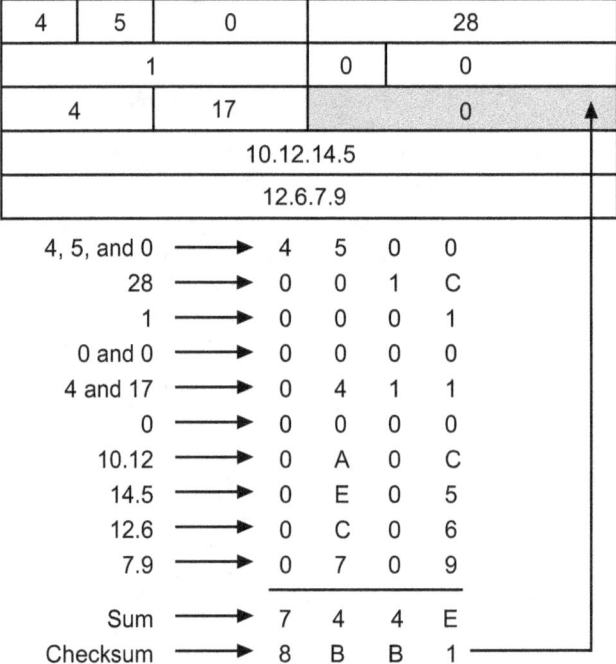

Fig. 3.24 : Example of checksum calculation of IPv4

3.3.4 Options

- The header of IPv4 datagram is of two parts i.e., Fixed part and Variable part.
- The fixed part is of 20 bytes long and variable part is maximum of 40 bytes.
- Options are not required for a datagram, they are used for network testing and debugging.
- Fig. 3.25 shows types of options.

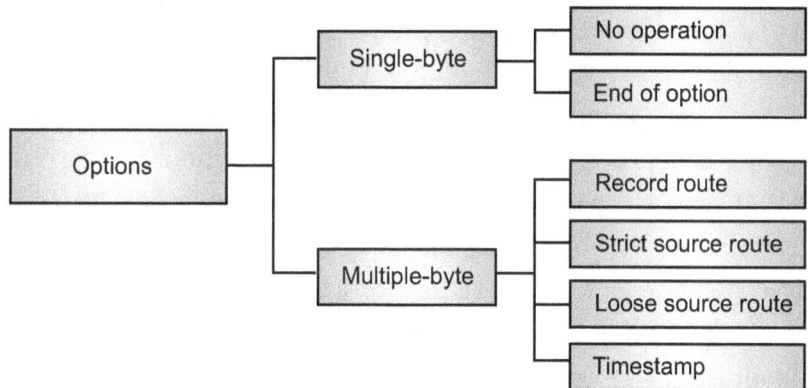

Fig. 3.25 : Options in IPv4

1. **No Operation :** A no-operation option is a 1 byte option used as a filler between options.

2. **End of Option :** An end-of-option option is a 1 byte option used for padding at the end of the option field. It can only be used as the last option.

3. **Record Route :** A record route option is used to record the Internet routers that handle the datagram. It can list upto nine router addresses.

4. **Strict Source Route :** A strict source route option is used by the source to predetermine a route for the datagram as it travels through the Internet. The sender can choose a route with a specific types of service (e.g. minimize delay, maximum throughput). If a datagram specifies a strict source route, all the routers defined in the option must be visited by the datagram. If a address of a router is not mentioned in route list, it must not be visited. If datagram visits a route that is not on the list, datagram is discarded. If datagram arrives at the destination and some of the entries were not visited, it will be also discarded.

5. **Loose Source Route :** A loose source route option is similar to strict source route. Only one difference is, each router in the list must be visited, but the datagram can visit other routers also.

6. **Timestamp :** A timestamp option is used to record the time of datagram processing by a router. This can help users and managers to track the behaviour of the routers in the Internet. We can estimate time taken for a datagram to go from one router to another.

3.4 | ROUTING   (April 11; Oct. 14)

- One of the main function of the network layer is routing packets from the source machine to the destination machine.

- When a device has multiple paths to reach a destination, it always selects one path by preferring it over others. This selection process is termed as Routing.

- Routing is done by special network devices called routers or it can be done by means of software processes. The algorithms that choose the routes and data structures that they use are a major area of network layer design.

- Routing algorithm is part of network layer software. Routing algorithms are based on specific criteria (e.g. shortest path). Routing algorithm selects one path from multiple paths depending on certain criteria.

- Network layer software (routing algorithm) are responsible for deciding which output line an incoming packet should be transmitted on. If the subnet uses virtual circuits internally, routing decisions are made only for new virtual circuit is being set up.

- Every router has two processes inside it. One process handles every incoming packet, when it arrives looking up the outgoing line in routing table for a packet. This process is known as forwarding.

- The other process is responsible for creation and updation for routing tables, for which routing algorithms are used.

3.4.1 Properties of Routing Algorithm   (April 11)

- Routing is the process of forwarding of a packet in a network so that it reaches its intended destination.

- The main properties of routing are:

  1. **Correctness:** The routing should be done properly and correctly so that the packets may reach their proper destination.

  2. **Simplicity:** The routing should be done in a simple manner so that the overhead is as low as possible. With increasing complexity of the routing algorithms the overhead also increases.

  3. **Robustness:** Once, a major network becomes operative, it may be expected to run continuously for years without any failures. The algorithms designed for routing should be robust enough to handle hardware and software failures and should be able to cope with changes in the topology and traffic without requiring all jobs in all hosts to be aborted and the network rebooted every time some router goes down.

  4. **Stability:** The routing algorithms should be stable under all possible circumstances.

5. **Fairness:** Every node connected to the network should get a fair chance of transmitting their packets. This is generally done on a first come first serve basis.

6. **Optimality:** The routing algorithms should be optimal in terms of throughput and minimizing mean packet delays. Here there is a trade-off and one has to choose depending on his suitability.

- Suppose there is continuous traffic between A and A', B and B', C and C'. The communication in between these nodes will not interfere with each other. But it will stop completely the communication between P and P', which is unfair for P and P'. So some compromise between global efficiency and fairness to individual connection is needed.

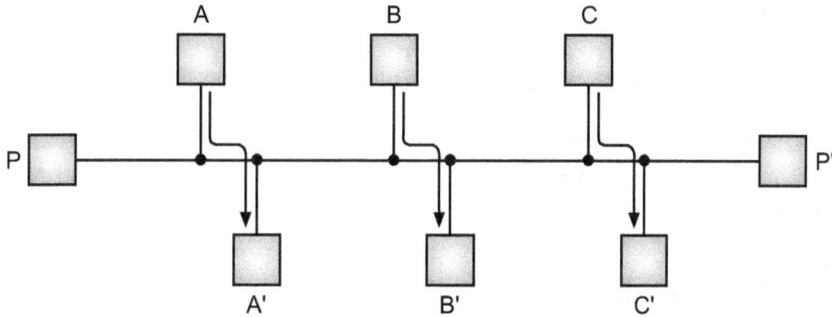

Fig. 3.26 : Conflict between fairness and optimality

3.4.2 Types of Routing Algorithm (Adaptive and Non-adaptive)

- Routing algorithms can be grouped into two different classes i.e., Non-adaptive routing algorithms, and Adaptive routing algorithms as discussed below.

1. **Non-adaptive Routing Algorithms :**

- Non-adaptive routing algorithms do not base their routing decisions on measurements or estimates of the current traffic and topology.

- Instead, the choice of the route to use to get from I to J (for all I and J) is computed in advance, off-line and downloaded to the routers when the network is booted. This routing is also called as static routing.

- This can be further classified as follows:

    (i) **Centralized:** In this type some central node in the network gets entire information about the network topology, about the traffic and about other nodes. This then transmits this information to the respective routers. The advantage of this is that only one node is required to keep the information. The disadvantage is that if the central node goes down the entire network is down, i.e. single point of failure.

(ii) **Isolated:** In this method the node decides the routing without seeking information from other nodes. The sending node does not know about the status of a particular link. The disadvantage is that the packet may be send through a congested route resulting in a delay. Some examples of this type of algorithm for routing are:

(a) **Hot Potato:** When a packet comes to a node, it tries to get rid of it as fast as it can, by putting it on the shortest output queue without regard to where that link leads. A variation of this algorithm is to combine static routing with the hot potato algorithm. When a packet arrives, the routing algorithm takes into account both the static weights of the links and the queue lengths.

(b) **Backward Learning:** In this method the routing tables at each node gets modified by information from the incoming packets. One way to implement backward learning is to include the identity of the source node in each packet, together with a hop counter that is incremented on each hop. When a node receives a packet in a particular line, it notes down the number of hops it has taken to reach it from the source node. If the previous value of hop count stored in the node is better than the current one then nothing is done but if the current value is better then the value is updated for future use. The problem with this is that when the best route goes down then it cannot recall the second best route to a particular node. Hence all the nodes have to forget the stored informations periodically and start all over again.

(iii) **Distributed:** In this the node receives information from its neighbouring nodes and then takes the decision about which way to send the packet. The disadvantage is that if in between the the interval it receives information and sends the paket something changes then the packet may be delayed.

2. **Adaptive Routing Algorithms :**

- Adaptive algorithms ,in contrast, change their routing decisions to reflect changes in the topology , and usually the traffic as well.

- Adaptive algorithms differ in where the get their information, when they change the routes, and what metric is used for optimization. They are also called dynamic routing.

- This can be further classified as:

(i) **Flooding:** Flooding adapts the technique in which every incoming packet is sent on every outgoing line except the one on which it arrived. One problem with this method is that packets may go in a loop. As a result of this a node may receive several copies of a particular packet which is undesirable. Some techniques adapted to overcome these problems are as follows:

(a) **Sequence Numbers:** Every packet is given a sequence number. When a node receives the packet it sees its source address and sequence number. If the node finds that it has sent the same packet earlier then it will not transmit the packet and will just discard it.

(b) **Hop Count:** Every packet has a hop count associated with it. This is decremented (or incremented) by one by each node which sees it. When the hop count becomes zero (or a maximum possible value) the packet is dropped.

(c) **Spanning Tree:** The packet is sent only on those links that lead to the destination by constructing a spanning tree routed at the source. This avoids loops in transmission but is possible only when all the intermediate nodes have knowledge of the network topology.

Flooding is not practical for general kinds of applications. But in cases where high degree of robustness is desired such as in military applications, flooding is of great help.

(ii) **Random Walk:** In this method a packet is sent by the node to one of its neighbours randomly. This algorithm is highly robust. When the network is highly interconnected, this algorithm has the property of making excellent use of alternative routes. It is usually implemented by sending the packet onto the least queued link.

3.5	CONGESTION CONTROL

3.5.1 Definition   (April 13)

- When too many packets are present in a subnet (or part of subnet), performance degrades. Packets sent are not equal to the packets received. This situation is called congestion.

- At very high traffic, performance collapses completely and almost no packets are delivered. Buffers get full, so packets are discarded leading to more retransmissions and less packets delivered to their destinations.

- Congestion thus tends to feed upon itself and become worse, leading to collapse of the system.

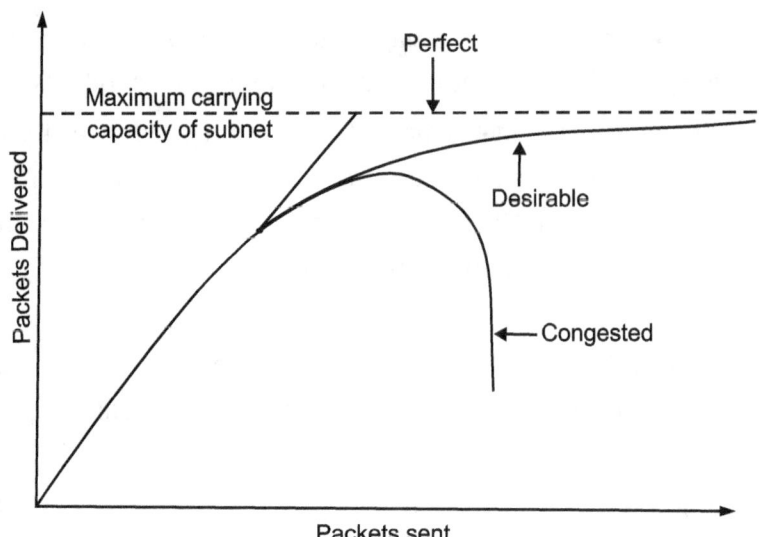

Fig. 3.27 : When too many packets are sent, congestion occurs and performance degrades

3.5.2 Reasons as Congestion

- Congestion can occur because of several reasons :
    1. Consider if suddenly at router, packets are arrived on three or four input lines and all of them need the same output line, then a queue is built up. If there is insufficient memory at router to hold the packets, congestion occurs and packets are lost. Adding more memory at router will not solve the problem.
    2. Slow processors can also cause congestion. If router's processor is slow, queues can build up, even though there is excess line capacity, congestion can occur.
    3. Similarly, low bandwidth lines can also cause congestion.

3.5.3 Difference Between Congestion Control and Flow Control

- There is a difference between flow control and congestion control.
    1. Congestion control has to do with making sure the subnet is able to carry the offered traffic. It is a global issue, involving the behaviour of all hosts, routers, the store and forwarding processing within the routers.
    2. Flow control in contrast, relates to the point-to-point traffic between a given sender and a given receiver. Flow control make sure that a fast sender cannot continually send packets faster than the receiver is able to cope it.
    3. The reason congestion and flow control are often confused is that some congestion control algorithm operate by sending messages back to various sources, telling them to "slow down". Thus a host can get a "slow down" message either because the receiver cannot handle the load or because the network cannot handle it.

3.5.4 General Principles of Congestion Control   (April 12, 13)

- Many problems in computer networks (complex systems) can be solved by control theory. Congestion Control refers to techniques and mechanisms that can either prevent congestion, before it happens, or remove congestion, after it has happened.
- Congestion control mechanisms are divided into two categories, one category prevents the congestion from happening and the other category removes congestion after it has taken place.
- Many congestion control algorithms are known in networking. In 1995 Yang and Reddy divide all algorithms into open loop or closed loop.
- They further divides the open loop algorithms into ones that works at the source and at the destination. The closed loop algorithms are also divided into two subcategories, explicit feedback and implicit feedback.
- In explicit feedback algorithms, the packets are sent back from the point of congestion to warn the source.
- In implicit feedback algorithm, the source makes a conclusion of congestion by making local observations, like time needed for acknowledgements to come back.

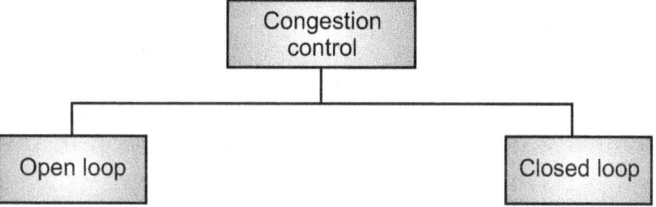

Fig. 3.28

1. **Open Loop Congestion Control :**   (April 12)
- Open loop solutions attempt to solve the problem by good design, making sure that it does not occur in the first place. Once, the system is up and running , midcourse corrections are not possible.
- Open loop solutions decides when to accept new traffic, when to discards packets and which ones. These solutions also make scheduling decisions at various points in the network. All these decisions are made in advance, without considering to the current state of the network.
2. **Closed Loop Congestion Control :**   (April 12)
- Closed loop solutions are based on feedback loop. This approach has three parts:
  (i)   Monitor the system to detect when and where congestion occurs.
  (ii) Pass this information to places where action can be taken.
  (iii) Adjust system operations to correct the problem.

- A subnet is monitored for congestion by many ways by a source or router. Some are:
  (i)   If the percentage of discarded packets due to lack of buffer space is more.
  (ii) The average queue length is more.
  (iii) The number of packets that time out and are retransmitted.
  (iv) The average packet delay
  (v)   The standard deviation of packet delay
  (vi) In all the cases, rising number shows growing congestion.

- The second step in closed loop solution is to transfer the information about congestion from where it is detected to the point where action is taken. A router detecting congestion pass the information about congestion to original source or sources by sending a packet. This extra packet also increases the load. By other methods information about congestion can also be passed.

- In every packet a bit is reserved for routers to fill in whenever congestion is detected. Whenever congestion is detected router fill in this bit of all outgoing packets, to inform the neighbors. Routers periodically asking each other about congestion by sending dummy packets to each other.

- In all feedback schemes, we can say that after knowing about congestion, the host will take appropriate actions to reduce it.

3.5.5 Congestion Prevention Policies

- Open loop systems are designed to minimize congestion in the first place. Open loop solutions supports many policies on different layers which affects congestion.

- Table 3.8 shows different data link, network and transport layer policies that can affect congestion.

Table 3.8 : Policies that affect congestion

Layer	Policies
Transport layer	• Retransmission policy • Out of order caching policy • Acknowledgement policy • Flow control policy • Time out determination
Network layer	• Virtual circuits versus datagram inside the subnet • Packet queuing and service policy • Packet discard policy • Routing algorithm • Packet lifetime management

Data link layer	• Retransmission policy • Out-of-order caching policy • Acknowledgement policy • Flow control policy

1. **Data Link Layer Policies:**

   (i) **Retransmission Policy :**

   • The retransmission policy is concerned with how fast a sender times out and what it transmits after timeout.

   • If one sender may timeout quickly and retransmits all outstanding packets using go back n, then it will put heavier load on the system than the sender using selective repeat.

   • If a receiver routinely discard all out of order packets, these packets will have to be retransmitted again, which creates extra load. With respect to congestion control, selective repeat is better than go back n.

   (ii) **Acknowledgement Policy:**

   • Acknowledgement policy also affects congestion.

   • If every packet is acknowledged immediately, it will create extra traffic and extra load. If piggybacking is used, extra time outs and retransmission may occur.

   (iii) **Flow Control Policy:**

   • A tight flow control scheme (small window) reduces the data rate and congestion is controlled.

2. **Network Layer Policies :**

   (i) **Virtual circuits verses datagram inside the subnet:**

   • At network layer choice between virtual circuits and datagram affects congestion.

   • Many congestion control algorithms work only with virtual circuits and some work with only datagram subnets.

   (ii) **Packet queuing and service policy:**

   • Packet queuing and service policy relates to whether routers have one queue per input line, one queue per output line, or both.

   • It also relates to the order in which packets are processed, which method is used, round robin or priority based.

   (iii) **Packets discard policy:**

   • Discard policy tells which packet is dropped whenever there is no space.

   (iv) **Routing algorithm:**

   • A good routing algorithm can help to avoid congestion by spreading the traffic over all the lines, whereas a bad one can send too much traffic over already congested lines.

(v) **Packet lifetime management:**

- Packet lifetime related with how long a packet may live before being discarded.

- If it is too log, lost packets may clog up the work for long time, but if it is too short, packets may sometimes time out before reaching their destination.

3. **Transport Layer Policy :**

- In transport layer, all policies are same as data link layer except timeout determination. As transport layer deals with end to end communication issues are more complex.

- Determining the timeout interval is difficult because we cannot predict the transit time across the network. If the time out interval is too short, extra packets will be sent unnecessarily.

- If it is too long, congestion will be reduced but the response time will suffer whenever a packet is lost.

3.6 | NETWORK LAYER DEVICES : ROUTERS

- A router is a networking device that routes data packets between computer networks based on logical addressing (IP addressing). Routers normally connects LANs and WANs.

- Routers perform the "traffic directing" functions on the Internet. Router has routing tables, which are used to make routing decisions.

- A data packet is routed from one router to another through the networks that constitute the internetwork until it reaches its destination node.

- Router works on layer 3 (Network Layer) as shown in Fig. 3.29.

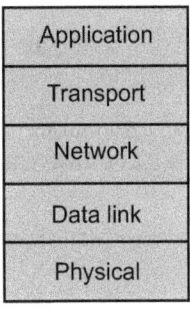 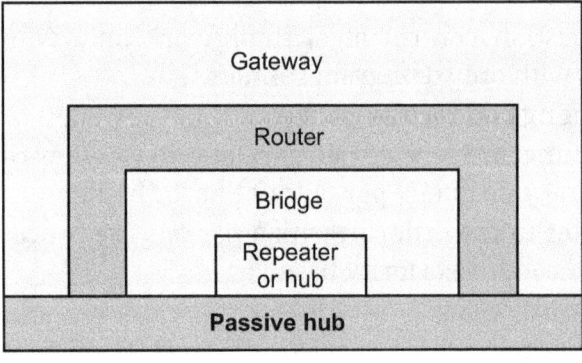 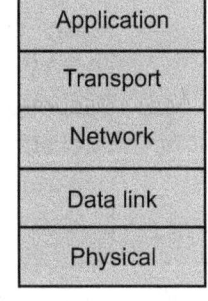

Fig. 3.29

Functions of Router :

1. **Route the packet:** A router uses a combination of hardware and software to "route" or "path" data from its source to its destination.

2. **Packet Forwarding:** Router maintains a routing table for all possible networks that can be reached. In the routing table, a router maintains subnet, Gateway, forwarding interface, timing etc. of the destination network.

3. **Packet Filtering:** Packet filtering is such like firewall. By which you can define which network can be entered and which network can be dropped. In easy word, It filters the packet on the basis of IP address, subnet, port no and protocols.

4. **Packet Switching :** To move packets from one interface to another to send the packet to its destination.

• Fig. 3.30 shows a part of the Internet that uses routers to connect LANs and WANs.

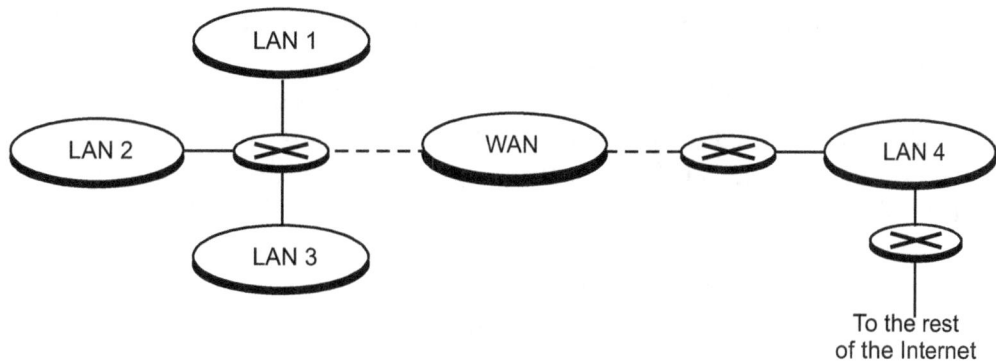

Fig. 3.30

Solved Problems :

Ex. 1. A packet has arrived with or m bit value of 0. Is this the first fragment, the last fragment, or a middle fragment ? Do we know if the packet was fragmented ?

Sol. : If the m bit is 0, it means there are no more fragments, the fragment is the last one. We cannot say if the original packet was fragmented or not. A non-fragmented packet is considered the last fragment.

Ex. 2. A packet has arrived with an m bit value of 1. Is this the first fragment, the last fragment or middle ?

Sol. : If the m bit is 1, it means that there is atleast one or more fragment. This fragment can be the first one or the middle one, but not the last one.

Ex. 3. A packet has arrived in which the offset value is 100, the value of HLEN is 5, and the value of the total length field is 100. What are the numbers of the first byte and last byte ?

Sol. : The first byte number is $100 \times 8 = 800$. The total length is 100 bytes and he header length is $5 \times 4 = 20$ bytes, which means that there are 80 bytes in this datagram. If the first byte number is 800, the last byte number is 879.

SUMMARY

➢ In the seven layer OSI model of computer networking, the network layer is layer 3rd. Network layer receives services from data link layer and gives services to transport layer.

➢ The network layer is responsible for the delivery of individual packets from the source to the destination host. This layer is also responsible for routing mechanism, addressing, internetworking, packetizing and fragmentation etc.

➢ The network design issues of network layer includes Store-and-Forward Packet Switching, the services provided to the transport layer, Internal design of the subnet, Routing, Congestion control, and Internetworking etc.

➢ Store and forward is a communication technique in which information is sent to an intermediate station where it is kept and sent at a later time to the final destination or to another intermediate station.

➢ For connection-oriented service, we need a virtual-circuit subnet. The idea behind virtual circuits is to avoid having to choose a new route for every packet sent. If connectionless service is offered, packets are injected into the subnet individually and routed independently of each other. No advance setup is needed.

➢ The packets transmitted by source computer may pass through several LANs or WANs before reaching at destination computer. To identify every device uniquely on Internet, we need a global addressing scheme, called as logical addressing.

➢ A logical address is given to all hosts connected to Internet and this logical address is called Internet Protocol (IP) Address.

➢ An IPv4 (Internet Protocol version 4) address is a 32-bit address that uniquely and universally defines the connection of a device such as a computer or a router to the Internet.

➢ IPv4 addressing uses the concept of classes. This architecture is called classful addressing.

➢ To overcome address depletion and give more organizations access to Internet, classless addressing was designed and implemented. No classes are used but the addresses are still granted in blocks.

➢ A better way to define block of addresses is to select any address in the block and the mask. The mask is 32 bit number in which the n left most bits are 1s and the 32-n right most bits are 0s.

➢ When classful addressing was used, subnetting was introduced. If an organization was granted a large block in class A or B, it could divide the addresses into several contiguous groups and assign each group to smaller network (subnets).

➢ Subnetting is the process of subnetting involves dividing a network up into smaller networks called subnets or sub networks. Each of these subnets has its own specific address.

➢ In supernetting, an organization can combine several class C blocks to create a larger range of addresses. In other words, several networks are combined to create a supernetwork or a supernet.

➢ Supernetting is an addressing scheme in which several class C blocks can be combined to create a larger range of addresses.

➢ Network Address Translation (NAT) is a methodology of remapping one IP address space into another by modifying network address information in Internet Protocol (IP) datagram packet headers while they are in transit across a traffic routing device.

➢ A translation table has only two columns i.e., the private address and the external address (destination address for a packet).

➢ IPv4 is defined and specified in IETF publication RCF 791.

➢ A datagram can be defined as "a self-contained, independent entity of data carrying sufficient information to be routed from the source to the destination computer without reliance on earlier exchanges between this source and destination computer and the transporting network."

➢ In IPv4, packets are called as datagrams.

➢ The Internet Protocol (IP) implements datagram fragmentation, breaking it into smaller pieces, so that packets may be formed that can pass through a link with a smaller Maximum Transmission Unit (MTU) than the original datagram size.

➢ To compute checksum in IPv4, the value of the checksum field is set to 0. Then the entire header is divided into 16 bit sections and added together. The result (sum) is complemented and inserted into the checksum field. The checksum covers only the header, not the data.

➢ The header of IPv4 datagram is of two parts : Fixed part and Variable part. The fixed part is of 20 bytes long and variable part is maximum of 40 bytes. Options are not required for a datagram, they are used for network testing and debugging.

➢ When a device has multiple paths to reach a destination, it always selects one path by preferring it over others. This selection process is termed as routing.

➢ Routing algorithm is part of network layer software. Routing algorithms are based on specific criteria (e.g. shortest path). Routing algorithm selects one path from multiple paths depending on certain criteria.

➢ The main properties of routing are i.e., simplicity, robustness, stability, correctness, fairness and optimality.

➢ Routing algorithms can be grouped into two classes i.e., Non-adaptive routing algorithms (do not base their routing decisions on measurements or estimates of the current traffic and topology) and Adaptive routing algorithms (change their routing decisions to reflect changes in the topology, and usually the traffic as well).

➢ Flooding adapts the technique in which every incoming packet is sent on every outgoing line except the one on which it arrived.

➢ In Random Walk method a packet is sent by the node to one of its neighbours randomly. This algorithm is highly robust.

➢ When too many packets are present in a subnet, performance degrades, a situation called congestion.

➢ Network congestion occurs when a link or node is carrying so much data that its quality of service deteriorates. Typical effects include queuing delay, packet loss or the blocking of new connections.

➢ Congestion control has to make sure that the subnet is able to carry the offered load. It is a global issue, involving the behavior of all hosts and routers.

➢ In open loop congestion control method, policies are used to prevent the congestion before it happens. Congestion control is handled either by the source or by the destination. Closed loop congestion control mechanisms try to remove the congestion after it happens.

➢ There are many policies on different layers that affect congestion like the Retransmission policy is concerned with how fast a sender times out and what it transmits after timeout, Acknowledgement policy also affects congestion. If every packet is acknowledged immediately, it will create extra traffic and extra load, Discard policy tells which packet is dropped whenever there is no space.

➢ Router works on layer 3 (Network Layer) of OSI model. A router is a networking device that forwards data packets between computer networks. Routers perform the "traffic directing" functions on the Internet.

➢ A router is a three-layer device that routes packets based on their logical addresses (host-to-host addressing). A router normally connects LANs and WANs in the Internet and has a routing table that is used for making decisions about the route.

PRACTICE QUESTIONS

1. List the network layer services.
2. Define Netid and Hostid.
3. Define internetworking and routing.
4. What is multicasting ?
5. How to find classes of IP address in binary and dotted decimal notations ?
6. List the differences between virtual circuit and datagram subnet.
7. List the properties of routing algorithm.
8. Define non-adaptive and adaptive routing algorithm.
9. What is logical address ?
10. What is classful addressing ?
11. Define classless addressing.

12. Define subnetting.
13. Define supernetting.
14. Why time to live field is required in IP datagram.
15. What is congestion ?
16. List the data link layer policies for congestion control.
17. How closed loop solutions uses concept of feedback.
18. What is a use of timestamp option ?
19. Explain the task performed by network layer.
20. Discuss the store and forward packet switching.

Problems :

1. Change the following IP addresses from binary notation to dotted decimal notation :
   (a) 01111111 11110000 01100111 11111001
   (b) 10101111 11000111 11111000 00011101
   (c) 11011111 10110000 00011111 01011101
   (d) 11100000 11110111 1100011 01111101

2. Find the class, netid and host id of the IP address :
   (a) 114.34.12.8   (b) 127.24.6.10   (c) 240.34.54.15
   (d) 230.34.2.1   (e) 237.14.2.10   (f) 129.14.6.8
   (g) 114.30.2.8

3. Change the IP addresses given in question 2 from dotted decimal to binary notation.

4. An ISP is granted a block of addresses starting with 140.80.0.0/16. The ISP wants to distribute these blocks to 2600 customers as follows :
   (a) The first group has 200 medium size businesses, each needs 16 addresses.
   (b) The second group has 400 small businesses, each needs 8 addresses.
   (c) The third group has 2000 households, each needs 4 addresses.
   Design the sub-blocks and give the slash notation for each sub-block. Find out how many addresses are still available after these allocations.

5. Find the range of addresses in the following blocks :
   (a) 200.17.21.128/27   (b) 200.17.21.128/25
   (c) 17.34.16.0/23   (d) 123.56.77.32/29

6. An organization is granted the block 211.17.180.0/24. The administrator wants to create 32 subnets :
   (a) Find the subnet mask.
   (b) Find the number of addresses in each subnet.
   (c) Find the first and last addresses in subnet 1.
   (d) Find the first and last addresses in subnet 32.

7. A host is sending 100 datagrams to another host. If the identification number of the first datagram is 1024. What is the identification number of the last ?

8. The value of the total length field in an IPv4 datagram is 36 and the value of the header length field is 5. How many bytes of data is the packet carrying ?

UNIVERSITY QUESTIONS AND ANSWERS

April 2011

1. What is the need of network address translation ? How NAT router maintains translation table ?   [5 M]

Ans. Please refer to Section 3.2.6.

2. Explain IPv4 fragmentation process in detail.   [5 M]

Ans. Please refer to Section 3.3.1.

3. What is routing ? Explain the desirable characteristics of routing algorithms.
                                                                          [5 M]

Ans. Please refer to Sections 3.4 and 3.4.1.

October 2011

1. The value of the total length field in an IPV4 datagram is 36 and the value of the header length field is 5. How many bytes of data is the packet carrying ?
                                                                          [1 M]

Ans. Please refer Solved Problems.

2. Why network address translation is needed ? How it is implemented ? [5 M]

Ans. Please refer to Section 3.2.6.

3. Discuss classful addressing in detail.   [5 M]

Ans. Please refer to Section 3.2.2.

April 2012

1. Define sub netting.   [1 M]

Ans. Please refer to Section 3.2.3.

2. Distinguish between open-loop and closed-loop congestion control.   [5 M]

Ans. Please refer to Section 3.5.4 Points (1) and (2).

October 2012

1. Find out class, Netid and Hostid of : IP address 126.25.21.1.   [1 M]

Ans. Please refer to Page 3.13.

2. Draw the structure of IPV4 datagram and explain its fields.   [5 M]

Ans. Please refer to Section 3.3.1.

April 2013

1. What is congestion ? Which congestion prevention policies are used in Data Link Layer Protocol ?   [5 M]

Ans. Please refer to Sections 3.5.1 and 3.5.4.

2. A company is granted the block 164.25.40.0126 which contains 64 addresses. The company wants to divide these addresses into three groups, containing 32, 16 and 16 addresses respectively. Design the subnets.   [5 M]

Ans. Please refer Solved Problems.

October 2014

1. State any two goals in the designing of network layer services.   [1 M]

Ans. Please refer to Section 3.0.

2. Change the following IPv4 addresses from binary notation to dotted-decimal notation.

    10000001   00001011   00001011   11101111

    11000001   10000011   00011011   11111111   [1 M]

Ans. Please refer to Section 3.2.1 Point (2).

3. State the responsibility of routing algorithm. Explain nonadaptive and adaptive classes of routing algorithms.   [5 M]

Ans. Please refer to Section 3.4.

4. Explain the fields related to fragmentation in IPV4 protocol.   [5 M]

Ans. Please refer to Section 3.3.2.

5. State different rules used for assigning IP address blocks.   [2 M]

Ans. Please refer to Section 3.2.5.

April 2015

1. Find out the class, Netid and Hostid of IP address 130.140.10.2.   [1 M]

Ans. Please refer to Solved problems and Page 3.13.

2. Define subnetting.   [1 M]

Ans. Please refer to Section 3.2.3.

3. Differentiate between virtual circuit and datagram subnet.   [5 M]

Ans. Please refer to Section 3.1.5.

4. For the given IP address 205.16.37.39/28 in some block of address, calculate : Address mask, first and last address of the block and number of address in the block.   [5 M]

Ans. Please refer to Section 3.2.5.

Address Mapping

Contents ...

Objectives...

- To Understand Address Mapping Concepts
- To Sutdy ARP, RARP, BOOTP, DHCP Protocols

4.0   INTRODUCTION

- In the previous Chapter, we discussed about IP (Internet Protocol) as the main protocol of network layer.

- We also know IP is a best effort delivery protocol, which does not provide error control and flow control. It is a host to host protocol using logical addressing. To make IP more useful, we need the help of other protocols.

- Protocols are needed to create a mapping between physical and logical addresses. IP packet uses logical (host to host) addresses. When IP packet is given to Data link

---

layer, it needs to be encapsulated in a frame, which needs physical addresses (node to node).

- ARP (Address Resolution Protocol) is designed for this purpose. Sometimes, reverse mapping - mapping a physical address to a logical address is also needed. RARP protocol is used for this purpose.

4.1 | ADDRESS MAPPING

- An Internet is a combination of physical networks connected by routers. To reach upto the destination, a packet may pass through several different physical networks. The hosts and routers are recognized at the network layer by their logical (IP) addresses.

- Packets pass through physical networks to reach up to hosts and routers. At physical layer, the host and routers are recognized by their physical addresses.

- A physical address is local address, which is unique for that network. It is usually implemented on hardware. An example of physical address is the 48 bit MAC address, which is imprinted on the NIC (network interface card) installed inside the host or router.

- For delivery of a packet to the host or router, we requires both addressing : Physical and Logical. Mapping of a logical address to a physical address and vice versa is needed. This mapping can be done by using static or dynamic mapping.

- In static mapping, a table is stored in each machine on the network. This table associates a logical address with a physical address. Each machine that knows the IP address of another machine and wants to know its physical address can check in the table. But this method has some limitations, because physical addresses may change in the following ways :

  1. If NIC of a machine is changed, its physical address changes.

  2. In some LANs, such as Local Talk, the physical address changes every time the computer is turned on.

  3. A mobile computer can move from one physical network to another, every time its physical address changes.

- To implement these changes, static mapping table must be updated periodically, which is not feasible. So we use dynamic mapping, in which each time a machine knows one of the two addresses, it can use protocols like ARP or RARP to find the other one.

4.2 ADDRESS RESOLUTION PROTOCOL (ARP)   (April 11, 12)

- ARP is a protocol for mapping an Internet Protocol address (IP address) to a physical machine address that is recognized in the local network.

- When a host or router wants to send a packet to another host or router, by using DNS, it has IP address of the receiver. But IP datagram must be encapsulated in a frame to pass through the physical network.

- Sender needs the physical address of the receiver. Sender sends an ARP query packet. The packet includes the physical and IP address of the sender and the IP address of the receiver. Here, we assumes that sender does not know the physical address of receiver. This query is broadcasted over the network.

- Every host on the network receives this request and process it. But only the intended recipient recognizes its IP address and sends back ARP response packet.

- The response packet contains the recipients IP and physical addresses. The packet is unicasted directly to the sender since recipient knows about sender's logical and physical addresses.

- This concept is shown in Fig. 4.1.

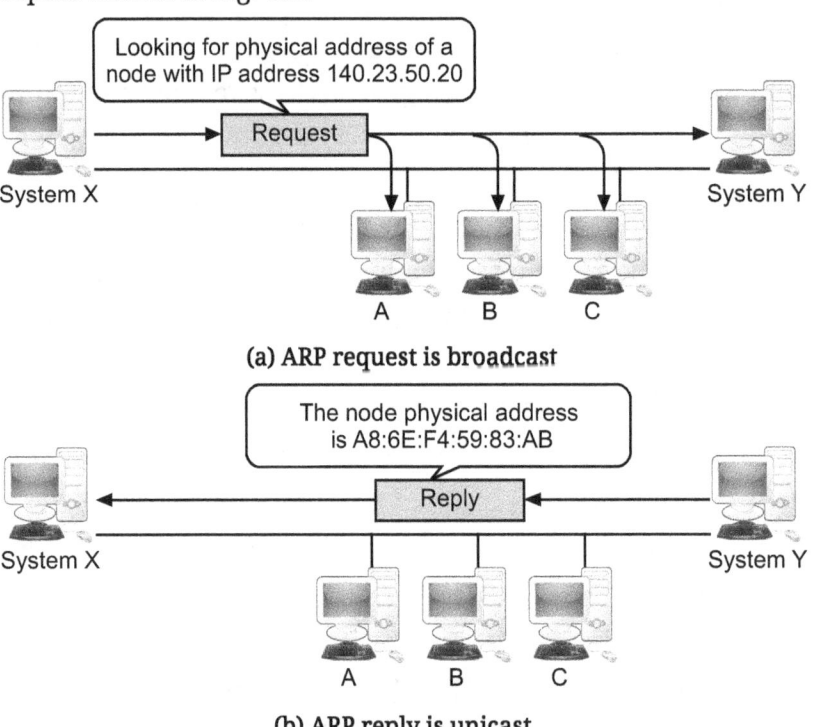

(a) ARP request is broadcast

(b) ARP reply is unicast

Fig. 4.1 : ARP operation

- In Fig. 4.1 (a), we can say, system X wants to communicate with system Y with IP address 140.23.50.20. But system X don't know the physical address of system Y, so it uses ARP broadcast service of the protocol and broadcast ARP request to ask about the physical address.

- This request is received by every system on that computer network. But only system Y gives reply as shown in Fig. 4.1 (b). System Y sends ARP reply packet which contains its physical address and unicast it to system X.

4.2.1 Cache Memory

- If computer X wants to send several packets to computer Y, computer X don't know the physical address of computer Y, then several times computer X has to broadcast the ARP request to computer Y, which is inefficient.

- ARP can be useful if the ARP reply is kept in cache memory for a while. Because a system normally sends several packets to the same destination. X system that receives an ARP reply stores the mapping in the cache memory.

- The reply is stored for 20 – 30 minutes unless the space in the cache is exhausted. Before sending the ARP request, the system first checks its cache to see if binding is stored or not.

4.2.2 ARP Packet Format   (Oct. 12)

- Fig. 4.2 shows ARP packet format.

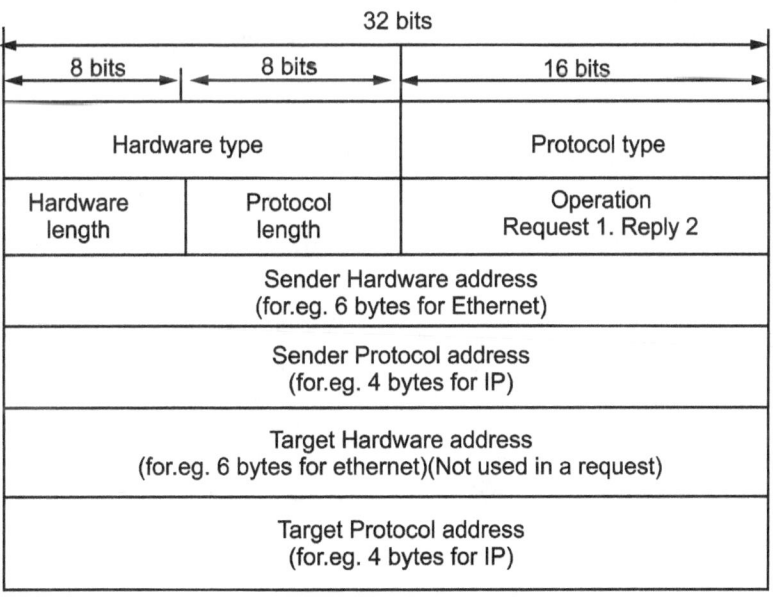

Fig. 4.2 : ARP packet format

- The fields used are :

  1. **Hardware Type :** This 16 bit field defines the type of the network on which ARP is running. Each LAN has been assigned an integer based on its type. For example : Ethernet is 1.

  2. **Protocol Type :** This 16 bit field defines the protocol. ARP can be used with any higher level protocol.

  3. **Hardware Length :** This 8 bit field defines the length of the physical address in bytes. For example : Ethernet has value 6.

  4. **Protocol Length :** This 8 bit field defines the length of the logical address in bytes. For example : IPv4 has value 4.

  5. **Operation :** This 16 bit field defines the type of packet. Two packet types are ARP request (1) and ARP reply (2).

  6. **Sender Hardware Address :** This variable length field defines the physical address of the sender. For example : For Ethernet, it is 6 bytes long.

  7. **Sender Protocol Address :** This variable length field defines the logical (IP) address of the sender. For IP, this field is 4 bytes long.

  8. **Target Hardware Address :** This variable length field defines the physical address of the target. For ARP request, this field is all Os because the sender does not know the physical address of the target.

  9. **Target Protocol Address :** This variable length field defines the logical (IP) address of the target. For IPv4, this field is 4 bytes long.

4.2.3 Encapsulation

- An ARP packet is encapsulated into a data link frame.
- Fig. 4.3 shows an ARP packet is encapsulated in an Ethernet frame.
- Type field indicates that the data carried by the frame are an ARP packet.

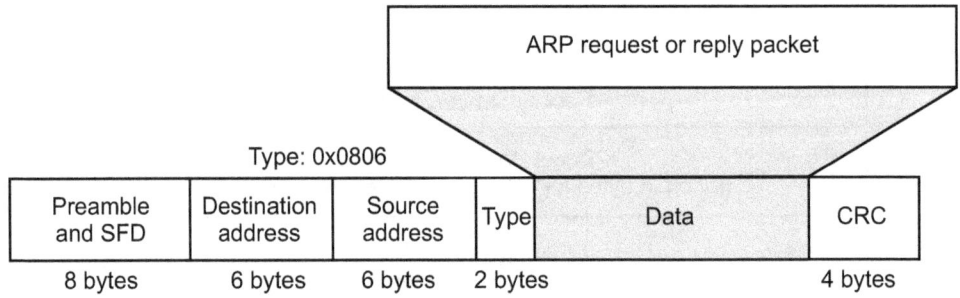

Fig. 4.3 : Encapsulation of ARP packet

4.2.4 Operation

- Now, let us talk about how ARP functions on an Internet. First, we will discuss the steps involved and then we discuss four cases in which a host or router needs to use ARP.

- The steps are :

  Step 1: The sender knows the IP address of the target.

  Step 2: IP asks ARP to create ARP request message. In request message, sender physical address, sender IP address and the target IP address are filled. The target physical address field is filled with 0s.

  Step 3: The message is passed to the data link layer. Data link layer encapsulates it in a frame by using the physical address of the sender as the source address and the physical broadcast address as the destination address.

  Step 4: Every host or router receives the frame. All machines discards it, except the targeted computer.

  Step 5: The target machine replies with an ARP message that contains its physical address. This message is unicast.

  Step 6: The sender receives the reply and knows the physical address of targeted machine.

  Step 7: The IP datagram, which carries data for the target machine, is now encapsulated in a frame and is unicast to the destination.

4.2.5 Four Different Cases   (Oct. 11, 14; April 12)

- As shown in Fig. 4.4, four different cases requires the services of ARP. These are :

  Case 1: The sender is a host and wants to send a packet to another host on the same network. In this case, the logical address must be mapped to a physical address of destination mentioned in IP datagram.

  Case 2: The sender is a host and wants to send a packet to another host on another network. In such situation, the host looks at its routing table and finds the IP address of the next hop (router) for this destination. If it does not have a routing table, it looks for the IP address of the default router. The IP address of the router becomes the logical address that must be mapped to a physical address.

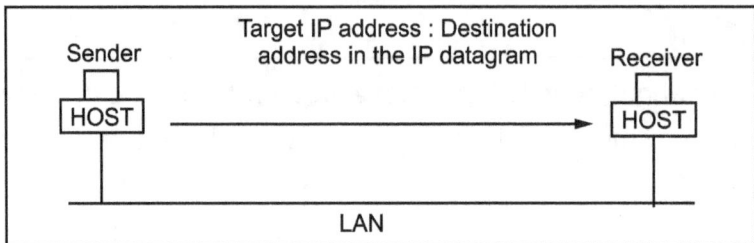

(a) Case 1 : A host has packet to send to another host on the same network

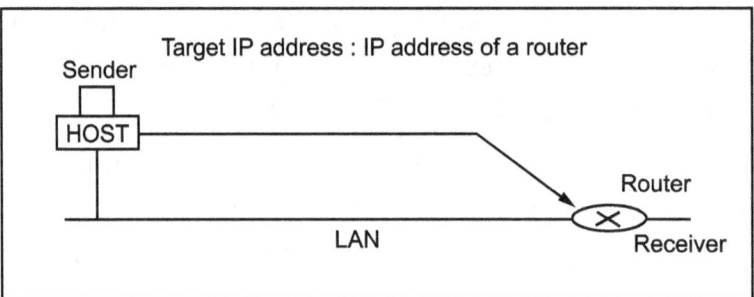

(b) Case 2 : A host wants to send a packet to another host on another network. It must first be delivered to a router

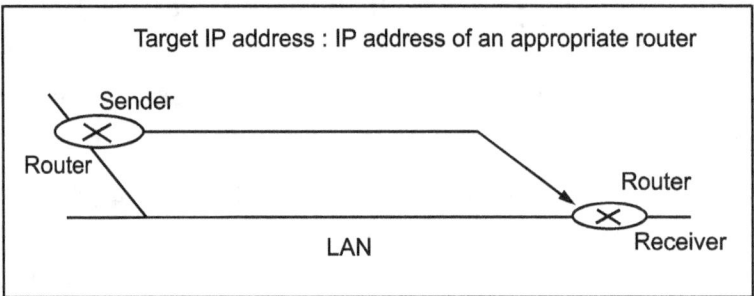

(c) Case 3 : A router receives a packet to be sent to a host to another network. It must be first delivered to the appropriate router

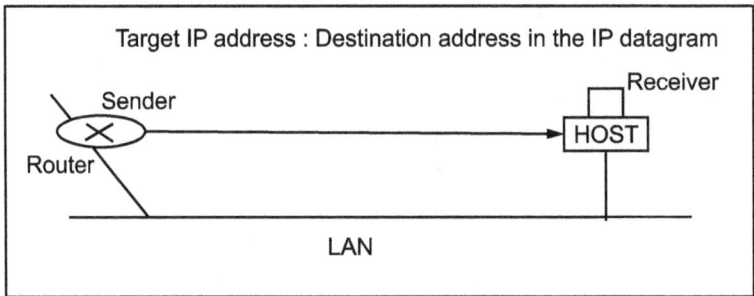

(d) Case 4 : A router receives a packet to be sent to a host on the same network

Fig. 4.4

Case 3: Router is a sender that has received a datagram destined for a host on another network. It checks its routing table and finds IP address of next router. IP address of next address becomes the logical address that must be mapped to the physical address.

Case 4: Sender is a router, who received a datagram destined for a host on the same network. The destination IP address of the datagram becomes the logical address that must be mapped to the physical address.

Ex. 1 : Hosts A and B are from same Ethernet network. Host A having IP address 110.23.43.21 and physical address B4 : 34 : 50 : 10 : 20 : 30 and Host B having IP address 110.23.43.32 and physical address A2 : 6E : F4 : 59 : 83 : AB. A don't know B's physical address. Show the ARP request and reply packets.

Sol. :

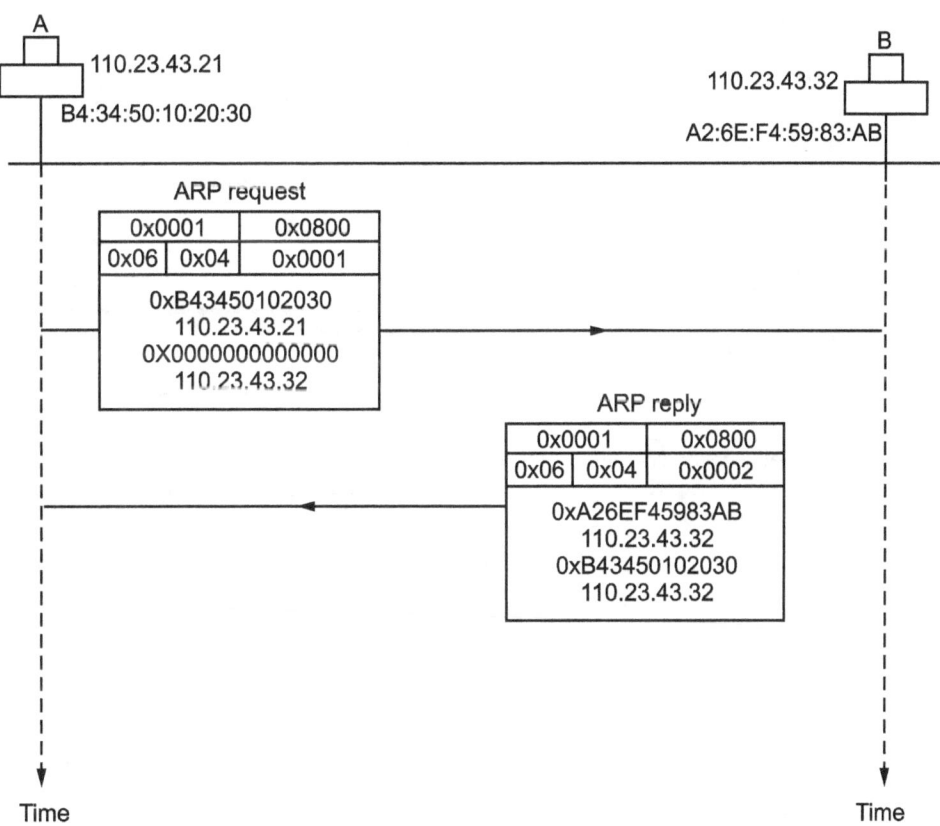

Fig. 4.5 : Example – ARP request and reply

4.2.6 Proxy ARP   (Oct. 14; April 15)

- Proxy ARP is the technique in which one host, usually a router, answers ARP requests intended for another machine. By "faking" its identity, the router accepts responsibility for routing packets to the "real" destination.

- Proxy ARP can help machines on a subnet reach remote subnets without the need to configure routing or a default gateway.

- Proxy ARP is defined in RFC 1027.

- Proxy ARP is used to create subnetting effect. A proxy ARP is an ARP that acts on behalf of a set of host. Whenever a router running a proxy ARP receives an ARP request of IP address of one of these hosts, the router sends an ARP reply of its own physical address. After the router receives the actual IP packet, it sends the packet to the appropriate host or router.

- This concept is shown in Fig. 4.6. Whenever, a request for 141.23.56.10, 141.23.56.11 and 141.23.56.12, these hosts coming from subnet A proxy router immediate sends its own physical address as a reply.

- When the proxy router receives the IP packet, it sends the packet to the appropriate host. Proxy router is able to do so because it knows both addresses of the connected hosts.

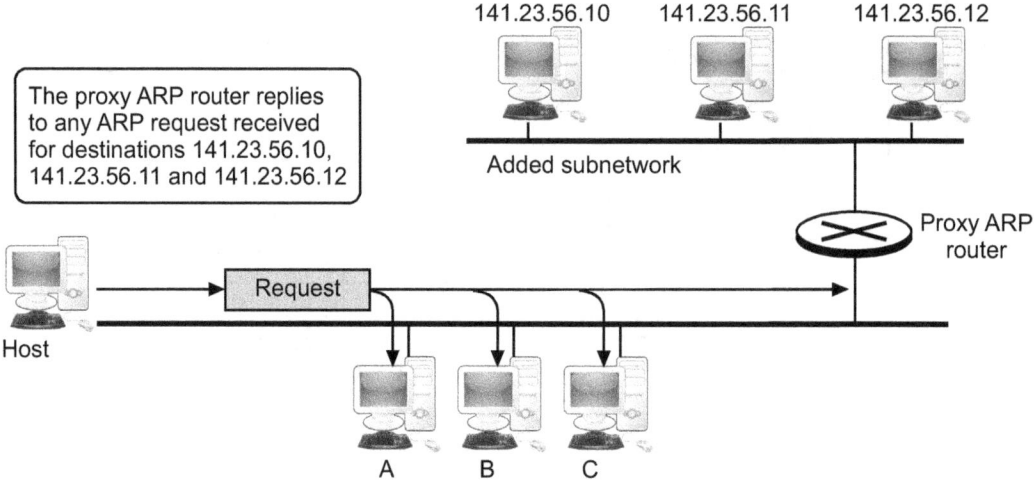

Fig. 4.6 : Proxy ARP

Advantages of Proxy ARP :

1. Proxy ARP must be used on the network where IP hosts are not configured with a default gateway or do not have any routing intelligence.

2. Proxy ARP can be added to a single router on a network and does not disturb the routing tables of the other routers on the network.

Disadvantages of Proxy ARP :

1. It increases the amount of ARP traffic on network segment.

2. Hosts need larger ARP tables in order to handle IP-to-MAC address mappings.

3. Security can be undermined. A machine can claim to be another in order to intercept packets, an act called "spoofing."

4. It does not work for networks that do not use ARP for address resolution.

5. It does not generalize to all network topologies. For example, more than one router that connects two physical networks.

4.2.7 Mapping Physical to Logical Address (RARP, BOOTP and DHCP) (Oct. 12)

- Sometimes, a host knows its physical address, but needs to know its logical address. We requires mapping of physical to logical address. This may happens in two situations :

  1. A diskless workstation is just booted. It can find its physical address by checking NIC, but it does not know its IP address.

  2. An organization does not have enough IP addresses to assign to each station, it needs to assign IP addresses on demand. The station who needs IP address can send its physical address and ask for IP address.

- In such type of situations, we are having three different solutions i.e., protocols RARP, BOOTP and DHCP. In this chapter, we discuss this protocols.

4.2.7.1 RARP

- Reverse Address Resolution Protocol (RARP) is used to find logical address of a computer which knows only its physical address.

- Every computer and router is assigned one or more IP addresses. These IP addresses are unique on that network and independent of physical address.

- To create IP datagram (packet), computer or router needs to know its IP address, usually read from its configuration file stored on a disk file.

- But whenever a diskless workstation is booted, it uses ROM, which are installed by manufacturer. Manufacturer cannot include the IP address in ROM because they have to be assigned by the network administrator.

- The diskless workstation can get its physical address by reading NIC. It can then use the physical address to get logical address by using the RARP protocol. A RARP request is created and then broadcasted on the network.

- Another machine on that network that knows all IP addresses will respond with the RARP reply. The requesting machine must be running a RARP client program and the responding machine must be running a RARP server program.

- Because of the serious problems RARP is almost obsolete and BOOTP and DHCP, are replacing RARP.

- Fig. 4.7 shows RARP operation.

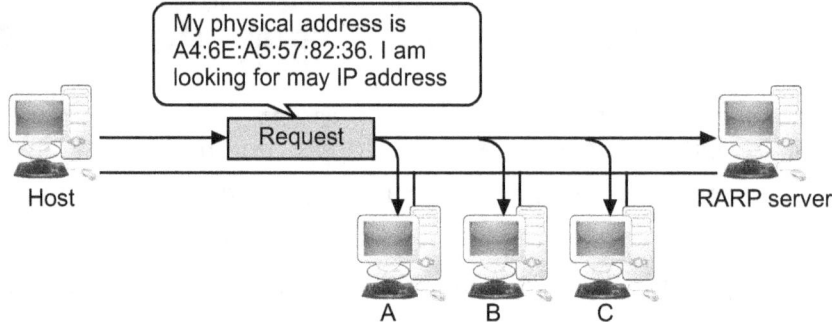

(a) RARP request is broadcast

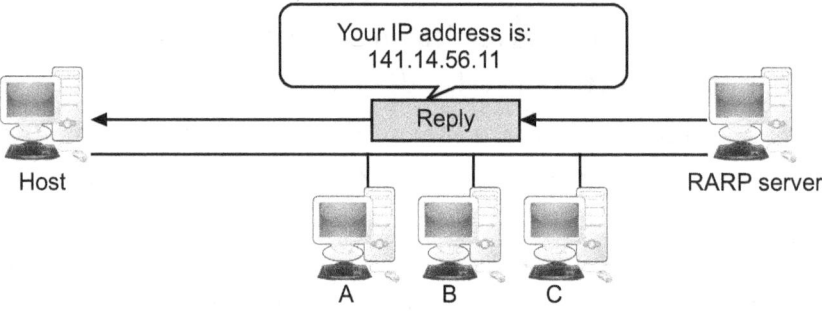

(b) RARP reply is unicast

Fig. 4.7

4.2.7.2 BOOTP

- The Bootstrap Protocol (BOOTP) is a client/server protocol.

- BOOTP is used to provide physical address to logical address mapping. The *BOOTP* was originally defined in RFC 951 standard. BOOTP is an application layer protocol.

- The administrator may put the client and the server on the same network or on different networks, as shown in Fig. 4.8.

1. **Client and Server in the Same Network:**

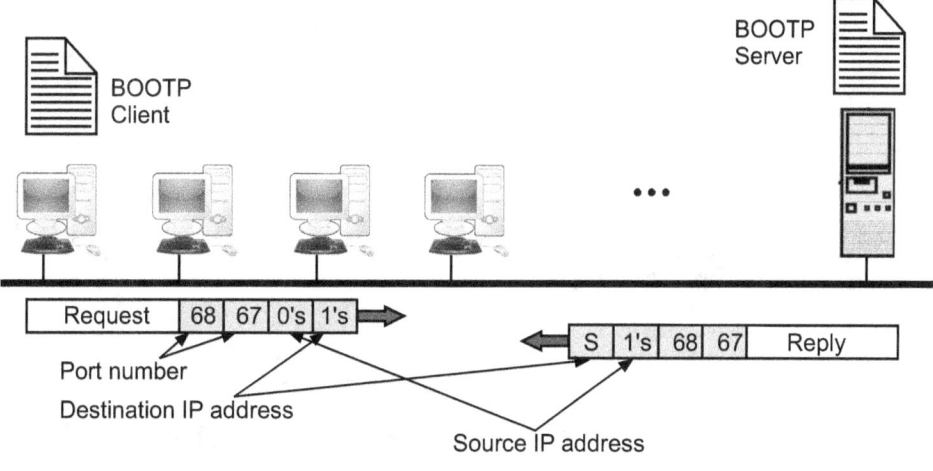

Fig. 4.8

- Operations of BOOTP for client and server in the same network, (Refer Fig. 4.8):
  (i) The BOOTP server issues a passive open command on UDP port number 67 and waits for a client.
  (ii) A booted client issues an active open command on port number 68. The message is encapsualted in a UDP user datagram, using the destination and source port number 67 and 68. The UDP user datagram is encapsulated in an IP datagram. The client uses all 0s as the source IP address and all 1s as the destination IP address.
  (iii) The server responds with either a broadcast or a unicast message using a UDP source and destination port numbers 67 and 68.

2. **Client and Server on Two Different Networks:**

- An IP address with all 1s is broadcast within a network. A host or a router needs to be configured as a relay agent to relay the message to other networks.
- The relay agent knows the unicast address of the BOOTP server. When the relay agent receives a broadcast request message, it sends the message to the BOOTP server and send the reply back when it gets the replay message from the server.
- The advantage of BOOTP over RARP is that it is client/server application layer protocol.
- A client and server can be from different networks. BOOTP request is broadcasted and IP broadcast datagram cannot passed from a router, which is a network layer device. To solve this problem one of the host or router is configured in application layer amd called as relay agent.

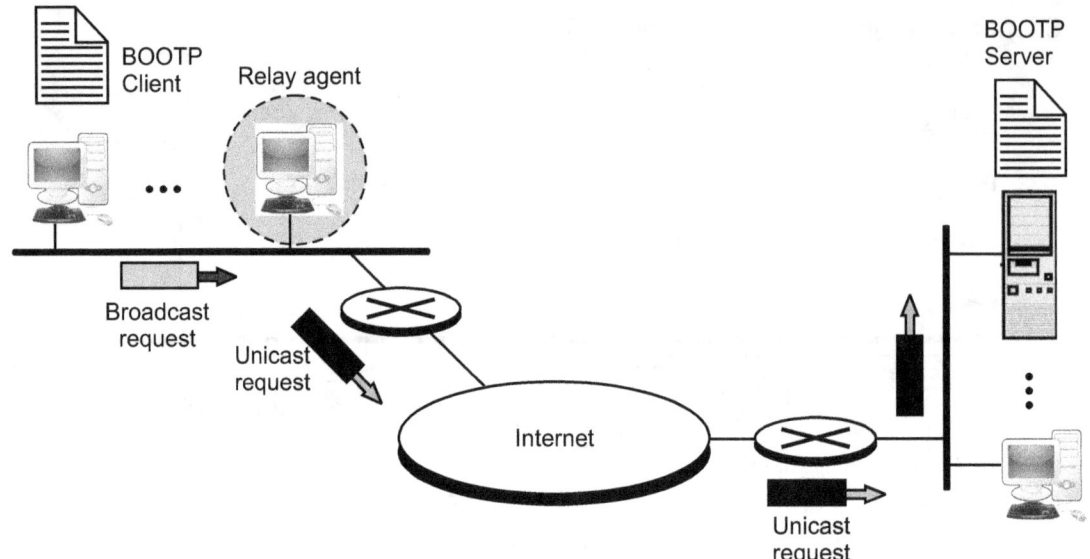

Fig. 4.9

- The relay agent knows the unicast address of BOOTP server. When it receives such broadcast packet, it encapsulate such packet in a unicast datagram and sends it to the BOOTP server. BOOTP server sends response, which is deliver to appropriate client by relay agent.

4.2.7.3 DHCP

- BOOTP is a static protocol, it provides binding between the physical address and the IP address of the client which is already exists. This binding is predetermined. But if a host moves from one physical network to other or it wants temporary IP address, BOOTP is not useful.
- The Dynamic Host Configuration Protocol (DHCP) is used for providing static as well as dynamic address allocation that can be manual or automatic.

1. **Static Address Allocation:**
- In static allocation DHCP works same as BOOTP.
- A DHCP server has a database that statically binds physical addresses to IP addresses.
- Even a BOOTP client can request a static address from a DHCP server.

2. **Dynamic Address Allocation:**
- DHCP has a static and dynamic database.
- Dynamic database is with pool of IP addresses. When a DHCP client sends a request to DHCP server, the server first checks in static database.
- If a binding of requested physical address is available, the IP address is return to the requesting host. But if the binding is not available in static database, the server

selects one IP address from pool of IP addresses and assigns that IP address to the client, and makes an entry in the database. Such assignment of IP address from pool is purely temporary.

- DHCP server issues a lease for a specific time. When lease expires, client can renew it or get another IP address.

3. **Manual and Automatic Configuration:**

- In BOOTP mapping of IP addresses to physical addresses needs to be done manually. But DHCP allows both manual and automatic configurations.

- Static addresses are created manually, dynamic addresses are created automatically.

Difference between BOOTP and DHCP:

Sr. No.	BOOTP	DHCP
1.	Static mappings.	Dynamic mappings.
2.	Permanent assignment.	Lease.
3.	Designed prior to DHCP.	Designed after BOOTP.
4.	Supports a limited number of client configuration parameters called vendor extensions.	Supports a larger and extensible set of client configuration parameters called options.
5.	Describe a two-phase bootstrap configuration process as follows : (i) Clients contact BOOTP servers to perform address determination and boot file name selection. (ii) Clients contact Trivial File Transfer Protocol (TFTP) servers to perform file transfer of their boot image.	Describes a single-phase boot configuration process whereby a DHCP client negotiates with a DHCP server to determine its IP address and obtain any other initial configuration details it needs for network operation.
6.	BOOTP clients do not rebind or renew configuration with the BOOTP server except when the system restarts.	DHCP clients do not require a system restart to rebind or renew configuration with the DHCP server. Instead, clients automatically enter a rebinding state at set timed intervals to renew their leased address allocation with the DHCP server. This process occurs in the background and is transparent to the user.

SUMMARY

➢ The delivery of a packet to a host or a router requires two levels of addressing: logical and physical. We need to be able to map a logical address to its corresponding physical address and vice versa. These can be done by using either static mapping (involves in the creation of a table that associates a logical address with a physical address) or dynamic mapping (each time a machine knows one of the two addresses (logical or physical), it can use a protocol to find the other one).

➢ ARP (Address Resolution Protocol) is a protocol for mapping an Internet Protocol address (IP address) to a physical machine address that is recognized in the local network. For example, in IP Version 4, the most common level of IP in use today, an address is 32 bits long.

➢ An ARP packet is encapsulated into a data link frame.

➢ Proxy ARP is defined in RFC 1027. Proxy ARP is the technique in which one host, usually a router, answers ARP requests intended for another machine. By "faking" its identity, the router accepts responsibility for routing packets to the "real" destination. Proxy ARP can help machines on a subnet reach remote subnets without the need to configure routing or a default gateway.

➢ RARP (Reverse Address Resolution Protocol) is used to find logical address of a computer which knows only its physical address. Every computer and router is assigned an IP address, which are unique on that network and independent of physical address. To create IP datagram (packet), computer or router needs to know its IP address. IP address of a machine is usually read from its configuration file stored on a disk file.

➢ The BOOTP (Bootstrap Protocol) was originally defined in RFC 951. The BOOTP is a computer networking protocol used in Internet Protocol networks to automatically assign an IP address to network devices from a configuration server.

➢ Dynamic Host Configuration Protocol (DHCP) is a client/server protocol that automatically provides an Internet Protocol (IP) host with its IP address and other related configuration information such as the subnet mask and default gateway.

PRACTICE QUESTIONS

1. What are the types of addresses ?
2. State the difference between logical address and physical address.
3. Explain the mapping of logical to physical address.
4. Explain the role of cache memory in ARP.
5. Explain ARP in detail.
6. What is encapsulation w.r.t to ARP ?

7. What are the four different cases in which a host or a router needs to use ARP ?

8. Explain proxy ARP.

9. What is RARP ?

10. Explain BOOTP in detail.

UNIVERSITY QUESTIONS AND ANSWERS

April 2011

1. How cache memory speeds up ARP operation ?   [1 M]

Ans. Please refer to Section 4.2.1.

2. What is address resolution ? Explain all steps required for a host or router needs to use ARP.   [5 M]

Ans. Please refer to Section 4.2.

October 2011

1. Discuss four different cases requires the services of ARP.   [5 M]

Ans. Please refer to Section 4.2.5.

April 2012

1. What is the purpose of ARP ?   [1 M]

Ans. Please refer to Section 4.2.

2. Explain four cases of using ARP.   [5 M]

Ans. Please refer to Section 4.2.5.

October 2012

1. What is the purpose of RARP ?   [1 M]

Ans. Please refer to Section 4.2.7.1.

2. Explain ARP packet format.   [5 M]

Ans. Please refer to Section 4.2.2.

October 2014

1. Why proxy ARP technique is used ? Define proxy ARP.   [1 M]

Ans. Please refer to Section 4.2.6.

2. State different cases in which the services of ARP can be used.   [2 M]

Ans. Please refer to Section 4.2.5.

April 2015

1. What is proxy ARP ?   [2 M]

Ans. Please refer to Section 4.2.6.

CHAPTER 5

The Transport Layer

Contents ...

Objectives...

- To Understand Transport Layer
- To Study UDP and TCP Protocols

5.0 INTRODUCTION   (April 15)

- Transport layer, layer number four (4) in the TCP/IP model is responsible for process-to-process delivery. To achieve the process-to-process delivery, transport layer supports three protocols i.e., UDP, TCP, SCTP.

- In this chapter we discussed two protocols UDP and TCP in details.

5.1 │ PROCESS-TO-PROCESS DELIVERY

- We know that, the data link layer is responsible for delivery of frames between two neighboring nodes over a link. This is called node-to-node delivery.
- The network layer is responsible for delivery of datagram between two hosts. This is called host-to-host delivery.
- Real communication takes place between two processes (application programs) in a network. This is called process-to process delivery.
- The transport layer is responsible for process-to-process delivery the delivery of a packet, part of a message, from one process to another.
- At the transport layer, we need a transport layer address, called a port number, to choose among multiple processes running on the destination host.
- In the Internet model, the port numbers are 16-bit integers between 0 and 65,535.
- The client program defines itself with a port number, chosen randomly by the transport layer software running on the client host. This is the ephemeral port number.
- The server process must also define itself with a port number. This port number, however, cannot be chosen randomly.
- On source and destination, several processes are running simultaneously. To complete the delivery, mechanism is required to deliver data from one of these processes running on the source host to the corresponding destination host.
- The transport layer is responsible for process-to-process delivery, the delivery of a packet, part of a message, from one process to another.
- Fig. 5.1 shows these three types of deliveries.

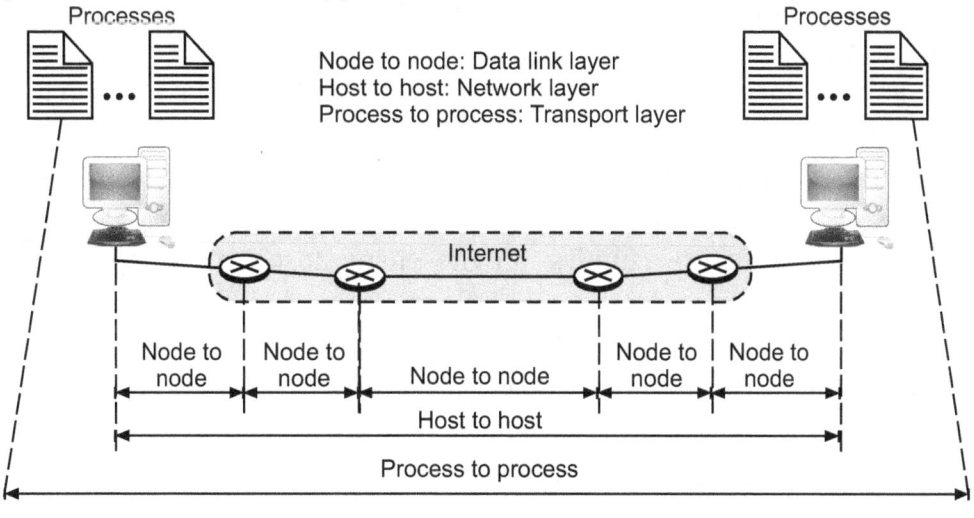

Fig. 5.1

5.1.1 Client/Server Paradigm

- The most common method to achieve process to process communication is through the client/server paradigm.

- A process on the local host, called a client, needs services from a process on the remote host called a server. The client and server machines can run several applications programs simultaneously.

- Both processes (client and server) have a same name. For example, to get the day and time from a remote machine, we need a day time client process running on the local host and day time server process running on a remote machine.

- For communication in between local and remote hosts, we must define :
  1. Local host.
  2. Local process.
  3. Remote host
  4. Remote Process.

Addressing :

- To deliver the data, we need address. At data link layer, we need physical (MAC) address. A frame in the data link layer needs a destination MAC address for delivery and source MAC address for reply.

- At the network layer, we need a IP address. A datagram in the network layer needs a destination. IP address for delivery and the source IP address for the destination's reply.

- At transport layer, we need transport layer address called port address. We know that many processes are running on source and destination. To identify uniquely, we requires port addresses. Every process is running on a port. The destination port number is needed for delivery, the source port number is needed for the reply.

- In the Internet model, port numbers are 16 bit integers between 0 and 65535. The client program defines itself with a port number, chosen randomly by the transport layer software running on the client host. This is ephemeral port (temporary) number.

- The server process must also define itself with a port number. The Internet has decided to use universal port numbers for servers, these are called well known port numbers (permanent).

- All server processes intend to communicate over the network are equipped with well-known Transport Service Access Points (TSAPs) also known as port numbers.

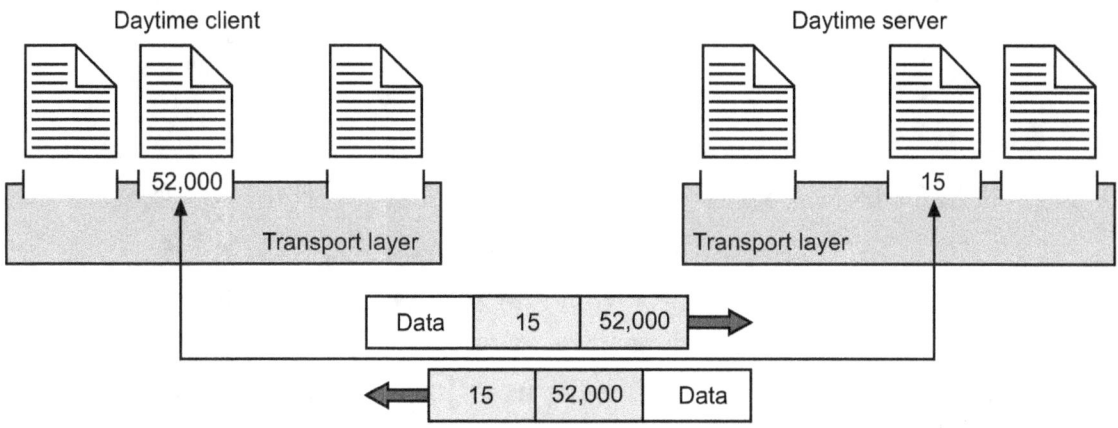

Fig. 5.2

- The role of destination IP address is to define the host among the different hosts. Once the host has been selected, role of port number starts, the port number defines one of the processes on this particular host. This is shown in Fig. 5.3.

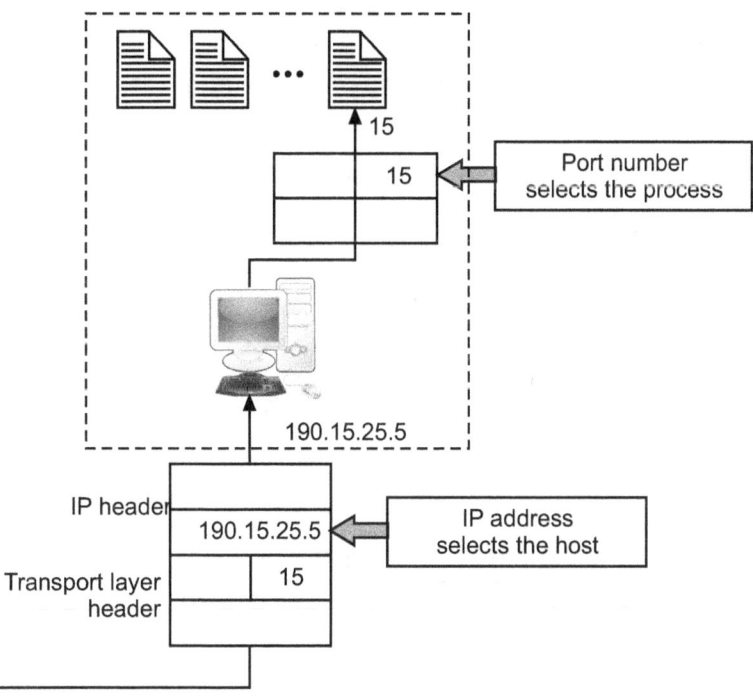

Fig. 5.3

IANA Ranges :

- The IANA (Internet Assigned Number Authority) has divided the port numbers into three ranges as shown in Fig. 5.4.

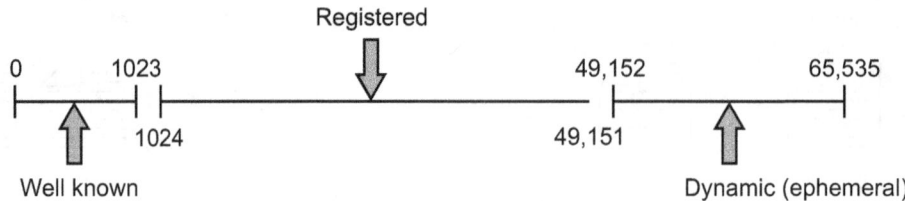

Fig. 5.4 : IANA ranges

1. **Well known ports :** The ports from 0 to 1023 are assigned and controlled by IANA. These are well known ports.

2. **Registered ports :** The ports ranging from 1024 to 49151 are not assigned or controlled by IANA. They can be registered with IANA to avoid duplication.

3. **Dynamic ports (ephemeral ports) :** The ports ranging from 49,152 to 65,535 are neither controlled nor registered. They can be used by any process. These are ephemeral ports.

Socket Addresses :

• Transport layer provides process-to-process delivery. Process-to-process delivery needs two identifiers, IP address and port number at both ends to make a connection.

• The combination of an IP address and a port number is called a socket address.

• The client socket address shows client process uniquely and server socket address shows server process uniquely.

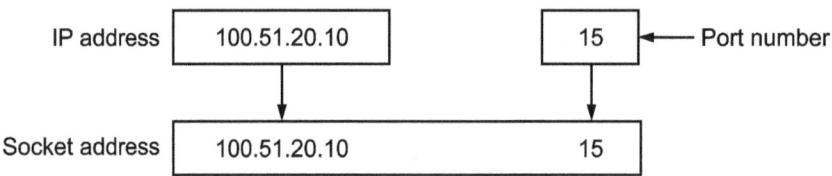

Fig. 5.5 : Socket address

5.1.2 Multiplexing and Demultiplexing

• Multiplexing and De-multiplexing are the two very important functions that are performed by transport Layer.

Multiplexing :

• Transport layer at the sender side receives data from different applications , but there is only one transport protocol, which encapsulates every packet with a transport Layer header and pass it on to the underlying Network Layer. This is many-to-one relationship. This job of transport layer is known as Multiplexing.

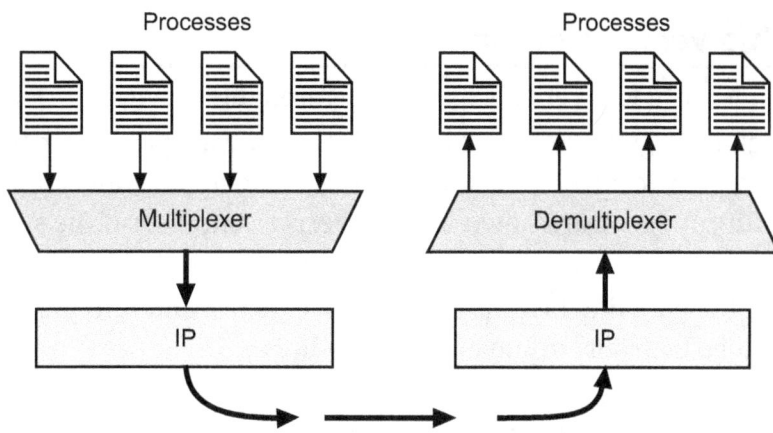

Fig. 5.6 : Multiplexing and demultiplexing

Demultiplexing :

- At receiver, situation is opposite, the relationship is one-to-many and requires demultiplexing.

- Transport layer receives packet from network layer. After removing the header, transport layer delivers each message to the appropriate process as per port number.

5.1.3 Connectionless Versus Connection Oriented Service

- Transport layer protocols can either be connectionless or connection oriented.

1. **Connectionless Service :**

- In a connectionless service, the packets are sent from one machine to another without connection establishment or connection release.

- The packets may arrive without order or they may be lost or delayed. Packets are not numbered. No acknowledgement is processed.

- UDP is transport layer's connectionless protocol.

2. **Connection - Oriented Service :**

- In a connection oriented service, connection is established first and then data are transferred in between sender and receiver. After end of data transfer, connection is released.

- TCP and SCTP, these two transport layer protocols are connection oriented.

5.1.4 Reliable versus Unreliable   (Oct. 12)

- Transport layer provides reliable as well as unreliable services.
- If the application layer program needs reliability, transport layer uses a reliable protocol with error control and flow control. If the application program does not need reliability, it may use its own flow and error control or if the service does not demand flow and error control, transport layer uses unreliable UDP protocol.
- Reliability at the data link layer is between two nodes, and reliability between two ends is provided by transport layer as shown in Fig. 5.7.

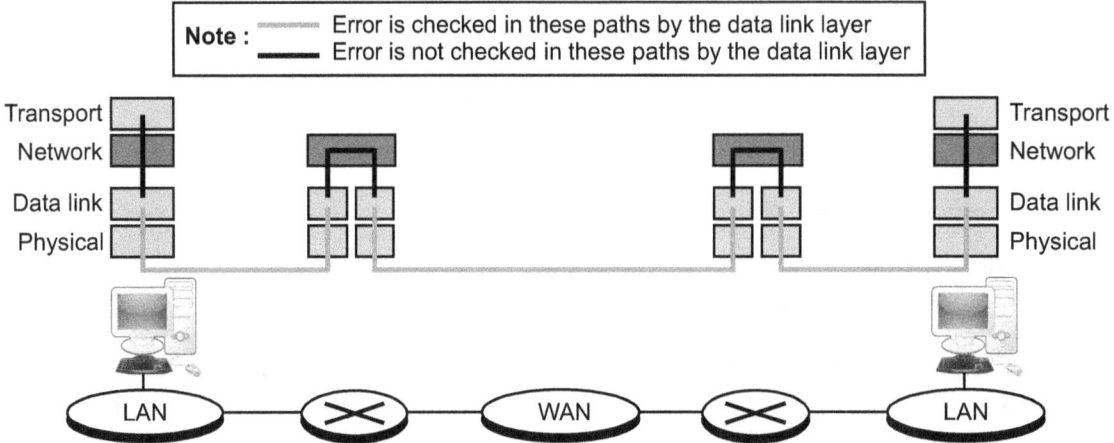

Fig. 5.7 : Error control of data link and transport layer

Three Protocols:

- In the Internet model, transport layer supports three protocols TCP, SCTP and UDP. Out of which TCP and SCTP are connection oriented and reliable and UDP is connectionless and unreliable.
- Though data link layer is reliable and provides error and flow control, we need reliability at transport layer also. Data link layer provides reliability between two nodes and transport layer provides reliability between two ends. Since, the network layer is unreliable, we need reliability at transport layer.

5.2 USER DATAGRAM PROTOCOL (UDP)   (Oct. 12)

- The UDP is one of the core members of the Internet protocol suite. The protocol was designed by David P. Reed in 1980 and formally defined in RFC 768 standard.
- UDP is a connectionless, unreliable Transport Layer protocol.
- UDP does not add anything to the services of IP except to provide process-to-process communication instead of host-to-host communication. Also, it performs very limited error checking.

- UDP is powerless protocol. But it is very simple protocol, using minimum overhead. If a process wants to send a small message and does not care much about reliability, it can use UDP.

- UDP is stateless protocol. It is suitable protocol for streaming applications such as VoIP, multimedia streaming.

5.2.1 Datagram Format   (Oct. 14)

- UDP packets, called as user datagrams, have a fixed-size header of 8 bytes.

- Fig. 5.8 shows the format of a user datagram.

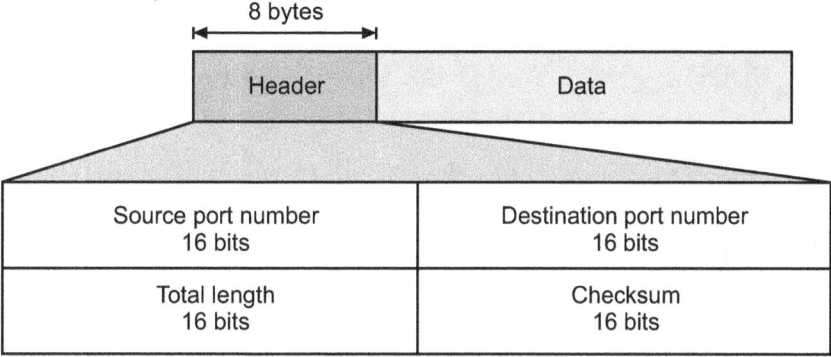

Fig. 5.8 : User datagram format

- UDP header contains four main parameters:

1. **Source Port Number:** This 16 bit field is used by the process running on the source host which wants to make communication. Port number can range from 0 to 65,535. If a client is sending a request, generally the port number is a ephemeral port number. If server is sending response port number is well known port number.

2. **Destination Port:** This 16 bit is used by the process running on the destination host. If the destination host is server, the port number is well known port number. If destination host is client, the port number is an ephemeral port number.

3. **Length:** This 16 bit field defines the total length of the user datagram, header plus data. This field is actually not necessary, because UDP is encapsulated in IP. IP has total length and header length fields.

   So, UDP length = IP length − IP header's length

4. **Checksum:** This 16 bit field is used to detect errors over the entire user datagram. The checksum field we will discuss in detailed.

- Some well known ports used by UDP are given in Table 5.1.

Table 5.1 : Some well known ports used by UDP

Port	Protocol	Description
7	Echo	Echoes a received datagram back to the sender.
9	Discard	Discards any datagram that is received.
11	Users	Active users.
13	Day time	Returns the date and time.
17	Quote	Returns a quote of the day.
53	Name server	Domain name service.
67	BOOTPs	This is the server port to download the bootstrap information.
68	BOOTPc	This is the client port to download bootstrap information.
69	TFTP	Trivial File Transfer Protocol.
111	RPC	Remote Procedure Call.
123	NTP	Network Time Protocol.
161	SNMP	Simple Network Management Protocol.

5.2.2 Checksum   (Oct. 11, 14)

- UDP provides checksums for data integrity, and port numbers for addressing different functions at the source and destination of the datagram.

- The UDP checksum calculation is different from IP. UDP's checksum includes three sections : a pseudoheader, the UDP header and the data coming from application layer.

- The pseudoheader is the part of the header of the IP packet in which the user datagram is to be encapsulated with some fields filled with 0s.

- If the checksum does not include the pseudoheader, a user datagram may arrive safe and sound. If the IP header is corrupted, it may be delivered to the wrong host.

- The protocol field is added to confirm that the packet belongs to UDP. The value of protocol for UDP is 17. If this value is changed during transmission, the checksum calculation at the receiver will detect it and UDP drops the packet.

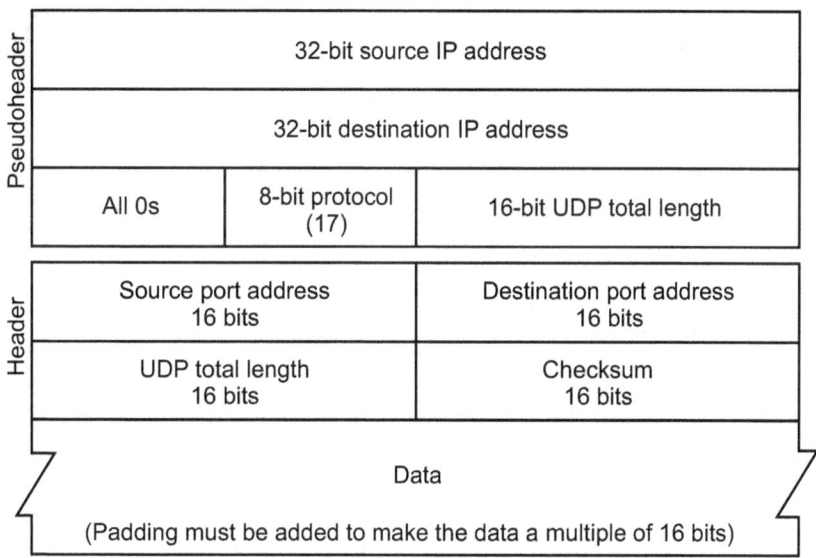

Fig. 5.9 : Pseudoheader for checksum calculation

- The calculation of checksum and its inclusion in a user datagram are optional. If checksum is not calculated, the field is filled with 1s.

Example : Fig. 5.10 shows the checksum calculation for a very small user datagram with only 7 bytes of data. Since the data is odd, padding is added for checksum calculation. The pseudoheader as well as the padding will be dropped when the user datagram is delivered to IP.

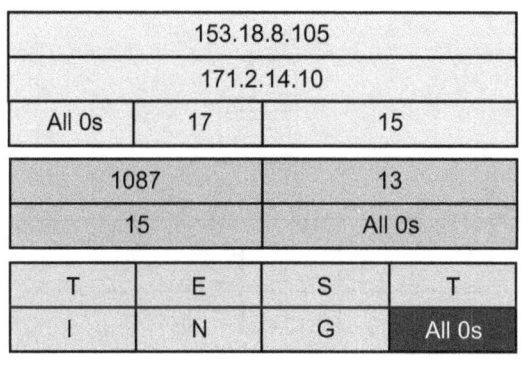
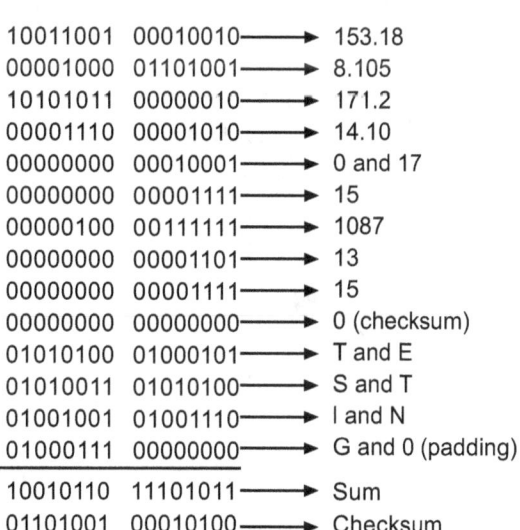

Fig. 5.10 : Checksum calculation of a simple UDP user datagram

5.2.3 UDP Operations   (Oct. 11, April 12)

- UDP uses concepts common to the transport layer. These concepts are explained below :

1. **Connectionless Services:**
   - UDP provides connectionless service. The user datagram are not numbered. There is no connection establishment and no connection termination between both ends. Every user datagram is independent datagram, they can travel on a different path.
   - The process that uses UDP cannot send a stream of data to UDP, instead each request must be small enough to fit into one user datagram. Only those processes sending short messages should use UDP.

2. **Flow and Error Control:**
   - UDP is simple, unreliable transport protocol, which not provides error and flow control.
   - Since, there is no flow control, the receiver may overflow with incoming messages. Since, there is no error control, the sender does not know if a message has been lost or duplicated.
   - Absence of flow and error control means that the process using UDP should provide these mechanisms.

3. **Encapsulation and Decapsulation:**
   - To send a message from one process to another, the UDP protocol encapsulates and decapsulates messages in an IP datagram.

4. **Queuing:**
   - In UDP, queues are associated with ports as shown in Fig. 5.11.

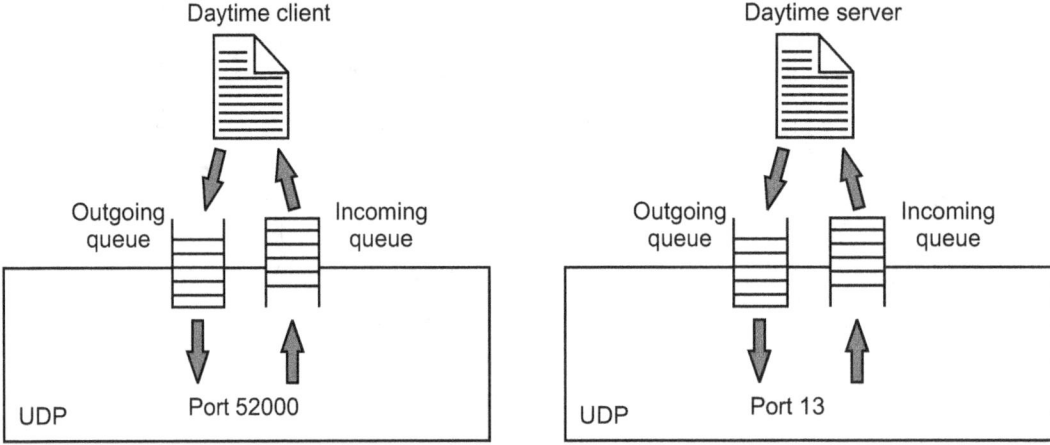

Fig. 5.11

- o   At the client site, when a process starts, it requests a port number from the Operating System (OS).
- o   An incoming and an outgoing queues associated with each process is created.
- Even if a process wants to communicate with multiple processes, it obtains only one port number and one outgoing and one incoming queue. Queues works as long as the process is running, when the process terminates, the queues are destroyed.
- The client process can send messages to the outgoing queue by using the source port number. UDP removes the messages one by one and after adding the UDP header, delivers it to IP. If outgoing queue is overflow, the operating system ask the client process to wait before sending any messages.
- When a message arrives for a client, UDP checks the destination port number and a queue which is created for such port. If there is such queue, UDP sends the received user datagram to the end of the queue. If such queue is not created, UDP discards such datagram. An incoming queue can overflow, if this happens, UDP drops the user datagram.
- At the server site, the mechanism for creating queues is different. When server starts running, incoming and outgoing queues are created. When message arrives for a server, UDP checks for port number, if there is queue created for port number UDP sends the received datagram to the end of the queue. If there is no such queue, UDP discards the user datagram. If incoming queue is overflow, UDP drops the packets.
- When server wants to send message to the client, it sends message to the outgoing queue by using the source port number specified in the request. UDP removes messages one by one, adds UDP header and delivers them to IP. If outgoing queue is overflow, the operating system asks the server to wait before sending more messages.

5.2.4 Use of UDP   (April 12, 15)

- Following are the uses of UDP protocol :
  1. UDP is suitable for a process that requires simple request response communication with little concern for flow control and error control.
  2. UDP is suitable for a process having inbuilt error control and flow control mechanisms, for example, TFTP (Trivial File Transfer Protocol).
  3. UDP is used for route updating protocols such as RIP (Routing Information Protocol).

4. UDP is suitable for multicasting, TCP not.

5. UDP is used for management processes such as SNMP (Simple Network Management Protocol).

5.3 | TRANSMISSION CONTROL PROTOCOL (TCP)   (April 13)

- The TCP is one of the most important protocols of Internet Protocols suite. TCP is most widely used protocol for data transmission in communication network such as Internet.
- TCP is reliable and connection oriented protocol.
- TCP creates a virtual connection between two TCPs to send data. The receiver always sends either positive or negative acknowledgement about the data packet to the sender, so that the sender always has right clue about whether the data packet is reached the destination or it needs to resend it.
- In addition, TCP uses flow and error control mechanisms. All these features makes TCP a reliable protocol.

5.3.1 TCP Services   (April 13)

- Let us discuss the services offered by TCP to the process at the application layer.

1. **Process-to-process Communication :**

- Like UDP, TCP provides process-to-process communication using port numbers.
- Table 5.2 shows some well-known port numbers used by TCP.

Table 5.2 : Well known ports used by TCP

Port	Protocol	Description
7	Echo	Echoes a received datagram back to the sender.
9	Discard	Discards any datagram that is received.
11	Users	Active users.
13	Day time	Returns the date and time.
17	Quote	Returns a quote of the day.
19	Chargen	Returns a string of characters.
20	FTP, Data	File Transfer Protocol (data connection).
21	FTP, Control	File Transfer Protocol (control connection).
23	TELNET	Terminal Network.

Contd..

25	SMTP	Simple Mail Transfer Protocol.
53	DNS	Doman Name Server.
67	BOOTP	Bootstrap Protocol.
80	HTTP	Hypertext Transfer Protocol.
111	RPC	Remote Procedure Call.

2. **Stream Delivery Service :** (Oct. 14; April 15)

- TCP is a stream oriented protocol. TCP allows the sending process to deliver data as a stream of bytes and allows the receiving process to obtain data as a stream of bytes.
- TCP creates an environment in which the two processes seem to be connected by an imaginary "tube". This tube carries data across the Internet. This imaginary environment is shown in Fig. 5.12.
- The sending process produces the stream of bytes and the receiving process reads data from it.

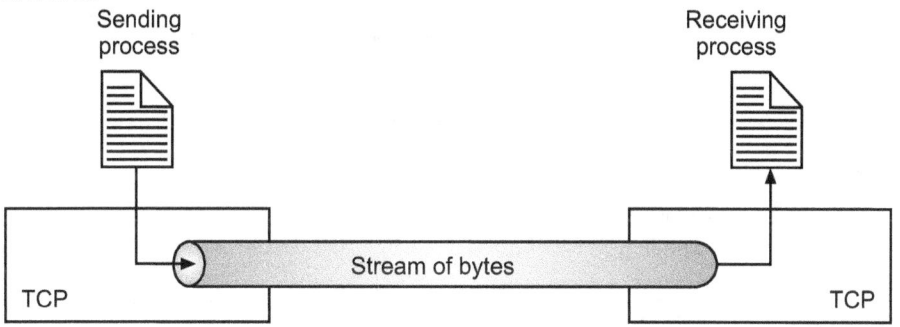

Fig. 5.12 : Stream delivery

3. **Sending and Receiving Buffers :**

- TCP requires buffers for data storage, since the sending and receiving processes may not write or read data at the same speed.
- There are two buffers, sending buffer and receiving buffer, one for each.
- Fig. 5.13 shows the movement of the data in one direction. At the sending side, buffer is divided into three sections. The white section is empty, that can be filled by the sending process.
- The cross-section area shows bytes are sent but not yet acknowledged. TCP keeps these bytes in the buffer until it receives an acknowledgement. The dotted area contains bytes to be sent by sending TCP.
- At receiver, the operation is simpler. The circular buffer is divided into two areas, white and dotted one. The white area contains empty buffers to be filled by bytes received from the network layer.

- The dotted section contains received bytes that can be read by the receiving process. When the byte is read, that part of buffer becomes empty.

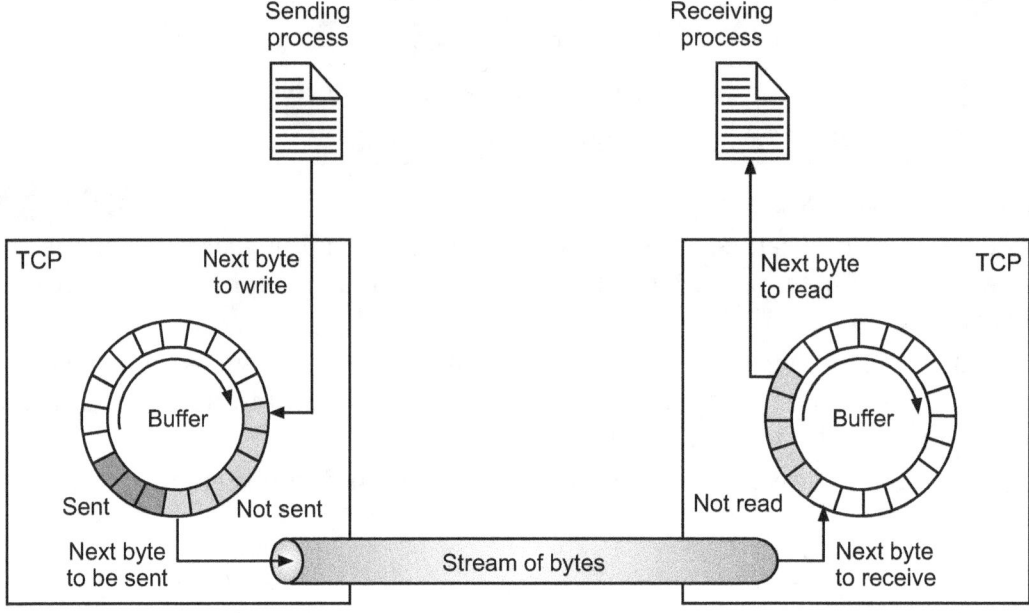

Fig. 5.13 : Sending and receiving buffers

4. Segments :

- Fig. 5.14 shows segments in TCP.

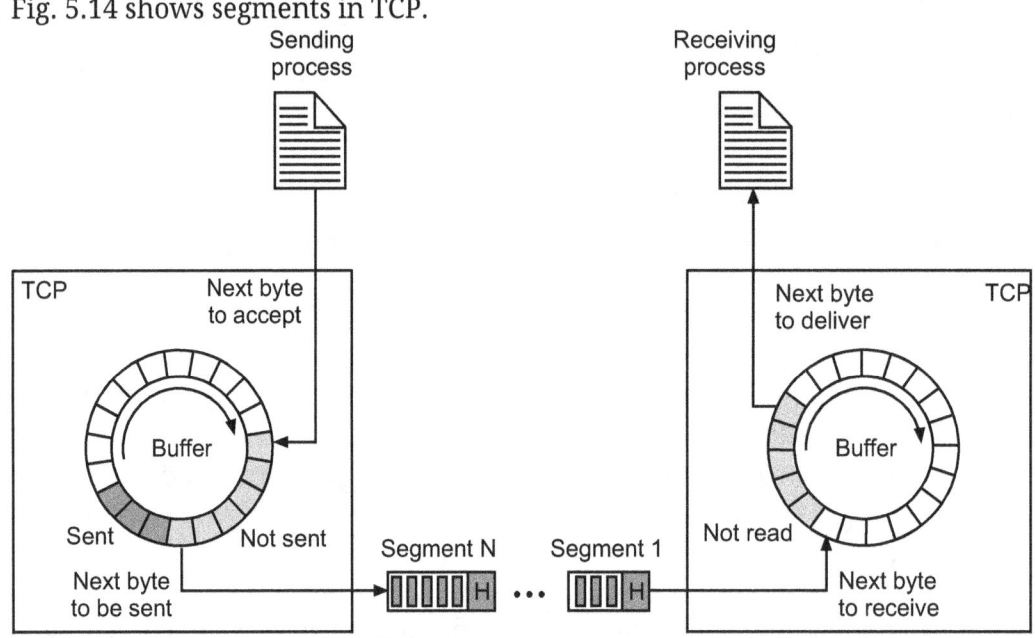

Fig. 5.14 : TCP segments

- IP provides services to TCP. IP protocol needs to send data in packets, not as a stream of bytes. At transport layer, TCP groups a number of bytes together into packets called a segment.

- TCP adds header to each segment and delivers it to IP, for transmission. The segments are encapsulated in IP datagram and transmitted.

5. **Full Duplex Communication :**

- TCP offers full duplex communication in which data can flow in both directions at the same time.

6. **Connection Oriented Service :**

- TCP is a connection oriented protocol. When a process at site A wants to send and receive data from another process at site B, the following occurs :

   (i)   The two TCPs establish a connection between them.

   (ii) Data are exchanged in both directions.

   (iii) The connection is terminated.

7. **Reliable Service :**

- TCP is connection oriented and reliable protocol. It uses acknowledgement to check the arrival of data.

5.4 | TCP FEATURES   (April 11)

- To provide the services mentioned above, TCP has several features that are explained below :

1. **Numbering System :**

- TCP software keeps track of segment (packets) transmitted and received. But there is no number value in the segment header.

- There are two fields i.e., sequence number and the acknowledgement number. These two fields refer to the byte number and not the segment number.

2. **Byte Number :**

- TCP numbers all data bytes that are transmitted in a connection.

- Numbering is independent in each direction. The numbering starts with a randomly generated number.

3. **Sequence Number :**

- The value in the sequence number field of a segment defines the number of the first byte contained in that segment. When a segment carries a combination of data and control information (piggybacking), it uses a sequence number.

- If a segment does not carry user data, it does not logically define a sequence number. The field is there but value is not valid. Randomly generated sequence numbers are used. If it is x then first byte sequence number is x+1.

4.   **Acknowledgement Number :**
- Communication in TCP is full duplex. Both communication parties send and receive data at the same time.
- Every party starting with a different sequence number. Each party also uses an acknowledgment number to confirm the bytes it has received.
- The value of the acknowledgement field in a segment defines the number of the next byte a party expects to receive. The acknowledgement number is cumulative.

5.   **Flow Control :**
- TCP provides flow control mechanism. The receiver of data controls the amount of data that are to be sent by the sender. By doing this, receiver is not swamped by data sent by the sender.
- The numbering system allows TCP to use a byte oriented flow control.

6.   **Error Control :**
- For providing reliable service, TCP uses error control mechanism. Error control is byte oriented.

7.   **Congestion Control :**
- TCP also provides congestion control. Receiver not only control the amount of data sent by the sender (flow control), but it is also determined by the level of congestion in the network.

5.5 | TCP SEGMENT FORMAT   (April 13)

- A packet in TCP is called as a segment. The format is shown in Fig. 5.15.

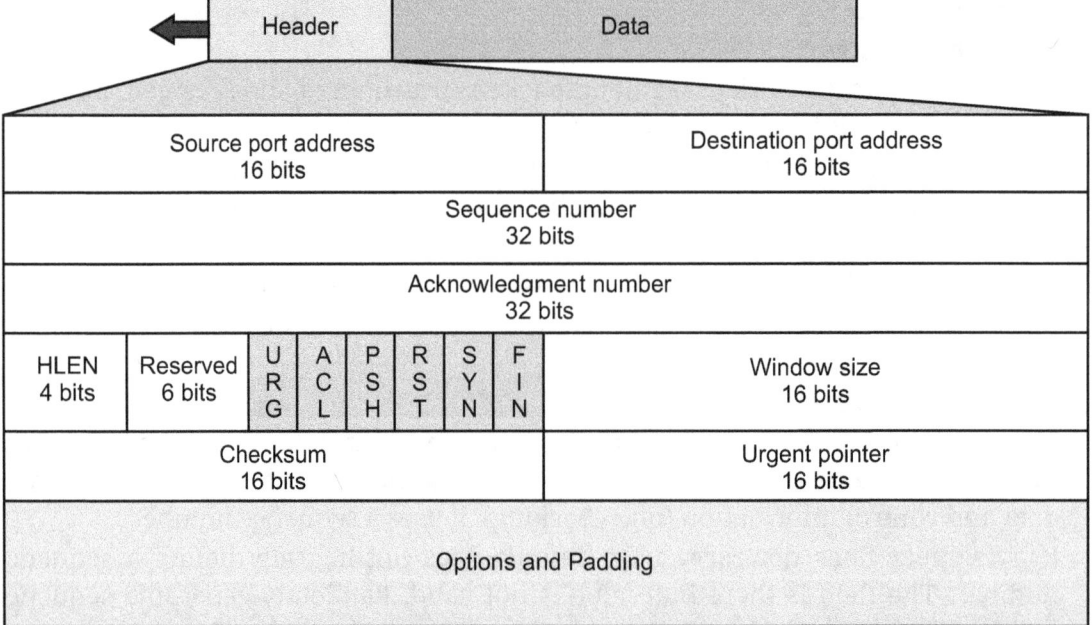

Fig. 5.15 : TCP segment format

- The segment consists of a 20 to 60 byte header, followed by data from application layer. The header is of 20 bytes if no options are used and upto 60 bytes if it contains options.
- Fig. 5.15 shows following fields of TCP segment format:
  1. **Source Port address:** This 16 bit field defines the port number of the application program in the host that is sending the segment.
  2. **Destination Port address:** This 16 bit field defines the port number of the application program in the host who is receiving the segment.
  3. **Sequence number:** This 32 bit field defines the number assigned to the first byte of data contained in the segment.
  4. **Acknowledgement number:** This 32 bit field defines the byte number that the receiver of the segment is expecting to receive from other party.
  5. **Header length:** This 4 bit field defines length of the header. The length of the header can range between 20 to 60 bytes.
  6. **Reserved:** This 6 bit field is reserved for future use.
  7. **Control:** This field defines 6 different control bits or flags as shown in fig. . One or more flags can be set at a time.

Note :   URG : Urgent pointer is valid   RST : Reset the connection
           ACK : Acknowledgement is valid   SYN : Synchronize sequence number
           PSH : Request for push   FIN : Terminate the connection

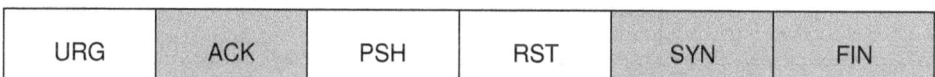

Fig. 5.16 : Control fields

- These bits enable flow control connection establishment and termination, connection abortion, and the mode of data transfer in TCP.
- The brief description of each bits is shown in Table 5.3.

Table 5.3 : Description of flage in the control field

Flag	Description
URG	The value of the urgent pointer field is valid.
ACK	The value of the acknowledgment field is valid.
PSH	Push the data.
RST	Reset the connection.
SYN	Synchronize sequence number during connection.
FIN	Terminate the connection.

8. **Windows Size:** This 16 bit field defines the size of the window in bytes, that other party must maintain. It is used for flow control between two stations and indicates the amount of buffer (in bytes) the receiver has allocated for a segment, i.e. how much data is the receiver expecting.

9. **Checksum:** This 16 bit field contains the checksum used for error control.

10. **Urgent Pointer:** This 16 bit field s valid only if the urgent flag is set, it is used when the segment contains urgent data.

11. **Option:** There can be up to 40 bytes of optional information in the TCP header. It facilitates additional options which are not covered by the regular header. Option field is always described in 32-bit words. If this field contains data less than 32-bit, padding is used to cover the remaining bits to reach 32-bit boundary.

Difference between TCP and UDP:

Sr. No.	Terms	TCP	UDP
1.	Acronym for	Transmission Control Protocol.	User Datagram Protocol.
2.	Connection	TCP is a connection-oriented protocol.	UDP is a connectionless protocol.
3.	Speed of transfer	The speed for TCP is slower than UDP.	UDP is faster because there is no error-checking for packets.
4.	Header Size	TCP header size is 20 bytes.	UDP Header size is 8 bytes.
5.	Weight	TCP is heavy-weight. TCP requires three packets to set up a socket connection, before any user data can be sent. TCP handles reliability and congestion control.	UDP is lightweight. There is no ordering of messages, no tracking connections, etc. It is a small transport layer designed on top of IP.
6.	Data Flow Control	TCP does Flow Control. TCP requires three packets to set up a socket connection, before any user data can be sent. TCP handles reliability and congestion control.	UDP does not have an option for flow control.

Contd...

7.	Error Checking	TCP does error checking	UDP does error checking, but no recovery options.
8.	Reliability and Acknowledgements	Unreliable best-effort delivery without acknowledgements.	Reliable delivery of message all data is acknowledged.
9.	Retransmissions	Not performed. Application must detect lost data and retransmit if needed.	Delivery of all data is managed, and lost data is retransmitted automatically.
10.	Overhead	Very low	Low, but higher than UDP.
11.	Data Quantity Suitability	Small to moderate amounts of data.	Small to very large amounts of data.

SUMMARY

➢ In OSI Model the 4th layer is the Transport Layer. This layer manages end to end (source to destination) (process to process) message delivery in a network.

➢ The transport layer is responsible for process-to-process delivery - the delivery of a packet, part of a message, from one process to another.

➢ There are several ways to achieve process to process communication. The most common one is through the client/server paradigm. A process on the local host, called a client, needs services from a process usually on the remote host called a server.

➢ Process-to-process delivery in Transport layer needs two identifiers, IP address and port number at both ends to make a connection. The combination of an IP address and a port number is called a socket address.

➢ Multiplexing and De-multiplexing are the two very important functions that are performed by Transport Layer.

➢ Transport layer at the sender side receives data from different applications, encapsulates every packet with a transport layer header and pass it on to the underlying network layer. This job of transport layer is known as Multiplexing.

➢ At the receiver's side, the transport gathers the data, examines it socket and passes the data to the correct Application. This is known as De-multiplexing.

➢ In a connection oriented service, connection is established first and then data are transferred in between sender and receiver. In a connectionless service, the packets are sent from one machine to another without connection establishment or connection release.

➢ Transport layer provides reliable as well as unreliable services. If the application layer program needs reliability, transport layer uses a reliable protocol with error control and flow control. If the application program does not need reliability, it may use its own flow and error control or if the service does not demand flow and error control, transport layer uses unreliable UDP protocol.

➢ The UDP protocol was designed by David P. Reed in 1980 and formally defined in RFC 768. The UDP (User Datagram Protocol) is one of the core members of the Internet protocol suite.

➢ UDP is a connectionless, unreliable Transport Layer protocol.

➢ TCP (Transmission Control Protocol) is most widely used protocol for data transmission in communication network such as Internet.

➢ TCP is a reliable and stream oriented protocol.

➢ Various TCP Services are Process-to-process Communication, Stream Delivery Service, Sending and Receiving Buffers, Segments, Full Duplex Communication, Connection Oriented Service and Reliable Service.

➢ TCP has several features Number System, Byte Number, Sequence Number, Acknowledgement Number, Flow Control, Error Control and Congestion Control.

➢ A packet in TCP is called as a segment.

PRACTICE QUESTIONS

1. Explain the process-to-process delivery in detail.
2. Explain the addressing in transport layer.
3. Describe the multiplexing and demultiplexing used in transport layer.
4. Explain the connectionless service and connection-oriented service.
5. Explain UDP in detail.
6. What is TCP ?
7. Explain the various services of TCP.
8. Describe the features of TCP.
9. Explain the TCP segment format.

UNIVERSITY QUESTIONS AND ANSWERS

April 2011

1. Explain the different features supported by TCP.   [5 M]

Ans. Please refer to Section 5.4.

October 2011

1. Explain three sections used in UDP checksum. Which common concepts are used in UDP operation ?   [5 M]

Ans. Please refer to Section 5.2.2 and 5.2.3.

April 2012

1.   Give two applications of UDP.   [1 M]

Ans. Please refer to Section 5.2.4.

2.   Explain UDP operation in brief.   [5 M]

Ans. Please refer to Section 5.2.3.

October 2012

1.   "The UDP is called a connectionless, unreliable transport protocol". Justify.

                                                                     [1 M]

Ans. Please refer to Section 5.2.

2.   Distinguish between reliable and unreliable services.   [5 M]

Ans. Please refer to Section 5.1.4.

April 2013

1.   What is window size of TCP segment ?   [1 M]

Ans. Please refer to Section 5.5.

2.   Which services are provided by TCP to application layer ? Explain it.   [5 M]

Ans. Please refer to Section 5.3.1.

October 2014

1.   What is a role of pseudoheader in the UDP checksum calculation ?   [1 M]

Ans. Please refer to Section 5.2.2.

2.   Write a note on stream delivery service of TCP.   [5 M]

Ans. Please refer to Section 5.3.1 Point (2).

3.   Explain the different fields of UDP datagram.   [4 M]

Ans. Please refer to Section 5.2.1.

April 2015

1.   State any two applications of UDP.   [1 M]

Ans. Please refer to Section 5.2.4.

2.   Explain duties performed by Transport layer.   [5 M]

Ans. Please refer to Section 5.0.

3.   Explain stream delivery and byte segment service of TCP protocol.   [5 M]

Ans. Please refer to Section 5.3.1 Point (2).

CHAPTER 6

The Application Layer

Contents ...

Objectives...

- To Understand Application Layer
- To Study E-mail, FTP, HTTP etc.
- To Learn WWW and Gateways Concepts

6.0 | INTRODUCTION

- We knew that the Application Layer is the top most layer in OSI and TCP/IP layered model.
- The application layer is responsible for providing services to the user and user applications.
- Application layer provide user interfaces and support for services such as DNS, e-mail, file transfer and access, access to system resources, surfing the world wide web (www) and network management.
- In this chapter, we will discuss services supported by the application layer.

6.1 | DOMAIN NAME SYSTEM (DNS)   (Oct. 12)

- Application layer supports several applications that follow the client/server environment. The client/server programs can be divided into two categories i.e., programs which are directly used by user like e-mail and those that support other application program.
- DNS is a supporting program used by other applications like e-mail.
- We know that network layer provides unique identification and source to destination delivery for a host on the Internet. For this, network layer uses its own IP protocol (for source to destination delivery) and IP addressing (for unique identification).
- However, people prefer to use names instead of numeric addresses. Therefore, we need a system that can map a name to an address or an address to a name.
- When the Internet was small, mapping was done by using a host file. Every host stores these hosts file on its disk and update it periodically from a master file. This file had two columns i.e., name and address.
- When a program or a user wanted to map a name to an address, the host consulted the host file and found the mapping.
- Today, since the size of Internet is so large and growing day-by-day, the host file becomes too large to store on every host. It would also be impossible to update all host files every time there was a change.

- One solution to this problem is, instead of storing the host file on every computer, the host file is stored on single computer and allows access to this centralized information to every computer who needs mapping. But it will create large traffic on the Internet and number of users will not get the mapping. So this solution also not works.

- Another solution is, instead of storing this huge information on single computer, divide this huge information into smaller parts and store each part on a different computer. The host that needs mapping can contact the closest computer holding the needed information. This method is Doman Name System (DNS).

- Domain Name Systems (DNS) is mechanisms that assign easy to remember names to IP address.

- Domain is a large group of computers on the Internet. Under this scheme each computer has an IP address and a domain name.

- Domains have been made on the base of organization type or geographical locations, e.g., the domain name google.com (where, .com indicates that Google is a commercial organization).

- Fig. 6.1 shows an example of how a DNS client/server program supports a user to find IP address.

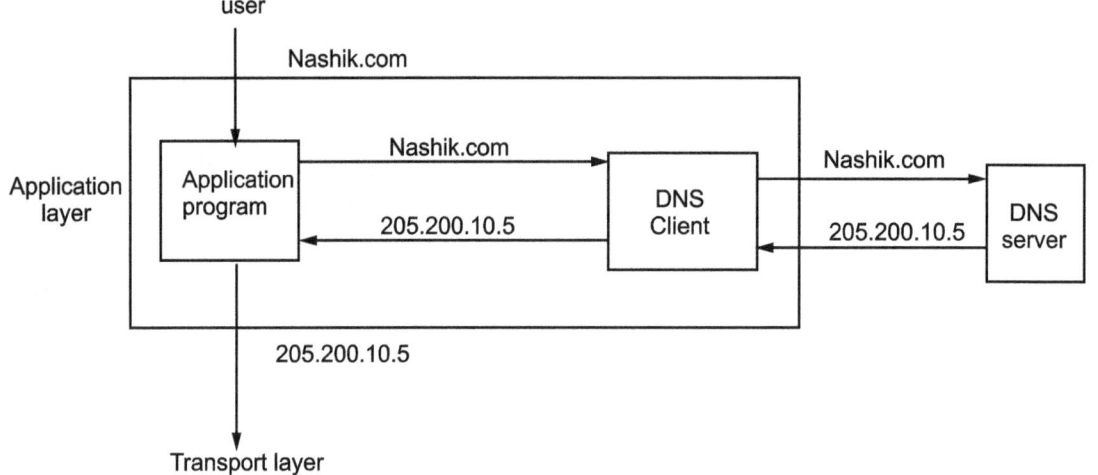

Fig. 6.1 : Example of using DNS service

6.1.1 Name Space

- The names assigned to machines must be carefully selected. The names must be unique because the addresses are unique.

- A name space that maps each address to a unique name can be organized in two ways i.e., flat or hierarchical.

1. **Flat Name Space :**
*   In flat name space, a name is assigned to an address. A name in this space is a sequence of characters without structure.
*   The names may or may not have common section. But this name space cannot be used in Internet because ambiguity and duplication is not avoided.
*   For example, a url nashik or rediff or google.

2. **Hierarchical Name Space :**
*   In hierarchical name space, every name is made up of several parts. The first part can define the nature or organization, the second part defines name of organization and third part defines departments in the organization, if any and so on.
*   A central authority can assign the part of the name that defines nature of the organization and name of organization. The organization can add suffixes or prefixes to the name.
*   These names are unique and cannot be duplicated.

    For examples : nashik.com,   rediff.com,   kthmcollege.edu,   pune.com, webdreamworkindia.com etc.

6.1.2 Domain Name Space

*   The domain name space refers a hierarchy in the internet naming structure. This hierarchy has multiple levels (from 0 to 127), with a root at the top.
*   The Fig. 6.2 shows the domain name space hierarchy.

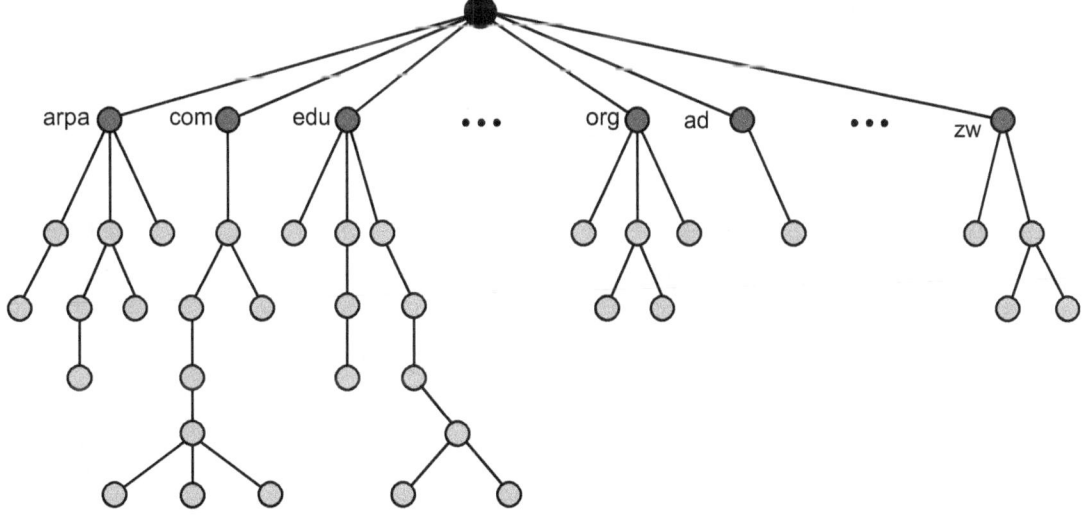

Fig. 6.2 : Domain name space

- To have a hierarchical name space, a domain name space was designed. The names are defined in an inverted-tree structure with root at the top. The tree can have maximum 128 levels.

Label :

- Each node in the tree has a label, which is a string with a maximum of 63 characters. The root label is null string.

Domain Name :

- Every node in the tree has a domain name. A full domain name is a sequence of labels separated by dots (.).

- Domain names are always read from the node upto the root. Fig. 6.3 shows some domain names.

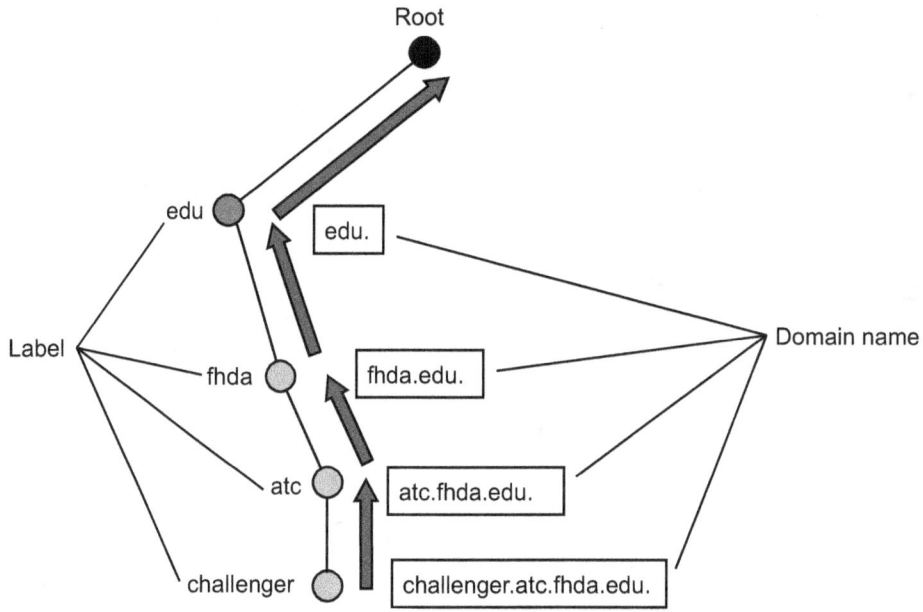

Fig. 6.3 : Domain names and labels

1. **Fully Qualified Domain Name :**   **(Oct. 12)**
   - If a label is terminated by a null string, it is called a Fully Qualified Domain Name (FQDN).
   - FQDN contains full name and all labels of a host.
   - For example : unipune.ernet.in, unipune.ac.in., kthmcollege.com etc.

2. **Partially Qualified Domain Name :**   **(Oct. 12)**
   - If a label is not terminated by a null string, it is called a Partially Qualified Domain Name (PQDN).

- A PQDN starts from a node, but it does not reach the root.
- For example : unipune.

3. **Domain :**
   - A domain is a subtree of the domain name space.
   - The name of the domain is the domain name of the node at the top of the subtree. A domain may be divided into sub-domains.

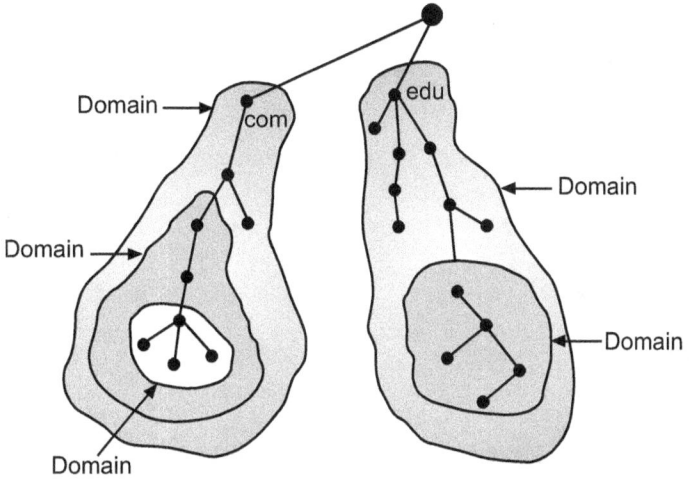

Fig. 6.4 : Domains

- Domain Name is a symbolic string associated with an IP address.
- There are several domain names available; some of them are generic such as .com, .edu, .gov, .net etc, while some country level domain names such as .au, .in, .za, .us etc.

6.1.3 Distribution of Name Space

- The information contained in the domain name space must be stored. Storing this huge information on single computer is inefficient and unreliable.
- It is inefficient because all users from the world send their requests to this computer, which places a heavy load. If this computer fails then data becomes inaccessible, so it is unreliable.
- The solution of above problem is to distribute the information among many computers called DNS Servers.

Hierarchy of Name Servers :

- Name server contains the DNS database.
- DNS database comprises of various names and their corresponding IP addresses. Since it is not possible for a single server to maintain entire DNS database, therefore, the information is distributed among many DNS servers.

- Hierarchy of server is same as hierarchy of names.
- The entire name space is divided into the zones.

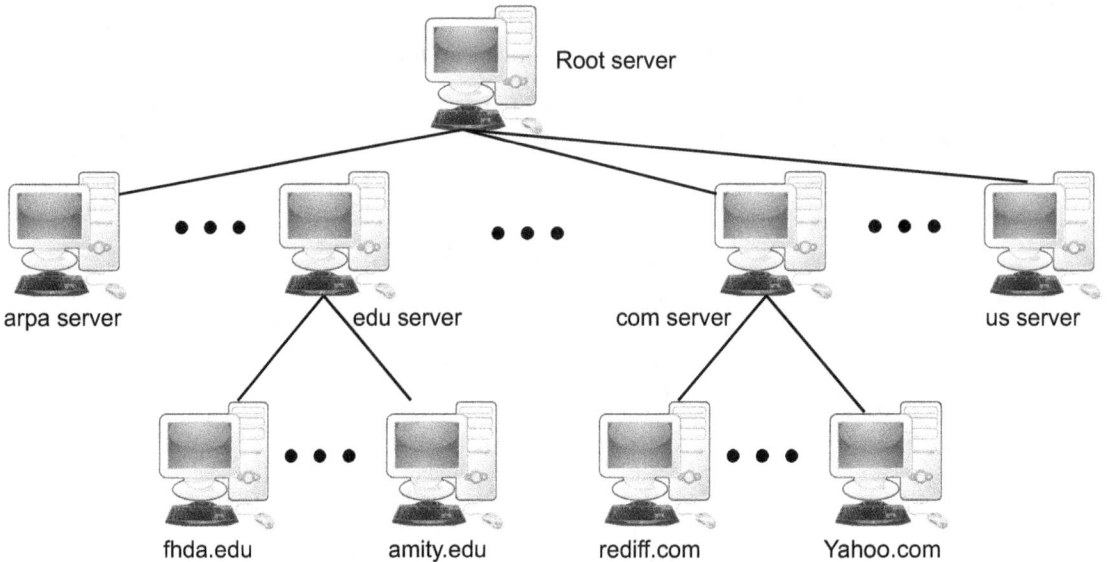

Fig. 6.5 : Hierarchy of name servers

- DNS allows domains to be divided further into sub-domains. Each server can be responsible for either a large or small domain. We have hierarchy of servers in the same way as hierarchy of names.

Zone :

- Since, the complete domain name hierarchy cannot be stored on a single server, it is divided among many servers.
- What a server is responsible for or has authority over is called a zone.

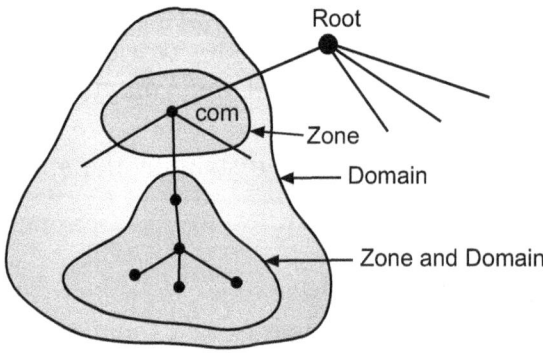

Fig. 6.6 : Zones and domains

- If a server accepts responsibility for a domain and does not divide the domain into smaller domains (sub-domains), the "domain" and the 'zone" refers to the same thing.
- The server makes a database called a zone file and keeps all the information for every node under that domain.

Root Server :

- Root Server is the top level server which consists of the entire DNS tree. It does not contain the information about domains but delegates the authority to the other server.
- Root server is a server whose zone consists of the whole tree. There are several root servers, each covering the whole domain name space.
- These servers are distributed all around the world. These servers usually does not store any information about domain.

Primary and Secondary Servers :

- DNS defines two types of servers i.e. Primary and Secondary.

1. Primary Servers :

- A primary server is a server that stores a file about the zone for which it is an authority.
- It is responsible for creating, maintaining and updating the zone file. It stores the zone file on a local disk.

2. Secondary Server :

- A secondary server is a server that transfers all information from the primary server.
- When the secondary downloads information from the primary, it is called zone transfer.

Zone Transfer :

- A primary server loads all information from the disk file; the secondary DNS Server loads all information from the primary server.
- When the primary DNS server downloads information from the secondary, it is called zone transfer.

6.1.4 DNS in the Internet

- In the Internet, the domain name space is divided into three different sections i.e., generic domains, country domains and the inverse domain.

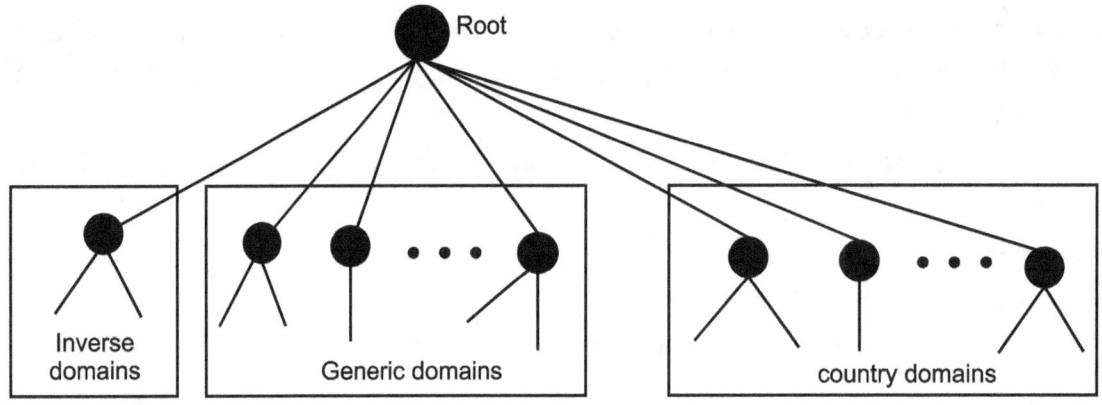

Fig. 6.7 : DNS used in the Internet

1. Generic Domains :   (April 13)

- The generic domains define registered host according to their generic behaviour.

- Fig. 6.8 generic domains.

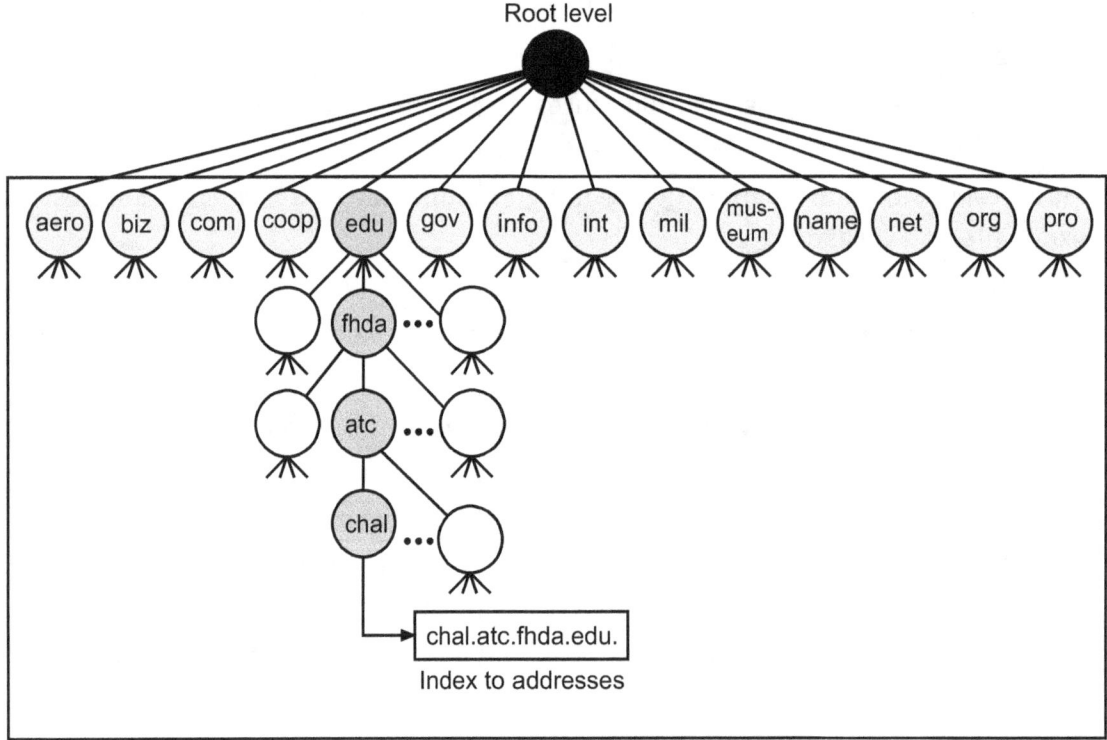

Fig. 6.8

- Table 6.1 gives list of labels used in generic domain.

Table 6.1 : Generic Domain Labels

Label	Description
aero	Airlines and aerospace companies.
biz	Business or firms.
com	Commercial organizations.
coop	Co-operative business organizations.
edu	Educational institutions.
gov	Government institutions.
info	Information service providers.
int	International organizations.
mil	Military groups.
museum	Museums and other non-profit organizations.
name	Personal names.
net	Network support centers.
org	Non-profit organizations.

2. **Country Domains :**

- Country domains uses two characters country abbreviations (e.g. in for India). Second labels can be organizational or national designations.

- Fig. 6.9 shows the country domains.

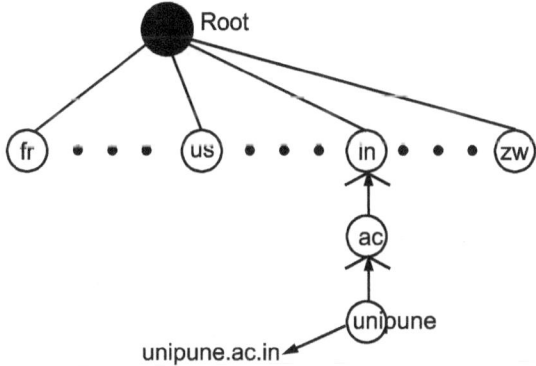

Fig. 6.9 : Country domains

3. **Inverse Domain :**

- The inverse domain is used to map an address to a name. This can be happen, for example, server want to check his authorized client.

- Fig. 6.10 shows example of inverse domain.

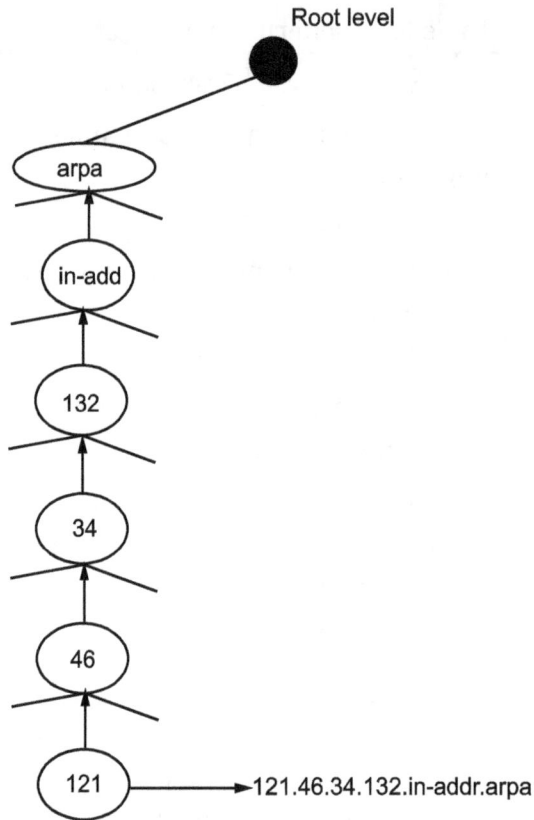

Fig. 6.10 : Inverse domain

6.1.5 Resolution   (Oct. 11)

- Mapping a name to an address or an address to a name is called name-address resolution.

Resolver :

- DNS is a client/server application. When a host requires mapping of name to an address or an address to a name, it calls DNS client called a resolver.

- The resolver accesses the closest DNS sever with mapping request. If the server knows the mapping, it gives it to resolver or it redirect the resolver to other server.

Mapping Names to Addresses :

- The resolver gives a domain name to the server and asks for the correct address. The server either checks the generic domains or the country domains for the mapping.

- Query is sent by the resolver to the local DNS server for resolution. If the local server cannot resolve the query, it either refers the resolver to other servers or asks other servers directly.

Mapping Addresses to Names :

- A client can send an IP address to a server to be mapped to a domain name.
- To answer such type of query, DNS server uses inverse domain.

Recursive Resolution :

- If the client (resolver) sends recursive query to the DNS server and expects the server to supply the final answer, if that server is the authority for the domain name, it checks the database and responds.
- If the server is not authority, it sends the request to another server and waits for response. If this server is authority, it responds, otherwise it sends the query to yet another server.
- When the query is finally resolved, the response travels back up to the requesting client. This is called recursive resolution and it is shown in Fig. 6.11.

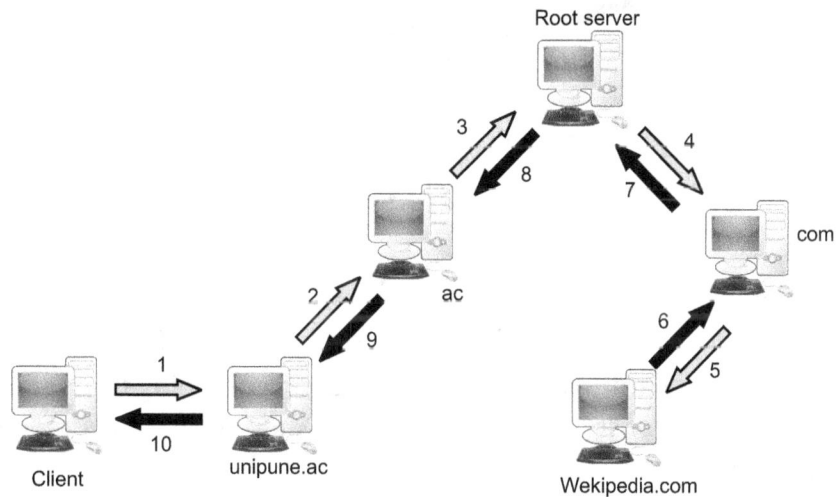

Fig. 6.11 : Recursive resolution

Iterative Resolution :

- If the client does not ask for a recursive query, the mapping can be iterative. If the server is authority for the name it gives reply to the client. Otherwise it returns the IP address of a server that it thinks can resolve the query.
- Now client again ask to that new server about mapping, if it knows, it gives reply, otherwise it gives the IP address of server which he thinks solve the query.

- Now, the client must repeat the query to the third server and so on. This process is called iterative resolution because the client repeats the same query to multiple servers. Fig. 6.12 shows iterative resolution.

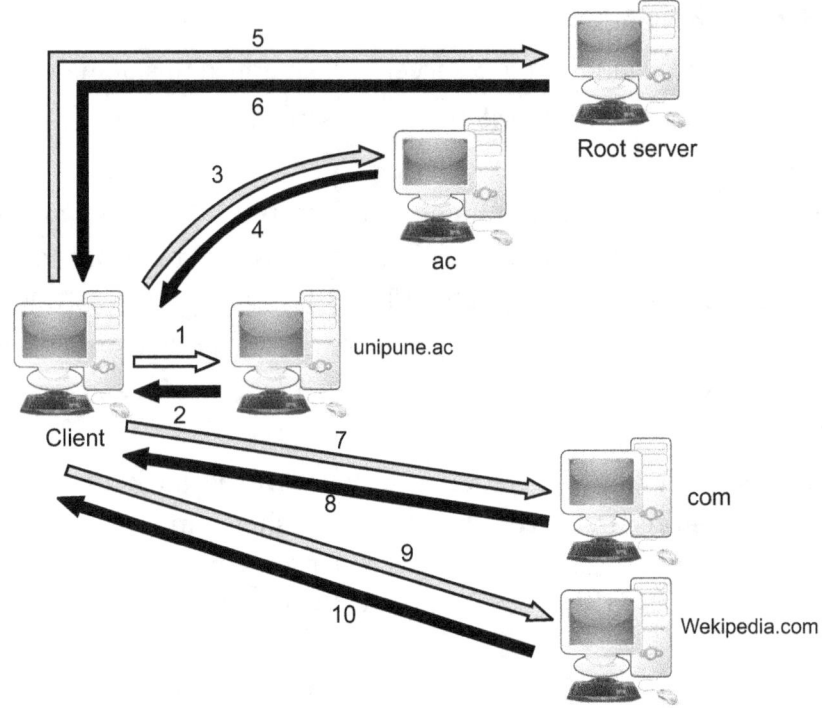

Fig. 6.12 : Iterative resolution

Caching :

- Every time when DNS server receives a request from client, it has to search in its database and then gives reply. If this search time reduces, efficiency increases.

- DNS use caching to do this. When a server asks for a mapping from another server and receives the response, it stores the information in its cache memory before sending it to the client.

- If the same or another client asks for the same mapping, it can check its cache memory and gives reply. The server marks such type of response as un-authoritative.

- Caching speeds up the resolution but sometimes it can also be problematic.

6.2 | E-MAIL

- The main task of the Internet is to provide services to users. E-mail is most popular application of Internet. E-mail is short form of electronic mail.

- At the beginning of the Internet, the messages sent by electronic mail were short and contains text only. Today, e-mails are much more complex and contains text, audio and video and one message can be sent to multiple recipients.
- We will study architecture of e-mail and the components of e-mail system in this section.

6.2.1 Architecture   (April 11, 13)

- To understand the architecture of e-mail, we will discuss four scenarios associated with e-mail system.

First Scenario :

- In this scenario, the sender and the receiver of the e-mail are users on the same system. Every user is having one mail box created by administrator.
- A mail box is a part of local hard disk. When user Amar (A) wants to send a message to another user Bhushan (B), Amar runs a User Agent (UA) program to create mail and store it in Bhushan's mail box.
- Every mail has sender's and recipient mail addresses. Bhushan can read the contents of his mail box at his convenience, using a user agent.
- When the sender and the receiver of an e-mail are on the same system, we need only two user agents. This is shown in Fig. 6.13.

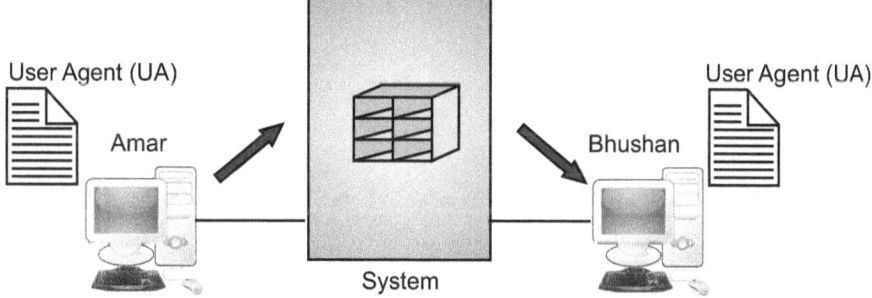

Fig. 6.13 : First scenario in electronic mail

Second Scenario :

- In the second scenario, the sender and receiver of the e-mail are users from different systems. The message is sent over the Internet. Thus, we need two user agents and pair of MTAs (client and server).
- Amar, the sender uses user agent program to send her message at her own site. Bhushan, the receiver needs user agent program to retrieve messages stored in the mail box of the system at his site.
- To send the message from Amar's site to Bhushan's site, two Message Transfer Agents (MTAs) are needed, one client and one server. This is shown in Fig. 6.14.

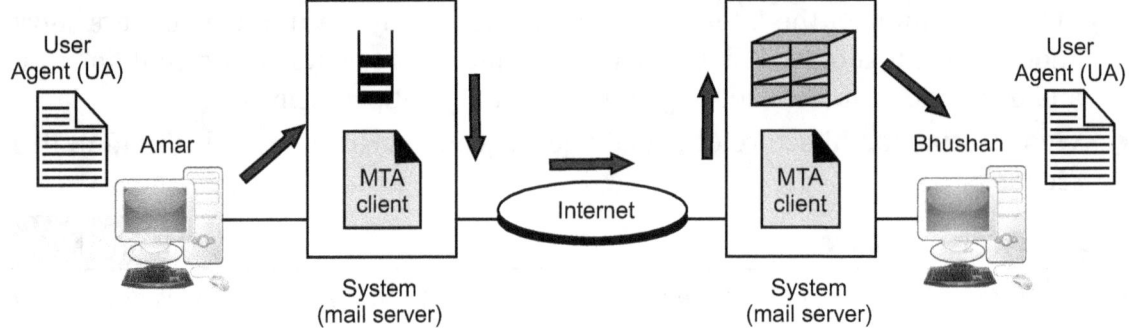

Fig. 6.14 : Second scenario in electronic mail

Third Scenario :

- In this scenario, Bhushan, the receiver is directly connected to his system. Amar, the sender is separated from him system. He is connected to the system via dial up modem or DSL etc.

- Amar uses user agent to prepare his message.

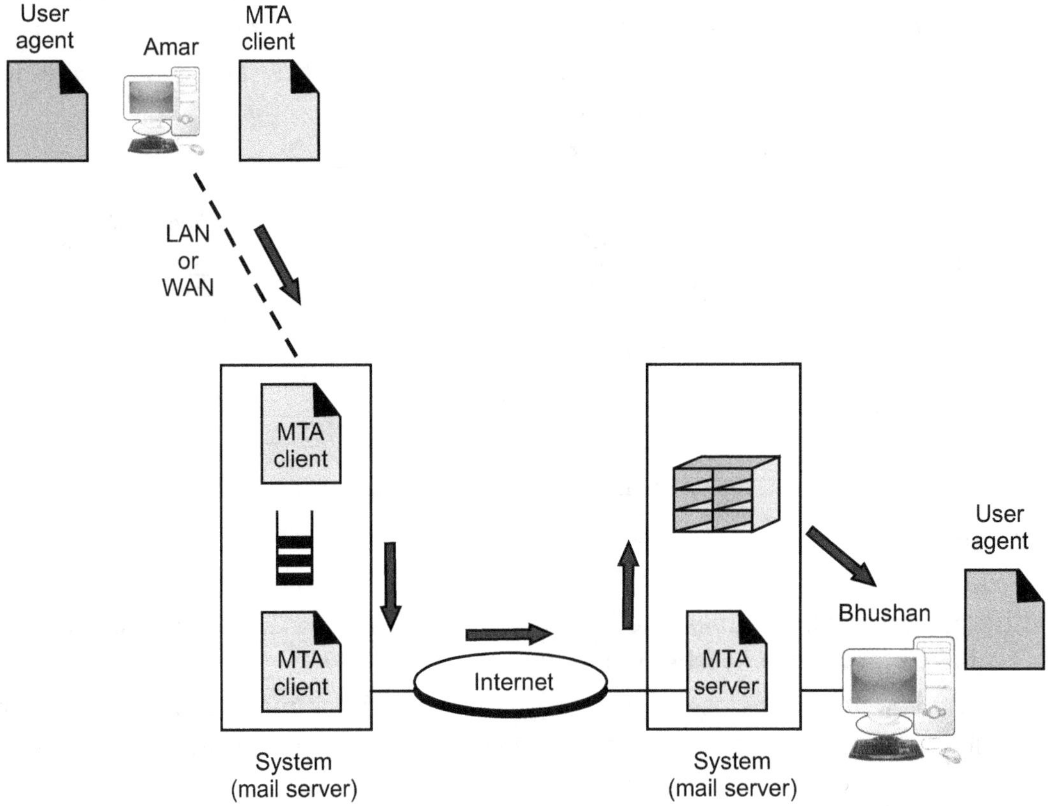

Fig. 6.15 : Third scenario in electronic mail

- The message is now send through the LAN or WAN. This is done by using pair of message transfer agent (client and server). MTA client establishes a connection with MTA server. MTA client then send the message to the system at Bhushan's site.

- System receives it and stores it in Bhushan's mail box. As per his convenience, Bhushan uses his user agent to retrieve his message. Note that, when the sender is connected to the mail server via a LAN or a WAN, we need two UAs and two pairs of MTAs (client and server).

Fourth Scenario :

- In the fourth and most common scenario, Bhushan, the receiver is also connected to his mail server by a WAN or LAN. When the message is arrived at Bhushan's server, he retrieves it by using another set of client/server agents also called as Message Access Agents (MAAs).

- Bhushan uses MAA client to retrieve the message. The MAA client pulls the messages from the mail server and pushes them into a special MAA server.

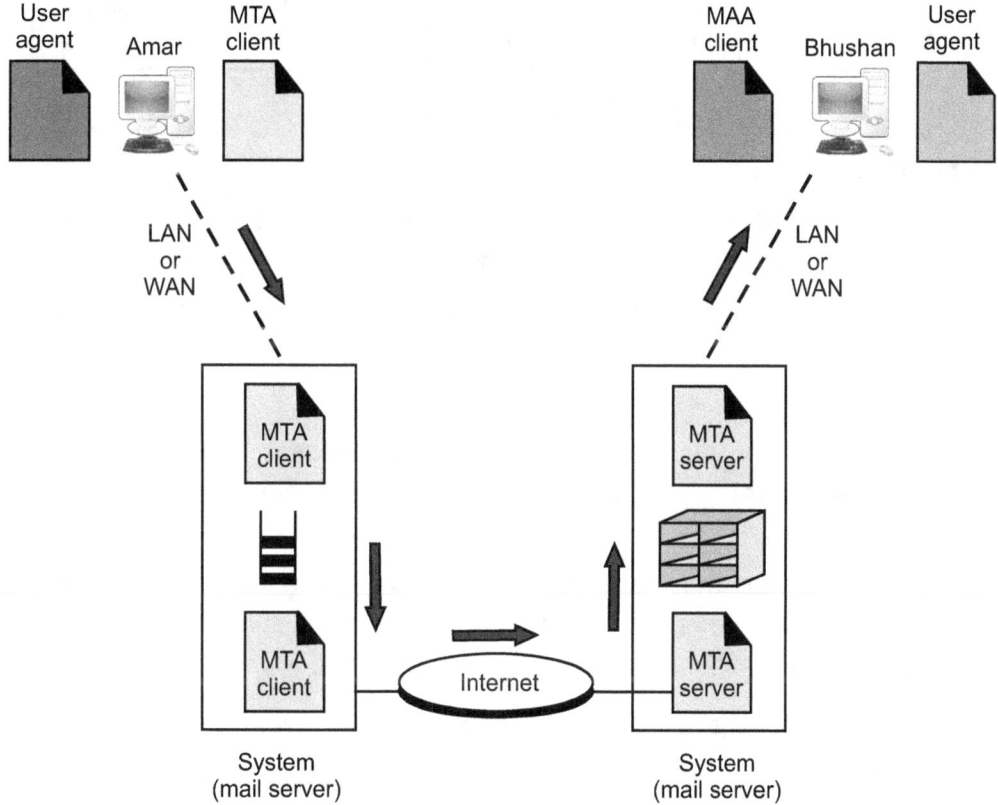

Fig. 6.16 : Fourth scenario in electronic mail

- Bhushan uses MAA client to retrieve messages from the MAA server.

- In short, we can say, when both sender and receiver are connected to the mail server via a LAN or WAN, we need two UAs, two pairs of MTAs, and a pair of MAAs. This is most common situation today, shown in Fig. 6.16.

6.2.2 User Agent   (April 11, 12; Oct. 11, 14)

- The first component of e-mail system is User Agent (UA). It provides services to user.

Services Provided by User Agent :

- A user agent is a software that provides following services shown in Fig. 6.17.

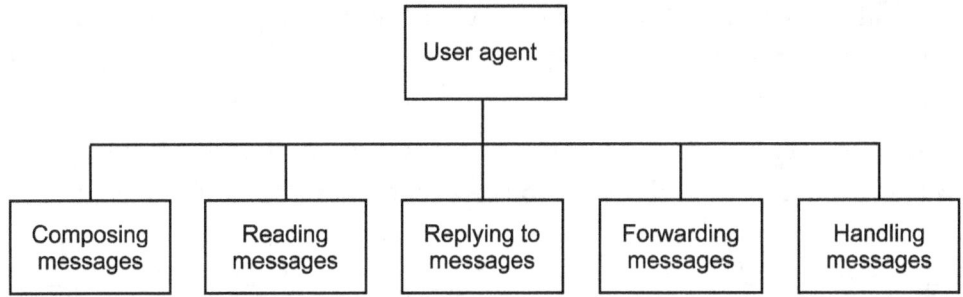

Fig. 6.17 : Services of user agent

1. Composing Messages :

- A user agent helps the user to compose (create) an e-mail. User agent provides a template on the screen, which helps the user.

- Some even have built in editor that can do spell checking, grammar checking, cut, copy, paste etc. text formatting functions.

2. Reading Messages :

- Next function of user agent is to read incoming messages. User agent first checks the mail in the incoming mail box. User agent shows a one line summary of every received mail.

- Every e-mail contains number field, flag showing status of e-mail like new, read, replied etc., size of message, the sender and the optional subject field.

3. Replying to Messages :

- After reading a message, user sent reply by using user agent.

- The user agent allows the user to reply to the original sender or to reply all recipients of the messages.

4. **Forwarding Messages :**

- User agent allows the receiver to forward the message, with or without extra comments, to a third party.

5. **Handling Mail Boxes :**

- A user agent creates two mail boxes i.e., inbox and outbox.
- Inbox keeps all the received e-mails until they are deleted by the user. The outbox keeps all the sent e-mails until the user deletes them.

Types of User Agent :   (Oct. 11, 14)

- User agent can be of two types :

1. **Command Driven :**

- Command driven user agents belong to the early days of e-mail.
- A command driven user agent normally accepts one character from the keyboard to perform its task, e.g. mail, pine and elm.

2. **GUI Based :**

- Modern user agents are GUI-based, which contains graphical user interface that allow the user to use keyboard and mouse, e.g. Outlook, Netscape, Eudora.

Sending Mail :

- To send mail, user creates a mail. E-mail has an envelope and a message as shown in Fig. 6.18.

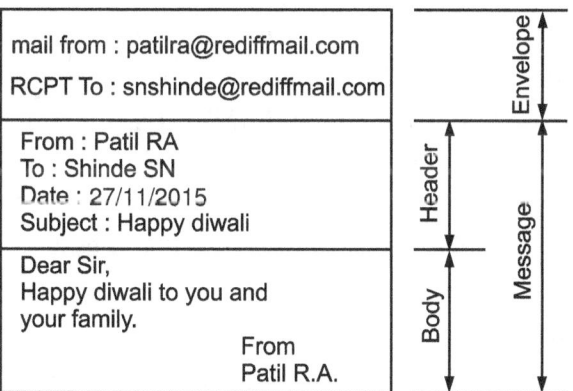

Fig. 6.18 : Format of e-mail

Envelope :

- The envelope contains sender and receiver addresses.

Message :

- Message contains header and body. In header, sender, receiver, date, subject of e-mail are defined. Body part contains actual information to be read by the recipient.

Receiving Mail :

- If user has a mail, UA informs the user. A list is displayed to the user in which summary of e-mail is mentioned.

- The user can selects any of the messages and display its contents on the screen.

Addresses :

- To deliver a mail, a mail handling system must use an addressing system with unique addresses.

- E-mail address contains two parts, local port and a domain name, separated by @ sign.

Fig. 6.19 : E-mail address

- Local port defines the name of user mail box. And domain name defines the name of mail server.

  For example:

MIME :

- E-mail system has one limitation, it can send messages only in NVT 7-bit ASCII. It cannot be used for languages like German, Russian, Chinese, Japanese and Hebrew. Also it cannot be used to send binary files or video or audio data.

- Multipurpose Internet Mail Extensions (MIME) is a protocol that allows non-ASCII data to be sent through e-mail.

- MIME transforms non-ASCII data at sender site to NVT ASCII and delivers them to the client MTA to be sent through the Internet. The message at the receiving site is transformed back to the original data.

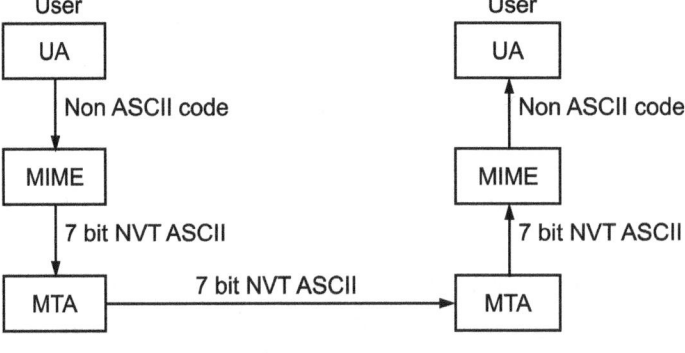

Fig. 6.20 : MIME

6.2.3 Message Transfer Agent : SMTP   (Oct. 11, 12; April 13)

- The mail transfer is done by message transfer agents. To send mail, a system must have client MTA and to receive mail, a system must have server MTA.

- The protocol that defines the communication between MTA client and MTA server is called Simple Mail Transfer Protocol (SMTP).

- SMTP is a TCP/IP protocol that specifies how computers exchange electronic mail.

- SMTP is used twice, between the sender and the sender's mail server and between the two mail servers.

- Another protocol i.e. POP3 or IMAP4 is needed between the mail server and the receiver.

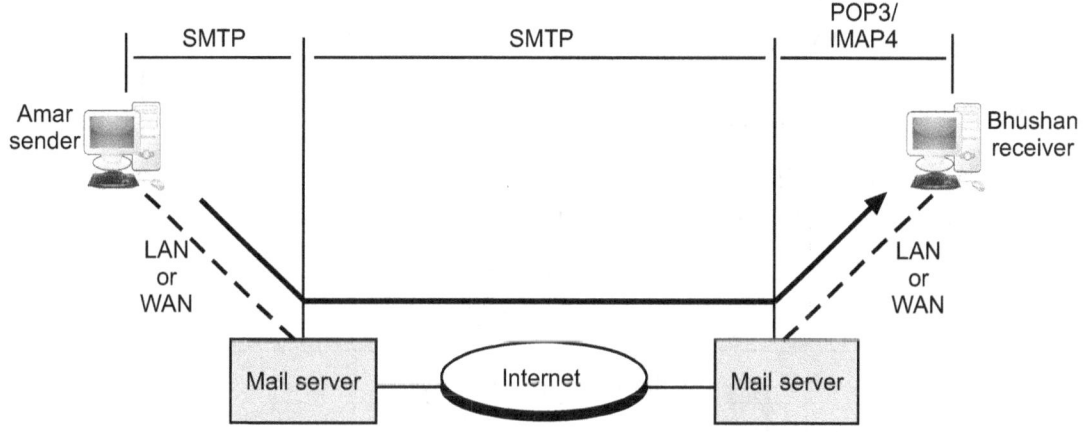

Fig. 6.21 : SMTP range, POP3 and IMAP4

Commands and Responses :

- SMTP uses commands and response to transfer messages between MTA client and MTA server.

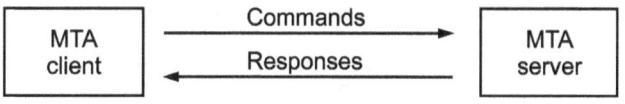

Fig. 6.22 : Commands and responses

- Commands are sent by client to server. Command consists of a keyword followed by zero or more arguments. SMTP uses 14 commands.

- Responses are sent from server to client. A response is a three digit code.

- Table 6.2 shows SMTP commands.

Table 6.2 : SMTP Commands

Keyword	Argument (s)
HELO	Sender's host name
MAIL FROM	Sender of the message
RCPT TO	Intended recipient of message
DATA	Body of the mail
QUIT	—
RSET	—
VRFY	Name of recipient to be verified
NOOP	—
TURN	—
EXPN	Mailing list to be expanded
HELP	Command name
SEND FROM	Intended recipient of the message
SMOL FROM	Intended recipient of the message
SMAL FROM	Intended recipient of the message

Table 6.3 : SMTP Responses

Code	Description
Positive Completion Reply	
211	System status or help reply
214	Help message
220	Service ready
221	Service closing transmission channel
250	Request command completed
251	User not local, the message will be forwarded
Positive Intermediate Reply	
354	Start mail input
Transient Negative Completion Reply	
421	Service is not available
450	Mail box not available
451	Command aborted : local error
452	Command aborted : insufficient storage

Permanent Negative Completion Reply	
500	Syntax error, unrecognized command
501	Syntax error in parameters or arguments
502	Command not implemented
503	Bad sequence of commands
504	Command temporarily not implemented
550	Command is not executed, mail box unavailable
551	User not local
552	Requested action aborted, exceeded storage location
553	Requested action not taken, mail box name not allowed
554	Transaction failed.

Mail Transfer Phases :

- Mail transfer occurs in three phases : connection establishment, mail transfer and connection termination.

- Now, let us see the typical SMTP procedure with an example :

```
$ telnet mail.rediffmail.com 25
Trying 70.168.78.100....
connected to mail.rediffmail.com (70.168.78.100).
...........................Connection Establishment............................
220 mta 13.rediffmail.com SMTP server reday Monday,15 Nov. 2010...
HELO mail·rediffmail.com
250 mta 13.rediffmail.com
...........................Mail Transfer............................
MAIL FROM : patilra@rediffmail.com
   250 sender <patilra@rediffmail.com> OK
RCPT TO : Shindesn@rediffmail.com
   250 Recipient <shindesn@rediffmail.com> OK
   DATA
   354 OK send data ending with <CRLF>.<CRLF>
FROM : Patil RA
TO : Shinde SN
Hi, How are you ?
...........................Connection Termiation............................
   250 message received : mail@rediffmail.com
QUIT
   221 mta 13.rediffmail.com SMTP server closing connection
   Connection closed by foreign host.
```

6.2.4 Message Access Agent : POP3 and IMAP4 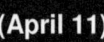 (April 11)

- SMTP is used in the first and second stage of mail delivery. SMTP is push protocol, it pushes the message from the client to the server, as shown in Fig. 6.21.

- The third stage needs a pull protocol from receiver to mail server. The third stage uses a message access agent. Now, two message access protocols are available i.e., Post Office Protocol (POP Version 3) and Internet Mail Access Protocol (IMAP Version 4).

- Fig. 6.21 shows these two protocols.

1. **POP3 :**

- Post Office Protocol (POP) is an application-layer Internet standard protocol used by local e-mail clients to retrieve e-mail from a remote server over a TCP/IP connection.

- POP supports simple download-and-delete requirements for access to remote mailboxes. A POP3 server listens on well-known port 110.

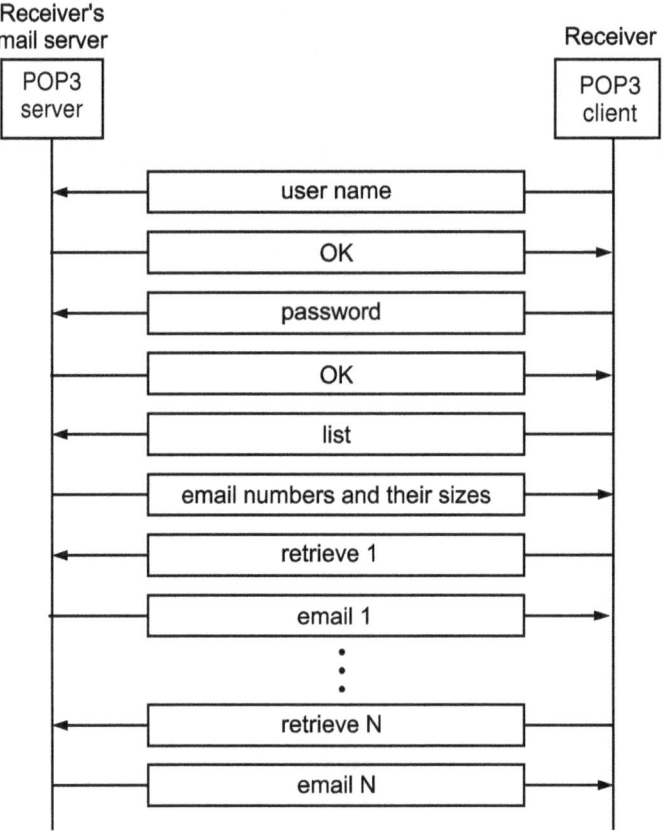

Fig. 6.23 : Exchange of commands and responses in POP3

- Post Office Protocol V3 (POP3) is simple protocol with limited functionality. The client POP3 software is installed on the recipient, the server POP3 software is installed on the server.
- Mail access starts with the client, when the user wants to access e-mail from the mail server to mail box. Client opens TCP connection on port 110. It then sends its user name and password to access the mail box. User can then retrieve the mail messages.
- Fig. 6.23 shows example of downloading using POP3.
- POP3 has two modes, the delete mode and the keep mode. In delete mode, the mail is deleted from the mail box after each retrieval. In the keep mode, the mail remains in the mail box after retrieval.

2. IMAP4 :

- IMAP stands for Internet Mail Access Protocol. It was first proposed in 1986.
- Another mail access protocol is Internet Mail Access Protocol V4 is similar to POP3 but is more powerful and more complex. POP3 not allows the user to organize mail on the server, the user cannot have different folders on the server.
- POP3 also does not allow the user to partially check the content of mail before downloading. All these drawbacks are overcomed in IMAP4.
- IMAP4 provides following functions :
    - (i) User can check e-mail header before downloading.
    - (ii) User can search the contents of the e-mail for a specific string of characters before downloading.
    - (iii) User can partially download e-mail.
    - (iv) A user can create, delete or rename mailboxes on the mail server.
    - (v) User can create a hierarchy of mailboxes in a folder for storage.

Comparison between POP and IMAP:

Sr. No.	POP	IMAP
1.	Generally used to support single client.	Designed to handle multiple clients.
2.	Messages are accessed offline.	Messages are accessed online although it also supports offline mode.
3.	POP does not allow search facility.	It offers ability to search emails.

Contd...

4.	All the messages have to be downloaded.	It allows selective transfer of messages to the client.
5.	Only one mailbox can be created on the server.	Multiple mailboxes can be created on the server.
6.	Not suitable for accessing non-mail data.	Suitable for accessing non-mail data i.e. attachment.
7.	POP commands are generally abbreviated into codes of three or four letters. Example : STAT.	IMAP commands are not abbreviated, they are full. Example : STATUS.
8.	It requires minimum use of server resources.	Clients are totally dependent on server.
9.	Mails once downloaded cannot be accessed from some other location.	Allows mails to be accessed from multiple locations.
10.	The e-mails are not downloaded automatically.	Users can view the headings and sender of e-mails and then decide to download.
11.	POP requires less internet usage time.	IMAP requires more internet usage time.

6.2.5 Web Based Mail   (April 13)

- Some websites provide e-mail service to anyone who accesses the site, such as Rediff, Yahoo, gmail etc. Mail transfer from Amar's browser to his mail server is through HTTP.

- Transfer of the message from sending mail server to the receiving mail server is by using SMTP. Message from the receiving server to Bob's browser is through HTTP.

- Webmail (or web-based email) is any email client implemented as a web application running on a web server.

- Examples of webmail software are Roundcube and SquirrelMail.

- In web-based mail transfer from sender's browser to mail server through HTTP.

- Transfer of message from sending mail server to receiving server still through SMTP.

- Message from receiving server (web server) to receiver browser is done through HTTP.

- Instead of POP3 and IMAP4, HTTP is used as MAA.

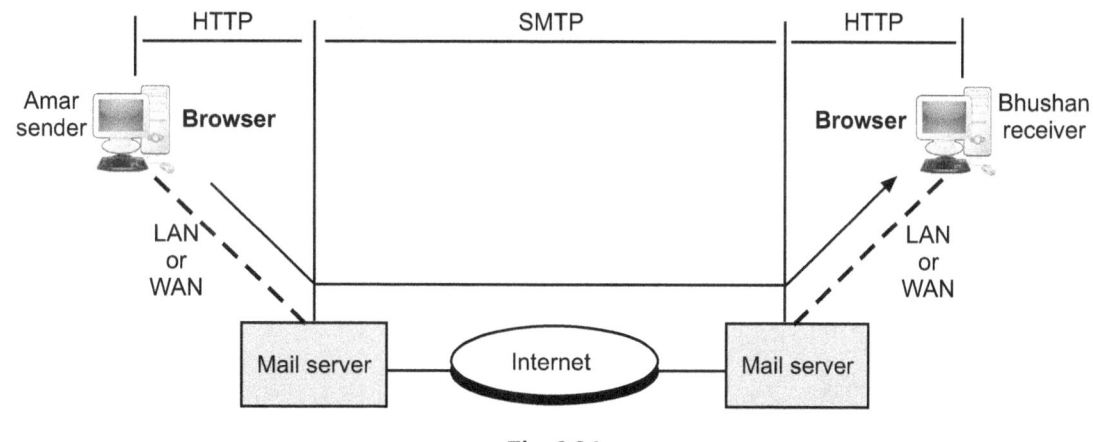

Fig. 6.24

6.3 | FILE TRANSFER PROTOCOL (FTP)   (April 13; Oct. 14)

- Transferring files from one computer to another is one of important task of network/internetworks.

- FTP is the standard mechanism provided by TCP/IP for copying (transferring) a file from one host to another.

- FTP short for "File Transfer Protocol," can transfer files between any computers that have an Internet connection, and also works between computers using totally different operating systems.

- Transferring files from a client computer to a server computer is called "uploading" and transferring from a server to a client is "downloading".

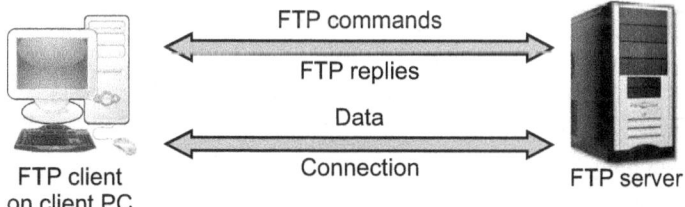

Fig. 6.25

- While transferring files from one system to another, several problems can be arises, e.g. two systems may use different file name conventions, two systems may have different ways to represent text and data. They may have different directory structures etc. All these compatibility problems are solved by FTP.

- FTP is a client/server application. FTP establishes two connections between hosts. One connection for data transfer and other for control information (commands and responses).

- FTP uses the services of TCP. It needs two TCP connections. The well known port 21 is used for the control connection and the well known port 20 is used for data connection.
- Fig. 6.26 shows the basic model of FTP.
- The client has three components :
  1. User interface.
  2. Client control process.
  3. Data transfer process.
- The server has two components :
  1. Control process.
  2. Data transfer process.
- Control connection is made between control processes and data connection is made between data transfer processes. First control connection is established and then data connection.
- While the control connection is open, data connection can be opened and closed many times if number of files are transferred.

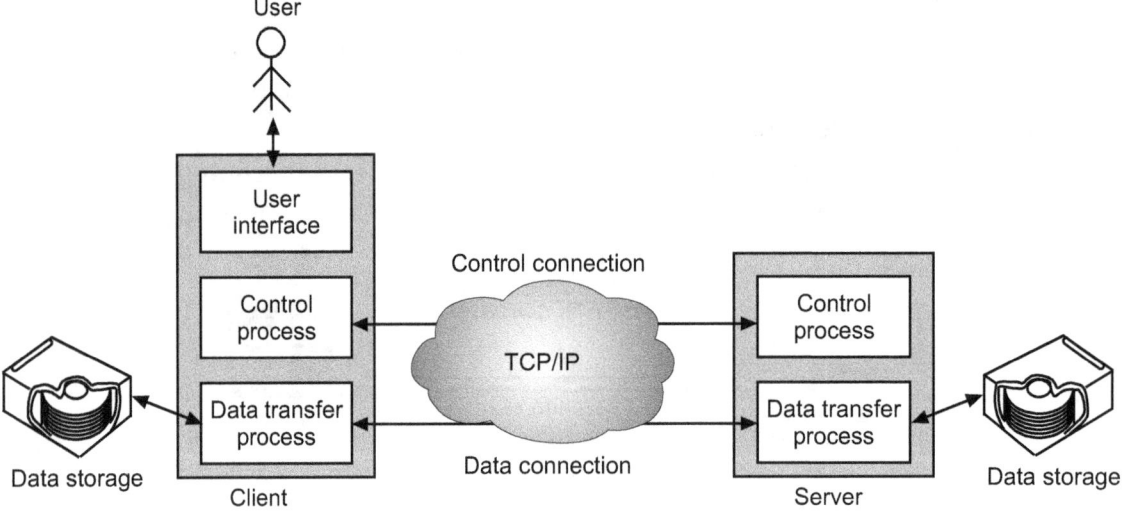

Fig. 6.26 : Basic model of FTP

6.3.1 Communication in FTP

- Communication with an FTP server is done through two connections, a control connection, and a data connection.

6.3.1.1 Communication Over Control Connection

- The control connection is always the first connection established with an FTP server.
- The control connection's purpose is to allow clients to connect and to send commands to the server (and receive server responses).
- FTP uses 7 bit ASCII character set over the control connection. On control connection, communication is achieved through commands and responses.
- Every command or response is one short line, so we need not worry about file format or file structure. Every line is terminated with carriage return and line feed, end of line token.

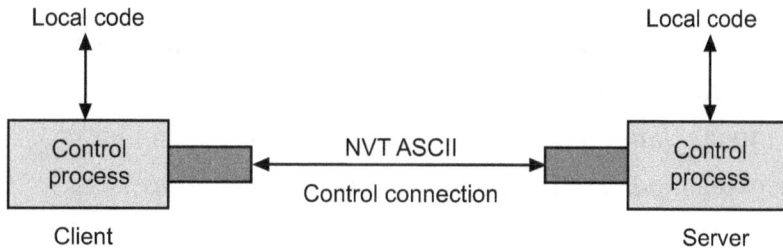

Fig. 6.27 : Control connection

6.3.1.2 Communication Over Data Connection

- Files are transferred using data connection. File transfer over data connection is under the control of control connection.
- File transfer in FTP means, a file is to be copied from server to the client (retrieving a file).
  - ○ A file is to be copied from the client to the server (storing a file).
  - ○ A list of directory or file names is to be sent from server to the client.
- The compatibility problem between client and server must be solved by defining three attributes of communication i.e., File type, Data structure and Transmission mode.

1. **File Type :**

- FTP can transfer one of the following types across data connection : ASCII file, EBCDIC file or image file.
  - (a) The ASCII file is default format for transferring text files.
  - (b) If one of two machines uses EBCDIC encoding, the file can be transferred using EBCDIC encoding.
  - (c) The image file is the default format for transferring binary files.

2. **Data Structure :**

- FTP allows three different data structure of a file : File structure, Record structure and Page structure.

  (a) **File structure :** File has no structure, it is continuous stream of bytes.

  (b) **Record structure :** File is divided into records.

  (c) **Page structure :** The file is divided into pages, each page having page number and page header.

3. **Transmission Mode :**

- FTP supports three transmission modes : Stream mode, Block mode and Compressed mode.

  (a) **Stream mode :** Stream mode is default mode. Data are delivered from FTP to TCP as a continuous stream of bytes.

  (b) **Block mode :** Data can be delivered from FTP to TCP in blocks.

  (c) **Compressed mode :** If the file is big, data can be compressed.

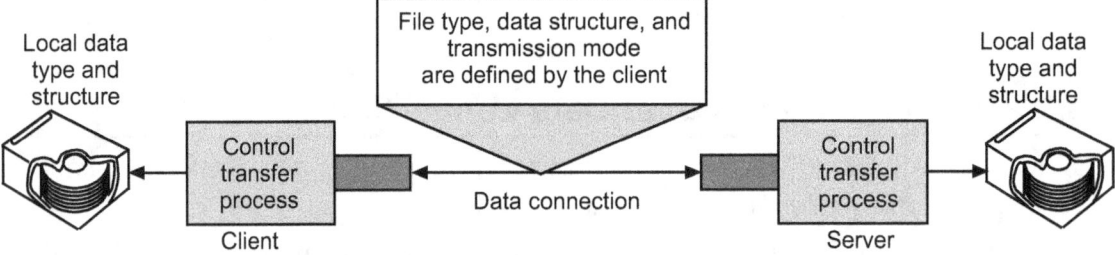

Fig. 6.28 : Communication over data connection

6.3.2 Anonymous FTP

- To use FTP, a user needs account and password on the remote server. Anonymous FTP allows users without having account on server. Some sites have a set of files available for public access, to enable anonymous FTP.

- To access these files, user need not have account, he can use anonymous as user name and guest as the password.

6.4 WWW (WORLD WIDE WEB)

- The WWW is a repository of information linked together from points all over the world. This information consists of text, graphics, audio and video etc. are connected by hyperlinks.

- WWW provides flexibility, portability and user friendly features.
- HTTP is a protocol, which is used to retrieve information from the web.

6.4.1 Architecture   (Oct. 12; April 15)

- WWW is a client/server service. Client uses a browser software to access an information stored on web server. Every web server contains one or more documents known as web pages.
- Each web page can contain a link to other page of the same site or other site (server). When client needs some information from a particular server, it sends request to that server.
- Server find that information and send it to the client in the form of web document.

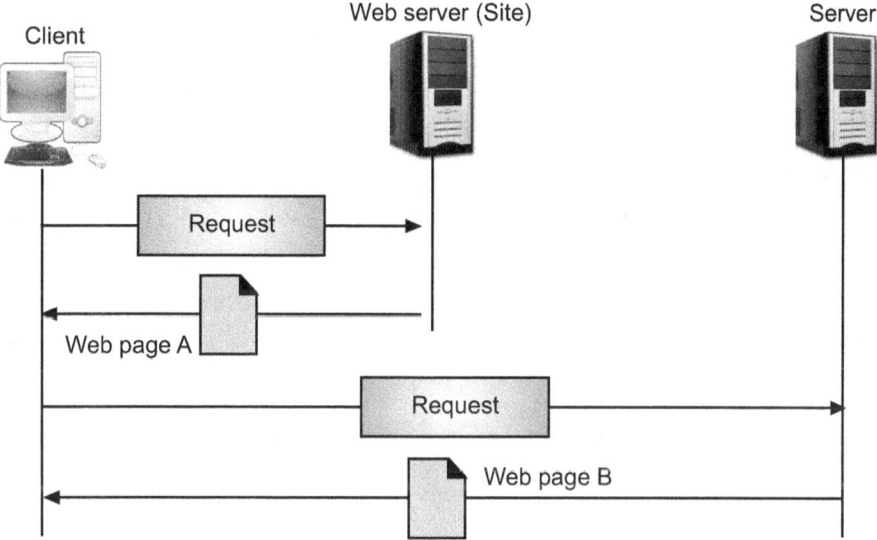

Fig. 6.29 : Architecture of www

1. Client (Browser) :

- Many vendors offer variety of browsers that interpret and display a web document.
- Every browser consists of three parts i.e., a controller, client protocol and interpreters.
- The controller receives input from keyboard or mouse and use client program to access the document. After that controller uses one of the interpreters to display the document.

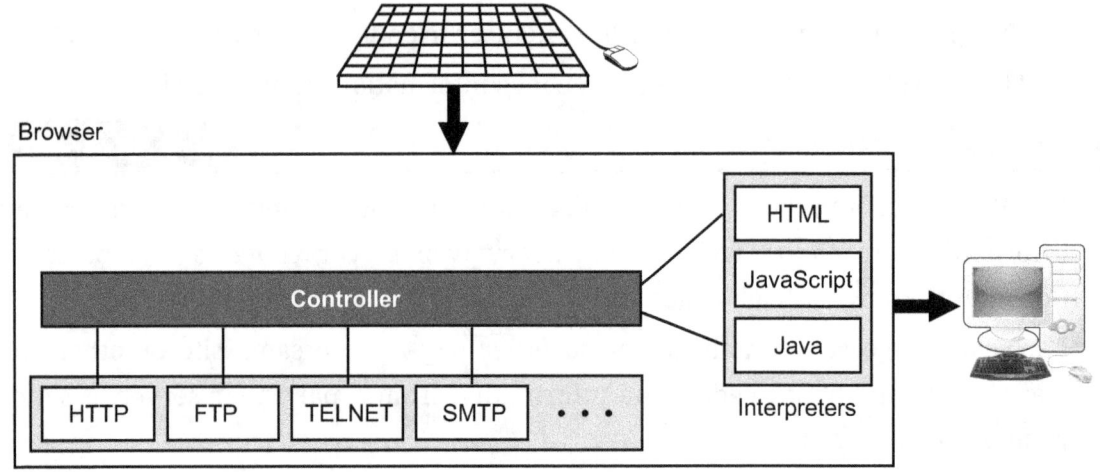

Fig. 6.30 : Browser

2. Server :

- The web pages are stored on the server. When client request comes, the corresponding document is sent to the client.

Uniform Resource Locator (URL):   **(April 15)**

- A client wants to access web pages need an address known as a uniform resource locator (URL).

- The URL contains four things : Protocol, Host Computer, Port and Path, (See Fig. 6.31).

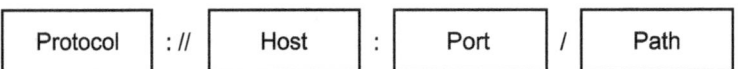

Fig. 6.31 : URL

- The host is the server on which information is stored. Port number gives port number of the server, it is optional. Path is the path name of the file where the information is stored.

- For example : rediff.com/news, google.com etc.

3. Cookies :

- The www uses HTTP protocol, which is a client/server protocol.

- Today, the www has other functions like :

  (a) Some websites need to allow access to registered clients only.

  (b) Websites are used for e-commerce purpose.

  (c) Some websites are used as portals.

  (d) Some are just advertising.

- For these purpose, the cookie mechanism is used :
  (i)   A cookie is small program which server stores in the client machine to identify the client.
  (ii) An e-commerce website uses a cookie for its client shoppers. When a client selects an item and inserts it into cart, cookie contains information about that item.
  (iii) Cookie is also used by advertising agencies.

6.4.2 Web Documents

- The information stored on web servers is in the form of documents.
- The documents in the www can be grouped into three broad categories i.e., Static document, Dynamic document and Active document.

1. Static Documents :

- The static documents are fixed content documents that are created and stored in a server i.e. their content does not change by the user.
- When user sends a request, it can get only a copy of the document. The user can then use browser to display the document.

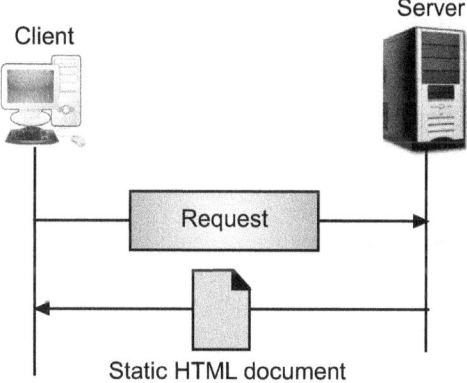

Fig. 6.32 : Static document

2. Dynamic Documents :

- A dynamic document is created by a web server, whenever a browser request the documents.
- When request comes at web server, it runs an application program or script and output is sent to the browser as a response.
- The content of the dynamic document vary from one request to another.
- For dynamic documents various, techniques like dynamic HTML, CGI, PHP, ASP etc. are used.

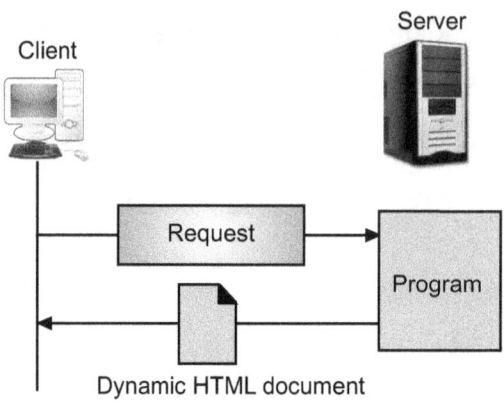

Fig. 6.33 : Dynamic document

- One good example of a dynamic page is the results of a search.-The client asks for some set of data from the server, a program runs at the server and creates a page of results for the client, and ships it back.

3. **Active Documents :**

- In many cases, we need a program or a script to be run at the client site and generate, the documents. Such documents are called active documents.

- For example, a program that interacts with a user (creation of e-mail account). For active documents, techniques like java scripts are used.

- Active documents are sometimes referred to as client-site dynamic documents.

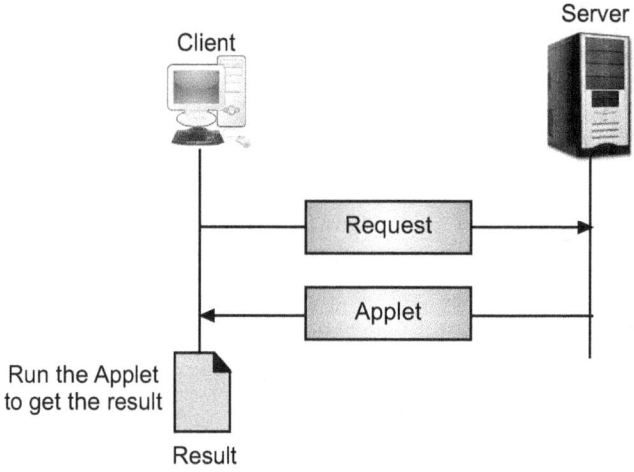

Fig. 6.34 : Active document

- Active documents are those that actually run at the client site. These are often written in Java.

- Examples abound on the Net, if you have a Java-enabled browser, and are using a platform that supports Java. These programs actually run at the client site, and so are called active.

- Java applets can perform a wide range of functions from telling time to calculating the actual price and payments on a new car.

6.5 | HTTP   (April 13)

- The HyperText Transfer Protocol (HTTP) is a main protocol used to access data on WWW.

- HTTP works as a combination of FTP and SMTP. It is similar to FTP because it transfers files and uses the services of TCP.

- HTTP is like SMTP because the data transferred between the client and the server looks like SMTP messages.

- HTTP is a communication protocol. It defines mechanism for communication between browser and the web server.

- It is also called request and response protocol because the communication between browser and server takes place in request and response pairs.

6.5.1 HTTP Transaction

- HTTP traffic consists of requests and responses.

- All HTTP traffic can be associated with the task of requesting content or responding to those requests.

- Every HTTP message sent from a Web browser to a Web server is classified as an HTTP request, whereas every message sent from a Web server to a Web browser is classified as an HTTP response.

- HTTP is often referred to as a stateless protocol. Although this is accurate, it does little to explain the nature of the Web.

- All this means, however, is that each transaction is atomic, and there is nothing required by HTTP that associates one request with another.

- A transaction refers to a single HTTP request and the corresponding HTTP response.

- Fig. 6.35 shows HTTP transaction between the client and server.

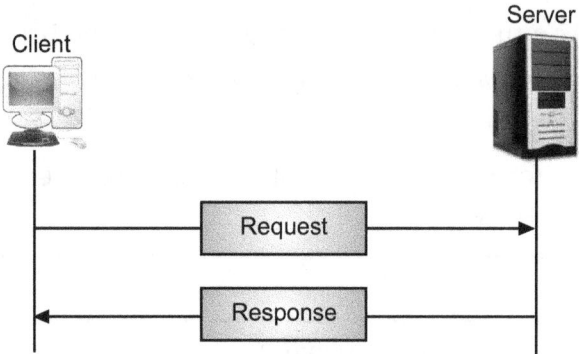

Fig. 6.35 : HTTP transaction

- The format of request and response messages are similar. Request message consist of request line, a header and sometimes a body. A response message consists of a status line, a header and sometimes a body.

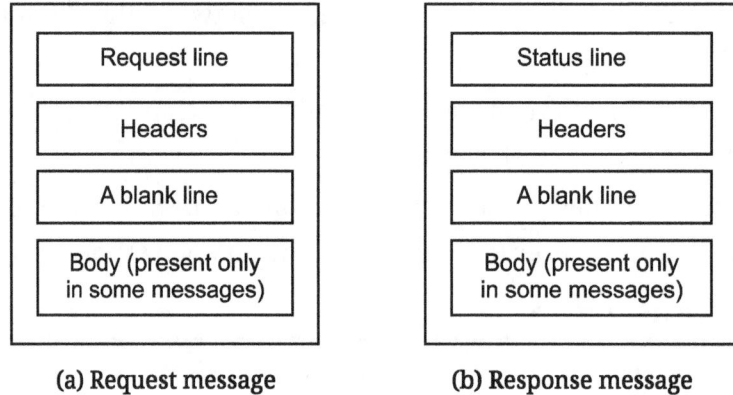

(a) Request message   (b) Response message

Fig. 6.36 : Request and response messages

Request and Status Lines :

- The first line in request message is called a request line, the first line in response message is called status line.

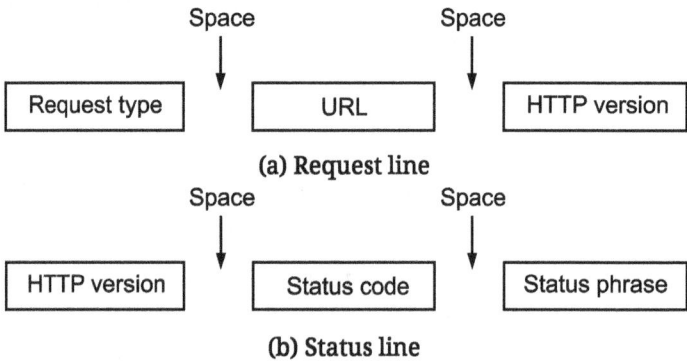

Fig. 6.37 : Request and status line

Request Type :

*   The request type is categorized into methods. Some methods are :   **(April 15)**

    1.   **GET** : To retrieve a document from server.
    2.   **HEAD** : Request information about a document but not the document itself.
    3.   **POST** : Sends some information from the client to the server.
    4.   **PUT** : Sends a document from the server to the client.
    5.   **TRACE** : Echoes the incoming request.
    6.   **CONNECT** : Reserved.
    7.   **PATCH** : It contains a list of differences which should be implemented in the existing file.
    8.   **MOVE** : Moves a file to another location.
    9.   **OPTION** : Inquires about available options.

    URL : URL of web documents.

    Version : The current version of HTTP is 1.1.

    Status code : This field is used in the response message.

*   It is similar to FTP and SMTP. It consists of three digits. The codes starting from 1 are informational, 2 are success, 3 are redirection, 4 are client error and starting from 5 are server error.

Header :

*   The header exchanges information between client and server. Each header line has a header name, a colon, a space and header value.

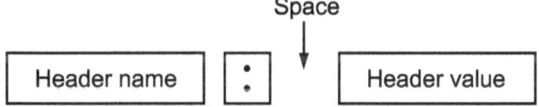

Fig. 6.38 : Header format

*   Header is divided into four categories :

    1.   **General Header** : General header gives general information about the message and present in request and response message.
    2.   **Request Header** : It can present only in a request message. It specifies the client configuration and client's preferred document format.
    3.   **Response Header** : It is present only in response message. It specifies the server's configuration and special information about the request.
    4.   **Entity Header** : Entity header gives information about the body of the document.

Body :

- The body can be present in a request or response message. It contains the document to be sent or received.

- For example: (1) Client sends a GET request for an image file with the path/user /bin/image1. Request does not have a body. The response message contains the status line and four lines of header.

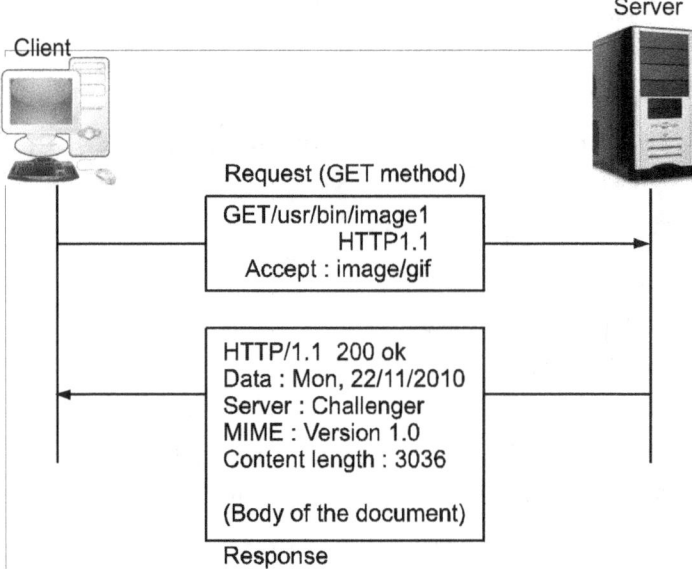

Fig. 6.39

(2) The client wants to send data to the server by using POST method.

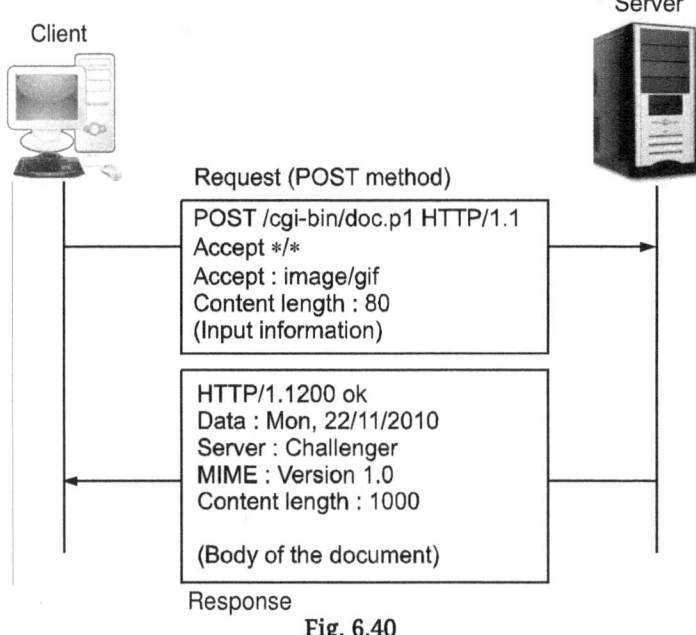

Fig. 6.40

6.5.2 Persistent Versus Non-persistent Connection

- HTTP prior to version 1.1 specified a non-persistent connection, while in version 1.1, persistent connection is default one.

1. **Non-persistent Connection :**

- In a non-persistent connection, one TCP connection is made for each request/response.

- For N different pictures in different files, the connection must be opened and closed N times. This strategy creates high overhead on the server.

- Following steps are involved in this strategy :

   Step 1: The client opens a TCP connection and sends a request.

   Step 2: The server sends the response and closes the connection.

   Step 3: The client reads the data until it encounters an end of file marker, it then closes the connection.

2. **Persistent Connection :**

- HTTP version 1.1 supports persistent connection. HTTP persistent connection, also called HTTP keep-alive, or HTTP connection reuse, is the idea of using a single TCP connection to send and receive multiple HTTP requests/responses, as opposed to opening a new connection for every single request/response pair.

- The newer HTTP/2 protocol uses the same idea and takes it further to allow multiple concurrent requests/responses to be multiplexed over a single connection.

- In a persistent connection, the server leaves the connection open for more requests after sending a response. If client request then server closes the connection or if time out reached.

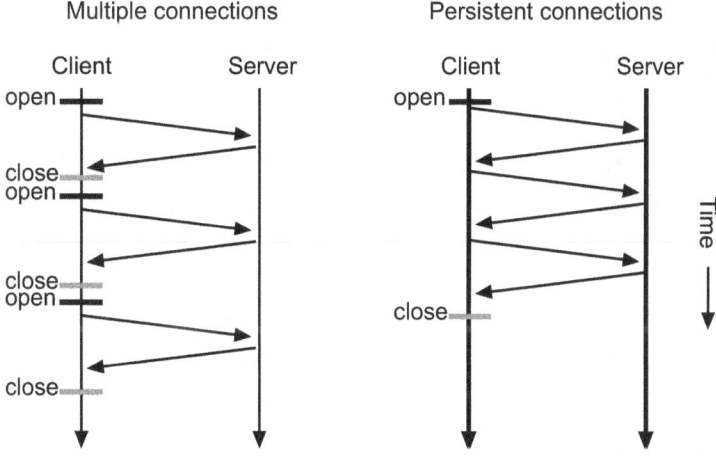

Fig. 6.41

6.5.3 Proxy Server

- HTTP supports proxy servers. Proxy servers reduces the load on original server, traffic is decreased and improves latency. When client sends a request to servers it passes from proxy server. Proxy server checks it cache. If response is found, it is given to client. If not found, proxy sends the request to the original server.

- Incoming responses are sent to the proxy server and stored for future requests from other clients. To use proxy server, client must be configured to proxy server.

Process of Proxy Server:

1. The HTTP client sends a request to the HTTP Proxy.
2. The HTTP Proxy connects the HTTP Server.
3. The HTTP Server sends back the answer to the HTTP Proxy.
4. The HTTP Proxy sends back this answer to the HTTP client.

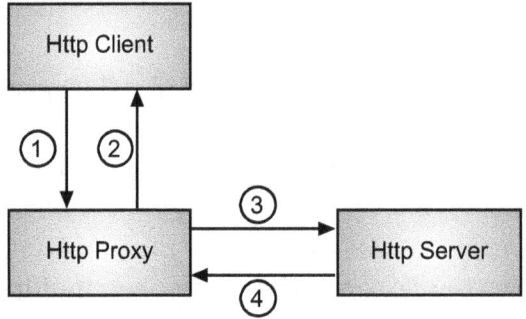

Fig. 6.42

Difference Between FTP and HTTP :

Sr. No.	FTP	HTTP
1.	FTP stands for File Transfer Protocol.	HTTP stands for Hypertext Transfer Protocol.
2.	FTP, as the name implies, is used in transferring files from one computer to another.	The purpose of HTTP is to serve as a means of accessing the world wide web. Websites are accessed using http with the help of browsers.
3.	FTP is more efficient in transferring larger files.	HTTP is more efficient for transferring smaller files such as web pages.
4.	FTP can send data both in ASCII and Binary Format.	HTTP only uses Binary Format.

Contd...

5.	FTP does not supports pipelining.	HTTP supports pipelining.
6.	FTP is a member of the TCP/IP suite of protocols, used to copy files between two computers on the Internet.	The HTTP protocol used to transfer information on the World Wide Web.
7.	FTP uses TCP port 21 to transfer files from one host to another host over the TCP network.	HTTP uses port 80.

6.6 │ GATEWAYS (TRANSPORT & APPLICATION)   (Oct. 12; April 15)

- The term gateway is applied to any device, system, or software application that can perform the function of translating data from one format to another. The key feature of a gateway is that it converts the format of the data, not the data itself.
- Gateway work at all 7 layers of the OSI model.
- Gateway is a network device which interconnects two heterogeneous networks.
- Gateway is a connectivity link between two networks that use dissimilar protocols and architecture.
- A gateway is a network element that acts as an entrance point to another network. For example an access gateway is a gateway between telephony network and other network such as internet.
- A gateway is generally a work station or server. It is a two-way path between networks.
- Gateway is used to connect different types of networks.
- Fig. 6.43 shows a gateway connecting an Systems Network Architecture (SNA) network (IBM) to a NetWare network (Novell).

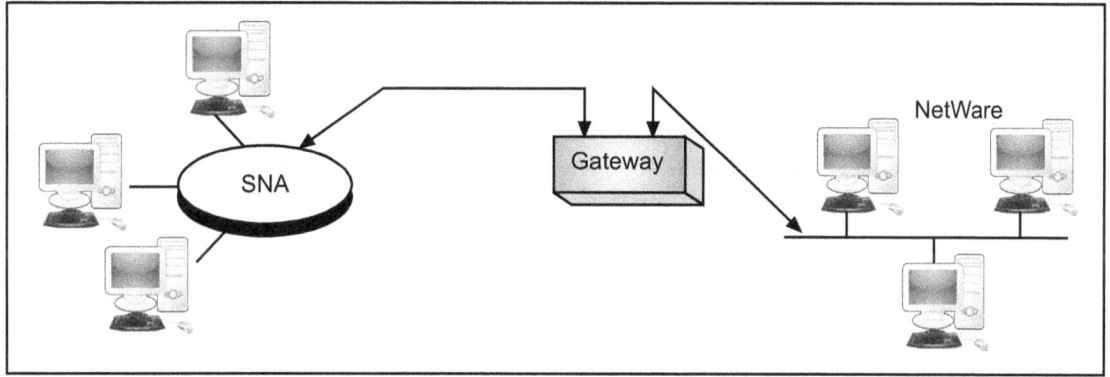

Fig. 6.43

- Basically there are two types of gateways (1) Transport gateway and (2) Application gateway. The former is for transport layer and the later is for application layer.
- Transport gateways connect two computers that use different connection oriented transport protocol. It can copy the packets to one connection to other, reformatting them as need be.
- Transport gateways make a connection between two networks at the transport layer.
- Application gateways connect two parts of an application in the application layer, e.g., sending e-mail between two machines using different mail formats.
- Application level gateways, also called proxies, are similar to circuit level gateways except that they are application specific.
- They can filter packets at the application layer of the OSI model. Incoming outgoing packets at the application layer of the OSI model. Incoming or outgoing packets cannot access services for which there is no proxy.
- Fig. 6.44 shows application level gateway.

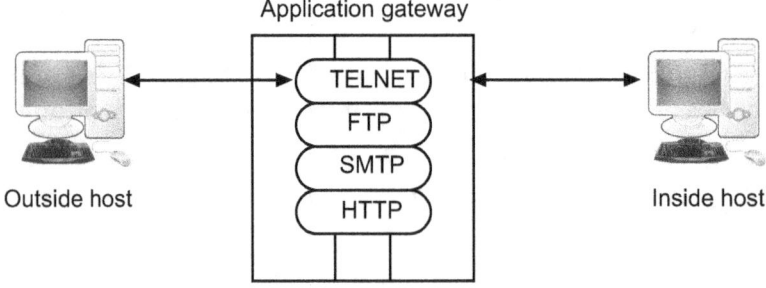

Fig. 6.44 : Application gateway

Advantages :

1. Application gateway provides high level of security than packet filters.
2. Easy to configure.
3. They can hide the private network topology.
4. It support user level authentication.
5. Capability to examine the all traffic in detail.

Disadvantages:

1. High impact on network performance.
2. Slower in operation because of processing overheads.
3. Not transparent to users.

SUMMARY

➤ It is the top most layer of OSI Model. It performs Mail Services, Directory Services, File Transfer, Access and Management (FTAM) etc. functions.

➤ Domain Name Systems (DNS) is mechanisms that assign easy to remember names to IP address. Domain is a large group of computers on the Internet. Under this scheme each computer has an IP address and a domain name.

➤ The domain name space refers a hierarchy in the internet naming structure. This hierarchy has multiple levels (from 0 to 127), with a root at the top.

➤ A name space that maps each address to a unique name can be organized in two ways flat name space (a name is assigned to an address and a name in this space is a sequence of characters without structure.) or hierarchical name space (every name is made up of several parts. The first part can define the nature or organization, the second part defines name of organization and third part defines departments in the organization, if any and so on).

➤ Domain Name is a symbolic string associated with an IP address. A full domain name is a sequence of labels separated by dots (.).

➤ There are several domain names available; some of them are generic such as .com (Commercial business), .edu (Education), .gov (Government), .net (Networking organization) etc., while some country level domain names such as .au (Australia), .in (India), .us (United States) etc.

➤ There are two types of domain names i.e., Fully Qualified Domain Name (FQDN) and Partially Qualified Domain Name (PQDN). If a label is terminated by a null string, it is called a FQDN. If a label is not terminated by a null string, it is called a PQDN.

➤ Name server contains the DNS database. This database comprises of various names and their corresponding IP addresses.

➤ Zone is collection of nodes (sub domains) under the main domain. The server maintains a database called zone file for every zone.

➤ In the Internet, the domain name space is divided into three different sections like generic domains, country domains and the inverse domain.

➤ The generic domains define registered host according to their generic behavior like .biz (Business or firms), .int (International organizations), .mil (Military groups), .org (Non-profit organizations) etc.

➤ Country domains use two characters country abbreviations such as uk for United Kingdom.

➤ The inverse domain is used to map an address to a name. This can be happen, for example, server want to check his authorized client.

➤ Mapping a name to an address or an address to a name is called name-address resolution.

➤ When a host requires mapping of name to an address or an address to a name, it calls DNS client called a resolver. The resolver accesses the closest DNS sever with mapping request.

➤ E-mail is short for electronic mail. The main task of the Internet is to provide services to users. E-mail is most popular application of Internet.

➤ Services of UA include Composing Messages, Reading Messages, Replying to Messages, Forwarding Messages and Handling Mail Boxes.

➤ Multipurpose Internet Mail Extensions (MIME) is a protocol that allows non-ASCII data to be sent through e-mail.

➤ The mail transfer is done by Message Transfer Agents (MTA). To send mail, a system must have client MTA and to receive mail, a system must have server MTA.

➤ The protocol that defines the communication between MTA client and MTA server is called Simple Mail Transfer Protocol (SMTP). SMTP is a TCP/IP protocol that specifies how computers exchange electronic mail.

➤ SMTP uses commands and response to transfer messages between MTA client and MTA server.

➤ Commands are sent by client to server. Command consists of a keyword followed by zero or more arguments. SMTP uses 14 commands. Responses are sent from server to client.

➤ Post Office Protocol (POP) is an application-layer Internet standard protocol used by local e-mail clients to retrieve e-mail from a remote server over a TCP/IP connection. Post Office Protocol V3 (POP3) is simple protocol with limited functionality.

➤ IMAP stands for Internet Mail Access Protocol. POP3 also does not allow the user to partially check the content of mail before downloading. All these drawbacks are overcome in IMAP4.

➤ Webmail (or web-based email) is any email client implemented as a web application running on a web server. Examples of webmail software are Roundcube and SquirrelMail.

➤ FTP short for File Transfer Protocol. FTP can transfer files between any computers that have an Internet connection, and also works between computers using totally different operating systems.

➤ The WWW (World Wide Web) is a repository of information linked together from points all over the world. This information consists of text, graphics, audio and video etc. are connected by hyperlinks.

➤ WWW is a client/server service. Client uses a browser software to access an information stored on web server.

➤ A cookie is small program which server stores in the client machine to identify the client.

➤ The information stored on web servers is in the form of documents. The documents in the www can be grouped into three broad categories i.e., Static document (are fixed content documents that are created and stored in a server i.e. their content does not change by the user), Dynamic document (created by a web server, whenever a browser request the documents) and Active document (a program or a script to be run at the client site and generate, the documents).

➤ The HyperText Transfer Protocol (HTTP) is a main protocol used to access data on www. HTTP works as a combination of FTP and SMTP. It is similar to FTP because it transfers files and uses the services of TCP.

➤ HTTP traffic consists of requests and responses. All HTTP traffic can be associated with the task of requesting content or responding to those requests. Every HTTP message sent from a Web browser to a Web server is classified as an HTTP request, whereas every message sent from a Web server to a Web browser is classified as an HTTP response.

➤ HTTP are contains two connections i.e., persistent connection and non-persistent connection.

➤ In a non-persistent connection, one TCP connection is made for each request/response. For N different pictures in different files, the connection must be opened and closed N times.

➤ HTTP version 1.1 supports persistent connection. HTTP persistent connection, also called HTTP keep-alive, or HTTP connection reuse, is the idea of using a single TCP connection to send and receive multiple HTTP requests/responses, as opposed to opening a new connection for every single request/response pair.

➤ HTTP supports proxy servers. Proxy servers reduces the load on original server, traffic is decreased and improves latency.

➤ Gateway works at all 7 layers of the OSI model. It is a network device which interconnects two heterogeneous networks.

➤ Basically there are two types of gateways Transport gateway and application gateway.

➤ Transport gateways connect two computers that use different connection oriented transport protocol. It can copy the packets to one connection to other, reformatting them as need be.

➤ Application gateways understand the format and contents of the data and translate messages from one form to another e.g. an e-mail gateway could translate internet messages to an SMS messages on mobile phone.

PRACTICE QUESTIONS

1. What is domain name system ?
2. Write short note on DNS in internet.
3. Explain resolution in DNS.
4. Explain the e-mail architecture.
5. What is User Agent ? Describe the services provided by user agent.
6. Write a short note on MIME.
7. Explain message transfer agent SMTP.
8. Describe various commands of SMTP.
9. Explain POP3 and IMAP4.
10. What is FTP ? Explain in detail.
11. How does communication takes place over control connection and over data connection ?
12. What is anonymous FTP ?
13. Explain the architecture of www.
14. Explain the terms : (a) Browser, (b) Server, (c) URL, (d) Cookies.
15. Explain various web documents.
16. Write a note on HTTP.
17. Explain non-persistent and persistent connection in HTTP.
18. Explain proxy server.

UNIVERSITY QUESTIONS AND ANSWERS

April 2011

1. List the services of user agent.   [1 M]
Ans. Please refer to Section 6.2.2.
2. Discuss POP3 and IMAP4 message access protocols.   [5 M]
Ans. Please refer to Section 6.2.4.
3. Explain any two scenarios of email architecture.   [5 M]
Ans. Please refer to Section 6.2.1.

October 2011

1. List the types of user agent.   [1 M]
Ans. Please refer to Section 6.2.2.
2. Explain recursive, iterative resolution and caching used in DNS.   [5 M]
Ans. Please refer to Section 6.1.5.

April 2012

1. Write a short SMTP.   [5 M]
Ans. Please refer to Section 6.2.3.
2. Explain services provided by User Agent.   [5 M]
Ans. Please refer to Section 6.2.2.

October 2012

1.   "Why do we need POP 3 or IMAP 4 for electronic mail ?   [1 M]
Ans. Please refer to Section 6.2.3.
2.   Distinguish between FQDN and PQDN.   [1 M]
Ans. Please refer to Section 6.2.3 Points (1) and (2).
3.   Define Gateway.   [1 M]
Ans. Please refer to Section 6.6.
4.   Explain detail architecture of WWW.   [5 M]
Ans. Please refer to Section 6.4.1.
5.   Write note on secure DNS.   [5 M]
Ans. Please refer to Section 6.1.

April 2013

1.   What is generic domain ?   [1 M]
Ans. Please refer to Section 6.1.4 Point (1).
2.   Give port number of HTTP, SMTP.   [1 M]
Ans. Please refer to Sections 6.2.3 and 6.5.
3.   Which pull protocol is used to retrieve message from mail server? Explain in
     detail.   [5 M]
Ans. Please refer to Section 6.2.5.
4.   Explain the most common scenario used in Email Architecture.   [5 M]
Ans. Please refer to Section 6.2.1.

October 2014

1.   List different types of transmission modes used by FTP to transfer a file
     across the data connection.   [1 M]
Ans. Please refer to Section 6.3.
2.   Write a note on different types of user agents.   [4 M]
Ans. Please refer to Section 6.2.2.

April 2015

1.   Which file types can be transferred on FTP ?   [1 M]
Ans. Please refer to Section 6.3.
2.   Name the four terms define by the URL.   [1 M]
Ans. Please refer to Page 6.31.
3.   Discuss different methods used in HTTP request message.   [5 M]
Ans. Please refer to Page 6.35.
4.   Explain in detail architecture of WWW.   [4 M]
Ans. Please refer to Section 6.4.1.
5.   Write a note on Gateway.   [4 M]
Ans. Please refer to Section 6.6.

❖ ❖ ❖

Network Security

Contents ...

Objectives...

- To Understand Network Security Concept
- To Learn Cryptography
- To Study Web and Mobile Security
- To Learn Social Issues in Networking

7.0 | INTRODUCTION

- Computer security means to protect information. It deals with prevention and detection of unauthorized actions by users of a computer.

- Network security issues include protecting data from unauthorized access, protecting data from damage and development and implementing policies and procedures for recovery from breaches and data losses.

- Network security is a specialized field in computer networking that involves securing a computer network infrastructure.

- Today, millions of people are using computer networks for banking, ticket reservation, shopping, for social networking and filing their tax returns etc. People have realized that data on computer is an extremely important aspect of modern life.

- Security becomes an important issue, when data is transmitted between applications on a network, it can be read by unauthorized users (intruder).

- An intruder can capture credit card details as they travel from the client to the server. Even the merchant who receives credit card details can misuse it. Several serious issues exist related to network security. No one can deny the importance of security in data communication and networking.

- Security in networking is based on cryptography. Cryptography is the science and art of achieving security by encoding messages to make them non-readable. Cryptography can provide confidentiality, integrity, authentication and non-repudiation of messages.

- In this chapter, we will discuss only the basic concepts of network security.

7.1 | Security Services

- Security is a fundamental component of every network design. When planning, building, and operating a network, you should understand the importance of a strong security policy.

- Network security consists of the policies adopted to prevent and monitor authorized access, misuse, modification, or denial of a computer network and network-accessible resources.
- Network security involves the authorization of access to data in a network, which is controlled by the network administrator.
- Network security can provide one of the five services as illustrated in Fig. 7.1.
- Four of these network security services are related to the message exchanged i.e., message confidentiality, integrity, authentication, and non-repudiation. The fifth service of network security provides entity authentication or identification.

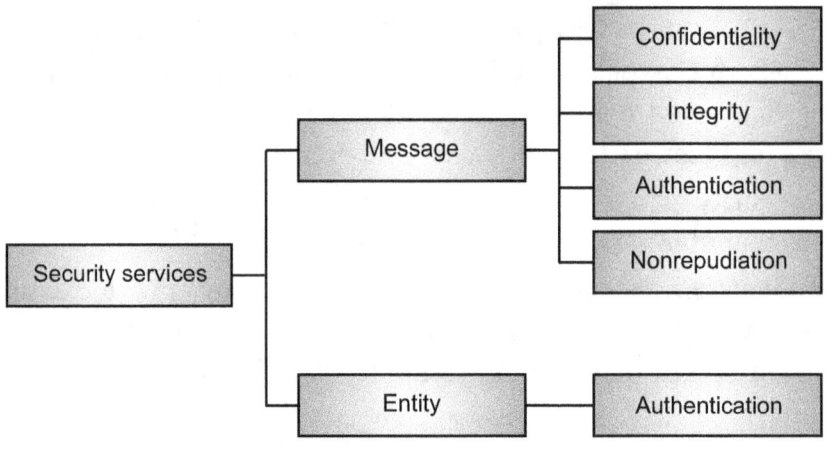

Fig. 7.1

- Fig. 7.1 Shows following types of services.
  1. **Confidentiality:** The principle of confidentiality specifies that only the sender and the intended recipient(s) should be able to access the content of a message. Example of compromising the confidentiality is shown in Fig 7.2.

     Example of this could be a confidential email message sent by A to B which is accessed by C, without the permission or knowledge of A and B. This type of attack is called as interception.

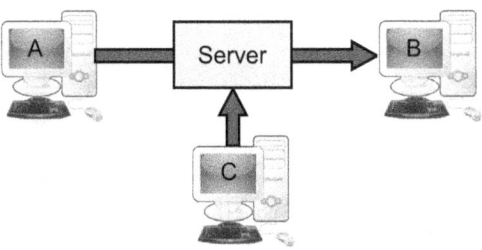

Fig. 7.2: Loss of confidentiality

2. **Integrity:** When the contents of a message are changed after the sender sends it, but before it reaches the intended recipient, the integrity of a message is lost. This type of attack is called as modification.

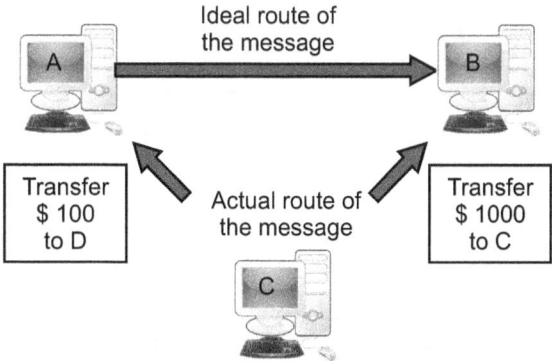

Fig. 7.3 : Loss of integrity

3. **Authentication:** Authentication mechanism help establish proof of identities. The authentication process ensures that the origin of an electronic message or document is correctly identified. For example, consider user C, posing as user A, sending a funds transfer request(from A's account to C's account) to bank B. The bank may transfer the funds from A's account to C's account, thinking that user A has requested for the fund transfer. This type of attack is called as fabrication.

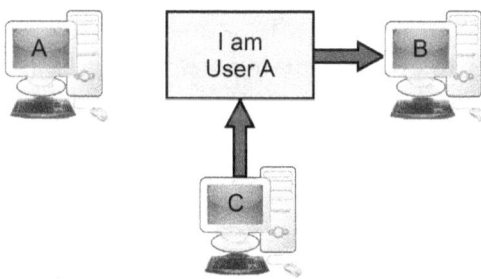

Fig. 7.4 : Absence of authentication

4. **Non-repudiation:** There are situations where a user sends a message, and later on refuses that he/she sent that message. Consider user A send a funds transfer request to bank B. After the bank performs the funds transfer as per A's instructions, A could claim that he never sent funds transfer instructions to bank. Thus A denies funds transfer instruction. The principle of non-repudiation defeats such possibilities of denying something, having done it.

5. **Entity (User) Authentication:** In entity authentication or user authentication the entity or user is verified prior to access the system resources. Consider user A want to access his bank account needs to be authenticated during the logging process.

7.2 | MESSAGE CONFIDENTIALITY

- To achieve the message confidentiality or privacy one technique is used from thousands of years, i.e. encryption.

- In technical terms, the process of encoding plain text message into cipher text message is called encryption.

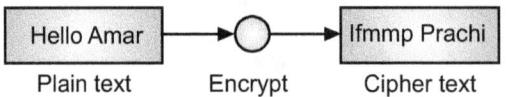

Fig. 7.5 : Encryption

- The reverse process of transforming cipher text message back to plain text messages is called decryption.

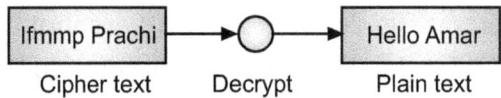

Fig. 7.6 : Decryption

- In communication a plain text signifies a message that can be understood by the sender, the recipient, and also by anyone else who gets an access to that message.

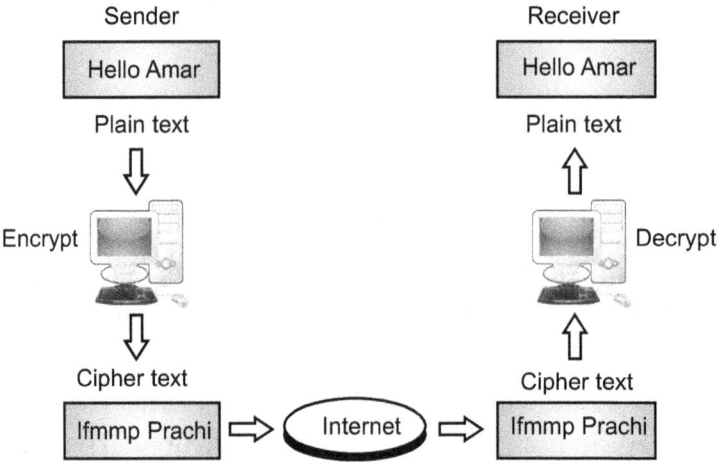

Fig. 7.7 : Encryption and decryption in the real world

- When a plain text message is codified using any suitable scheme, the resulting message is called as cipher text.

- The message must be encrypted at the sender site and decrypted at the receiver site. This can be done using either symmetric-key cryptography or asymmetric-key cryptography.

7.2.1 Confidentiality with Symmetric Key Cryptography

- As we know, to achieve encryption we can use symmetric key or asymmetric key cryptography.

- In symmetric key cryptography, same key is used by sender for encryption and by receiver for decryption respectively. Here sender and receiver needs to share a secrete symmetric key.

- In the past when data exchange was between two specific persons, it was possible to personally exchange the secret keys. But now a days, communication by using computers and users seating at two different locations in the world, exchanging a key personally becomes highly impossible.

- A solution is required for key sharing. This can done using a session key. A session key is one that is used only for the duration of one session. This session key is exchanged using asymmetric key cryptography.

- Fig. 7.8 shows the use of session symmetric key for sending confidential message from Amar to Bhushan and vice versa.

- In the Fig. 7.8 one shared key is used in both directions. But using two different keys for each direction is more secured.

- For long message, symmetric key cryptography is very fast and more efficient than asymmetric key cryptography.

- Fig. 7.8 shows the use of a session symmetric key for sending confidential messages from Amar to Bhushan and vice versa.

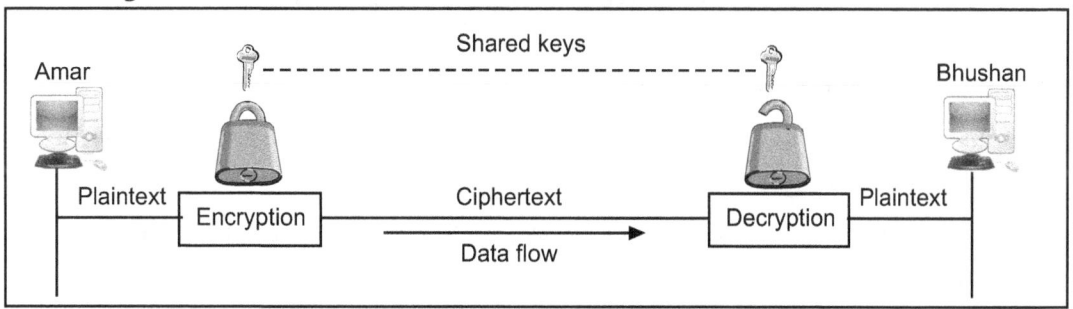

(a) A shared secret key can be used in Amar-Bhushan communication

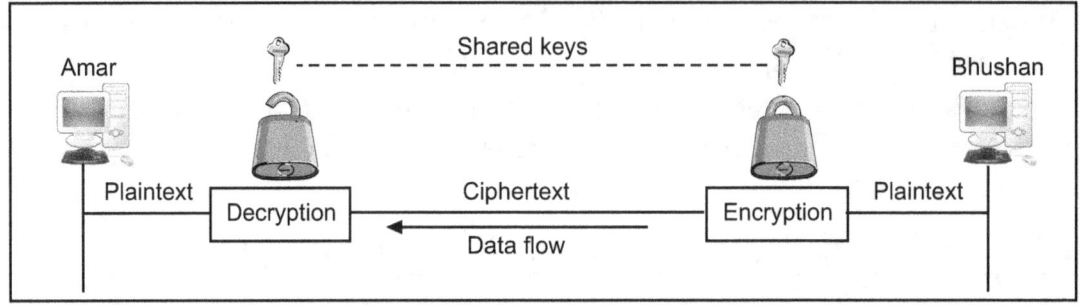

(b) A different shared secret key is recommended in Bhushan-Amar communication

Fig. 7.8

7.2.2 Confidentiality with Asymmetric Key Cryptography

- Symmetric key cryptography is fast and efficient. However it suffers from a big disadvantage of the problem of key exchange.

- Asymmetric key cryptography solve this problem. Here, each communicating party uses two keys to form a key pair. One key (the private key) remains with the party, and the other key (the public key) is shared with everybody by announcing it publically.

- One key is used for encryption and only the other corresponding key must be used for decryption. No other key can decrypt the message, not even the original key used for encryption.

- Consider, Amar and Bhushan wants to do secure communication by using asymmetric key cryptography. Both of them needs a pair of key. Public key, known to all and private key known to themselves only.

- Asymmetric key cryptography works as follows:

  1. When Amar wants to send a message to Bhushan, he encrypts the message using Bhushan's public key. This is possible because Amar knows Bhushan's public key.

  2. Amar sends encrypted message to Bhushan.

  3. Bhushan decrypts Amar's message by using his own private key, which is known to him only.

  4. Similarly Bhushan can send a message to Amar, exactly reverse step take place.

- Fig. 7.9 message confidentiality using asymmetric keys.

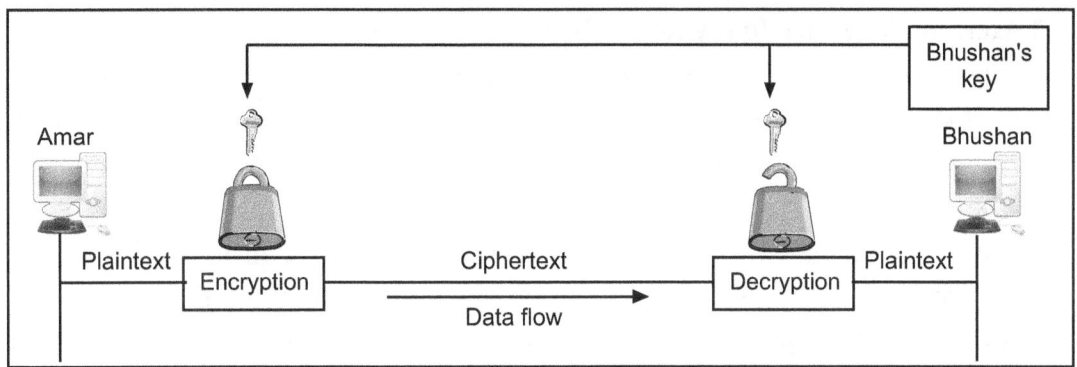

(a) Bhushan's keys are used in Amar-Bhushan communication

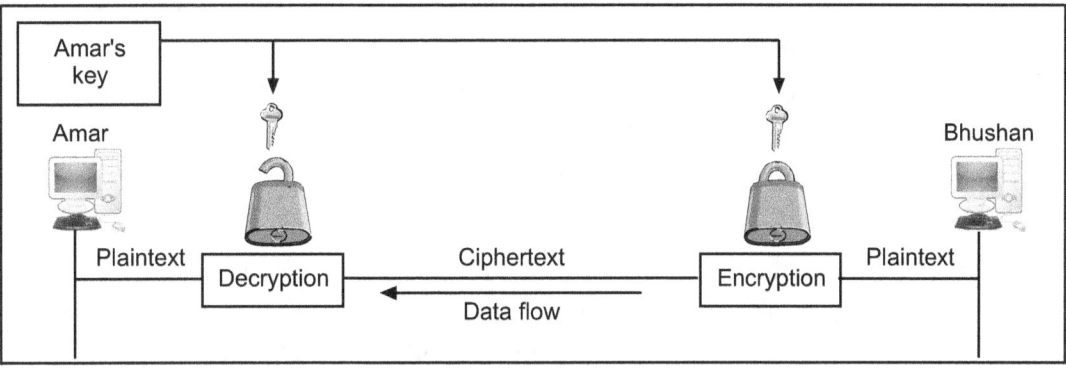

(b) Amar's keys are used in Bhushan-Amar communication

Fig. 7.9

7.3 | CRYPTOGRAPHY   (Oct. 11, 14; April 15)

- Cryptography is a technique to provide message confidentiality.

- The term cryptography is a Greek word which means "secret writing".

- It is an art and science of transforming messages so as to make them secure and immune to attacks.

- Cryptography involves the process of encryption and decryption. This process is depicted.

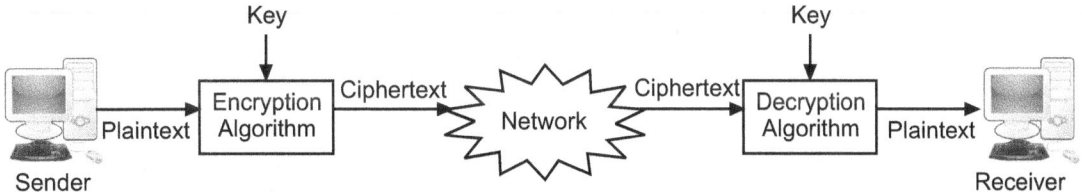

Fig. 7.10: Cryptography

- The terminology used in cryptography is given below:

  1. **Plaintext and Ciphertext:** The original message, before being transformed, is called plaintext. After the message is transformed, it is called ciphertext. It is the scrambled message produced as output. It depends upon the plaintext and the key.

  2. **Encryption algorithm:** The encryption algorithm is the algorithm that performs various substitutions and transformations on the plaintext. Encryption is the process of changing plaintext into cipher text. We refer to encryption and decryption algorithms as ciphers. a cipher (or cypher) is an algorithm for performing encryption or decryption, a series of well-defined steps that can be followed as a procedure.

  3. **Decryption algorithm:** The process of changing Ciphertext into plain text is known as decryption. Decryption algorithm is essentially the encryption algorithm run in reverse. It takes the Ciphertext and the key and produces the original plaintext.

  4. **Key:** A key is a number (or a set of numbers) that the cipher, as an algorithm, operates on. It also acts as input to the encryption algorithm. The exact substitutions and transformations performed by the algorithm depend on the key. Thus a key is a number or a set of number that the algorithm uses to perform encryption and decryption.

7.3.1 Encryption Model   (April 13)

- Cryptography is the art and science of achieving security by encoding messages to make them non-readable.

- Cryptanalysis is the technique of decoding messages from a non-readable format back to readable format without knowing how they were initially converted from readable format to non-readable format.

- Cryptology is a combination of cryptography and cryptanalysis. In the early days, cryptography is used to be performed by using manual techniques. Today, computers perform these cryptographic functions making the process faster and secure.

- Cleartext or plaintext signifies a message that can be understood by the sender, the recipient and also by anyone else who gets an access to that message.

- When a plaintext message is codified using any suitable scheme, the resulting message is called as ciphertext.

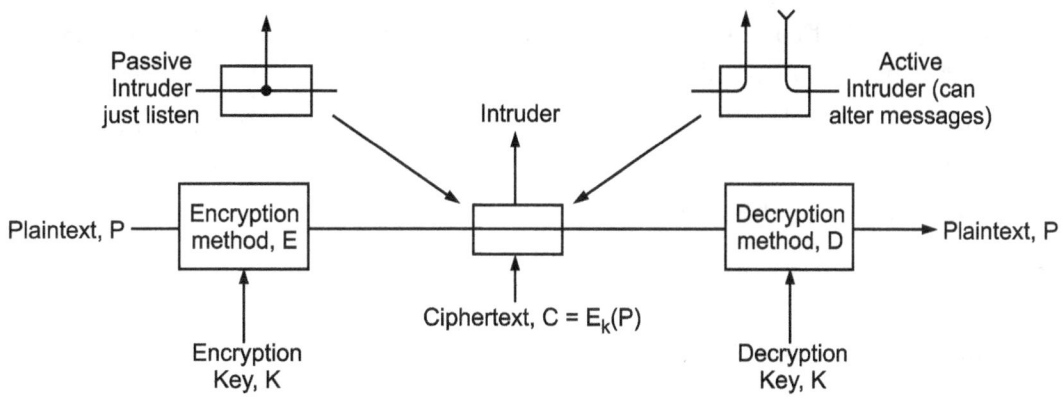

Fig. 7.11 : Encryption model (for symmetric key encryption)

- In Fig. 7.11, encryption model is shown, where plaintext P, is encrypted by using a key K. At receiver, the receiver again uses the same key (symmetric key encryption) for decryption to obtain plaintext back.

- In cryptology, algorithm and key are two very important aspects. Key must be kept as a secret.

- There are two primary ways in which a plaintext message can be codified to obtain the corresponding ciphertext :

  1. Substitution cipher and

  2. Transposition cipher.

7.3.2 Substitution Cipher   (Oct. 14)

- In a substitution cipher, each letter or group of letters are replaced by another letter or group of letters to disguise it.

- One of the oldest substitution cipher is Caesar cipher. In this method, A will be replaced by D, B will be replaced by E. C will be replaced by F and so on.

- **For example :**

  Plaintext : A B C D E F G H I J K L M N O P Q R S T U V W X Y Z

  Ciphertext : D E F G H I J K L M N O P Q R S T U V W X Y Z A B C

- Using this method, NASHIK becomes QDVKLN

- In the modified version of Caeser cipher, alphabet A can be replaced by any other alphabet in the English alphabet set (i.e. B through Z). Thus, for each alphabet, we have 25 possibilities of replacement.

- Another method is mono-alphabetic cipher. In this method, random substitution is used. This means that in a given plain text message, each A can be replaced by any other alphabet (B through Z), each B can also be replaced by any other random alphabet (A or C through Z) and so on. It also means, we are having $(26 \times 25 \times 24 \times 23 \times \ldots \times 2)$ or 4×10^{26} possibilities.

Example : By using Caesar cipher, transform the message 'Happy birthday to you'.

Solution :

Plaintext : Happy birthday to you

Key :   Character + 3

Caesar cipher : kdssb eluwkgdb wr brx

- In substitution cipher's other methods, like polygram substitution cipher, polyalphabetic substitution cipher, playfair cipher, hill cipher etc. are also used.

7.3.3 Transposition Cipher   (Oct. 14)

- Transposition ciphers differ from substitution ciphers. Transposition ciphers do not simply replace one alphabet with another. They also perform some permutation over to the plaintext alphabet.

- The next example is of common transposition method, the columnar transposition. In this method, one key is used which does not contain any repeated letters.

Example : Plaintext : Please transfer one million dollar to my swiss bank account six two two.

Key : MEGABUCK.

Solution : Steps :

1. Write the key and give numbers to the alphabets.

2. Write the plaintext horizontally, in rows, padded to fill the matrix if the need be.

3. Write the ciphertext by columns, starting with the column whose key letter is lowest.

M	E	G	A	B	U	C	K
7	4	5	1	2	8	3	6
P	l	e	a	s	e	t	r
A	n	s	f	e	r	o	n
E	m	i	l	l	i	o	n
D	o	l	l	a	r	s	t
O	m	y	s	w	i	s	s
B	a	n	k	a	c	c	o
U	n	t	s	i	x	t	w
O	t	w	o	a	b	c	d

Cipher text : AFLLSKSOSELAWAIATODSSCTCLNMOMANTESILYNTWRNNTS OWDPAEDOBUOERIRICXB

Example : Consider a plaintext : "How are you when you arrived ?" By using a key NCBTZQARX, use transposition cipher on the plaintext.

Solution : Use transposition cipher on the plaintext.

N	C	B	T	Z	Q	A	R	X
4	3	2	7	9	5	1	6	8
H	o	w	a	R	e	y	o	u
w	h	e	n	Y	o	u	a	r
r	i	v	e	D	a	b	c	d

Ciphertext : YUBWEVOHIHWREOAOACAHEURD

7.4 | TWO FUNDAMENTAL CRYPTOGRAPHIC PRINCIPLES

(Oct. 11; April 15)

- Two fundamental principles are underlying to all cryptographic system, they are Redundancy and Freshness.

1. Redundancy :

- First principle in every cryptographic system is all encrypted messages must contain some redundancy. We know that passive intruders cannot decrypt the messages. But active intruder can cause a massive amount of trouble, even though intruder cannot understand the messages.

- To understand this, let us see an example, Consider a company with large range of product. Company decided to use ordering messages which consist of 16 byte customer name followed by a 3 byte data field. Last 3 bytes are encrypted with a key known only to the customer and the company.

- Passive intruders cannot decrypt the message, since it is not knowing the key. However, passive intruders can make guesses about the text. Now consider a recently fixed employee who wants to take a revenge, he takes customers list and writes a program to generate fictitious orders using real customer names. This ex-employee is not having the keys of customers so not able to encrypt it but can cause massive amount of trouble to the company. Company's server may not be able to find which records are valid and which are not.

- To prevent this, some additional information should be added to every record/every message. All messages must contain considerable redundancy so that active intruders cannot send random junk and have it be interpreted as a valid message.

2. **Freshness :**

- The second cryptographic principle is that some measures must be taken to ensure that each message received can be verified as being fresh, that is, sent very recently. This measure is needed to prevent active intruders from playing back old message.

- One such measure is including in every message a timestamp valid only for, say, 10 seconds. The receiver can then just keep messages around for 10 seconds, to compare newly arrived messages to previous ones to filter out duplicates.

- Messages older than 10 seconds can be thrown out, since any replays sent more than 10 seconds later will be rejected as too old.

7.5 | COMMUNICATION SECURITY : FIREWALLS (April 12, 13)

- In this section, we will look at communication security, that is, how to get the bits secretly and without modification from source to destination.

- The dramatic rise and progress of the Internet has opened possibilities that no one would have thought of.

- We can connect any computer in the world to any other computer, no matter how far the two are located from each other. This is a great advantage for individuals and corporate as well.

- But because of this, two kinds of attacks are also possible, these are :

  1. Most corporations have large amounts of valuable and confidential data in their networks. Leaking of this critical information to competitors can be a great setback.

  2. Insider can also leak out the information as well as there is a danger of viruses, worms entering a corporate network to create havoc.

- As a result of these dangers, we must have mechanisms which can ensure that the inside information remains safe and also prevent the outside attackers from entering inside a corporate network. This is where a firewall comes into picture.

- One of the most basic and easily implemented methods of network security is the firewall.

- The main purpose of a firewall is to separate a secure area from a less secure area and to control communications between the two.

- Firewall also controlling inbound and outbound communications on anything from a single machine to an entire network.

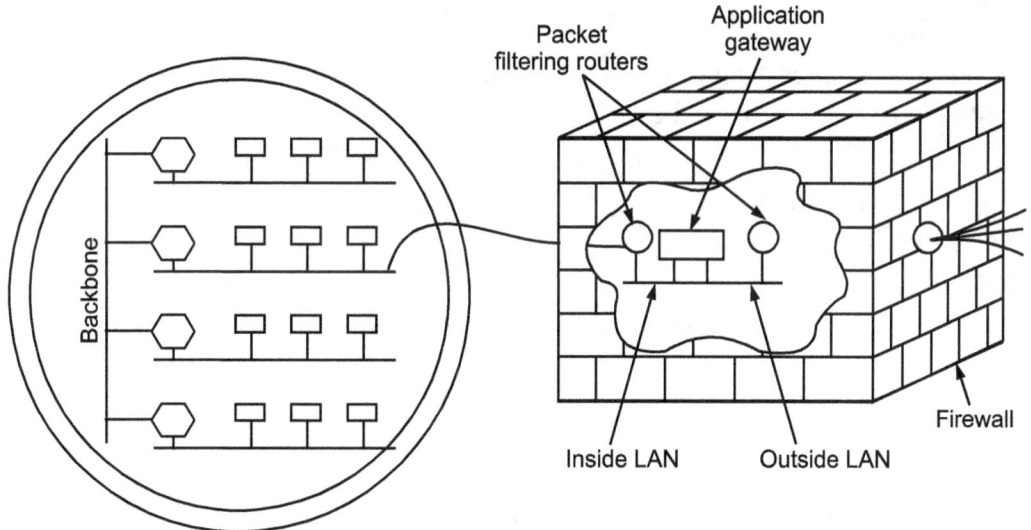

Fig. 7.12 : A firewall consisting of two packet filters and an application gateway

- A firewall can be compared with a policeman standing outside VIP person's house. This policeman usually keeps an eye on and physically checks every person that enters into or come out of the house.

- A firewall acts like the policeman, it guards a corporate network by standing between the network and outside world. All traffic between the network and the Internet in either direction must pass through the firewall. The firewall decides if the traffic can be allowed to flow or whether it must be stopped from proceeding further.

- A firewall can serve the following functions:
  1. Limit Internet access to e-mail only, so that no other types of information can pass between the intranet and the Internet.
  2. Control who can telnet into your intranet (a method of logging in remotely).
  3. Limit what other kinds of traffic can pass between your intranet and the Internet.

- Based on the criteria used for filtering traffic, firewalls are generally classified into two types as shown in Fig. 7.13.

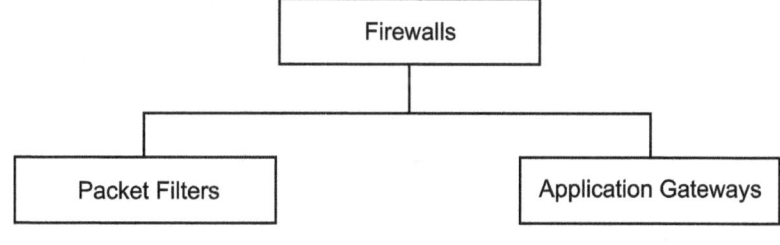

Fig. 7.13 : Types of firewalls

1. Packet Filter :

- Packet filter applies a set of rules to each packet and based on the outcome decides to either forward or discard the packet.
- It is also called as screening router or screening filter. Such a firewall implementation involves a router, which is configured to filter packets going in either direction.
- The filtering rules are based on a number of fields in the IP and TCP/UDP headers, such as source and destination IP addresses, IP protocol field, TCP/UDP port numbers.

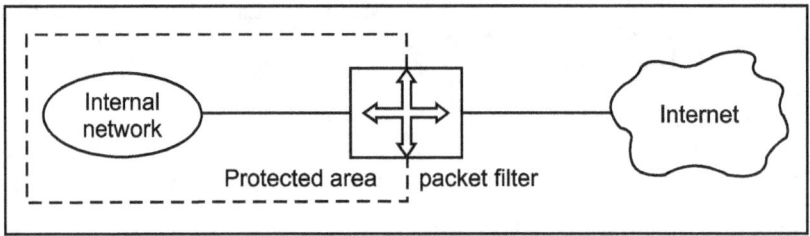

Fig. 7.14 : Packet filter

Advantages:

(i) The biggest advantage of packet filtering firewalls is cost and lower resource usage and best suited for smaller networks.

Disadvantage:

(i) Packet filtering firewalls can work only on the network layer and these firewalls do not support complex rule based models. And it's also vulnerable to spoofing in some Cases.

2. Application Gateways :

- Application gateway is also called as a proxy server.
- Application gateways are generally more secure than packet filters.
- The disadvantage of application gateways is the overhead in terms of connections.

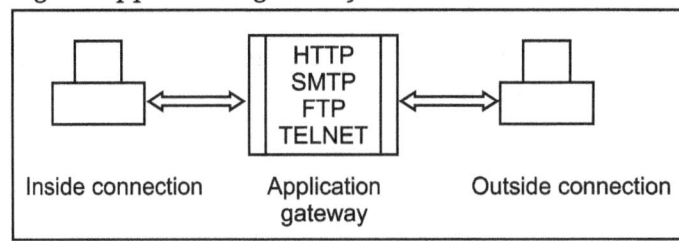

Fig. 7.15 : Application gateways

Advantages:

(i) Better logging handling of traffic.

(ii) Highest level of security.

Disadvantages:

(i) A poor implementation that relies on the underlying as Inetd daemon will suffer from a severe limitation to the number of allowed connections in today's demanding high simultaneous session environment.

(ii) Complex setup of application firewall needs more and detailed attentions to the applications that use the gateway.

7.6 | WEB SECURITY

- Web security is very important issue, because of modern nature of attack. The web is where most of the intruders resides.

- Web security can be roughly divided into three parts :

    1. How are objects and resources named securely ?

    2. How can secure authenticated connections be established ?

    3. What happens when a web site sends a client a piece of executable code?

- In this section, we will discuss web security threats and their mechanisms.

7.6.1 Threats

- A threat, in the context of computer security, refers to anything that has the potential to cause serious harm to a computer system.

- It can be defined as "threats are anything (e.g., object, substance, human, etc.) that are capable of acting against an asset in a manner that can result in harm".

- There are several types of problems and threats related with web security. Let us study some of the examples related with this :

    1. The home page of number of organizations has been attacked and replaced by a new home page.

    2. Number of sites have been brought down by denial-of-service attack, in which the hacker floods the site with traffic and it becomes unable to respond to the queries.

    3. A mirror image of a web site can also be created by a hacker.

    4. E-commerce web site is hacked to know the credit card details of the customers.

    5. Fake announcement about share's prices, fake prizes etc., can be done by the hackers.

- Threats are potentials for vulnerabilities to turn into attacks on computer systems, networks, and more. They can put individuals' computer systems and business computers at risk, so vulnerabilities have to be fixed so that attackers cannot infiltrate the system and cause damage.

- Network-delivered threats are typically of two basic types:

   1. **Passive Network Threats:** Activities such as wiretapping and idle scans that are designed to intercept traffic traveling through the network.

   2. **Active Network Threats:** Activities such as Denial of Service (DoS) attacks and SQL injection attacks where the attacker is attempting to execute commands to disrupt the network's normal operation.

- Now, we will discuss some technical issues related to web security.

7.6.2 Secure Naming

- Suppose, Amar wants to visit Bhushan's web site. She types Bhushan's URL and then a web page appears. But there is no guarantee about this web page has come from Bhushan's server only.

- A man in the middle attack is possible in this case. Trudy, the intruder may intercepts Amar's message and in response may send a fake page to Amar. There are several ways by which the intruder can intercept Amar's request and modify the response. One method is DNS spoofing, discussed in next section.

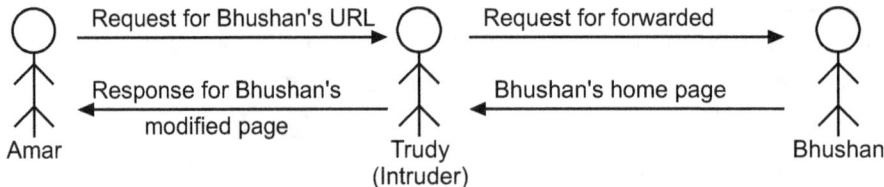

7. 16 : Man in the middle attack

7.6.3 DNS Spoofing   (April 11)

- Using the Domain Name System (DNS), people can identify web sites with human readable names (e.g. rediff.com) and computers can continue to treat them as IP addresses (e.g. 121.10.80.67). DNS server maintains the mapping between domain names and corresponding IP addresses. DNS server is usually located with the ISP. DNS spoofing or DNS poisoning works as follows :

   1. Suppose Bhushan's domain name is www.Bhushan.com and the IP address is 100.10.10.10. In the DNS server, the entry is maintained as,

      www.Bhushan.com 100.10.10.10

   2. The attacker trudy manages to hack and replace the IP address of Bhushan with his own e.g. 100.10.20.30 in the DNS server. Now entry becomes, www.Bhushan.com 100.10.20.30

3. When Amar wants to communicate with Bhushan's site, his browser queries the DNS server maintained by his ISP for Bhushan's IP address, providing it the domain name www.Bhushan.com. Amar gets the replaced (Trudy's) IP address, 100.10.20.30.

4. Now Amar starts communicating with Trudy, believing that she is communicating with Bhushan.

- Such DNS spoofing attacks are common and cause a lot of havoc. A protocol called secure DNS and self certifying names are used to thwart such attacks.

7.6.4 Secure DNS   (April 11; Oct. 14)

- In 1994, IETF a working group was introduced to make DNS fundamentally secure. This project is known as DNSsec (DNS security).

- DNSsec is conceptually simple. It is based on public-key cryptography. Every DNS zone has a public/private key pair i.e., when A wants to send a message to B, A encrypts the message with B's public key.

- When this public-private key method (asymmetric key cryptography) is used, public key is known to all but private key is known to the owner only. If message is encrypted by public key, it is decrypted by corresponding private key or vice versa. So when A sends a message encrypted by B's public key, it is decrypted with only B's private key, not even B's public key.

- All information sent by DNS server is encrypted with the sender's private key, so the receiver can verify its authenticity.

- DNSsec offers three fundamental services :

   1. **Proof of where the data originated :** This verifies that the data being returned has been approved by the zone's owner.

   2. **Public key distribution :** It is useful for storing and retrieving public keys securely.

   3. **Transaction and request authentication :** It is needed to guard against playback and spoofing attacks.

Resource Record Sets :

- DNS records are grouped into sets called RRSets (Resource Record Sets), with all the records having the same name, class and type being grouped together in a set.

- RRSets may contain multiple A records. For this, digital signature and hashing is used, which is beyond the scope of this syllabus.

- DNSsec introduces several new record types :
  1. **Key record :** This record holds the public key of a zone, user, host, or other principal, the cryptographic algorithm used for signing, the protocol used for transmission and few other bits. Public key is also stored.
  2. **SIG record :** It holds the signed hash according to the algorithm specified in the KEY record. The signature applies to all the records in the RRSet. It also stores the time when the signature begins its period of validity and when it expires.
  3. **CERT record :** It stores digital certificates for verifying the authenticity of domain.

7.6.5 Self Certifying Names

- Secure DNS is not the only method for securing names. Another different approach is used in the secure file system.
- In this project, the authors designed a secure, scalable, worldwide file system, without modifying standard DNS and without using certificates or assuming the existence of a PKI.
- Each web server has a public/private key pair. Each URL contains a cryptographic hash to the server's name and public key as part of the URL, a colon and 32 character hash.
- Hash contains the server name followed by public key and the name of file.

  For example:

  http://www.bob.com:295hd8bfjkclmn780commady/photos/bob.jpg

  Fig. 7.16 : A self certifying URL containing a hash of server's name and public key

7.7 | MOBILE CODE SECURITY

- Mobile codes are small executable programs. In early days, web pages were static by using HTML only and not containing any executable code.
- Now-a-days, web pages contain small programs including Java applets, ActiveX controls and JavaScripts. Downloading and executing such mobile code is security risk. So various methods have been devised to minimize it.

7.7.1 Java Applet Security   (April 12; Oct. 14)

- Java applets are small Java programs compiled to a stack oriented machine language called Java Virtual Machine.

- They can be placed on a web page for downloading along with the page. After the page is loaded, the applets are inserted into a JVM interpreter inside the browser.

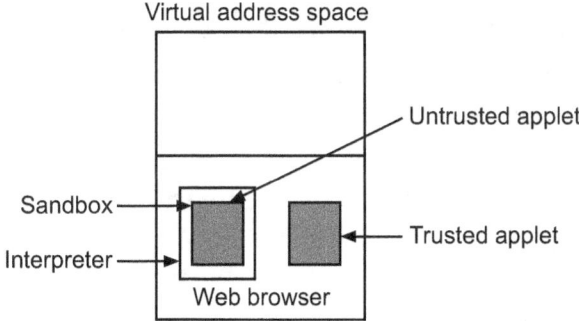

Fig. 7.17 : Applets can be interpreted by a web browser

7.7.2 ActiveX Security   (April 12)

- ActiveX controls are Pentium binary programs that can be embedded in web pages.

- When one of them is encountered, a check is made to see if it should be executed and if it passes the test, it is executed. It is not interpreted or sandboxed in anyway, so it has much power as any other user program and can potentially do great harm. Thus, all the security is in the decision whether to run the ActiveX Control.

- Microsoft uses code signing method for decision. Every ActiveX Control is a accompanied by a digital signature. The Microsoft system for verifying ActiveX control is called Authentic Code.

Difference between Java and ActiveX Approach :

- With Java approach, no attempt is made to determine who wrote the applet. A run time interpreter makes sure it does not do things the machine owner has said, applets may not do. With code signing, there is no attempt to monitor the mobile code's run time behaviour.

- If it came from a trusted source and has not been modified in transit. No attempt is made to see whether the code is malicious or not.

7.7.3 JavaScript Security

- JavaScript does not have any formal security model. Every browser handles security in a different way.

- For example, Netscape navigator V4 uses code signing model.

7.7.4 Viruses

- Viruses are another form of mobile code. The difference between a virus and ordinary mobile code is that viruses are written to reproduce themselves.

- When a virus arrives, it starts out by infecting executable programs on the disk. When one of these programs run, control is transferred to the virus, which usually tries to spread itself to other machines.

- Viruses have become huge problem on the Internet. There is no obvious solution, only the user can install a good antivirus software.

7.8 | SOCIAL ISSUES   (Oct. 11; April 13)

- The Internet and its security technology is an area where social issues, public policy and technology meet. We will examine three areas i.e., privacy, freedom of speech and copyright.

7.8.1 Privacy

- Privacy is on the public agenda from the last 200 years. In the 18th Century, if the government wanted/needed to check the documents of a citizen, it had to do so by actually sending a government official. Now-a-days, telephone companies and ISP make everything easy.

- Cryptography makes it possible for the users to encrypt data so that no one can read it. For government it becomes harder to know about data, so, some government restrict or forbid the use of cryptography.

7.8.2 Anonymous Remailers

- PGP, SSL and other technologies make it possible for two parties to establish secure, authenticated communication, free from third party.

- However, sometimes privacy is best served by not having authentication, in fact by making communication anonymous.

- The anonymity may be desired for point-to-point messages, newsgroups or both.

- People who wish to remain anonymous are :

  1. Political dissidents living under authoritarian regimes often wish to communicate anonymously to escape being jailed or killed.

  2. Wrongdoing in many corporate, educational, governmental and other organizations has often been exposed by whistleblowers, who frequently prefer to remain anonymously to avoid retribution.

3. People with unpopular social, political or religious views may wish to communicate with each other via e-mail or newsgroups without exposing themselves.

4. People may wish to discuss mental illness, sensitive issues, or being a member of a persecuted minority in a newsgroup without having to go public.

- Anonymous remailer is a server which allows users to create pseudonyms and send e-mail to the server, which is then re-mailed or re-posted to them using the pseudonym. So no one could tell where the message really came from.

- Many users who wish anonymity, chain their requests through multiple anonymous remailers as shown in Fig. 7.18.

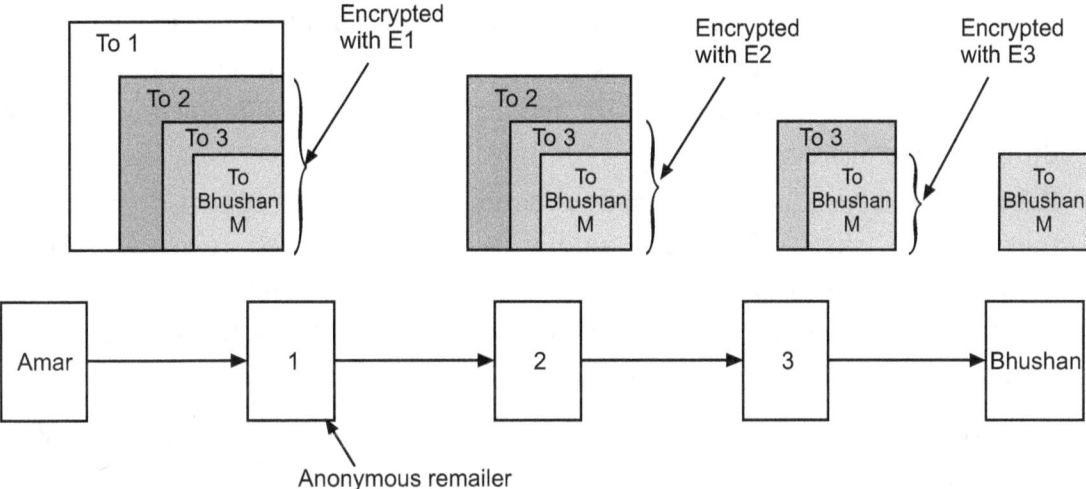

Fig. 7.18 : How Amar uses 3 remailers to send Bhushan a message

- For example, Amar wants to send a message M to Bhushan, so he uses three remailers. He composes the message M, and puts a header on it with Bhushan's e-mail address. Then he encrypts the whole thing with remailer 3's public key, E3. To this, he prepends a header with remailer 3's e-mail address in plaintext. This message is shown between remailers 2 and 3.

- Then he encrypts this message with remailer 2's publickey, E2 and adds plaintext header containing remailer 2's e-mail address. This message is shown between 1 and 2. Finally, he encrypts the entire message with remailer 1's public key, E1, and adds a plaintext header with remailer 1's e-mail address.

- When the message reaches at remailer 1, the outer header is stripped off. The body is decrypted and then e-mail is send to remailer 2. Same steps carried at other two remailers.

7.8.3 Freedom of Speech

- Freedom of speech is another social issue, which is opposite of censorship. Government wants to restrict what individuals can read and publish. But on web sites there are millions of pages which should be banned.

- Mostly the banned web sites may contain :

  1. Material inappropriate for children or teenagers.

  2. Hate aimed at various ethnic, religious, sexual or other groups.

  3. Information about democracy and democratic values.

  4. Accounts of historical events contradicting the government's version.

  5. Manuals for picking locks, building weapons, encrypting messages etc.

- The world wide web covers whole world, so it becomes difficult to enforce the censorship. Different countries are having different laws regarding different things related to security.

- Eternity service has been proposed to counter censorship. Its goal is to make sure that the published information cannot be depublished or rewritten. To use eternity service, the user specifies how long the material is to be preserved, pays a fee proportional to its duration and size and uploads it. Thereafter, no one can remove or edit it, not even the uploaded.

7.8.4 Steganography   (Oct. 12; April 15)

- It is the science of hiding information. Steganography is a technique that facilitates hiding of message that is to be kept secret inside other messages. This results in the concealment of the secret message itself.

- Historically, the sender used invisible ink, tiny pin punctures on specific characters, minute variations between handwritten characters, pencil marks on handwritten characters etc. Therefore, the science of hiding messages is called steganography.

- Now, people hide secret messages within graphic images. For example : Suppose that we have a secret message to send. We can take another image file and we can replace the last two right most bits of each byte of that image with (the next) two bits of our secret message.

- The resulting image would not look too different and yet carry a secret message inside. The receiver would perform the opposite tricks; it would read the last two bits of each byte of the image file and reconstruct the secret message.

- This concept is shown in Fig. 7.19.

```
1100101
0010100
1111111
0001111
```

Secret message   Original image   Resulting image
                        and its bits   and its bits

Fig. 7.19 : Example of Steganography

7.8.5 Copyright

- Copyright is a legal right created by the law of a country that grants the creator of an original work exclusive rights for its use and distribution. This is usually only for a limited time.

- Copyright is a form of intellectual property protection granted under particular country law to the creators of original works of ownership such as literary works including computer softwares, computer databases etc.

- The copyright notice consists of three elements. They are the "c" in a circle (©), the year of first publication, and the name of the owner of copyright.

Problems :

1. **By using substitution cipher, encrypt the following plaintext :**

   (a) **Plaintext :** "Another method is monoalphabetic cipher". Key : 4.

   (b) **Plaintext :** "Two fundamental principals are". Key : 7.

2. **By using transposition cipher, convert the following :**

   (a) **Plaintext :** "In computer terms, the concept of key range leads us to the principle of key size". Key : NCBTZQA.

   (b) **Plaintext :** "The reverse process of transforming ciphertext message back to plaintext message is called as decryption". Key : ZQARXPM.

SUMMARY

➢ Network security issues include protecting data from unauthorized access, protecting data from damage and development, and implementing policies and procedures for recovery from breaches and data losses.

➢ Network security consists of the policies adopted to prevent and monitor authorized access, misuse, modification, or denial of a computer network and network-accessible resources. Network security involves the authorization of access to data in a network, which is controlled by the network administrator.

➢ Network security can provide one of the five services like confidentiality, Integrity, Authentication, non-reproduction and Authentication.

➢ The term cryptography is a Greek word which means "secret writing". Cryptography is an art and science of transforming messages so as to make them secure and immune to attacks.

➢ Cryptanalysis is the technique of decoding messages from a non-readable format back to readable format without knowing how they were initially converted from readable format to non-readable format.

➢ Cryptology is a combination of cryptography and cryptanalysis. In the early days, cryptography is used to be performed by using manual techniques.

➢ There are two primary ways in which a plaintext message can be codified to obtain the corresponding ciphertext i.e., Substitution cipher and Transposition cipher.

➢ A substitution cipher replaces one symbol with another. A transposition cipher reorders (permutes) symbols in a block of symbols. In a transposition cipher, the key is a mapping between the position of the symbols in the plaintext and cipher text.

➢ Two fundamental principles are underlying to all cryptographic system are Redundancy and Freshness.

➢ We can divide all the cryptography algorithms (ciphers) into two groups: symmetric key also called as secret-key cryptography algorithms and asymmetric also called as public-key cryptography algorithms.

➢ In symmetric-key cryptography, the same key is used by both parties. The sender uses this key and an encryption algorithm to encrypt data; the receiver uses the same key and the corresponding decryption algorithm to decrypt the data.

➢ In asymmetric or public-key cryptography, there are two keys: a private key and a public key. The private key is kept by the receiver. The public key is announced to the public.

➢ One of the most basic and easily implemented methods of network security is the firewall. The main purpose of a firewall is to separate a secure area from a less secure area and to control communications between the two.

➢ Packet filter firewall maintains a filtering table that decides which packets are to be forwarded or discarded. A packet filter firewall filters at the network or transport layer.

➢ Application Gateways firewalls handle packets for each Internet service separately, usually by running a program called a proxy server, which accepts e-mail, Web, chat, newsgroup, and other packets from computers on the intranet, strips off the information that identifies the source of the packet, and passes it along to the Internet.

➢ Threats are anything (e.g., object, substance, human, etc.) that are capable of acting against an asset in a manner that can result in harm.

> DNS spoofing or DNS cache poisoning is a computer hacking attack, whereby data is introduced into a Domain Name System (DNS) resolver's cache, causing the name server to return an incorrect IP address, diverting traffic to the attacker's computer (or any other computer).

> In 1994, IETF a working group was introduced to make DNS fundamentally secure. This project is known as DNSsec (DNS security). DNSsec is based on public-key cryptography.

> Mobile codes are small executable programs.

> The Internet and its security technology is an area where social issues, public policy and technology meet. The three main areas are privacy, freedom of speech and copyright.

> Steganography is a technique that facilitates hiding of message that is to be kept secret inside other messages and this results in the concealment of the secret message itself.

PRACTICE QUESTIONS

1. Define the terms : (a) Cryptography, (b) Cryptanalysis, (c) Cryptology.
2. What is substitution cipher ?
3. What is transposition cipher ?
4. Explain the two fundamental cryptographic principles.
5. Write a note on firewalls.
6. What are the types of firewall ?
7. Describe the threats to web security.
8. What is DNS spoofing ?
9. Explain secure DNS.
10. Explain self certifying names.
11. Write a note on mobile code security.
12. What is an anonymous remailer ?
13. What is difference between Java Applet and ActiveX approach ?
14. What are services of DNSsec ?
15. Write a note on steganography.

UNIVERSITY QUESTIONS AND ANSWERS

April 2011

1. By using substitution cipher transform the message "Happy Birthday to You". Key is '5'. [1 M]

Ans. Please refer to Solved problems.

2. List the fundamental services offered by DNSsec. [1 M]

Ans. Please refer to Section 7.6.4.

3.   Explain the concept of DNS spoofing. Discuss the strategies used to prevent DNS spoofing.   [5 M]

Ans. Please refer to Section 7.6.3.

4.   By using transposition cipher convert the following:

Plaintext: "The reverse process of transforming ciphertext message back to plaintext message is called decryption".

Key : ZQARXPM   [5 M]

Ans. Please refer to Solved problems.

October 2011

1.   By using substitution cipher transform the message "difference between random access protocol with controlled access protocol". Key is '4'.   [1 M]

Ans. Please refer to Solved problems.

2.   By using transposition cipher convert the following :   [5 M]

Plain text : " Please transfer one million dollar to my Swiss bank account six two two".

Key : MEGABUCK.

Ans. Please refer to Solved problems.

3.   What is cryptography ? Explain two fundamental cryptographic principles.

[5 M]

Ans. Please refer to Sections 7. 3 and 7.4.

April 2012

1.   Which social issues are important in network security ? Explain any one. [5 M]

Ans. Please refer to Section 7.8.

2.   Explain components of Firewall.   [5 M]

Ans. Please refer to Section 7.5.

3.   Distinguish between Java applet and Active X control security.   [5 M]

Ans. Please refer to Sections 7.7.1 and 7.7.2.

October 2012

1.   "What is stegnography ?   [1 M]

Ans. Please refer to Section 7.8.4.

2.   Encrypt the following plain text transposition cipher :   [5 M]

Key : MAGNETIC

Plain text : transmit this message.

Ans. Please refer to Solved problems.

April 2013

1. Define cryptanalysis.   [1 M]

Ans. Please refer to Section 7.3.1.

2. What act as guard during communication security in an network ?   [1 M]

Ans. Please refer to Section 7.5.

3. Which social issues are important in network security ? Explain any one.

[5 M]

Ans. Please refer to Section 7.8.

October 2014

1. What do you mean by cipher ?   [1 M]

Ans. Please refer to Section 7.3.

2. State one line difference between Substitution ciphers and Transposition ciphers.   [1 M]

Ans. Please refer to Sections 7.3.2 and 7.3.3.

3. Write a note on Java Applet Security.   [5 m]

Ans. Please refer to Section 7.7.1.

4. What is RRSets ? Explain several new record types introduced by DNS sec.

[4 M]

Ans. Please refer to Section 7.6.4.

April 2015

1. By using substitution cipher transform the message :   [1 M]
    "WELCOME IN COMPUTER SCIENCE FIELD" Key is 5.

Ans. Please refer to Solved problems.

2. What is steganography ?   [1 M]

Ans. Please refer to Section 7.8.4.

3. What is cryptography ? Explain two fundamental cryptographic principles.

[5 M]

Ans. Please refer to Sections 7.3 and 7.4.

4. By using transposition cipher convert the following :
    Plain Text : "The key for encryption is Go back from border and the key for decryption is welcome to India"
    Key : ZQARXPM   [4 M]

Ans. Please refer to Solved problems.

www.ingramcontent.com/pod-product-compliance
Lightning Source LLC
Chambersburg PA
CBHW080727020726
47503CB00010B/2824

* 9 7 8 9 3 5 1 6 4 9 1 1 3 *